Also by Donald J. McGill

Talk Radio Mysteries
Featuring Jerry Jeremy

Novels
Tune in to Danger
Talked to Death

Short Stories
Deadly Vision
Disappearing Act

Watson and the Reality Crowd
Featuring Sherwood Holmes

Tune in to Danger

Donald J. McGill

A Talk Radio Mystery

The Dangerous Press
San Francisco MMXIV

Be sure to visit **www.Donald J. McGill.com** for the latest on Jerry Jeremy and his pals.

While you're there, if you can take a moment to let me know how you liked this book, I'd greatly appreciate the feedback.

djm

To Doris,

My first reader, with all my love.

Chapter 1.

I COULDN'T believe my ears.

Pamela Kay Paulson, the owner of KPMT Big Talk Radio, the same lady who'd invited me to lunch, was now telling me that my next career move might be on a bus out of town. "You'll be lucky to get a job doing the snow report in Alaska," was how she put it. I was as speechless as an up-and-coming talk show host can be.

"Listen, PK, I like the weather right here," I said. "It's good for my tan. Besides, I'm allergic to ice." We were seated at one of the many umbrella-shaded tables scattered around Pamela Kay's plus-sized swimming pool. A hundred feet away, the Pacific Ocean pounded on the rocky shore north of San Francisco. There wasn't an iceberg in sight and I wanted to keep it that way.

Earlier that day Pamela Kay had asked me to meet her for lunch and at the time I took it as a good thing. Even now, as the sun warmed us up and the ocean breeze cooled us down, as Ricardo, Pamela Kay's house pet—er, houseman—slinked over with drinks and canapés, an observer might take us for a couple of old friends sunning ourselves out in the...well, out in the sun. But then, that's California for you. They make you feel good while you're getting the boot. Don't let the karma hit you in the ass on the way out.

As my radio fans already know, my name is Jeremy Jeremy. That's right, double Jeremy. And my middle name's Jeremy too. That's what's on any important papers anyway, but my listeners all know me as Jerry. And thanks to me, KPMT radio is the seventh highest rated station from four to seven every evening Monday to Friday. Not counting the Spanish-language stations, of course. I haven't been able to break into that demographic yet, but if Pamela Kay was serious as she seemed to be, I'd better start learning to *hable* the lingo.

"MARGARITAS?" Ricardo had oozed up loaded down with a frosty pitcher, bowls of chips and guacamole, and glasses rimmed with salt and lime. He looked at me like maybe I didn't deserve any, but the boss lady gave him a nod. He poured and I gulped.

When I finally stopped choking, I realized Pamela Kay was still talking, "...you can't squat where you dip your taco chips, Jerry, but there you go, you're doing it. What in the living hell do you have against me?"

"Against you, Pamela Kay? Nothing, I like you, you're great. I even like taco chips." But I figured I'd skip the guacamole just in case this was a test.

For some reason Pamela Kay had the idea that I did something to annoy her, but for the life of me I couldn't imagine what it was. Sure, talk radio's no *60 Minutes*, but then neither is the traffic report, so this was a step up for me. I watched myself in her shades while she balled me out. A pale green reflection of the real me. Not a good look for a carrot-top. I was beginning to wonder if I'd overdosed on the suntan lotion when I realized Pamela Kay was still talking, "...you're screwing with my family and I for one plan to do something about it."

"Do something about what, Pamela Kay? Do what to me? Why me?"

"Here's what I'm going to do about it, Jerry. I'm going to have *you* do something about it, that's what."

"Sure, Pamela Kay, I'll do anything you want."

"And if you *don't* do something about it, you can kiss Big Talk Radio and your career *arriva*-motherfucking-*derchi* good-bye."

"But my contract..."

"Contracts are made to be broken, Jerry. Why do you think I keep Cardwell, Heilbrun and Wilshire on retainer?"

"The lawyers? Gee, you don't need to get tough, Mrs. P...."
Lunch wasn't going well and I hadn't had a bite to eat yet. I was beginning to eye the guacamole.

"You not only won't work in radio, you won't even be able

to get your old job back selling Charlie Wooten's cars. He said you were the worst salesman he ever had. Charlie had to buy a ton of advertising just so we'd give you a job and he'd be rid of you."

"Voice overs, commercials, that's my thing, not face to face selling—"

Charlie had sponsored my traffic reports back when I was at KDAB. I had made a name for myself taking the station's news van to the worst bottlenecks in the morning commute. I'd pull off the road and using a wireless mic interview commuters stuck in the gridlock. *"Good morning, this is Jerry Jeremy bringing you the traffic from right out in it...."*

It was pretty entertaining stuff and occasionally we got an interview we didn't need to bleep. The station manager called it the human interest angle. But one morning as the commute ground to a halt heading onto the Oakland Bay Bridge, so did my career.

I was doing my usual thing, having stepped out of the van to interview a nearby Toyota. Since cars weren't moving anyway, a few of my fans got out of their cars to say hello or take a picture with me, then a few more got out of their cars to see why everybody else was getting out of their cars. Before I knew it, a crowd of people in no hurry to get to work had gathered and traffic was stopped half way back to Sacramento.

In the distance I could hear sirens working their way through the jam up and I figured the KCTY traffic chopper circling overhead must have ratted me out. Anyhow, having heard that discretion is the better part of valor, I left the news van there and hitched a ride back to the City with the guy in the Toyota. Bottom line, the publicity was huge and like they say the only bad publicity is...well, you know.

I was in all the papers and the receptionist at KDAB said I generated more calls to the station than anybody ever. Yet in spite of all that, management just didn't see the upside. Before you could say unemployment insurance, I was collecting it.

As one door closes though, they say another opens. Probably the same "they" who said that discretion-valor thing. Anyway, after a slight detour I landed at KPMT radio and had been doing the evening drive show for just over a year when Pamela Kay Paulson gave me an early morning call. Maybe ten, ten-thirty, so naturally I was still dead to the world.

The telephone chased away the girl of my dreams as it rang me awake. The girl being that imaginary hottie you wished lived next door, all blonde and cheerleaderly. But addresses next to girls like that are only found in dreams I'm afraid. Anyway she was my kind of girl, it was my kind of neighborhood and for that matter it was my kind of dream.

"Hello? Oh...hi...Mrs. Paulson," I said shaking the sleep out of my ears. "Definitely. Yes, this is Jerry—

"Oh, no, no. Fine, really fine. Been up for hours—" I said.

"Sure, Freddy and Betty, great show—" I also said.

"Sure, Pamela Kay, just doing my morning workout—" I said that too.

Pamela Kay said she didn't want to interrupt my beauty sleep, but then she supposed I had been up anyway listening to Freddy and Betty's morning show. A team player would never miss the fair-haired morning duo. But mainly, Pamela Kay wanted to make sure it wouldn't be a problem for me to run up to her beach house in Marin for lunch.

I assured her she was right on all counts and rolled out of bed after she rang off. I showered and dressed up as much as a guy on the radio needs to, dropped the top on the Beamer and headed for the Golden Gate. The sun was shining, the wind ruffled my hair, it was all good.

The only other time I'd been invited to Pamela Kay's was for the annual Christmas bash she throws for our sponsors under the guise of an employee party. My takeaway from that occasion was not to let Pamela Kay catch me under the mistletoe again. Unless, of course, whispered promises and the morning drive slot were involved. A guy's gotta do what a guy's gotta do, right?

And Lord knows I'm just a guy.

"JERRY, you need to straighten out this goddamn' mess—it's all your goddamn' fault this happened."

When she stopped for a breath, I saw my chance; I don't argue with callers three hours a day for nothing. "Wait a minute, Pamela Kay—I don't even know which mess of mine you're talking about."

"My nephew Tony is in some kind of trouble and you're the cause of it." She picked up a chunk of gold and snapped a flame out of it, setting fire to a long, thin cigarette. "I'm going to tell you what it is you are going to have to do. But first I want you to listen closely so you know why I'm concerned. Pay attention now, I'm not one of your callers and I won't be taking my answer on the air. My nephew has approached a bank about borrowing money against his KPMT stock. What do you think of that, Jerry?"

"Well, of course I'll do what I can, but I'm sure I don't have that kind of ready cash to lend out, Pamela Kay. Why don't you just front him the dough?"

"Why the fuck indeed. Listen and try to get this straight, Jerry. He doesn't want anybody knowing about this. Especially me."

"I guess not."

"If I ever got wind of this—even the slightest hint—I would raise hell."

"Rightly so. And you got wind of it. How did you get wind of it?"

"The bank went to my lawyer, Leland Heilbrun, to get the stock grant settled, so Leland gave me a call. That's how it's set up, Jerry. Good thing too. See what can happen?"

I saw what could happen.

For a moment Pamela Kay was quiet, either a dramatic pause while this sank in or she was waiting for me to answer her. I didn't really think she was waiting for me, but it was dead air so I jumped right in.

"As I understand it, Pamela Kay, you're telling me Tony's hard up for cash and you don't want him borrowing from strangers, but don't want to give him the dough yourself...tell me again why you're talking to me and not Tony?"

"Because at the end of the goddamn' day," she explained, those sunglasses staring me down, "it's all your fucking fault. I keep turning it over in my mind and you're the one I keep coming back to."

"Why me? Mrs. Paulson, this doesn't make any sense."

"I may be stuck up here in Marin County, but I still have a few friends in the City. When I asked around, I found out Tony's been hanging around with someone and that someone is probably taking him for a ride—" Pamela Kay lowered her shades, the old eye to eye even worse than my pale green reflection, "—and you brought this person into our lives. And you'd goddamn' better get her out!"

All in all, I wished she'd left the glasses on.

"Mrs. Paulson—Pamela Kay—you must have me confused with the morning guys. I hardly even know Tony. I've been at KPMT a little over a year, and Tony and I have only ever talked when maybe we had lunch or drinks with some advertiser, somebody who wanted to do a commercial on my show. I don't think Tony will take advice from me on his girl troubles, Mrs. P."

"He doesn't need any of your damn' advice, Jerry. Your job is to unload the bitch that's soaking him." She leaned in very close. "Jerry, you put her and her pet dwarf in the picture and you need to get rid of them."

"Dwarf? A dwarf? That I.... I'm trying to understand, but you got to throw me a bone here, Missus P. Who or what are we talking about?"

"Who else, Jerry? Your goddamn' fortune teller. Remember that little show of yours last Halloween? The one that cost me fifty-eight thousand fucking dollars?"

Oh. *That* show.

Madame Zoroaster.

The psychic disaster.

"Oh, well, Pamela Kay...." I was fumbling around looking for a way out, hoping for maybe a small earthquake—something, anything to get me off the hook. "That really wasn't...I mean...."

"Listen, Jerry, I'm not going to hold that lawsuit over your head. It never even went to court," she waved it away, adding, "though I paid through the nose."

Thanks to our lawyer pal, Leland Heilbrun, again.

Heilbrun had kept the story out of the papers, but I guess Pamela Kay had to pay the price. Or at least KPMT did, which was the same thing. A Halloween theme show, a clairvoyant with a troll-like companion, a magician with a statuesque assistant, a disappearing diamond bracelet, and a couple of unhappy listeners. It all added up to Mrs. Paulson seeing fifty-eight large go up in smoke. I guess she had a right to take it personally, it being her fifty-eight grand.

"Jerry, focus please. You know who she is," Pamela Kay lit another cigarette. "You and that magician brought these crooks into the picture. Now they are taking Tony for a ride. They're hustling or blackmailing him or something and I want it to stop right now. For all I know they're making him pay to have a sit down dinner with his long dead parents or maybe Abraham Lincoln. I don't care what it is, it's your damn' fault."

"How can I stop them? They won't listen to me."

"I'm not even sure your listeners listen to you. But here's what I'm going to have you do—" She put the cigarette out in her margarita making Ricardo spring into action. New glass, new drink, ashtray closer. "One, you will find out what the hell is going on—why those two crooks came back to town and what they're doing with Tony."

That sounded like more than one, but I decided not to

press the point.

"Two, you will report back to me regularly with your findings and I will decide how to proceed."

"Look, Mrs. P, I don't think Madame Zoroaster likes me too much after she was on my show...not that it was my fault, I mean...but, they did tell me I would be sorry if I did them any more favors."

"Well, la-de-da. Maybe you can have her look into her goddamn' crystal ball and see what the fuck's gonna happen to you if you don't get this fixed."

Chapter 2.

WELL, that's me all over. Just a guy trying to get on with his life. Maybe with a little help now and then from the afterlife.

I really thought a Halloween call-in show where we connect you up with your dearly departed might give both the audience and the ratings a lift. And to keep things honest, a friend of mine who specializes in debunking the occult was also guesting. As a matter of fact it was really all The Great Rondini's fault, not mine.

At any rate, I had thought a change in format for once would be a good thing. All that political huffing and puffing gets a little stale after a while. Don't get me wrong, I make a good living as a right-wing talk show host, but the only party I want to get in is where they play music and serve cocktails.

Drinking, chasing women, acting silly—sounds a bit like the Democrats, doesn't it?

"*Robert from Milpitas, you're on the air....*"

"*Jerry, long time, first time. Gotta talk quick 'cause they may cut me off, but the cell phone companies are putting subliminal advertising in our phone calls. It's a high frequency only dogs can hear, but all of a sudden you get a craving to run out and buy an iPhone....*" I let him rant on while I tried to think of a way to make a few subliminal plugs myself.

My listeners are largely convinced that the nation is controlled by a secret group of powerful men who plan to wipeout freedom of speech, confiscate our weapons and enslave the population. As for me, I'm still not sure Google is all that bad. Anyway, if I'm doing my job right, the listeners should think I'm further right than the Grand Dragon. Funnier too, I hope. But the bottom line is I'm whatever KPMT, Big Talk Radio, wants me to be, left, right, or center. And believe me, they don't want left or center.

Not like I couldn't get another gig, but usually you have to wait until somebody dies. Take, for example, last year when I took a break from daily radio following that unfortunate experience at KDAB. I had been on the bench so long that I had memorized the 'Trainee Wanted' signs at McDonald's. I was picturing myself in an apron and a paper hat when I got a call from my old KDAB sponsor, Charlie Wooten. He's the head honcho at Charlie Wooten Imports. It's named after him because he's the guy who owns the place. A purveyor of the finest vehicles on four wheels, as I used to announce three times an hour for those folks in less fine vehicles fighting the morning traffic.

I must have done okay reading his spots though, because Charlie took a real liking to me. Introducing him to a couple of the young coeds interning at the station didn't hurt either. So when I was out of pocket—I'd already started thinking about living in my car, but the cost of parking was higher than my rent—Charlie hired me to do big things in the automotive trade. I became a Charlie Wooten sales executive at his dealership on Van Ness, "sales executive" being an entry level position. I got enough of a draw against future commissions to keep me off the streets, but I'd have to actually put a few citizens behind the wheel if I wanted to eat and keep the cable guy happy too. Anyway, California's supposed to be car crazy, so how hard could it be?

I had been there a couple of months when I got paged one morning to go to Charlie's office. It was too early for lunch, so I figured maybe I got paged by mistake. On my way I tried to remember what Charlie had told me about sales quotas and such. I also thought about how far unemployment insurance would go these days. I could probably snag that job bagging groceries. That and I'd be okay if I gave up living indoors.

"How 'bout a cigar, Jerry? Coffee? Raynee can fetch you a cup if you want. Hell, she can run right down to Starbucks if you want some of that faggity shit."

Charlie had his expansive mood on, waiving me to the big client chair. Raynee however didn't look all that happy about running down to Starbucks in six inch heels. One thing I gotta say about Charlie, at least he canned you in style. None of that business about security guards walking you out and such. Anyway I decided to take it like a man, no coffee and no last cigarette—er, cigar. I would have taken a blindfold if they'd offered one though. The begging and crying would come later.

"Listen here, Red, I gotta start right off apologizin'," Charlie started off, giving me a smile like I was a fleet buyer. "All the time you were doing the traffic I never thought of it, but you're the perfect guy," he waived his arm in my direction like he was showcasing a new Mercedes. His smile, pretty big to start with, was about to dislocate his jaw. "That traffic reporting you did back on KDAB was good and all, but it's confusing. All those freeway numbers, locations, times, all that. You're a creative guy...just maybe not so good with numbers. I saw you doing the pricing and the financing stuff here, and yeah, I gotta say you're no numbers man."

He raised an eyebrow and dropped the smile.

"Well, Charlie, I really thought the computer would straighten out any mistakes in the numbers," I said.

"Huh? Oh sure, Red. But for traffic you really need to fly a helicopter and that's sort of like the thing with the numbers. Not really *your* thing. I've ridden with you on a test drive—I gotta say it scared the shit outta me. How the hell could you expect to get away piloting a chopper?"

"I promise I won't fly a chopper, Charlie. But, listen, I'm not sure I'm following you. Is this about the traffic report or pushing your jalopies?"

"No, no, don't get confused, kiddo. Well, about the cars— maybe BMW won't need to open any new assembly lines because of you. But that's not what we're talking about here."

"It's not? Oh no, of course, not. I knew that. What are we talking about, Charlie?"

"Two words, Red," Charlie stuck the cigar between his teeth and managed a smile at the same time. "I've got just two words for you, kid."

I figured the first word was "You're" and that the other had to be one of those f-words. The suspense was unbearable.

"Talk radio."

Charlie leaned back in his big chair and laced his thick fingers behind his head. "I've been talking to KPMT and they want me as a sponsor pretty bad. But I've decided I want you to be a part of the deal."

"Just like that? I'm part of the deal? Voice overs or reading your ads or something? When I'm not selling cars, you mean?"

"Well, you're in the deal only if I sign on to advertise. But we gotta face it, kid, you're killing me on the showroom floor and radio's your thing. They say you can start this week-end doing an overnight shift as a tryout. Talk show host, you know, on one of them call-in shows."

"KPMT...KPMT...." I searched my memory banks, "Right-wing talk station isn't it, somewhere just this side of King George. Do they know I'm not too political?"

"Well, to be honest again, I told them you were TP. You know, a tea party conservative. Look, Red, it's the happening thing. You can pick up some buzzwords, listen to a couple of their shows and you'll get the idea. The nuttier you act the better. It seems pretty simple to me." By now Charlie had stopped smiling. He leaned forward and said in an imitation of a whisper, "I hear their guy on the evening commute is headed back to Wichita."

"Wow, when did he decide to do that?"

"He hasn't yet. But KPMT wants my business, so...."

"Oh. I get it," and I'd be on the *next* plane to Wichita if I didn't work out. "Of course, the only thing I know about politics, is that the guy with the best hair gets elected."

"No problem. You'll say you're a Libertarian. Nobody knows what the hell they stand for. You musta listened to Limbaugh or some of those other guys sometime. If you haven't, tune in anytime—somebody's always on the air. Listen for a couple of shows and that's all the training you'll need. Remember the crazier you act, the better you'll do."

"I can do crazy. 'I'm not really a lunatic; I just play one on the radio.'"

Chapter 3.

AFTER leaving Pamela Kay's I found my way back to the coast highway and headed south toward the Golden Gate Bridge. The sun was shining, the top was down, I had the wind in the hair thing going again, doing the limit plus ten—the kind of day that makes you want to just keep on going. The Beamer hugged the curves like Charlie Sheen at a Playmate convention.

I could make it down to Carmel-By-The-Sea in time for a late lunch. Find a room, see what's new in the galleries, walk on the beach. Or maybe keep on motoring down Big Sur way for a hot tub and a massage at Esalen. But I knew I wouldn't be doing any of those things now. My whole way of life was tottering on the brink.

So much for lunch with the boss.

Pamela Kay had finally run out of steam during the eating portion of the program. I pushed the mahi-mahi and endive salad around on my plate for a while, made suitably agreeable noises about helping with the fortune-telling fortune hunter and escaped from *chez* Paulson claiming I had to get prep'd for my show. I never did really eat, but the thought of Madame Zoroaster's being back in the picture had taken away my appetite anyway. She had almost cost me the show when I'd been on less than six months.

Now even Charlie Wooten might not have the sway to keep me in the lineup if the clairvoyant was somehow ripping off Pamela Kay's only nephew, money being even thicker than blood. If I couldn't get out of this in one piece, I'd wind up washing cars, not selling them.

"Hey, babe, I just had lunch with Pamela Kay Paulson and I'll be a little busy this afternoon, so call me back when you get this, love ya'. Oh yeah, this is Jerry."

There's nothing like voice mail for pouring out your heart. I was looking for a soft shoulder to cry on while I drove back to town, so I called my part-time girlfriend Jeanne Parker for a little sympathy. Aside from being my part-time girlfriend, Jeanne was a fulltime associate producer for the detestable Freddy and Betty morning show. We'd been seeing each other on and off for about three months—Jeanne and me that is, not Freddy and Betty and me. As a matter of fact, I make an effort never to see Freddy and Betty, and Jeanne says they can't see me at all. Being a cog in the morning show means Jeanne's a great early date but has to be asleep about an hour after my show goes off the air. That made for some rather hurried lovemaking. I suggested they put a futon in the KPMT coffee room, but Ned Tunney, our station manager, put the kibosh on it.

That pretty much left my window for romance between ten in the morning when Freddy and Betty wrapped and my airtime at four. And it didn't look like I was going to make it today.

Anyway, I had speed-dialed Jeanne's mobile from mine and wound up in her voice mail. Next, while I drove through the Marin headlands, I tried my pal Ronnie Green to see if I could spread my depression around a little. After all, wasn't he the guy who got me into this whole mess? More VM. I left him a rude but witty message saying I'd see him later at the Blue Sphinx. I could always depress him then.

When I got back to San Francisco it was still a couple of hours until show time so I parked in my building and ran up to change my shirt. Then I elevatored back down and walked along the Embarcadero to Battery Street where the KPMT studio overlooked a parking lot that overlooked the bay. I was hoping to catch Tony Paulson in his office, but dreading it also. Go straight to the horse's mouth, that's what they always say, but I had a feeling I might wind up being the horse's other end.

Tony's in charge of the KPMT sales department and is nice enough for a guy who got his vice presidency as a birthright. Mostly, he spends his time wining and dining KPMT's advertisers. A couple of times he's dragged me along so the sponsors could see me up close. After all, they pay my salary.

I always thought Tony showed his real talent in building the KPMT sales team. He mainly hires attractive young women to deal with the basically lecherous tradesmen we get as sponsors. An effective sales strategy if ever there was one. The ladies also add a lot to the office Christmas party as I recall.

I pushed open the big glass door with 'KPMT—Big Talk Radio' lettered on it. The afternoon guy was ranting through the ceiling speakers that carry the broadcast throughout the office. He was rattling everyone's eardrums as he made a beat down of some poor caller the centerpiece of his show. Rattling everyone's eardrums except for the folks in the broadcast studios. Back there you need a pair of headphone to hear the show.

The young man sitting at the reception desk had on headphones, but I doubted he was listening to the afternoon guy. He also had an amazing assortment of pins, earrings and nose studs stuck through various parts of his face and ears. He could probably tune in the station without a radio.

"Wassup, Michael?" I asked. To set off the brightwork, tattoo sleeves covered his arms. They reminded me of the Sunday funnies. I could have sworn one was *Garfield*.

Anyway, I tried out my best smile and in return, he ignored me. I couldn't be sure if he heard me, so I cleared my throat for a repeat run at him. This time I'd speak louder in case he'd suddenly gone blind and couldn't see me standing there. His lips moved but he wasn't talking to me. Maybe just singing along with a music download or pretending to be on the phone so I'd have to wait.

While I waited, I looked over to the office area in case Tony P. might be wandering around, maybe chasing a secretary or doing whatever a V.P. does. I did get to see Rita Silvano bending over the copy machine though. My lucky day.

Meanwhile the afternoon talent was going round the bend: *"...if you ever call here again you filthy, pinko, homo I'll get you in the parking lot and I'll rip your..."*

And this caller was actually on his side. Just kidding.

The lovely Ms. Silvano had disappeared, so I turned back to Michael. He was saying, "...I got to go. Some guy's waiting here...." A good cover-up if he was just listening to music on the earphones. He gave me a smile chock full of metal, looking somewhat like a crocodile with a mouthful of tinfoil.

"Hey, don't I know you?" he said thumbing through the station newsletter looking for my picture. "Jeremy Jeremy. It has Jeremy down twice. Some kind of typo, I guess."

"That's no typo, that's me. I'm probably on while you're down at the tattoo parlor; otherwise you'd be a fan.

Remember, kid, the station's paying you to listen to me."

"Four o'clock show, that's you," he seemed more enthused once he saw my head shrunk down to wallet size. "Kaa-rist! Is it almost four already?"

The speakers were blaring, "...*come down to the station and say that, you bag of...*"

I was about to tell Michael that I had come in early but decided it might be better just to leave things as they were; instead I told him he'd better get a hustle on if it was that late. "Before you get too wrapped up in chores for Uncle Neddy though, can you check if I can see Tony Paulson for a minute or two?"

"He can't right now."

"Somebody in there with him?"

"Nope."

"*...in favor of lesbians having babies, how does that work? Immaculate conception?" What the hell...*"

"Somebody expected momentarily then?"

"You're getting colder."

"I'm also getting older. Any idea when he'll be free?"

"Why didn't you ask? He's open all afternoon."

"*...Rosie on line four—Wait a minute, you're not one of those...*"

"But I can't go in?"

"Sure, you can go in, but—" wait for it, I could feel a punch line headed my way "—he's not in there now. Ha-ha. He isn't back from lunch yet..."

Michael was laughing it up, but not enough to get me to join in. Eventually he got the time figured out and penciled me in on the computer for a two-thirty with Tony. Assuming he made it back from lunch.

"*...arghh—you liberal son of a...*"

I took a breath and jumped into the deep end again, "Do you think Ned might be in now? Back from lunch and all? Not out riding the waves, is he?"

"Nah, Ned had me order in for him. A super burrito." Michael studied the computer screen like it held the answer to all life's problems. "His calendar is clear, and let's see...nope, he's not on the phone, though he could be texting somebody, but that's a chance we'll have to take. I'd say you should be able to just go right in." He had to be Pamela Kay's illegitimate issue.

Anyway, I strolled into the office suite, normally foreign territory to the broadcast talent. I had to pass Tony's office on my way to Ned's, so I stuck my head in just to make sure he wasn't hiding under the desk. He wasn't. His office was so tidy I doubted he really worked there. No papers scattered around, no notes or directories cluttering up the desk. The only thing on it was the ratings bible, neatly lined up and squared to the right front corner. Even the wastepaper basket looked like it had never been used.

"DUDE, ¿cómo estás?" Ned said looking up from the workbench he used as a desk. On it were a few hundred parts from what I'd guess was a washing machine. He wiped grimy fingers on his shirt and gave me a handshaking that would make Hulk Hogan wince.

"How's the show? Kinta and the Brat doing okay? They're the best we got." He flashed his pearly whites. "I keep thinking they should be on the morning show, but you need a good team too. Your numbers show you're holding your own in evening drive."

"Thanks, Ned. The team and the show are both doing great," I said, trying to massage some life back into my fingers. Behind his desk a giant surf board hung on the wall with "KMPT—Big Kahuna, Bigger Talk" painted on it. It had a caricature of Ned also, showing him balancing a beach bunny over his head while riding the crest of a wave. The fact that he was out of the closet hadn't seemed to make a difference.

"Did you catch my show the other day about home schooling? How it cuts down the cost of having all those teachers hanging around?"

"Aw hell, I must have missed that one, Jerry. You know, I have to arrive pretty early most days to be on hand for the morning show. You know—Freddy and Betty. Need to make sure everything goes okay since they pull in the big numbers."

"Oh yeah, sure, you got to keep an eye on those two," I said. "You don't want them screwing up."

Not to mention the early start gave Ned an excuse to cut out while the surf was still running at Ocean Beach. Still, in spite of the tie-dyed shirt and sandals, in spite of being openly gay, Ned was an elder statesman of conservative talk radio in San Francisco. He'd pioneered the lunatic fringe since the sixties. Next to the "Big Kahuna" board was a picture of a young, long-haired Ned giving Senator Barry Goldwater the hand crusher. Barry looked like he could take it.

I wanted to work up gradually to my reason for coming in.

I didn't want to be obvious. I figured I'd noodle around first, break the ice and all. I asked him, "So what's all this stuff on your desk? Things so bad you can't afford to call the Maytag repairman?"

Ned gave me a laugh. As station manager, he wants me to be entertaining, so he makes it a point to laugh at almost anything I say. He went into hysterics the last time I brought up my contract.

"This is way beyond what the Maytag repairman can salvage. It's one of our old cart machines I'm trying to get working. We've still got a lot on cartridge that hasn't been moved to digital yet."

"I wouldn't throw away the number for the Maytag man until you hear sound coming out of that thing." I fished an old putter out of an umbrella stand to have something in my hands and after a few air-putts, settled down in the big leather chair he kept next to a row of beat-up filing cabinets.

Ned was still chuckling to himself. I took it as a good sign. Then Ned said, "Michael buzzed me, he says you're trying to track down Tony. You seeing if he can set up a few more supermarket openings for you?" This time he laughed at his own joke.

"Nah, I think my license for the KPMT Talk-A-Van has expired. You could try the afternoon guy though, he seems pretty upbeat. But I am looking for Tony. I have something to discuss with him, not really radio stuff though."

"What's up? Anything I can help you with?" Ned looked up from the tangle of wires and gears on his desk. The sandy hair was a little thinner than I seemed to remember; his faded blue eyes looked even more bleached out. He'd probably had lean swimmers' muscles once, but now they were settling into chunky knots. Still, I wouldn't want to arm wrestle him. Not if I had to use that arm again.

"I need to touch base with Tony as a favor for Mrs. Paulson. Not really station business."

"Interesting. Pamela Kay not talking to her favorite nephew all of a sudden?" Ned looked at me, then back to the wires and stuff on his table. "I didn't know you knew the Paulsons all that well. Glad I hired you on, if you're that well connected."

"The strange thing is that I'm not." Maybe if I leveled a little, Ned might have some insight into Tony's doings. I had heard that they had been pretty thick once, and maybe they still were. "It's actually kind of embarrassing, but Mrs. P seems to think that I can read the mind of a mind reader. Or at least see what she's up to."

"Huh? Why you?"

"Well, you might remember. That spirit medium I had on the show about six months ago."

"Not Madame Zoroaster!" Ned's head popped up from the cart machine and he tried to choke off another laugh, not that this was the kind I wanted to get. But he couldn't hold back, letting it out and knocking a few parts to the floor.

Okay, fair is fair. Madame Zoroaster, the psychic disaster. Not one of the better chapters in my career.

Ned poked a little more at what Pamela Kay was up to in case he needed a little CYA. But he didn't know much about Tony or if Tony had hooked up with the Z-witch in some way.

"Tony and I used to be a lot closer, but you know how it goes—he's tied up with the sales side and I'm just trying to keep the expenses in line and the station on the air." Ned held up a handful of wires to take a better look at them. He pushed his glasses up on his forehead and squinted at the cart machine. In that moment, he went from being an over-aged surfer to a middle-aged guy just hanging in, not hanging ten.

"Tony did say he'd be working at home for the next few days. He should have his cell on or you could reach him at home if it's important," Ned finally said.

"Thanks, but I'm not sure I want to bother him at home. I'll try to catch him next time he's in."

I wondered if Ned and Tony might still be better pals than Ned was letting on. Ned was the salt of the earth and all that, but for a station manager who made it a habit to miss my show, he seemed kind of chummy today. Of course, he was interested in why Pamela Kay Paulson had come to me first.

If Ned and Tony were still pals, Ned would probably call Tony at home before I could get there, so I saw no point in calling ahead myself. I wandered over to a desk nobody was using and signed in on the computer. Tony's home number was listed in the station's directory and when I typed it into *Yahoo!* I got back an address.

Chapter 4.

TONY lived in Noe Valley, one of San Francisco's nicer neighborhoods. Very upscale with boutiques and restaurants, not to mention boutique restaurants. Gingerbread row houses built for working-class families after the Big One in '06 line the streets. They were thrown up cheek-to-cheek and designed to be affordable. Today you can pick one up for somewhere north of a million.

Since not many working men had cars in '06, needless to say parking was now at a premium. The streets were lined with Beamers, Mercs and Volvos. I had to circle Tony's block a three times until I caught a Porsche pulling out of a spot just a few doors down from his house. Lucky again—maybe I'd buy that lottery ticket.

Tony's silver SUV was parked right in front of number four thirty-two, the address I got on-line, so I guessed he really was working from home, not at the gym or working on his short game. My faith in mankind and upper management having been restored, I sat in my car trying to decide how best to approach him. I wanted to ask if he knew where Madame Z was and how I could get in touch with her. Maybe something to do with a sponsor, say I had an idea for a mortuary tie-in... Maybe Madame Zoroaster sits in at the wake. Imagine getting a message from the guest of honor right at his or her own funeral.

Before I could come up with a solid excuse for knocking on Tony's door, it opened and he came out walking fast. A girl in a fuzzy pink sweater was pedaling at top speed to keep up with him. She looked a lot like the girl I had been dreaming about earlier, the kind of girl I might dream about even when I wasn't sleeping. Watching her run after Tony I managed to work up a small pang of envy. So this is what Tony spent his day working on. I just hate to see the rich guys get the girls, too. Maybe wavy red hair, a straight nose and a mellow voice don't count for much anymore.

Of course, Tony might not be so rich anymore according to his aunt. But maybe the lady in pink forgot to Google his net worth before going after him. Still, I'd like to think she was just the Avon lady making a house call. And maybe the romance was over, since Tony gave her the cold shoulder when he hopped into the Lexus.

My dream girl crossed the street, dodging a car and got in a white compact that had an Econo-rents sticker on the bumper. She followed Tony and I followed her. I had thought Tony would be going downtown to the office, but I guessed wrong. Instead he turned onto 17th Street heading out toward the avenues and eventually the ocean. Maybe he wanted to catch Ned between waves.

The white compact didn't follow Tony though. She turned at Market heading downtown. I had a decision to make before I got to the light—turn left after Tony or follow the lady in pink. On the one hand, Tony might be on his way to meet Madame Zoroaster, and on the other—well, I had seen her in my dreams. If I hadn't had that little talk with Pamela Kay, I'd have been all about following dream girl, but duty called. Duty and a steady paycheck.

I had never tailed a car before, but it seemed pretty easy. Whenever I got stopped by a light, Tony got nailed by the next one so I could catch up. Same with cross traffic at the stop signs. Pretty soon we were out by Golden Gate Park, Tony passed by 19th Avenue which would have taken him north to the Golden Gate Bridge and Auntie's house in Stinson Beach. Instead he went straight on and I followed him almost to the ocean.

A stop light at 28th caught me, but this time Tony made the one up ahead. I saw him turn off in the distance and tried to catch up, but I got blocked in by a car waiting to turn from the wrong lane. By the time I got past and turned where Tony had, the silver Lexus was out of sight. Being a detective was a little trickier than I thought.

I drove around for a while, but didn't spot him anywhere. So since airtime was approaching, I decided to head back to the stable. I should have followed the blonde.

On the way downtown, I called Jeanne again, but again no

soap. I called every number I had except her fax, but all I got were a bunch of voice mail greetings. As far as I knew, I hadn't done anything to make her screen my calls, but sometimes it's hard to be sure.

"STAY tuned for more of the Jerry Jeremy show on Big Talk Radio—wait a minute—what am I saying? Not just Big Talk Radio—you're listening to the biggest mouth on Big Talk Radio. Down here at KPMT, I'm known for my big mouth, my big ears, my big feet and, well, let's stop while I'm ahead....

"And right now we're going to talk about something close to my heart, namely—your wallet. The government is taking money right out of it that you could be using to, oh let's say, lease a new BMW or Mercedes down at Charlie Wooten Imports...."

The show was zipping along nicely and even the callers were a notch above average. From four to seven I belong to the listeners, the callers and the sponsors. And they belong to me. I enrich the lives of our evening drive audience, improve their intellects and expand their understanding of the world in general. But mostly I distract them from the miserable commute they're stuck in. The hours fly by when I'm on the air and for the audience's sake alone, you want those hours to fly by.

Kinta White, my producer, was screening the calls and serving up puff balls for me to knock out of the park. During the last segment, we even had a good name-calling argument that had my board op, Brad the Brat, bleeping every other word.

At seven I signed off, gave Brad and Kinta a goodbye salute—

"Good show, guys."

"Good show, Jerry."

—and started driving back out to the avenues, to a spot not far from where I had tailed Tony earlier. Twenty minutes later I was rolling slowly past the Blue Sphinx, waiting to see if somebody would pull out of a parking space. The Sphinx has a blue neon pyramid out front that the owner got cheap when the wax museum was doing a remodel. It always puzzled me why the club was named the Blue *Sphinx* when the sign was actually a blue *pyramid*.

The club's main attraction though was not the sign; it was the steady line-up of magicians, hypnotists and illusionists appearing there five nights a week. Those magicians not actually performing on its stage or elsewhere hang out at the Sphinx, making it a kind of club for the sleight of hand. I was there to see the night's headliner and I don't mean his snappy show, although his assistant alone was worth the two drink minimum.

"LADIES and gentlemen, the management of the Blue Sphinx is proud to present the master of mystery, that maestro of mind reading, our conjurer extraordinaire...." And so the intro spieled on, then a puff of orange smoke clouded the stage and The Great Rondini materialized. Of course, I've known The Great One since he was just plain Ronnie Green living two houses down from where I grew up back in New Jersey.

I had made it a point to arrive at the Sphinx early enough to catch his act which I always enjoy, and not just because he's my pal. Truth is I like magic and like they say, behind every great magician is a beautiful assistant wearing a costume about the size of a cocktail napkin. The real magic is how she manages not to get arrested. The Great Rondini says magic is all about the art of misdirection, and I guess she does the job. When Satyra saunters around the stage, nobody's trying to see what Ronnie has up his sleeve. Like Cher, she has only one name, though I'm pretty sure the nuns back at St. Mary's didn't call her that.

Because we're old friends, The Great Rondini pops up on my radio show now and then. He can't do card tricks over the radio or read my callers' minds—those being pretty much illegible. Instead Ronnie comes on to pursue his favorite pastime, his favorite right after chatting up the girls who turn up at the Sphinx for the show. After girls, drugs and rock 'n' roll, Ronnie devotes himself to exposing assorted clairvoyants, faith healers and other phonies who pretend their mind games are for real. Remember that Madame Zoroaster? Guess who got me to put her on the air.

That time it got started when The Great Rondini got booked into the Exotic-Erotic Halloween Ball. That's the big bash down at the Cow Palace that used to be called the Hookers' Ball until the hookers threatened to sue. Still, the Ball—all music, magic and show your tattoo—draws several thousand celebrants each October. For the Ronster the opportunity to spread his greatness was golden. And for once Satyra would be overdressed. So far, so good. But then

Rondini decided the gig's promotion wasn't doing enough to make his magic magic and so he took matters into his own hands. Whenever Ronnie does that, I get a call.

"Listen, Jerry, I'm going to give you an idea that will take your little show to a new level." We had finished an early afternoon run in the park and were catching our respective breaths and a couple of micro-brews by Stow Lake. We flopped down in the grass under a spreading Jacaranda tree where we'd have a clear view of the jogging path, girl watching being right up there with busting fortune tellers in Ronnie's book.

"Me? A new level? I thought I was on the level," I said. "As a matter of fact, I'm known for being on the level. Well, mostly on the level."

"No, no, a new plateau, Junior, new heights of cultural exploration, a new way of seeing—"

"Seeing? I'm on the radio...hearing maybe. What is it, some new kind of podcast?"

"No, you're missing the point. Now watch my lips and—abracadabra—your audience will double. Triple maybe."

"On the same station? Higher ratings? A bigger share? I'm all ears. What's the 411? Give. What's your idea?"

"A call-in show for the dead."

"Ahh...a call-in show for the dead." I paused to let the words sink in. "And here, I thought you were going to say something silly. Look, you know how this radio thing is supposed to work, don't you? You know, we talk, they listen and then they run out and buy stuff we advertise?

"Maybe my audience is barely breathing, but they're not dead yet. Not quite dead. Does Arbitron send ratings diaries to the cemetery? Is that how Freddy and Betty manage to stay on the air?"

"Slow down, JJ," Ronnie wiped the beer I'd spilled off his leg. "The callers aren't dead, they call in and we have this clairvoyant see, and callers ask her to connect them through to their loved ones who have passed over."

"Uh-huh. And you came up with this all by yourself, no help from the guys down at the sanitarium." It wasn't all that bad an idea, but somewhere I thought I heard another shoe whistling through the air. "Where do all my ratings come from? Beyond the grave?"

"Well that's the beauty part. Jerry Jeremy doesn't have to do a damn' thing, because his good pal, The Great Rondini, will do all the heavy lifting. My plan is to have a couple of calls go by, the clairvoyant does her number for them, and then I will expose this phony medium for the fraud that she is. I will unmask her tricks, the shaking table, the knocking, the eerie lights—"

"This is radio, remember? Low budget radio. No special effects unless they're in the tape library," I said. "Besides where do we get a medium? Do we post it on Craig's List?"

"Strange that you should ask. Some of my fellow magicians tell me that there is a certain woman, origins unknown, who has set up shop here in town. She mostly tries to get some well-off sucker to introduce her around his social circle where she puts on an act and sets up her marks. They say she's pulling in some large donations."

"What's her name? Nancy Pelosi?"

"She calls herself Madame Zoroaster, a pseudonym I'd bet."

"I thought she was a clairvoyant."

"A fake clairvoyant, but a real pseudonym."

"So if I put her on the show, I'll be able to expose her as a fake, and all these people she's scamming will be grateful I showed them up as chumps. That's not so bad...."

"Uh, actually, Red, I'll expose her. It's your show, but you're just along for the ride when it comes to exposing."

"Sure, you're known for that. They still after you down in Bakersfield?"

"And while exposure is on our minds," Ronnie popped the top on a fresh brew, "I happen to be booked for the Exotic-Erotic Ball this year."

"So Satyra got the exotic-erotic part covered—what are you going to be doing?"

"Actually I was thinking"—uh-oh, here it comes—"we could do the call-in for the dead show right before the Ball on Halloween. Very seasonal and the station could promote the show all through October, even get some advertising tie-ins. Of course, my appearance would be gratis, you'd just need to put in a small plug for my Exotic-Erotic extravaganza whenever you promo your show."

"I guess raising the dead on my show won't be as scary as all that stuff about politics, war and gas prices, but what's in it for me?"

"I'll see that you get tickets to the Ball. You won't be the ugly step-sister left at home."

"The ugly step-sister went to the ball, Cinderella was left at home. Only the ugly step-sister didn't make Cinderella plug the ugly step-sister's act."

"Well, excuse me. I just thought you might want to help out a pal. I didn't ask for anything before I gave you a killer idea for your show."

"Well, maybe not, but we'll need to get Ned Tunney to give it the okay and see if Sales can do anything with it. What about Satyra? You planning to bring her along?"

"Could be, but I don't want to distract you from the business at hand."

"The 'business' being to plug your show?"

"Hey, Junior, one hand scratches the other, you know. You wash my back, I'll scratch yours...."

"Settle down, fella, I'm already spoken for."

"Really? Still dating that girl with the bad eyes? Don't worry, I'll bring Satyra anyway. I want to make sure she doesn't overdo on the Cuervo getting rid of the pre-show jitters. After all I want her sober for the Exotic-Erotic show."

"But won't that ruin your act?"

Chapter 5.

GHOSTS on the loose....

The undead walk among us....

People all wild and scary....

Well, maybe not scary in the normal sense, this being San Francisco. But it meant that Halloween had come at last.

In the City, it's all about trick or treating for the grown-ups, practically a bank holiday. Whole neighborhoods get into the swing of it. Streets get closed off and all the ghouls and goblins come out to play, not to mention the drag queens, motorcycle gangs, and pretty much anyone under the age of sixty. You got your normal, your paranormal and your abnormal running around here. And believe me, telling one from the other isn't easy.

In some neighborhoods, they even dress up the kids and send them door-to-door begging for candy.

My show went on at four o'clock as usual. We started off in my regular digs, Studio B, which closely resembles a glassed-in phone booth, if we still had phone booths. Like some kind of radio clown car, we normally squeeze in Brad's big control board, a couple of chairs, an assortment of consoles, cart machines, computers, phone buttons, and a couple of microphones on hanging off articulated armatures. And of course Brad the Brat too. It's so close if Brad has tacos for lunch, I'm the one who burps. Kinta White sits just outside the studio window, screening callers and punching up my cues on the computer.

Madame Zoroaster was scheduled for six o'clock, the last hour of the show. Since we couldn't all fit into Studio B, Brad and Kinta had set up a remote in the KPMT lobby. By six the lobby would be clear of on-lookers, most of the staff by then would be fighting traffic or waiting it out over cocktails at the Bridgeview Grotto.

For the first two hours Ronnie, Satyra, Brad and I sweated it out shoulder to shoulder in Studio B. Ronnie threw in some dish on magic and not more than a dozen plugs for his show. Satyra added the woman's touch and Brad missed cueing three commercials, apparently suffering from some of that misdirection stuff. Meanwhile I persevered:

"...so that was Marsha with the traffic report for those listeners not actually out there in it. There's some crazy school of thought that says commuter lanes will help and save gas in the bargain by encouraging car pools."

"Well, Jerry," Ronnie said, "a lot of people do pick up strangers hanging out at the bus stops and parking lots so they can use the commuter lane—"

"Reverse hitchhiking...in California the drivers solicit the riders."

"—and we all know what hitchhiking leads to."

"The car pool lane?"

For the séance, Brad and Kinta had re-arranged KPMT's lobby, pulling chairs around a low table in the reception area and hooking up a few mismatched microphones. We could hear the callers over the office speakers, but wouldn't be able to use our headsets. Gaffer's tape crisscrossed the floor, heaven forbid anybody should trip on the cables. Kinta would still screen the callers but Brad the Brat would have to connect them in the studio and communicate with me using hand signals through the studio window.

In spite of an early winter rain that had started Madame Zoroaster and Vigo Czak, her diminutive companion, appeared right on time. Rita Silvano from Sales had hung around to greet them, keeping thoughts of the copy machine running through my mind. Turns out Rita had actually sold some commercial tie-ins. During the newsbreak, everybody greeted everybody else, shaking hands and commenting on the weather before taking our places around the lobby table.

Madame Z. had either gone all out for Halloween or was more over-done than medium. Neon-streaked hair, make-up that would have embarrassed Vampira, a dozen or so rainbow-hued shawls and scarves over paisley skirts—she looked like the world's worst-dressed gypsy. Vigo was a full head shorter than she was and shorter still compared to everyone else. He had dressed entirely in black, probably to avoid clashing with his girlfriend's *couture*. Vigo's pale face seemed to float above his body like a death's head only scarier. They both had accents that sounded like they'd been lifted from a Bela Lugosi film. Words like "being" or "seeing" came out like "be-ink" and "see-ink".

From the overhead speakers we could hear the weather girl describing a rainstorm to the listeners caught out in it. Brad cued the last of the commercials, the lights in the lobby were dimmed and a few candles lit at Madame Zoroaster's request. I felt like young Abe Lincoln, trying to read off his clipboard by candle light. Brad held up his hand, fingers outstretched and counted down, one finger at a time. When only one was left, he pointed to me and I did my thing.

"Welcome back, folks. The time is now six-oh-eight and you are tuned in to a special edition of the Jerry Jeremy show – with me, Jerry Jeremy—on KPMT, Big Talk Radio." Good start. I got my name in twice. *"Tonight our guests will amaze you; some are living, some dead, and some we're not sure of."*

I went around the table introducing each guest and each one said his or her hellos or the equivalent. The Great Rondini managed to tell us where he was appearing again, Satyra repeated it, and Madame Zoroaster—*"Call me Madame Ilonya"*—gave out the address of her website. Two minutes into the segment and already it was a plug-fest. I ignored Vigo who didn't have a spot at the table anyway and I joined in with a promo for my upcoming appearance at the new food court over in the Pleasanton Mall.

"Tonight our listeners will call in, not to talk to any of us here in the studio, but to talk to someone who has already shucked off this mortal coil. Our signal will be going out not only to the Bay Area, but across time and space to a new dimension, going where no talk show has gone before. Madame Zoroaster, will be tuning in the spirit world, contacting those who have passed over. Up 'til now our signal only got as far as Fresno."

I told the listeners that this was for entertainment purposes only, a warning that our attorney insisted we say, and added, *"In case you're a little skeptical of Madame Zoroaster's powers, the Great Rondini and his beautiful assistant, Satyra, are here to spot any chicanery."*

Ronnie drew the battle lines saying, *"In years of research, I have found no conclusive proof of genuine clairvoyance."*

Madame Z gave him a smile that could freeze a duck in flight and said her piece, *"It is always so with non-believers, but cynics learn in sorrow to believe and non-believers wander eternally searching for something to believe in."*

I didn't quite catch the meaning of all that, but I was sure Ronnie would be on top of it. Time to move on.

"The way the séance will work is you—the listening audience—will determine who our guests from the other world will be. When you think of it, this might be the ultimate call-in."

I spent a few minutes setting up the bit and then turned to Madame Zoroaster, dropping into the bass range for the best effect, *"Madame Zoroaster,"* I sounded most auspicious, *"are you ready?"*

"READY? Jerry, are you kidding, I was born ready and I will die ready." She leaned forward resting her arms on the table, *"Everyone please touch hands around the table."*

I thought about telling the audience to lay their hands on their radios, but didn't want to have too much fun at Madame Z's expense.

Then Madame Zoroaster said, *"Your listeners might want to touch their radios to give us more psychic power."*

"Well...okay, you heard it here. If you're driving in traffic, you might want to just put one hand on the radio. But remember, it's bad luck to change the dial."

We sat holding hands, resting them on the low table. For extra psychic energy, Satyra rubbed her foot against my ankle. Czak hovered behind Madame Z while she closed her eyes and began to breathe deeply. In a few moments the breathing seemed to morph into light snoring. I was about to say something when she sat up and spoke—

"Oh, hear my pleas. Oh, To-Nohwa, please hear my pleas. You are my window to the other side. Tonight we seek your help in unearthing the secrets of the ancestors of our listening audience. Oh, To-Nohwa...."

AT about the time Madame Zoroaster was tickling the ghosts out of the studio woodwork, Tom Marshall, Pamela Kay Paulson's partner in Big Talk Radio, was headed home from a meeting at *chez Paulson* in Marin. The rain showering the City was a lot more severe in the North Bay, flooding streets and washing away a few trees. It closed in on Tom as he drove along the Shoreline Highway. Sheets of rain were fighting his wipers to a draw, his headlights barely picking out the lane reflectors, tires kicking up buckets of spray.

Officially known as US Route One, the highway snakes along the California coastline from Los Angeles nearly all the way to the Oregon border. Summertimes the tourists get spectacular ocean views from the headlands as the road twists through hills a hundred feet or more above the rocky shore. But on this Halloween night, Tom was straining just to see the road. Every few minutes, he bounced through a puddle which in turn shook out a few choice words about the weatherman.

And not just any weatherman, KPMT's weatherman. The KPMT's *new* weatherman. Not that he blamed him for the storm. That could happen to anybody. The new guy had called the nor'wester okay, giving a big update on the six o'clock report. What pissed off Tom was the lightning. Or more accurately KPMT's weatherman's prediction of possible lightning strikes.

Thunder and fucking lightning? In the fucking Bay Area? Where was this guy from—someplace in the Midwest? Kansas? An out-of-towner might not think too much of it, but the Bay Area gets about as much thunder and lightning as it does snow. The micro-climates or millibars or something. Why take chances? Why not just get the forecast off the newswire like everybody else?

Tom would call Ned Tunney in the morning to find out where he got this guy—Cleveland? Milwaukee? Had to be some place back east, some place with a twelve kilowatt transmitter and lousy weather. He spun the dial, flipping through stations to check if anybody else was featuring thunderstorms. Later the cops said it was still tuned to some golden oldies station. Tom had missed out on Madame Z's warning from beyond.

MAYBE it was time for me to change channels too.

Madame Z certainly wasn't getting her ghost of honor tuned in, in spite of some impassioned pleading.

"Let us know you hear our pleas! Pleease!"

Somewhere in the room a cell phone began to ring. Otherwise the silence was deadly. Ronnie now had a death grip on my left hand and Satyra's nails were drawing blood on the right. I was grasping for words to fill the dead air and Kinta had a wild look in his eyes.

Slowly, with an all-the-time-in-the-world easiness, Vigo Czak reached into his pocket and came up with the offending phone. He flicked it open and thumbed the answer button to kill the ring, then handed it to Ilonya without looking or listening.

"It's for you," went out to the listening audience.

She said, *"To-Nohwa, I knew you would call!"* And we all knew that's what she would say.

"What the he— er, heck are you pulling?" The Great One couldn't believe his eyes—it was the ghost in the Nokia trick!

"Madame Zoroaster, you can't fool our listeners, that's a cell phone," I said. I was nothing, if not quick. *"You can't take a call on the air! Not from a ghost. After all, this is a live call-in show!"*

"What did you expect, a crystal ball? Knocks on the table? Strange voices? I've got a sore throat already." She opened wide and pointed into her mouth. *"This is the twenty-first century. We have cell phones now. I know one spirit guide only uses instant messaging.*

"Now please, everyone concentrate on communicating with our guide. Tonight we have the honor of having the ancient spirit of the Indian chief To-Nohwa joining with us. You know, right here on the mobile. From other side. Long distance."

"Let's see the caller ID—" Ronnie made a grab for the phone, but Ilonya was too fast.

"The number's blocked, it's unlisted," she held the phone behind her back.

"Since when do spirits have unlisted numbers?"

"Since always. You think they call up the phone company to get a line installed? Quiet down, everyone. I'll need to pass on any questions to To-Nohwa over the mobile and I'll repeat the answers from beyond for the radio audience. Be calm, I do this all the time."

"Can we hear what he says? Is there a speakerphone button," Satyra asked.

"Sorry, it's a cheapie, free with two year contract, no speaker. Besides, without the gift, you would hear nothing. To-Nohwa, can you hear me now? Can you hear me now?"

"How many bars you think he's getting?"

"Sometimes the coverage is not so good. There are some very, very dead spots," she looked around the table to see if anybody wanted to argue that one. Then she went into her spiel, *"To-Nohwa knows of the past and of the future; he*

knows of the good and evil that people do—" who is this guy, The Shadow? *"—he knows that someone tonight has much to atone for."*

I thought she was looking at me.

"But To-Nohwa says that he is happy to be with us tonight and to make contact with the mortal plane. From the great beyond To-Nohwa asks 'Who is our first caller?'"

Brad pointed at me and I said, *"Caller on line one, please tell us who you are and what you would like to ask Mr. To-Nohwa."*

"My name is Cheryl and I'm calling from San Francisco," the disembodied voice floated out of the speakers overhead. The effect was pretty spooky all by itself.

A slick highway full of curves; Tom Marshall keeping it under forty in the rain. Better a little late than stuck in some god forsaken ditch. Or worse if it came to that....

Tom's imagination starts playing with words like hydroplane and traction. But the big Mercedes grips the wet pavement like a starving man gripping a T-bone steak. Tom brakes through a low spot full of rainwater. His eyes strain against an early winter dusk settling over the unlit highway, not a good time to go too fast.

A blinding flash lights up the cliffs and thunder shakes the car. Tom swerves involuntarily, then overcorrects jerking the wheel too far and has to pull the other way, willing the car to stay on the pavement. Damn' lightning. Goddamn' Midwesterners.

The rearview mirror frames a distant pair of headlights, high beams just visible through the rain. Another poor schmuck hoping to get home in one piece. Tom will definitely talk to Ned about the weather tomorrow.

"My mom died about eighteen months ago and I have never been able to locate her diamond bracelet. It was quite valuable; Dad had bought it when he cashed in his Polaroid stock."

I said, *"Polaroid, eh? I guess it must be an antique."*

"Uh sure, very, I think. What I want to know is whether my sister-in-law got her greedy hands on it. If that (bleep), Heather, didn't already grab it, could you ask my Mom's spirit where the heck she might have hid it? I can't find it anywhere. And Mom was a little out of it towards the end, if

you know what I mean."

"*Madame Zoroaster,*" I intoned in my best intonation, "*can To-Nohwa tell Cheryl the whereabouts of her mother's diamond bracelet?*"

Another long pause.

Dramatic effect? Can't think of a comeback? Forgot your lines? Speak already—the audience is liable to be tuning away in droves.

"*To-Nohwa wants to know if the letter 'P' means anything to you.*" This time Madame Zoroaster was doing the intoning. Jeez, her voice was deeper than mine now.

"*Letter 'P', you say...yeah, yeah. It's her initial, my mother's first initial. For Pearl. How did you know?*"

Ronnie jumped in at last, "*This could be a setup. We don't know who she is.*" Satyra nodded her support. I was wondering where they had been. I hadn't seen them leave and their bodies were still here, but they sure hadn't contributed much so far. Giving our crystal ball reader enough rope to hang herself, no doubt. The way things were going she'd probably do the Indian rope trick with it.

"*To-Nohwa has not only the knowledge, but also, the wisdom of the ages.*" Madame Zoroaster gave The Great Rondini and Satyra a look.

"*Can he answer my question, oh Madame I-forgot-your-name?*" Cheryl's voice came over the loudspeaker. "*Where's that damn' diamond bracelet?*"

Madame Z intoned again, "*To-Nohwa, did you hear the request of this lady caller—'where is the damn' bracelet?' Can you answer to her and put her heart to rest?*"

Why did I let Ronnie talk me into this? She's a total sham, which we already knew, but does she have to be so boring? Ronnie was supposed to supply the fireworks, stripping her right down to her combat boots. Figuratively, of course. Any real stripping would be up to me.

Madame Z had the cell phone pressed against her forehead now. "*Yes, To-Nohwa, I hear you loud and clear, four bars at least. I will deliver your message on to this pitiful caller.*" For a moment I thought the old Rondini was going to grab the cell phone away and show her what she could do with it. "*Cheryl, listen closely, To-Nohwa has the answer to your question. To-Nohwa says 'Beware the green-eyed monster. What is a sparkling piece of ice-cold stone compared to the love and warmth of your family? It doesn't matter in the infinite scheme of things whether the bracelet has been stolen or misplaced, if you are meant to have it, you will, but if not, not."*

A DIM line on the side of the road—the guard rail—barely visible, fencing off the darkness. Tom Marshall's headlights push into the downpour. Lightning freezes the cliffs in stark relief, the ocean below a panorama of turbulent water. Rain pounds the Mercedes' roof as the highway twists left, then bends right again. High beams in the rearview mirror closer now, traveling too fast, not safe, dangerously speeding.

A dip in the road surprises Tom. Tires airborne, losing their grip. Overcorrecting, Tom fights the wheel. Blinding headlights flair up in the mirror, a car pulling out to pass. Tom braking, but the other schmuck still cutting it too close. The rough shoulder bouncing the Merc, headlights exploding dots against roadside reflectors. Metal screeches against metal, car against car, Tom fighting for a place on the highway. The Mercedes eats up the shoulder, splinters the guardrail, airbag slams Tom against the seat, the big sedan in free-fall, a slow motion dive onto sea-washed rocks a hundred feet below.

*"*WHAT *the (bleep) kind of an answer is that?"* Cheryl shrieked. *"I pulled over on the side of the freeway to call you; I'm sitting here on the shoulder and a cop has pulled in behind me; I held on through the break, for crying out loud, and all I get is 'if I'm meant to have it'? I gotta have something more— send me a sign or something."*

"Okay, To-Nohwa hates to say it—but look in the space behind where the closet shelf meets the wall. It's wrapped in tissue paper."

"Wow, that's something all right! Which closet? Never mind—I can find it...Oh, hello officer...Dick, you got the registration? Officer, we're just leaving. You guys on the radio, I'm heading over right now. Thanks, Totem-pole and Madame whatever...."

Ronnie took up the cudgel, telling listeners that there would be no way to prove whether or not To-Nohwa's answers were correct and Madame Zoroaster counted on that. As far as coming up with the caller's mother's initial, To-Nohwa wasn't really that specific. Madame Z asked only about the letter 'P' which anybody could come up with some kind of a match for. That the mother's name was Pearl was just a lucky shot.

Ilonya refuted The Great Rondini by claiming she was just

the channel by which her spirit guide communicated with the folks back home. In the background, Vigo quietly cheered Ilonya on. Satyra and I sat there looking beautiful.

Finally, I broke the spell, *"Cheryl, I know you said you were jamming for Mom's house, but if you've got the car radio tuned in—and why wouldn't you—please call us back to let us know whether you found the valuable diamond bracelet left to you by Mom or whether Ilonya Zoroaster was wrong and therefore talking through her hat about this."*

From over Madame's shoulder, Vigo Czak gave me the ocular equivalent of the finger, although Ilonya was smiling calmly. In the studio, Brad was signaling me to break for a commercial. *"We need to shift gears now for some messages from this earthly plane. We'll be back in a minute or five, and have our next ghost encounter of the weird kind."* The Brat cued up the commercial and an overly upbeat jingle came bouncing out of the speakers.

During the break Kinta told us every phone line was lit up by people wanting to be connected to the spiritphone and we needed to move along more quickly. One woman offered him five hundred bucks or a night of pleasure for Ilonya's cell phone number, but K had to tell her that although he could be bought, the number couldn't. Mainly because he didn't know it. Vigo casually asked if Kinta had gotten the lady's callback.

After ten or twelve messages from the people who pay the bills, I got a countdown from Brad the Brat, introduced my guests again for anybody just joining the program, they all plugged their various gigs and websites—Madame Z had a toll-free number—and we started working through the callers. Between all the commercials, station ID's, introductions and plugs, it was a miracle that we got to any of the callers. But Madame Zoroaster was a real trooper, even if she was a fake medium. She plowed through one caller after another, To-Nohwa running to form with a few lucky hits on numbers and letters, but mostly keeping to answers that couldn't be proven either true or false.

Ronnie didn't have much to sink his teeth into, so he and Satyra described a number of tricks used by phony fortune tellers and mediums. Ilonya didn't seem particularly bothered by their exposé, gently insisting they had nothing on her and implying her tormentors would probably burn in hell.

No more diamond bracelets turned up missing, but we got several requests for predictions on the stock market and NFL football games, which Madame carefully answered with unhelpful aphorisms that sounded like something out of a fortune cookie. There were a few smart alecks trying to be funny that got past Kinta. I only hoped they weren't funnier than me.

And of course, some callers believed in the gag, and I was feeling a little guilty about Madame Z leading them on.

"Madame Zoroaster, can To-Nohwa tell us what it's like in the afterlife?"

"Madame Zoroaster, can you ask if my brother, Albert, is happy there in heaven?"

"Madame Zoroaster, my first wife died ten years ago and I re-married. When I pass on, which wife will I be spending eternity with? I don't think I could afford both."

Madame Zoroaster, in spite of the cell phone gimmick, was putting enough spin on the old hocus pocus to keep the rubes entertained, including the rubes around the table. Ronnie kept up with the chatter on how Ilonya was just making this stuff up. I played referee and had gotten into the spirit of things. Satyra simply sat there classing up the joint. During the breaks she asked Madame Z about horoscopes and the girls found something to bond over. The show was turning out okay even if Ronnie didn't get the goods on Ilonya. He did get to promote his show at the Exotic-Erotic Ball and seemed happy to settle for that. I couldn't ask for anything more. As we romped through the final segment, I was relaxed and thinking of booking a repeat performance.

"To-Nohwa has a special message for some one listening tonight. I see the letter 'c'. This is for you. You have a difficult journey in your future but you will find the grail you seek. I also see the letter 'm'..." Madame Z gave out a few more personal messages while Ronnie worked on a crossword puzzle he'd found lying around.

Somehow both The Great Rondini and Madame Zoroaster had come off great, neither one able to outdo the other, yet plenty of dishing in both directions. Kinta had done good screening the callers, and the callers themselves fit into the show like they were from central casting. As Ilonya wrapped up her final prognostication, I was thinking she definitely needed more air time. Not enough for her to have a show of her own, of course. And certainly not in my time slot. Unless I somehow managed to nudge Freddy and Betty out of morning drive time....

THE next day the big Mercedes was draining water from every pore, having been winched up from the surf by a couple of monster tow trucks. It rested on a narrow ridge of gravel near the broken guardrail. Parked near it on the shoulder were a couple of Crown Victoria police specials, the tow trucks, a Parks Department SUV and an insurance adjuster wearing jeans with a dress shirt and tie. Multiple pens in a pocket protector, too. The cops, the parkies, the truckers and several others had spent the morning getting the battered sedan off the rocks below. That and getting Marshall's broken body out and into the coroner's wagon. No cause of death until the autopsy would be completed, but everyone could see he was pretty beat up. They all agreed on one thing though—the resale value of the Merc was definitely nil.

Chapter 6.

"...AND let us know how you liked the show. While you stay tuned for the newest news, I'll be putting on my Halloween ball gown and heading down to the Exotic-Erotic shindig with The Great Rondini and the lovely Satyra—"

I was wrapping up when a commotion erupted at the front door. A somewhat agitated twosome pushed into the lobby and what was left of our séance. I was startled, having just spent an hour in the world of the other world; this better not be a visitation from the far side, avenging angels dropping by to even the score. No, this was for real. Somebody had forgotten to lock the lobby door and maybe the homeless were on a raiding party. Or maybe a couple of Freddy and Betty fans, coming to beat me to a pulp.

For some reason the intruders seemed to think that I was in charge. They kept calling my name and they didn't look like they were happy. I hoped they weren't one of our sponsors. I try to stay on the good side of the people who keep KPMT on the air. Tony Paulson likes it that way. I thought about hiding behind Satyra, since Ronnie had told me that she's an expert in tae kwon do. I remember something about a black belt. Or maybe black garter belt. I'm not sure, but I'm sure she can take care of herself either way.

As the man and woman stomped toward us, Kinta popped up and tried to earn his pay by heading them off. My man, definitely deserves a raise. I'd talk to Ned Tunney first thing, if I got out of here alive.

I was still on the air, but I decided to abandon ship. After all I don't get hazardous duty pay. I managed to slip around Kinta and the crazy people into the studio. I hated to abandon my guests too, but the unhappy couple wasn't calling for their blood so I figured they'd survive. The female half of the duo looked kind of shopworn, but underneath the makeup and frizzy hair, under the shapeless coat, she looked like she wasn't all that bad. Still I didn't think I ever dated her, so it couldn't be an irate husband. The guy had a strange look too—angry, but...well, who cares? I locked the studio door behind me.

"—just point that Jeremy jerk out to me—"

She did remind me of this coal miner's daughter I knew when I was back at WCOL in West Virginia, but I think she wound up marrying her brother or something.

"—he's going to pay for this! This station's going to pay, believe me—"

The Brat was flipping switches and pulling levers. Finally he looked my way and gave me the finger. Pointed it, that is. I pulled up the mic and said, "Well, folks, that's the show for another day. The commotion you heard was just our guests wishing each other well before going their separate ways."

The lobby mics were off now and the studio window was sound proof, so I watched the unfolding drama in pantomime. Kinta was being backed against the wall by the couple, who by now looked like candidates for his and her heart attacks. Madame Zoroaster and her dwarf had put the cell phone away and were edging toward then door.

"I'd just like to thank all our guests and callers tonight, you know who you are, and the great job by Brad, our engineer, and Kinta White, my producer, in making sure everything got on the air without a hitch."

The Great Rondini and Satyra had done their famous vanishing act and Kinta was herding the crazy people to the lobby table and chairs. Probably he'd be serving coffee and cake before you knew it. Meanwhile, Brad potted up the bumper music to close out the show. *"...stay tuned for the news, and don't forget to tune in tomorrow."*

I'd have liked to have stayed and seen Kinta schmoozing with the psychopaths, but it being Halloween and all, I quietly slipped out the back way. With any luck, Kinta would be having drinks with them before long and they wouldn't be waiting for me after school tomorrow. After all, this is San Francisco—we can turn anything into a good time and may old acquaintances be forgotten. Sorry, Kinta, I hate to be the ugly stepsister, but you don't get to go to the ball tonight.

Ronnie and Satyra had already flagged down a cab and I squeezed in with them. We were late enough to miss commuter traffic now but still early enough so the party-goers hadn't tied things up. The cabbie kept his foot on it like he had a hot date so we made good time. We got dropped and already there was quite a line at the main gate. However, we bypassed the crowd, Ronnie leading the way through the door reserved for performers, vendors and assorted roadies. While The Great Rondini and his assistant went to check where they were in the lineup, I moseyed into the Ballroom. It was the same place they hold the rodeos and political conventions. The difference is tonight you didn't need to watch where you stepped.

Although it was early, the place was filling up. As the night progressed, every inch would be packed with outrageous and—as advertised—exotic and erotic partygoers, dressed in everything from plastic wrap to white tie and tails. Men dressed like women, women dressed like men, and for the most part they wouldn't even be in costume. Already the crowd noise almost drowned out the seven or eight rock bands beginning to tune-up on stages scattered around the huge auditorium. The smell of the crowd, the roar of the...well, you get the idea.

Everybody seemed to be on their cell phones trying to locate somebody else already a part of the mob or soon would be. Everybody trying to talk over everybody else. Even folks walking next to one another found it easier to talk via cell than shout over the noise. I'm not usually a joiner, but I pulled out my phone and texted Jeanne who had promised to meet me here. Almost immediately, her ringtone told me she was calling me back. Nokia was playing our song.

"Babe, where are you? Did you get inside yet or are you still standing in the line?"

Jeanne said that she didn't like lines so she got in through the VIP entrance, picking up a free glass of bubbly along the way. I was guessing she must have really put on the old exotic and erotic tonight to get past the VIP entrance security. And what about the champers? How did she get that?

"I probably need to come rescue you if that's all the fun you're having," I said. "Give me a landmark."

A guy floating with the surge of the crowd bumped my arm sending the phone flying. I snarled at him and he gave me a not-my-fault shrug. Next time I'd try the growl. Meanwhile, a few dozen beauty queens of both persuasion, a wave of ladies dressed as strippers and strippers dressed as...well, more strippers, were trampling over my cell phone, accidentally kicking it across the floor. At this rate I'd not only lose the phone, but probably my girl as well. I dived into the crowd on my hands and knees after it. Feet and knees were everywhere, I got stepped on and sat on, but as the phone skittered along the floor, I skittered after it.

"Can you hear me now? Can you hear me now?"

Finally I had it. After it had been in close contact with the sticky stuff on the floor, I wasn't sure that I wanted it too close to my mouth, but I wiped most of the gum and popcorn off. Jeanne's voice was still rattling on like she never missed me, oblivious of what I'd been through to hold up my end of the conversation. "Honey," I said, "they almost killed me in here, not to mention how much this phone cost. Where are you? I think I'm gonna need some mouth-to-mouth resuscitation."

She finally caved, giving me her latitude and longitude, and I headed in what I thought was her direction. Right in front of the bandstand with the guys dressed as singing nuns. Not to be confused with the lesbian nuns doing the can-can review. It shouldn't have been hard to find them, but I needed to stop at the Roman orgy to ask for directions. To the all-male nuns, not the dancing lesbian nuns.

A three hundred pound woman dressed as Cleopatra untangled herself from a couple of gladiators, grabbed my arm and said to follow her. I hoped she was just a good Samaritan and I wasn't going to wind up a galley slave. As she barged through the crowd, wrestlers and strongmen moved aside, young ladies jumped out of her way, and an accountant or two got trampled.

I was beginning to get worried when—Hallelujah!—I heard the sound of angels' voices. Wait just a minute—the tune was right but the words were wrong. These were no angels—these were the singing nuns! My prayers had been answered so to speak.

Somehow all three hundred pounds of Cleo had vanished into the heaving throng leaving no trace except for an overturned beer cart. And then through a break in the crowd, I saw Jeanne. Wow! I could see why there was a crowd around her. She was dressed as the wicked witch of the Ba-Da-Bing Club. The requisite pointy hat, a witch's broom, curly-toed shoes, and very little in between. It worked; she cast a spell over me. I'd have to ask her how she managed to get here on the Muni bus.

We hugged and kissed and I suggested we head straight for my place, but instead we got plastic cups of some kind of blue-colored beer and decided to find Rondini before his act was over. I picked a sticky map off the floor which showed what acts were on what stages and located Ronnie's designated spot. I just needed a boy scout to lead the way, but I struck out in what I hoped was the right direction with Jeanne hanging on to my belt. From the number of times she ouched, I figured she'd be black and blue from all the pinching. It was definitely some costume.

Finally we found The Great One and his sidekick on a small dais where I imagine they must park the horses during rodeo week. And they hadn't bothered to fumigate.

"Rondini, what am I holding in my hand?" Satyra had braved the audience, probably getting some pinching of her own. She was twirling a brassiere—not her own—over her head and slightly slurring her words. Must have had a lot of jitter medicine. "See into my mind, Oh Great One. See what I am holding up. Or see what it holds up if you can."

"Something is coming through, I see—yes, the letter 'C' as in cup. This is something that belongs to a beautiful lady. In fact she feels naked without it." Big laugh from the crowd.

Satyra said, "Let's just say she uses it for more than moral support." More laughs.

"I think it is something better kept secret. And it may be a secret, a Victoria Secret to be more exact," and in a stage whisper, "her lacey bra!" This got a round of applause.

I knew they had worked out certain code words to let Ronnie know what Satyra was mentally telegraphing, but all in all, it was pretty effective. They used words like 'some one' if it was a woman and 'somebody' if it was a man. I'm not sure what they did for cross-dressers.

All Souls' Evening passed into night and then early morning. A few hours later, city sanitation workers would be sweeping up the beer cans and noise makers. In a few days, the stories would be all told, the outrageous will have faded into the past. Earlier Madame Z had said that the past was over, we should all look to the future. She forgot the other part— if things can possibly get worse, don't worry, they will.

Chapter 7.

"A LAWSUIT," I couldn't believe my ears. "They're suing me? How can they sue me? Don't I have insurance for that?"

I was tucked in Ned Tunney's office a few days after the séance with Ned himself, Tony Paulson and Leland Heilbrun, the station's lawyer. Heilbrun had spread a bunch of papers around, legal-sized stuff on onion-skin that might have been typed half a century ago. Heilbrun himself looked like a character out of a Dickens novel, chubby and balding with a big diamond ring on his pinky. As for the papers the only thing I saw was my name listed under 'Defendants' in letters about a foot high. And naturally, I figured I must be guilty.

Turns out KPMT was listed too, so Heilbrun had dropped everything, quill pen included, and came over to take a meeting. He was giving a lecture on the finer points of jurisprudence. "...not a leg to stand on. The transcripts show KPMT did nothing wrong. I—"

"That's fine for KPMT, what about me?"

"And who are you exactly?" I hoped that Ned or Tony might jump to my defense, but they just looked at Heilbrun for their cues.

"Don't worry, Jeremy," he said, "you're just an employee here, the station indemnifies you for any content on your show just as long as you don't exceed established policy."

"I didn't, I swear I didn't do what it was you said."

"No, of course, it only means if you say something for which the FCC fines KPMT, they can take it out of your salary."

Leland continued with the lowdown on the lawsuit. He threw in a few Latin words just to show that he learned something at Stanford, but basically he laid it out like this: Madame Zoroaster, the psychic disaster, in spite of doing a pretty good show, turned loose a Frankenstein monster in the form of Heather and Dick Rubenstein's lawyer. Based upon the late Pearl Strathan's will, her daughters were to share equally in all her assets and worldly possessions, largely consisting of a five-carat diamond bracelet. As portrayed by the Rubenstein attorney, KPMT aided and abetted Mrs. Rubenstein's sister, Cheryl Strathan, in illegally, et cetera, et cetera, blah, blah, blah.

The short version is that when Dick and Heather got to the deceased's house, they met the greedy sister coming out. Sister Cheryl said she had just come by to see if the realtor had left flyers for the house on the dining room table as previously arranged (they were). Cheryl also says no, she didn't see hear them on the radio, and she has to skedaddle. Heather goes in, finds no jewels and can't get a hold of Cheryl who it turns out suddenly blew town. She was believed to have absconded with the bracelet because KPMT broadcast its whereabouts to the entire Bay Area.

Leland pooh-poohed it, said it didn't hold water, worst case he ever saw. Said we should settle, maybe fifty or sixty grand worth. Mother Strathan apparently had had the bracelet appraised for insurance purposes a couple years back and it came out closer to one hundred K. But as Leland said, it was the worst case ever. I guessed he meant it was fifty-eight thousand dollars worse.

"I agree," Tony said. "It's worth it not to get dragged through the courts."

"Goddamn' activist judges," Ned growled. "That's what we've come to. Paying off for some family dispute. Why doesn't she sue her sister instead of us? Get the ring back that way? With the judges today, we don't stand a chance."

"Exactly," I said.

"Maybe I'll do a show on 'em," I said.

"We'll take a stand," I said.

"Don't say anything more," Ned said.

So the upshot, pending Pamela Kay's okay, was mean sister Cheryl gets to pawn the ring someplace down in Mexico, Mr. and Mrs. Rubenstein get the cash, Ma gets to rest in peace. I hoped I'd get to keep my job, fifty or sixty large being some nice bling to drop on a couple of listeners without even a radio contest promo.

Tom Marshall's death had made the Rubenstein's scam

pretty much of a side issue though. The brain trust wasn't interested in spending a lot of time on it since they needed to deal with the changes brought about by Mr. Marshall's demise. He had been one of the original partners and there was speculation that his share might be bought out by a media conglomerate.

Marshall had spent a lot more time in the office than Mrs. P, but with my schedule I only had the chance to chat with him once or twice. He seemed like a nice guy, but I didn't know him well enough to really say. He had a family and all, but I skipped the funeral so didn't get to meet them either. Because his death distracted everybody from the diamond bracelet and the settlement, the Marshall family's cloud had a silver lining for me anyway.

The final settlement turned out to be fifty-eight thousand dollars, and like I said, it all blew over pretty quickly. I was feeling guilty anyway, so I volunteered to do about a million promos and mall appearances for the station over the winter and spring. Some magician friend of Ronnie's said that Ilonya Zoroaster and Vigo were working the Mexico cruise lines out of San Diego. Maybe they hoped to find the diamond bracelet down there; after all, she has powers beyond mortal comprehension. Anyway, on the show, I stuck with playing it straight, bashing the liberals.

Pamela Kay Paulson had the big Christmas bash at her Stinson Beach mansion, the winter rains came and went, and Jeanne was still prostituting her talents on the Freddy and Betty show. I heard the F and B team might even be getting a syndication deal. The winter of my discontent, no doubt.

Still spring, then summer eventually came, I had pretty much forgotten the psychic disaster, my ratings were solid enough that I leased a BMW convertible, and whenever Jeanne and I could sync up our bedtimes, we did a lot of heavy breathing.

So here I was, sitting at the bar in The Blue Sphinx watching The Great Rondini's act. I felt like somehow life had rewound itself back to last fall, back to Ilonya Zoroaster and tied it in to Pamela Kay's favorite nephew to boot. When Ronnie's act finished up, the audience started to clear out and I was able to snag a table where Ronnie and Satyra joined me.

We all ordered drinks and I started in on my tale of woe. I told them about my meeting with Pamela Kay, about Tony and the fortune teller, and how I might need a job in a hurry. Satyra suggested I put on her belly dancer costume and be

Rondini's stooge. She'd be happy to go back to waiting tables—the tips were better and she wouldn't catch so many colds.

"Well, Junior," Ronnie was saying, "I see you have a lot behind you. And, believe me from behind there a quite a lot to see."

"Thanks for making me feel better. On top of everything, now I have to start actually going to the gym." I had a membership, I had the gym togs, I even dated a Pilates instructor once. If The Great Rondini was trying to cheer me up, it was another amazing illusion.

"Don't worry, Jerry," Satyra said, "I'm sure Ronnie's seen more of your behind than I have, but I always thought it was fine. Of course, I'm pretty broad minded."

"Thanks, babe, I feel a lot better now. And the good news is I won't be eating all those meals when I'm unemployed. I'll get so thin my behind is liable to wind up in front."

"Well, you're not fired yet," she said. "Ronnie, what are we going to do for this guy?"

"Well, let's try to figure out how to do what the boss lady wants Jerry to do."

Could that be my old pal, Ronnie Green, actually coming up with a plan to help? Meanwhile Satyra whistled up the waiter for another round of drinks.

In spite of Satyra's being hot enough to melt glass and Ronnie's penchant for chasing anything in a thirty-six double-D, he's never tried the old magic on her. He keeps it under control because the act can't afford to lose her. As Ronnie says if they hooked up romantically, he'd wind up married to her and next thing you know she'd be asking for the cape off his back in divorce court. She'd be out of the act and he'd lose half his audience as well as half his income. I might not hang around as much either.

"I find it puzzling," Ronnie was saying, "that Madame Zoroaster has hooked up with Tony Paulson. They could hardly have known each other. They never even met before, as far as we know."

"Maybe Mr. Paulson took one of those Mexican Riviera cruises last winter and they got to reminiscing about old times," Satyra said. "Like, when she got the radio station sued. Could be the start of a beautiful friendship. Well, maybe not that beautiful."

"Who played the Bogart part? Madame Z? Anyway, I recall that Tony went skiing, not cruising."

"Maybe they met at a pick-up bar. I'm not saying who

picked who up though."

"It's a thought, Satyra. Not a pretty one, but a thought none the less. He's rich and good looking, and she's one step up from the bride of Frankenstein."

"Maybe they're kinky, she likes to be spanked, or he does."

"Not the Tony I know, he's pretty straight laced around the office."

"...'around the office,'" Satyra echoed my words, "but you never know what somebody is like in the bedroom until they have you strapped to the bedposts."

"While all the palaver is interesting," Ronnie said, "I think we're going to have to concentrate on what we really know, beginning with a missing diamond bracelet."

"It's not really missing," I said, "it's the sister who took it that's missing.... Say, I'll bet Ilonya ran into her down in Baja or someplace."

"How would she even recognize her," Ronnie asked. "She only saw the other sister for a minute at the radio station, the night of the show."

"Maybe they're twins."

"I don't think so, mainly because I don't think there is any sister."

No wonder we're pals. Ronnie already had figured an angle. The Great One laid out The Great Hypothesis like he was Sherlock Holmes back from the grave. He explained away the ghosts, the ring, and why Ilonya and Vigo spent the winter on cruise ships aside from working on their tans and having a captive audience. As he laid it out, it seemed to make sense, although I was a little the worse for the mojitos by that time. Satyra must have set it up with the waitress to keep filling the empties until the radio guy runs out of dough.

"Boss, that's why you're the boss. You've nailed it in one," Satyra was beaming at the showoff. "No wonder I put up with your crap, you're a genius when it comes to underhanded shit."

"Elementary, my dear Miss Watson," Ronnie said. "But the one thing that doesn't fit is why Tony Paulson would have anything to do with them. You'd think he would want to stay far away from Ilonya Zoroaster after what she cost the station."

"Could be he's just trying to get close enough to them to find out how they did the scam, but somehow I don't think so," I said. "Mrs. P made it sound like he's being taken for a ride. But then again, maybe he is a sucker for a gal with blue streaked hair. Though there are plenty of them around in this town."

"You know, Red," Ronnie stared into space and tented his fingers, "it's been a while since I was on your show—quite a while—and to be honest, I'm still more than a little sore about Madame Zoroaster slipping through my fingers the last time."

Oh-oh, I thought I heard another shoe dropping.

"Listen, Jerry," Ronnie leaned in close while Satyra pushed up against me from the other side so the only way out was under the table. "I'm beginning to get the germ of an idea about how to handle this. Just the merest glimmer, a seed to sow and water. But the good part is it happens to be right down our line of work."

Satyra pressed, Ronnie leaned, his voice whispered to keep any stray gypsies from reporting back to Madame Z. "Since the Ilonya's back in town, let's give her an encore performance, get her back on your show. This time we nail her on that diamond bracelet scam."

"How do we know she won't nail us for another fifty-eight g's, old pal o' mine?"

"This time we'll go in loaded for bear, we'll get the evidence beforehand. How about this—you could track down the Rubensteins, whoever they really are. More then likely they were just shills, probably local actors, not even good enough to be full time swindlers. With your background and connections, you should be able to find them. You've been in jail before, haven't you?"

"Only because you run faster."

"Well, sure, I'm in shape; you couldn't make it over that last fence. Lucky it was only the cops and not her father."

"Sure, I have all the luck. Now, I not only need to save Tony from a lady with crystal balls, I have to get another séance going after the station got screwed from the last one like that."

"Well, JJ, we're just here trying to help you out. You know I could turn Satyra loose on you to help you forget your troubles, but no, that wouldn't be right. It wouldn't make the problem go away."

"Maybe not, but I'd be the happiest guy in the unemployment line."

"No, little man, no," Rondini said. "This girl's many charms are not the answer."

"They're not?"

"Oh, too bad, Jerry," Satyra whispered in my ear.

"Whatever Madame Zoroaster has on Paulson," Ronnie said, "when I expose how she duped you—"

Duped me?

"—last Halloween, her and her little pal will either head back to Mexico or have the cops all over them. Fraud is still a crime in this town. Unless you don't get caught, of course."

"So we nail her on this and she gets scared off from whatever she has on Tony, I get to keep my show, Mrs. P thinks I'm a hero—"

"Well, only part of a hero, Red. Remember, I'm doing all the heavy lifting."

Satyra signaled the waiter for another round.

Ronnie and Satyra promised to put out feelers in their circles to see if anyone had heard anything about Madame Zoroaster building up a private practice. Someone suggested that the phony Rubensteins might still be working for her or may have worked as shills for one of the local magicians before. More heavy lifting for The Great Rondini.

Meanwhile, Ronnie and Satyra had the impression I had connections to the local show biz community and could run down any actors that might have been used for the scam. I figured I could Google 'diamond bracelet scams' and get a pile of names. Maybe Rubenstein really was their name. Or maybe I'd win the lottery and buy my own radio station.

Once upon a time, Ronnie had this act where he'd hypnotize people from the audience. The act really put people to sleep only this time it was on purpose. I thought he learned hypnosis just to improve his batting average at the singles bars, but he must have used it on me that night. That, and the drinks and Satyra all over me, I would have agreed to sharing my apartment and my girl with him. Well, maybe not my apartment.

So we'd rewind back to the Halloween show for real—The Great Rondini, Madame Zoroaster, and if we could find them, Mother Pearl's little girl and her son-in-law. Rondini would get a ton of free publicity. We'd expose the fakes, thereby scaring them off from Tony Paulson. This would make me a star in the eyes of Pamela Kay Paulson and with any luck Jeanne and I would be bedding down regularly at eight p.m. because Freddy and Betty would be back in Toledo and I would be getting up with Jeanne to do the morning drive.

Chapter 8.

I SLEPT until ten o'clock on Thursday morning, then went downstairs to drop off my dry cleaning and relax over a cappuccino at the coffee shop. It looked to be another real scorcher for this city; high seventies, low eighties were predicted by the KPMT weatherman. I got a *Chronicle* off the news rack and picked a table out on the sidewalk. Since I get to sleep in every day, the morning rush was over and the sun had burned off the fog if there had been any. Ain't life grand?

Even by the light of day, Ronnie's idea didn't seem so bad. The real trick would be tracking down Madame Zoroaster. I wasn't certain whether she wanted to be found, but if the cops weren't after her for raising the dead, she might be tempted to get some exposure on the radio. The last time she had actually come off pretty well in spite Ronnie's vow to show her up. She had a good radio voice, accent aside, and related well to the listeners. I thought she might have a future on the air. Until she skipped out with a fistful of hot diamonds, that is.

I still had most of the day free before time for my show so I decided to put some thought into finding Ilonya Zoroaster. There's a lot to be said for not having a real eight to five job. It gives a person time for special projects like this. If I was still working the day shift at Charlie Wooten's, I'd never be able to find her. But if I was working the dealership and had one of the shop's big SUVs, Madame Z better hope I didn't see her before she saw me. Not unless she could really read my mind.

All the same, if I wanted to hold on to my job, I needed to know how Tony Paulson fit into the picture. And if Paulson was involved with Madame Zoroaster, there's a good chance he might know how to get in touch with her.

The last time I tried catching Tony at the office, I got stuck talking to Ned. Not that Ned isn't my favorite station manager, but I didn't want to have him prying into the little job Mrs. Paulson gave me. So I called the main number where Michael the illustrated man picked up. I said hello and had to explain exactly who I was again. He gave me a song and a dance, but the short version was that Tony wasn't in and wasn't expected. I thought about offering him a Hamilton to cut the crap, when he volunteered that Tony was working from home today. But he couldn't give out Tony's home address. Not that I cared; I already had it, but I wasn't telling him.

Beamer time, top down. I headed back out to Noe Valley, cruising up Market. As I left downtown behind I picked up a little speed and figured time was on my side. Mrs. Paulson had wanted me just to find out what was going on and report back for further instructions, so I hoped I wasn't getting too far ahead of the curve with the exposé of Madame Zoroaster.

If a little knowledge was a dangerous thing, this would be...well, I'm not sure what it would be. The one thing I know about radio is that he who is hottest in the ratings department is king of the air and can pretty much get away with anything. And to get the ratings you gotta stand out from the crowd. Exposing a swindle on the show, the print media would have to cover that. People would tune-in in droves, drive time droves. Maybe snag a Pulitzer or some kind of radio Emmy, if there is such a thing.

A girl on a bike shouted something to me as she bounced over the curb. Close call, good thing she didn't bang into the car. She chucked a water bottle my way, but it was way high too and hit the gutter across the street.

I made the light and turned down Sanchez. My mind was still on the show. What would be the downside of a psychic return engagement? What's the worst that could happen? Ronnie had come up dry on how Ilonya and Tony were linked—we both just assumed it was a swindle. Suppose instead, that Tony was head over heels in love with Ilonya, and that was why he was giving her everything but the loose change in his sofa. He might not like us throwing dirt on his beloved. But a big romance didn't seem to play, Tony was always dodging the local supermodels, most of whom had taken a shot at him. Madame Zoroaster was not in that league, unless maybe she had read that book on hypnotism.

No, the down side would be that she had him believing in her mumbo jumbo. If that was the case and we showed up

Madame Z, then Tony would look like some kind of a jerk. Since the messenger is the one traditionally shot, making Tony look like a jerk seemed like something we should avoid at all costs. The Great Rondini could wind up pulling his rabbits out of a hat down on the BART platform. At least he has a craft and can get that much work; I'd be feeling up vending machines for lost change.

I turned up Tony's block and started looking for a place to park. San Francisco has been blessed with twice as many cars as parking spots, so that at any one time there are half a million cars circling the block, looking for parking. It's probably why they have drive-by shootings—the gang bangers can't find a spot. This time I took a chance on parking in a bus stop on the corner.

As I walked up to Tony's front steps, the Lady in Pink, the one I had seen yesterday, came barreling down. She was a pastel blur, running past me toward the street. Today the Lady in Pink was wearing fashionable lime, but I hardly noticed. She swept by me with a quick, "Pardon me!" and a hint of limey perfume.

As I turned to watch her, she slipped between the parked cars and dashed into the street. From the corner of my eye, I glimpsed a flash of darkness and I saw her stepping out in front of it. I shouted to warn her as the dark truck accelerated down on her. She was the classic deer caught in the headlights, frozen to the spot. Something inside me took over and I leaped between the cars toward her, but I wasn't going to get there in time. In my mind I saw her run down a second before I could pull her back, then suddenly; she twisted toward me and jumped. I grabbed her arm and some lime green fabric and pulled her close. The slipstream whipped us around as the truck swerved within inches of us, never slowing. I held on tight as our momentum carried us onto the trunk of a parked car.

It was a tossup as to who was shaking more, but I was trembling for more than one reason. I was half on top of her on the parked car and I didn't want to get off. Just when I thought about checking her vital signs to make sure she was okay, the Lady in Lime pushed me away.

"Hold on," I said, "I'm trying to help. Are you okay?"

"Oh my God, that asshole almost ran me down," she said, looking at the empty street where the truck had gone. She looked ready to give way so I put my arm around her in a gentlemanly fashion. Just to steady her. We were close for a moment, then she broke free again. In that instant I missed her warmth and softness.

"Did you get the license number?" she looked up at me. Big blue eyes that I didn't want to disappoint.

"Sorry, I couldn't get to my pencil. I was pretty much focused on trying to save your life." The blue eyes looked swell against her tan and the curly blonde hair. Forget the license plate, I only had eyes for her.

"Damn! We could have reported it to the police if we had the license number." She ran her fingers through her hair, tousling it like she was trying to clear her mind. Then, she made me feel good by saying, "I guess I owe you a big thank you. If you hadn't been there, I would have been roadkill."

"Well, they might have stopped to help if they hit you."

"I don't think so. Shit! They were out to get me. And I know why."

I hoped it wasn't because she was hooked up with Tony Paulson. This was the second time I saw her coming out of his house. And she was infinitely more attractive than Madame Zoroaster; I was hoping she wasn't the gypsy's kid sister or something. On the other hand, if she was Tony's girl, I might run him down myself.

I looked down the block again where the truck had disappeared, but this time I noticed something that got my stomach churning even more than almost being run down. My beautiful convertible had a long scratch on the driver's side. The bad guys had scraped along the parked cars when they tried to hit us. I went over to take a closer look and the Pastel Lady came with me.

"Your car?"

"Yes, she's all mine and the leasing company's. The nicest car I've ever had."

"I'm sure they can buff it out. I'll be glad to be a witness for you if the insurance company gives you any grief."

"No, it's not that. I'm sure I'm covered. It's just that until now my baby was a virgin."

"Oh."

"Now I know how a guy with teen-age daughters feels. There's a coffee place down on the corner. I need a coffee to quiet my nerves," I said. "Come on, I'm buying."

I took her by the elbow and guided her down the block, like I was some kind of overgrown Boy Scout. Truth be told, I liked walking with her. I decided I'd kill myself if she was Tony's girl.

The coffee shop was named 'Grounds for Divorce'. Maybe the owners couldn't agree on a name, but in a case like thus, who gets the beans? Anyway the kids behind the counter were too upbeat and happy to be the unhappy couple. I suspected the teenager at the cash register was combating coffee nerves with a little ganja during her breaks.

We ordered lattes and while things were brewing, told each other the weather was fine but maybe too hot for the City. Then we sat down at a small table out on the sidewalk. I kept trying my charm smile on her and kept wishing I hadn't left my shades in the car. I didn't want her to start getting antsy the way I kept staring at her. I was hoping she wouldn't wonder if she missed getting run down only to wind up at coffee with some kind of a psycho. Anyway, I thought I'd better get down to cases and find out who she was and what she was to Tony. If she was just the Avon lady trying to catch him at home, I'd know that I hit the jackpot.

"With all the excitement out there, I didn't get a chance to introduce myself. My name's Jerry Jeremy."

"Oh, of course. I thought you looked familiar," she seemed to shrink away. Guys on the radio don't usually look familiar. I hoped she didn't already know Rondini. "That must be why you just happened to be there. I might have known." She had that same look Mrs. Paulson had when she threatened to fire me. Like I was roadkill.

"Whoa! Hold on. Didn't you just thank me for saving your life? Maybe you've confused me with another Jerry Jeremy. I'm the one with the double moniker—Jeremy Jeremy from the radio show, get it? You know, the red-haired one?"

"I know exactly who you are."

"Did Tony Paulson say something bad about me?"

"Tony Paulson? No, he never said anything about you. As a matter of fact, he won't talk to me at all."

"Really?" suddenly things were looking up. "Then why are you mad at me?"

"I know who you are. You have a talk show on KPMT and you're all buddy-buddy with those boho's up at his house."

"Wait a second," I knocked over my cup. "Paulson hardly knows I'm alive. And as for being buddy-buddy, I don't even know what a boho is."

I sopped up the spreading coffee before much of it dripped onto her lap.

"I've never even been in his house," I said. "Definitely not with a boho. Right now, I'd like to be your buddy." I crossed my fingers under the table so Jeanne wouldn't count against me as either a buddy or a boho. "A few minutes ago, I saw somebody I didn't want see flattened like a pancake before I got to meet her and I tried to do something about it. You were coming from Paulson's, so I thought maybe you were a buddy of his."

"Well, maybe I'm wrong, but you must have been headed up to his place. Why else would you be out here?"

"Well I'm not selling magazine subscriptions door to door. But the reason I'm here is because he might know how I can get in touch with a certain psychic."

She looked at me for a minute and made a decision. She sipped her latte and said, "Listen, I'm sure you must know Tom Marshall?"

"Sure, he was one of the owners at KPMT. He died a while back in some kind of accident. I don't get to mix with the bosses much, so I didn't get to know him very well. I remember we shared a few laughs at a station get-together once. He seemed like a good guy."

"He *was* a good guy," the Pastel Lady said. "He was my dad."

The silence was ringing in my ears and I was trying to come up with something appropriate when she leaned closer to me, close enough that her perfume left me panting. She said, "I'm Christy Marshall. I was away at school when he was murdered—"

"Murdered?"

"You saw what just happened to me. I think that my father was killed and the Paulsons stood to gain from it."

"The Paulsons?"

"They took advantage of my mother after Dad's death."

"Your mother?"

"Don't keep repeating everything I say."

"Repeating? Er, I mean, I thought they said that your dad died in an accident."

"That's the story they want everyone to believe. I believed it at first. But there are a lot of strange things about it that have turned up. My mother wanted me to finish school so I held off looking into this until now. But I graduated this year and I'm going to do whatever it takes to find his killers. If I can't get justice for Dad, I'll settle for getting even somehow."

"Jeez," I didn't know what to say really. But that doesn't stop a good talk show host. "So you think the Paulsons had something to do with your father's death—"

"Murder."

"Sure, but the Paulsons? Weren't they all partners?"

"That's just it, Dad was going to sell his share of the radio station. The Paulsons—Pamela Kay Paulson really—as his partner had right of first refusal, but she couldn't or wouldn't meet the price he could get on the open market. So Dad was planning to sell it to a third party for a very good price."

"So you think the Paulsons killed him to keep him from selling? Wouldn't his estate, your mom I guess, just do the same thing?"

"Here's the thing—in case of a partner's death, their agreement called for the remaining partners to buy up the dead partner's share at a low price, one fixed years ago when they started KPMT. Which is what happened. Mom got cheated out of the real value of Dad's share."

"But couldn't that have gone the other way if Pamela Kay died?"

"I'm not questioning that, it wasn't a good business deal, but you're right it could have gone either way."

"Sure, it could. Either way."

"What tipped me off was the timing. Very convenient that he gets killed the night before he was to sign his share over to a big media outfit. And the police report—his car, what was left of it, showed signs of damage from another car that Mom says wasn't there before."

"And when you heard my name, you thought I might be on their side?"

"You do work for them, don't you?" Christy Marshall patted her lips with a napkin, then picked up her purse and started to rise.

"Hey, where're you going?" I got up too. I started to bus the empty cups, but Christy took off down the street so I dropped the dishes on the closest table. The people sitting there started to say something, but I was already heading down the street too.

I caught up with her and got her to slow down enough to plead my case.

"Look, I have a show on KPMT. One that I like having, one that pays the bills and then some, but I'm not quite the company man you think I am."

"But you were headed to Mr. Paulson's house, weren't you?"

"Sure, but only because I'm looking for somebody and he may know where they are."

"Good luck, he won't even talk to me."

"Well, he may not talk to me either since I'm trying to repeat a show just like the one I almost got fired for."

"They wanted to fire you? Maybe you aren't a company man after all." By now we were strolling along the sun dappled sidewalk like pals again.

"Yeah, it's a long story and I'd like to tell it to you someday, but suffice it to say I'm looking for a psychic called Madame Zoroaster to see if I can get her on my show again."

"You almost got fired, so now you're trying to get fired by having her on again?"

"No, no, that's not the plan. I'm trying to get Madame Zoroaster back on the air so that my magician friend and I can expose her as a fake and a phony. But I can't book her if I can't find her. It's a complicated situation, but I have reason to suspect that Tony may be able to give me a lead on where to find Madame Zoroaster."

"It's not that complicated, Jerry. If you want to see Madame Zoroaster, just ring Tony Paulson's doorbell."

Chapter 9.

"Long time, no seer," I said to Vigo Czak. His eyebrows arched in surprise; otherwise he remained his deadpan self. He must have forgotten the rule about seeing who's there before opening the door. Or maybe he was too short to reach the peephole. Czak exchanged hellos with Christy and added a bewildered smile to the lifted eyebrows.

"Mr. Jeremy, Madame had said she saw you in a dream recently," he recovered nicely. "You were being torn apart, chained to two cable cars headed in opposite directions. On the California line, I believe she said."

"Sweet dreams. But I never take public transit. Where is the old girl anyway? I'd like to chat with her."

"Ilonya? Why did you look for her here," Vigo asked. "Aren't you here to see Mr. Paulson? That's what the young lady said before and we told her that Mr. Paulson was out."

"Sure, Ms. Marshall and I are dying to talk to Tony, but you and the psychic will do until he comes home."

It was looking like Pamela Kay had been right about Ilonya having her hooks into Tony, which in turn led to my being right about Tony knowing where to find her. Meanwhile Christy and I brushed past the diminutive Dracula into the foyer, looking around.

"I know Madame Zoroaster is here because she came to the door when I called a few minutes ago," Christy said, elbowing Vigo aside.

By now we were at the door to the inner sanctum, the living room off the foyer. It looked like an ad for a Ralph Lauren country manor—leather easy chairs, Navajo rugs and hunting prints. I expected to see a moose head over the fireplace. Ilonya Zoroaster was sitting at a desk playing what looked like a complicated computer game. She looked up at us and said, "I was expecting you, Jerry. But I didn't think you were bringing a date."

"That part of your crystal ball must have been cloudy."

"Not really. Ned Tunney called yesterday, said you were trying to set up a meeting with Mr. Paulson." She pronounced "trying" as "tryink", "meeting'" was "meetink."

"He didn't say you were bringing anybody," she added.

"I guess Ned needs a refresher on predicting the future. Miss Marshall and I just teamed up. She wants to meet with Tony about another matter, but I was actually 'lookink' for you."

"For me? I really didn't see that coming. I'll have to get a tune-up, maybe."

"Maybe. I see you felt good enough to make a return visit to the City."

"I consider it my second home, after Budapest."

"I see your English has improved since you answered the door before," Christy said.

"Yes, thank you. I could not talk when I met you earlier. My spirit guide had not completely released me."

"Sure, I hate it when that happens."

"Now, ladies, let's move on," I said. "We're all here together. Let's sit down."

Christy and I sunk into a man-sized love seat covered in a flower print. Ilonya turned her chair to face us and smiled while Vigo stood beside her, deadpanned again.

"I'm glad to see you smiling," I said. "I thought maybe you wouldn't want to see me after last Halloween."

"And why would that be? We received very good exposure on your show. I was surprised that that many people listened to you."

Hmmmm....

"I guess we were both confused then," I said. "I'm a little surprised though to find you here at Tony's. I didn't know you even knew him."

"I know a great many people. Many of them feel very close to me in a short time. Tony is one of them."

"And he left you here while he went out," Christy asked.

"We are his house guests," Vigo lisped.

"Houseguests. Who'd a guessed," I said. They really had moved in on Tony. Bag and baggage. "You know when he'll be back? He might be interested in what I wanted to see you about. And Ms. Marshall wants to see him on another matter anyway."

"As I tried to explain to Miss Marshall, Mr. Paulson went out earlier and did not confide with either of us as to his destination or his return. Frankly, I also hoped to get a few moments to discuss something with him, but...well, you know...."

"Come on, Ilonya, I thought you were supposed to know all and see all."

"Perhaps, at times I do, but not so much for the quick answer, even for when I am asking the question," she tossed her tangled hair with her fingers. The polish on her nails was a shade of purple so dark it was almost black.

"Would anyone like to have a cold drink," Vigo asked us, practicing the good host role for when he became a full-time houseboy. Since these row houses were built with no air conditioning or insulation, the living room was starting to get warm. The windows looked to be painted shut so there was nary a breeze to stir up the dust. We all told Vigo we'd like a cold drink and he vanished down the hallway.

"So, Madame Zoroaster, how do you known Tony," Christy asked.

"Please, call me Ilonya, and," pointing toward the back of the house, "that is Vigo, my assistant and companion."

"Thanks, Ilonya. So how *do* you know Tony?"

"You know, Miss Marshall—"

"Please, call me Christy."

"Christy then, that's a good question. As we say in my business, I knew him long before I met him, but that's not what you want to know. Of course, Tony had heard my name as a result of my being on his radio station. Unfortunately he doesn't seem to be a regular listener to your show, Jerry, so he missed the actual broadcast. I think Tony said it is his schedule that keeps him from listening in, business you understand."

"Sure, like they say in the Mafia, 'Louie, it's just business,' then you get the kiss of death."

"How droll you are, Jerry. But to answer Christy's question, while I was traveling recently, I had a presentment, a kind of vision that brought me to Tony. I had never met him before, but I was entrusted to bring him the fruits of my vision. I think the spirits chose me for this task, because I had been on his station. Maybe they thought he would listen to me after my great success on your show."

"Some success. My show was almost cancelled. And the station had to pay out a big settlement to straighten out your success."

"That had nothing to do with Madame," Vigo said, returning with a tray of drinks balanced on one hand. "Her spirit guide provides the knowledge; what people do with it is up to them."

"Your view is perhaps the narrowest interpretation of the truth, Jerry, but the truth comes in many forms," Ilonya said in a calming voice, like you might use talking to a crazy person. If you ever do. I just wasn't sure which one of us was crazy. She continued, "I think I have brought Tony to an understanding of the mysteries of the other world. Tony holds nothing against me."

Okay, you and I recognize a straight line, but she's from out of town. I just said, "Sure, and Tony's pals are my pals. We're all pals now. It's all water under the bridge. So tell me, what was it that won Tony over, some vision you saw or maybe something only you and he know?"

"Jerry, darling (darlink), you must realize that I'm like a priest who hears confessions. I cannot reveal what is given to me to know unless Tony himself releases me to speak. My lips are not only sealed, they are stapled shut."

"I wouldn't to get you excommunicated from the witches' union. I just wondered, but no matter. I'm really glad that the stars are in alignment, or whatever they do, for you and Tony. But to tell the truth, I was hoping to get in touch with you anyway—"

"We can always be reached through our website," Vigo jumped in. He was becoming a regular chatterbox. "Anywhere or at any time. Just send us an e-mail and our staff will reply by same within forty-eight hours."

A fucking website? A goddamn' staff? I soldiered on. "—because I wanted to get you back on the show. An encore appearance."

"But you expressed concern about our previous visit to your show." Vigo interrupted the grown-ups again. I wondered if I should have Christy slap him down.

"I said it all before, it's like the ebbing tide—all water under the bridge. If Tony's cool with you guys, who am I, et cetera, et cetera."

Ilonya sipped her drink and looked over at Christy. "What is Miss Marshall's role in all of this?"

"Please, call me Christy. I'm here just to see Mr. Paulson.

On an unrelated matter."

Madame Zoroaster turned to Vigo Czak this time and asked, "Vigo, what is your opinion? Is this something we should pursue with Jerry?"

"I would like very much to be on the radio again," Vigo answered, pressing his cold glass against his forehead. Vigo kept talking, "We found many new believers as a result of Mr. Jeremy's previous show. On-line horoscopes alone almost doubled. Who knew there was that kind of an audience?"

So business was booming. I didn't want to be around when they went public though. Madame Zoroaster watched me pull out a handkerchief and pat the perspiration from my forehead. Then she asked, "When is it that you would like to have my appearance on your show? My schedule is very busy, business being quite good (goot)."

"Well, Ilonya, I don't have a date right now, but I'd like it to be as soon as possible. I still need to get the station to say okay, but I don't think that would be a problem, not if Tony Paulson is one of your fans." And not if it would spring the boy from the hold you've got on him. Pamela Kay would get behind that.

"Would you have the beautiful lady magician on, too," Vigo asked. "You know, Jerry, the one from last time."

"Truth be told, she's just the magician's assistant. Although I have to agree that she's the memorable one. Her straight man, The Great Rondini, is technically the magician."

"Yes, The Great...but will she be there, the assistant?"

"I don't think Rondini would go anywhere without her and you can count on him being there."

"Then in the absence of any unforeseen difficulties, I will agree to be on." Ilonya graced us with a smile, though it wasn't one of her strong points. Braces must not have been all that big a thing back in Transylvania. Not with all those vampires. "Of course, Tony will need to make his approval known. But, I'll make a prediction that he will approve."

Chapter 10.

So we had pretty much used up the small talk. I had hit it out of the park tracking down Madame Zoroaster and talking her into coming back on the show. On top of that I had gotten friendly with Christy Marshall and that alone was enough to make my day. But now we were sitting in a warm room in a sunny Victorian row house, waiting for its owner to show up.

I watched the mantle clock ticking toward show time, hoping that Tony would turn up soon. I guessed Christy would sit here all day to get her shot at Tony. But I wanted to get my shot at Christy before I had to head to work. I was planning on making plans with her for dinner if she was up for it. I'd see if I could close the deal on Madame Zoroaster's appearance and try to pry more info about her out of Tony some other time. After all, he might even show up at work one of these days. Besides, if Ronnie and I could expose her as a phony on the show, it might not really matter what she had on Tony.

I excused myself to use the bathroom where I splashed some cold water on my face and combed my hair. I took a chance and tried calling Jeanne on my cell, but all I got was her voicemail. I left a message setting up my regrets for the evening in case I got to meet up with Christy Marshall after my show. I was really interested in her story about her old man too. Accident or murder? I thought maybe I could help her out, maybe see if Marshall's former partner, Pamela Kay Paulson, had any doubts about it really being an accident.

By the time I got back to the living room, the prodigal nephew had returned. He had taken my seat next to Christy, so I just leaned against the doorjamb. It looked like they had been introduced and were making friends in a hurry.

"...Tom was really a great guy," Tony was saying. He glanced up and gave me a nod as though my materializing from the hallway was a usual thing. "I can't see that anybody would want to do anything to harm him, Christy."

"Well I don't want to stir up bad feelings, but surely you can see that your aunt benefited greatly by being able to buy out my father's share of the station."

"That might be so, but if I remember rightly that was a provision in their partnership agreement; it could have been the other way around." Tony was leaning well into Christy's space now, but not in threatening way. I'd have preferred that. If he kissed her, I decided I really would sock him. He said, "I don't think my aunt was the only one that benefited either. But it's still quite a stretch to suggest there might have been foul play."

"Maybe not," I stepped in, "but somebody isn't playing by the rules. You know anybody drives a black pickup truck, a big Dodge, I think? Tinted windows?"

"No, I can't think of anyone."

"Well, somebody in a truck like that tried to run down Christy right on your doorstep."

"On my steps?"

"No, not *on* the steps," Christy said. "I had just come from here. I had just stepped out on the street to look for a cab back downtown."

"So it could have just been a careless driver?" Tony asked. "Probably some kid not watching the road. Probably texting someone or watching a movie on his iPhone."

"It didn't look that way to me," I spoke up. "I had a clear view and that truck definitely looked like it took a swipe at Christy. It didn't look like some kid's car either. Lucky for Christy they were a second too soon. If she had taken another step out in street and she would have gotten hit.

"As it was, they put a nasty scratch in my door panel. And I'm pretty sure that my insurance company won't take that lying down. I've got a very low deductible."

"I am sure that someone killed my father," Christy said. "And today someone tried to kill me. I think they tried to run me down to keep me from looking into Dad's death."

So while Christy was plugging away about her dad's death, I was trying to think of how to get back to the séance.

"...Dad's car was pretty smashed up, but the initial report by the highway patrol said another car might have been involved," Christy was saying. "He was returning from your aunt's place in Stinson Beach that evening. I was wondering if you happened to be at that meeting, Mr. Paulson."

"No, I wasn't there. I didn't find out about your father's accident until the next day when Aunt Pam called with the news. You don't think I could have had anything to do with that, do you?" Tony seemed shocked that anyone could think he was even remotely near Marin County that night. At least that's how he acted. Or maybe overacted. "I can't remember exactly, but since it was the end of October, I probably worked late on my accounts for the month-end reports, and then I know that I wound up at a party with some friends later on."

"I don't remember seeing any lights in the office area when we wrapped the show that evening," I said. "Madame Zoroaster and Vigo were there too for the séance. But they wouldn't have known you then, would they?"

"Come on, Jerry," Tony pleaded, "by then I was headed home, I didn't get a chance to listen to your show. I'm sorry, jeez, kill me. I had to put on a costume for the party I was going to. It was Halloween after all."

"I thought you had the dial on your car radio super-glued to KPMT."

"Well, no, I didn't have my car. I remember I took a taxi. I think the car was in the shop for some reason. The driver probably had some Spanish language station on."

"You should have made him change the station. Those guys are killing us in the ratings. Anyway, something doesn't smell right and it's not just my deodorant breaking down in here."

Chapter 11.

"*...A FEW weeks ago I was headed home from the KPMT studios when I saw something that would make Lance Armstrong wish he'd taken up roller-blading. On the last Friday of the month they have this Critical Mess thing. What it is, is—*

"*What? Oh, Brad tells me it's called Critical Mass not Critical Mess, but he takes BART so he's got problems of his own.*

"*So anyway, this Critical Mess—or Mass—is a bunch of pinko guys and gals who couldn't get dates on Friday night, so they all get together on bikes to ride around the main thoroughfares in the city. And believe me, after a hard week's work, you really don't want to see some of these people in stretch pants.*

"*But here they all are in their fancy biking shirts and padded shorts—some guys wear the padding in front, if you know what I mean—and they form peddle packs of fifty or a hundred or two hundred bikers, ignoring traffic signals, pedestrians and trying their best to jam up the commuter flow.*

"*They say they don't block traffic, they are the traffic, but let's face it, they are just a bunch of bikers who have found a way to tweak the noses of the hard-working men and women who drive in and pay their twenty bucks a day for parking. Like that's not enough punishment.*

"*Let's hear what you think, right after these messages. This is Jerry Jeremy on KPMT, Big Talk Radio...*"

Ahh, back on the air where the only threats were from my listeners. After I had dragged Christy out of the Paulson nuthouse, I convinced her to let me drive her back downtown since she'd turned in her rental and was cabbing it. She was staying at the Hyatt Regency which wasn't far from my place anyway. During the drive, Christy was pretty quiet so I used the opportunity to tell her my life story. Well, mostly just the good parts. Since the good parts didn't take all that long to cover, we spent a lot of time watching buildings going by.

For a guy who makes his living with his mouth, I wasn't doing all that well with Christy. To fill in the dead air, I started giving her a more detailed account of all the stations I had been at and the jobs I had held. Sports, traffic, shock jock.... She could only take so much of that, so before I'd got very far, she started opening up.

"Jerry, I don't understand why you stopped me from questioning Tony Paulson. I thought I could pin him down and get something new."

"I don't think the direct approach works with Tony. I've got more going on than I can say right now, but while I'm working on exposing Madame Zoroaster, I can still help you find out more about your dad. Take my word for it, there are wheels within wheels here. And Tony did say he doesn't really have an alibi for the time in question. Not unless that mysterious Spanish-speaking cab driver turns up."

I glanced at Christy and she looked to be deep in thought. Even thinking, she looked great. A car horn squawked bringing my attention back to the wheel just in time to see a lady in the oncoming lane give us the one-finger salute. Her other hand held a eyebrow pencil so I guessed she must have been steering with her knees. But at least she was watching the road.

"Anyway, I think I can get more out of Tony, and maybe Pamela Kay too, with my séance idea," I said. "I want to get Madame Zoroaster back for an encore and expose her as a fake. But since Tony is her new best friend, we may be able to use the séance to pull the Paulsons in and stir things up in your dad's case."

"But how can you make her go along with the scheme?" Christy asked. "Like you say, Tony's a friend of hers so she won't want to do anything to harm him. I wonder just how good friends they are; just a mutual interest in the occult or something more physical?"

"Ugh, don't go there. I don't even want to think about that."

"Eeuw...that would be awful," Christy laughed. At least she

laughed now; that's one for the home team. "But they are connected somehow. It wouldn't surprise me if she tells us the spirits say it was only an accident."

"Well, I've got a little spirit world juice of my own that I can throw at the Madame and Mister Paulson. And I wouldn't want to meet mine in a dark alley any night soon."

I made Christy promise to tune in to my show when I dropped her at the Hyatt Regency across from the Ferry Building. Even better, she agreed to meet me for dinner afterwards. I still had some time to kill before the show but decided I'd go in early. I had been putting off making some voiceovers Ned had been pestering me for. I figured if Brad the Brat was in, he wouldn't mind setting me up to record them. I also thought he might not mind setting me up with a recorder small enough to fit in my pocket.

Christy's hotel was just a few blocks from KPMT and my condo was only a couple of blocks the other way, but rather than waste time going home, I headed to work. If things went well with Christy, we might be driving out to watch the sun set over the ocean later. Just off the Embarcadero by the station, a roach coach was packing up to leave, so I got his spot and picked up a chicken taco in the bargain.

The next hour was spent recording about five minutes of "live" commercials. My sponsors really didn't like having their commercials flubbed, so we recorded them in advance, making sure they were spontaneous, live and edited to perfection. I still had a little time left before the show when Bart and I finished recording and I decided to use it wisely for once. I Googled for info on Tom Marshall's short drive off the Marin headlands. It didn't take long to discover that it was a federal case—the stretch of highway runs through the Golden Gate National Recreation Area—but that was as far as I got.

Michael's annoying squawk came over the paging system. "Mister Jeremy, pick up line three, pul-eeze. It's your main squeeze." So much for privacy. I picked up line three. The speakers bleated, "Was that a secret? Sorry, call on line three, pul-eeze."

"All right, I've picked up already," I yelled at the ceiling and to the phone I purred, "Hello baby, is that you?"

"Is it me? That's the question. Or maybe the question should be 'is this the famous talk show host, Jerry Jeremy?' I thought maybe some little green men had swooped down in their UFO and plucked you off the face of the earth," Jeanne Parker replied.

From her tone I was beginning to think something might be a little bumpy between us, though I didn't have a clue why she would be pissed. Fortunately, she began to fill me in, "I actually got through to you right now on only about my eightieth try this week. Don't you ever check your messages? I have been trying to reach you for days."

"Uh, well, the coverage is terrible up here in the saucer," I said, trying to remember if I actually had remembered to check for messages on voicemail, e-mail, instant messaging, text messaging, pagers and maybe mental telepathy. "But as I remember it, I've been calling you and you've been screening. You haven't picked me up. I gave up leaving you voicemails when you never returned my calls. If I wanted to be ignored, I could call my agent."

"Check your messages, babe. I did call you back."

"Oh...really? Well, then there must be something wrong with this cell phone. I'll get it checked in the morning."

"How sweet of you. You'd go to all that trouble just for little ol' me. Make sure to check your DVR while you're at it."

"You left a message on my TiVo?"

"Well, not exactly. Look, Jerry, we need to talk."

Uh-oh. She'd already found out about Christy—maybe she ought to be the detective. I figured I'd gut it out though. "We're talking now."

"Not over the phone, Jerry. In person."

"Jeanne, that's why I've been trying to call you. No can do tonight. Besides with our schedules we'd only have an hour between my show and your bedtime."

"Oh, really? And I thought a quick blowjob during the news break was a romantic evening for you. A whole hour with me shouldn't put too much dent in your day."

"It's not that I don't want to. But Tony Paulson has set up a meeting with a potential sponsor. Dinner and drinks, you know. Could mean some bucks for good old Big Talk Radio."

"Oh? I always heard Tony didn't like you meeting the sponsors. At least that's the dish during morning drive. Don't tell me Tony found somebody besides Charlie Wooten who likes your show."

"Hey, my show's doing okay. You tell Dumb and Dumber to keep their opinions to their selves." I couldn't believe my ears. As far as Jeanne knew, she was still my girlfriend. "You defend me when they start up, don't you?"

"Jerry, I only work there. I can't argue with the talent." I had a few choice remarks about Freddy and Betty but held my breath. It wouldn't do to be overheard in the office; after all I'm a company man.

"Jerry, you there? I can't hear you," Jeanne said. "My mobile's fading. Before the signal's gone I need to tell you I can't make it tonight either. 'Cause I'm out of town. I have been for the past three days. If you had listened to your messages, you'd know that."

I made a mental note to check my messages, but the good news was I could meet Christy without any interference tonight.

"So let's hook up tomorrow after your show," Jeanne was saying. "I'll call you to set up a time and place. Make sure you check your messages..." Her signal seemed to fade and both the connection and Jeanne were gone.

Tonight I was free for an evening with Christy, but things might get a little trickier. If I was a hit with Christy, tomorrow night I might be double booked. Well, like they say, tomorrow is another day.

"...I KNOW a lot of you out there have kids and are more than a little concerned about what's going on in our school system.

"No, not the drugs and the sex and the disrespect for authority—and that's only the teachers. God knows what the kids are up to.

"No, what concerns me are some of the new things I see happening. Not those brought on by rampant homosexuality, free love and radical political activists—that's just our kids trying to find their way. No, I'm talking about that insidious group of individuals who influence our educational, industrial and governmental institutions at almost every level.

"That's right, folks, I'm talking about scientists.

"A bunch of four-eyed know-it-alls in lab coats who think that...well, they think that they know it all. Bad enough to say your ancestors were chimpanzees perched on some branch of your family tree, these guys are literally making monkeys out of us.

"You've been to school. Or at least you're probably working on your high-school equivalency. You've been sent to detention before, just like the rest of us. That practical joke you pulled in Mrs. Bundy's English class, the one with the paper bag and the whoopee cushion, anyone might have done that. So I know you're all for a basic education. Sure, we all

have some gaps, but that's what spell checkers are for.

"So what I'm talking about is a new study that says Artic temperatures reached their highest levels in 2000 years. I can just see Santa's elves lolling around by the pool instead of slaving away in his workshop. And what's the deal with giving away all those toys? Some kind of communist plot? Re-gifting okay, but let's hope they never take the capitalist profit motive out of Christmas.

"Anyway, what makes them think the ice was icier two thousand years ago? I happen to know the thermometer was only invented about four-hundred years ago. Besides I'm pretty sure they didn't have weather reports back then; it's not like the Eskimos could tune in Al Roker. And even if the North Pole is having a heat wave it's still colder than anywhere else, except maybe my agent's heart. Why even here in Fog City, things haven't changed since Mark Twain claimed the coldest winter he ever spent was a summer in San Francisco.

"Even so, the liberals are using something they call 'global warming' to push their green conspiracy. Not so long ago the only green they went for was the wearing of on Saint Paddy's Day. So I say what's wrong with things warming up? We could use more beach weather..."

IT was a good show. One caller even got a twelve-minute yelling match going with three other listeners. The more time they use, the less time yours truly needs to fill. Anyway, the time sped by and for most of the show I didn't even think about Christy, except during news breaks and commercials. That means about half the time.

We were to meet at the Ferry Building which was across Justin Herman Plaza from Christy's hotel and only a few blocks away from the station. Remodeled into a downtown arcade of fine food and produce a few years back, the Ferry Building had one of the City's hottest restaurants.

I was able to get a last minute reservation even though the restaurant was always booked for weeks in advance. Somehow they seemed to get the impression I'd be plugging them on my show in the coming days. Well, let's face it, Rondini gets plugged so I can get a pass on the cover charge at the Sphinx. And the food there is crummy.

When I stepped into the main arcade I spotted Christy coming out of Book Passages. She gave me a smile like I was a long lost friend and we air kissed each other. Long, lingering air kisses; I couldn't wait until we got down to the real thing. She had changed from the pastel sweater and skirt to a kind of silky Chinese style jacket and slacks. I took it as a good thing that she had dressed up a little for me.

I took her hand in mine while we strolled over to the restaurant. It was Vietnamese modern in both food and furniture, and even better, they recognized my name and seated us right away. A couple of plugs, right time, right place.

A moment later, the waiter, very tall and very skinny, glided up, told us his name was Rafael, and lucky us, he'd be our waiter tonight. "This evening, our specials are..." and he rattled off fish cheeks with earlobes, and tofu mushrooms in octopus gravy, and things with glass noodles and things with garlicky oysters and at about this point both my head and my stomach were churning.

Christy kept nodding like she understood what he was saying, but Rafael stayed focused on me with a patient smile on his fish face like he was encouraging the slow kid in the class. "...a few more minutes? Let me know if you have any questions. Any questions at all. Any." He looked down on me, an unblinking, unswerving stare.

Under that kind of pressure I made a quick decision, ordering tofu-laced pork buns and a plate of beef rolled in peanut leaves for starters. Rafael said I did "very good" and slipped away while Christy and I went back to studying the menu for potential entrees.

Our sake martinis made it to the table and we relaxed into the drinks. Through windows facing the Bay, we watched as the sun slanted across the bay and the last ferry started its commuter run to Vallejo. When our second round arrived, I figured Christy might be loosened up enough to loosen up about herself.

"I was away at school when Dad was killed, my senior year at U of A, that's the University of Arizona, Jerry. I had wanted to stay here to help Mom afterward, but she insisted I go back to Tucson to finish up."

"Smart lady, your mom."

"Now I wished I hadn't. What got me suspicious was that Mom got a raw deal when she sold Dad's share of KPMT. Dad still owned almost half of the business, but when the Paulson's bought up Dad's stock, Mom only got half the price per share that that car dealer paid when they sold him his ten percent."

"Uh, a car dealer, you say? I thought your dad and Pamela

Kay were equal partners with maybe a few shares for Tony as the idiot nephew and some non-voting stock in the hands of the investment bankers who bankrolled them."

"Well, that may have been the case originally, but as I heard Dad tell it around the dinner table, every now and then when there was a good deal, they would sell off a little of their holdings. It was maybe about a year ago that they brought the car dealer in. Wasn't that about the time your show got picked up?"

I gave her a smile; I was still wondering about Charlie and how I got my break. I couldn't believe I was bad enough at selling cars that he'd buy into the station just to get rid of me.

She said, "I think it was tied to some kind of big advertising campaign. They not only got the money for the stock, but the station made money on the advertising."

"And have you decided," Rafael said, arranging plates of appetizers in front of us, "or have you just been watching the pretty boats?"

He spent a minute adjusting the water glasses and the silverware, swapping plates and crumbing the tablecloth, while Christy and I went back to the menus to order our main courses.

Since the only Vietnamese food in Tucson came with guacamole, Christy asked me to order for both of us. I did a quick scan, took a wild guess or two, and Rafael told me I was very good again. I asked him to pick a wine that went with everything, hoping he wouldn't go over forty bucks. If he did, it was coming out of his tip.

"Listen, Christy, do you remember if that car dealer was named Charlie Wooten?" I didn't really need to ask. Charlie had done me a solid, but there appeared to be more to it than what he had said. I just couldn't have been that bad a salesman. "Never mind, I know it was Charlie. He got me the gig at KPMT."

"Oh yeah, I think I remember Dad being a little annoyed about having to hire someone, but I guess your friend insisted. I guess that must have been you," Christy paused to nibble on a shrimp, then said, "not that you didn't deserve the job. It's just how it came about, I think."

"What did you think of the show this evening?"

"Oh, Jerry, I'm sorry. I got tied up on the phone with Mom and then it was time to get ready to meet you, so I never really got a chance. But I bet it was a good show."

"Well, I tried extra hard because I thought you were

listening."

That got her laughing again.

"Well, maybe it was just a regular show...." I was glad she took it as a joke, because I didn't want to come off as a dork. Luckily Rafael and his helpers showed up with plates and bowls, artistic arrangements of duck and scallions and crispy potatoes, fish with swirls of sauces making design statements. I hoped it tasted half as good as it looked.

We concentrated on our plates for a while, taking a break from the radio dish. Christy tasted her entree and I tasted mine, then we switched and tried each other's, deciding on the ones we liked best and if we'd have to come back for them. It began to be like a real date, just a boy and a girl enjoying the moment. Somehow I never know when to leave well enough alone.

My goal was to offer up my services in shining armor if she was really in trouble. After all, I pride myself on going out of my way for a pretty girl.

I said, "So when your dad died, the Paulsons—Pamela Kay I guess—bought his share of KPMT from your mom? Maybe she should have just held onto it. Pamela Kay just hangs out in Stinson Beach while the profits roll in. Couldn't your mother have done the same?"

"Apparently not. Mom said there was some kind of clause in the partnership agreement that gave the surviving owners the option of buying out any partner that dies. That lawyer the station uses, Mr. Heilbrun, went over all this with Mom at the time. I talked to him myself from Tucson a few weeks ago."

"So then it wasn't a swindle?" I asked.

"I don't have any problem with the survivor clause per se, Jerry. It's the way they agreed to do business, Dad included. But I got really mad when I found out from Mom how little she got for a successful media outlet in the fourth largest radio market in the country."

I nodded encouraging and dug into some raw fish served with grilled papaya. Christy had finished off her meal without my noticing her taking a bite, chewing or talking with her mouth full. God, she's classy.

"When I decided to look into the sale, I couldn't get Mrs. Paulson or anybody else to talk to me about it. Mr. Heilbrun seemed to be giving me the run around, but he finally agreed to a meeting—I'm seeing him tomorrow."

I said, "Leland handled my contract. He seemed like a nice enough guy."

"Oh, I'm sure he is. Like I say, Dad had agreed to the survivor's clause when he signed the partnership papers. The funny thing is that Dad was planning on selling his share of the station anyway. Now the other partners had right of first refusal if any partner were to sell, but they had to match whatever offer was on the table. And I understand from what Mom says that he had a good offer from a large media chain. I'm convinced it would have been for a much higher valuation than my mother was given."

"Well, if your father's partners actually benefited from his death," I said trying to chop stick some glass noodles that were as slippery as glass, "it could indicate a motive, but jeez, it doesn't really prove foul play. On the other hand, I saw somebody try to run you down today—I'm sure of that."

"It's not the motive alone; Heilbrun and the Paulsons could have just taken advantage of the situation. But Mom received a copy of the CHP accident report a couple of months ago. And what do you think it had in it? It said that there were paint scrapes on Dad's car from another vehicle that could have been involved. I have a copy of the report that I can show you."

"That's okay, I'm already a believer. Any proof that the scrapes happened just then? Maybe somebody scraped him in a parking lot."

"Dad was always so careful with his Mercedes. Mom is sure that there were no scrapes when Dad left home that morning, and he never mentioned anything to her when they talked just before he headed up to meet with Mrs. Paulson."

"Still, I think it's what the cops call circumstantial. No hard evidence that anyone from the station was involved. On the other hand, they always say, 'Cherchez la dinero!'"

We agreed that Christy's dad dying just as he was making a deal to sell his stake in KPMT and Mrs. Paulson getting to buy it cheap instead looked like a motive. I had some reservations about Pamela Kay being a hit woman though. In this case, a hit-and-run woman I guess. But maybe somebody else stood to gain.

Freddy and Betty? Could be the new partners had crossed paths with them before; I wouldn't doubt it. If they were involved, I might need to help nail them. Anyway, Christy Marshall needed some help about now and I decided I was the guy to lend her a hand.

She was saying, "When I talked to the police they thought I was crazy. Besides no one was sure whose jurisdiction it was since it happened in a national park. The local Smokey the Bear types aren't really up to a homicide investigation. Plus, the trail is cold and no one but Mom and I are interested now."

"That might have been true until today," I said, "but I saw you almost get run down and somebody has to do something to protect visitors to our fair city. And in your case, I want that somebody to be me."

"Jerry, that would be wonderful," Christy said giving me a look like kids give Santa Claus, "but I don't want to drag you into something that could jeopardize your position at the station."

"What? You gotta be kidding. Big Talk Radio couldn't get along without me."

Chapter 12.

IN spite of the unhappy set of circumstances that brought us together and all that talk about murder, the gentle twilight and romantic setting cast their spell on me and to some degree on Christy. We walked along the edge of the Bay toward the lights of the Oakland-Bay Bridge. A thousand lights reflected off the water. I held Christy's hand. When we got to the Oldenburg sculpture 'Cupid's Span,' a half buried sixty-foot high bow-and-arrow, I put my arms around her and we kissed.

The breeze off the bay was starting to get chilly, so we huddled together on the way back to her hotel. We didn't talk much and for once, the dead air was okay. I left her at the hotel elevators and this time I just kissed her cheek. From the lobby I watched the glass elevator take her up. I hoped she was watching back so I gave her a brief salute.

A FOGGY sunshine streamed through the windows and prodded me awake. I usually draw the blinds at night so my alarm clock has a reason to be sitting on the nightstand. But having forgotten to set the alarm, forgetting the blinds evened things out. Who says two wrongs don't make a right?

Besides I had wanted to get an early start anyway. Calling Jeanne crossed my mind. I wanted to see if she was still sore at me and to break our date for tonight. That might be tricky so I decided to wait until later.

It was still too early to call Ronnie. He works later than I do and sleeps later. If he gets woken up before noon, he can pretty much be a grouch. So, with some time to kill, you should pardon the expression, I decided to start on my fitness program. After all, I wanted to look good for Christy.

Properly clothed and shod, I headed along the Embarcadero jogging briskly. I figured I might even pass by 'Cupid's Span' and bring back the memory of last night. I passed the big bow and arrow and kept jogging until I got to the ball park. At that point it was time to start looking for a cab back.

No luck, so I had to hoof it both ways. I managed to work up a sweat though it was still foggy and cool. On the typical San Francisco summer morning, a high fog covers the sky, burning off around noon. The temperature stays in the low sixties until then. Once the fog evaporates though, it hits the high sixties. The sun floats in clear, crystalline skies and stays that way until my show is about half done. Then the super-heated Central Valley pulls the fog back through the Golden Gate, air-conditioning the City once more. I used to do the weather.

By the time I got back to my apartment, said sun was breaking through and it was time to give Ronnie a wake-up call. I stopped by the coffee shop for a latte and then headed for the elevator. I settled in with my caffeine fix and dialed The Great One who, as it turned out, was up and about, having already gotten a call from the Amazing Ming.

"Hold on to your bonnet, Junior," he opened with. "You remember Ming, the Chinese mind reader? Did a telepathy act built around a Chinese vase?"

"A Ming vase?"

"No, he buys them at Target. That aside, he told me how a year or so back he used an actress planted in the audience as a shill. You know the 'have you ever met me before' come-on? They worked it pretty good as I recall—"

"Listen, Ronnie, I bet it was a great trick, but I need to talk about my upcoming séance show," while I spoke I browsed the refrigerator in case something microwavable had somehow been left in there.

"—hold on, kid, I'm getting to the good part," Ronnie said, "the gal Ming used was a small time actress named Rhonda Ridgeway. She'd apparently been in a few productions at the Geary Theater and maybe some work for the Magic Theater out at Fort Mason. Not real magic, just the magic of theater in an old warehouse. You know, Sam Shepard or something."

"Yeah, he's great, but I how did she get hooked up with Ming the mind reader. Seems a bit of a come down from Sammy-boy."

"Well, maybe she was playing the role of the producer's

girlfriend and they broke up, I don't know. God, I'd bet that Sam Shepard could script a great magic act if he put his mind to it. Of course, I'd have to show him how to make it work. You don't know him by any chance?"

"Know Sam Shepard? Listen, Ronnie, how would I know him?"

"You're in show business."

"So are you, Ronnie, more than me even."

"Hey, you don't suppose you could get him on your show. It would be a great opportunity for me to meet him. He might buy into writing a magic play for the Magic Theater. I could help him come up with the gags and actually work them in the play. This is exciting."

"Before you take it to Broadway, let's get back to why I'm calling you."

"That's what I was saying—word on the street, around the Amazing Ming's neighborhood anyway, is that Mrs. Rubenstein was really this Rhonda Ridgeway."

"Ming the Mirthless's shill was also Madame Zoroaster's? What is she, typecast?"

"Listen, Ming e-mailed me one of his old publicity stills that showed her with him. It's hard to be definite, she's pretty good looking in his photo, but dowdied up a little it could be Mrs. Rubenstein. She's an actress—she could pull it together."

"Great! I can feel it all coming together now. My show will be great, Pamela Kay will get off my case, and if this was a perfect world, she'll offer me the morning drive slot."

"Well, hold on, Red. Nothing's exactly perfect. I know you think I really do work magic, but all I have so far is a name. We still need to locate Miss Ridgeway."

"Locate? Listen, Ronnie, don't they have an actor's directory or something that you could look her up in?"

"Jerry, they might just have something like that. If not, they should."

"They should, huh?"

"You sure you don't know anybody who might know Sam Shepard?"

So the morning drive show didn't look to be dropping into my lap just yet. Before Ronnie hung-up, he promised to work on locating the elusive Rhonda Ridgeway if I would do the same. Ming had put his prodigious extra-sensory powers to work and vaguely recalled Rhonda had left the act because she had found herself a rich boyfriend. Ming wasn't sure but thought the rich boyfriend also might have been married. Due to the late hours and low pay that shilling provided, Rhonda Ridgeway saw the married man as a better deal. Maybe she thought he would leave his wife for her or maybe she thought he could get her a part on the stage. Maybe she thought pigs could fly.

Anyway Ronnie e-mailed me her picture posing next to The Amazing Ming and I Googled her. Google knew a lot Rhonda Ridgeways, but most of them couldn't have been my Rhonda Ridgeway. A New Jersey massage therapist seemed very popular but not the gal I was seeking, a dog trainer in Montana and a ceramic artist in Texas were dead ends also. Several sites had photos you wouldn't want your mother to see and that I hoped weren't of our gal.

There were a lot of non-pornographic Rhonda Ridgeway snaps that didn't match ours either, but I looked close just to make sure. And then—bingo.

Our Rhonda Ridgeway popped out of a cast picture for a play called *Gatos* which seemed to be based on *Cats* only without the music. Maybe they just meowed through the lyrics. The play had run last summer right here in River City. It had been put on by a theater troop called the Nuevo Hispanic Shakespeare Players.

There was a cast photo in cat drag and another one during rehearsal when they were in what they thought passed for street clothing. I played around with the images, zooming back and forth to make sure. There she was—a rat dressed as a cat. Better looking than I remembered Mrs. Rubinstein being, but still our lady rat. She matched the Ming photo, but I'd have recognized her anyway.

I searched on-line for the Nuevo Hispanic Shakespeare Players and got a few hits listing them in with some other small theater and dance groups, but not much detail. Not that I really cared about their artistic vision, however I did find a phone number. It was an old listing so no telling if they'd kept up with the phone bill, but I dialed it and an answering machine with a cultured voice told me rehearsals would start last week on *Un Streetcar Llamado Desire*. The voice also said auditions would be held at the Mission Paradise Theater until a date about three weeks ago. I guess the cultured voice hadn't gotten around to updating the recording. He invited me to leave a message if I wasn't a bill collector or a salesman, but I decided to hang up instead.

Since auditions were over, I had missed my chance for that, but maybe they would be into rehearsals by now, right there at the good old Mission Paradise.

My knowledge of actual show business, and particularly the theater, was a little hazy although I had met and interviewed a few actors. Still, I was pretty sure that most actors, unless they hit it big on Geary Street, spent their spare time waiting on the dinner crowds in one of San Francisco's many restaurants. So the Nuevo Hispanic Shakespeare Players' rehearsal would need to be over by three or four o'clock to let them get to their evening day jobs on time. Come to think of it that was my schedule too.

Timing being everything, I decided to cruise over to the Mission Paradise out on 26th Street where they held those auditions. Maybe I could say I wanted to audition even if the date had passed—better late than never. But I didn't want to actually audition; if I got a role, I'd have to go back to waiting on tables. Of course there was no guarantee that the Players would still be at the Mission Paradise. Or even that the theater hadn't been turned into a Costco by now. But I had some time to kill and I might get lucky. Ronnie wasn't the only one working on this. As a matter of fact I thought I was doing pretty good.

I felt a little bad that I wasn't hanging with Christy, but she was going to have KPMT's attorney give her the old soft shoe this morning and I'd have only slowed things down. At least that's what Leland Heilbrun said when he negotiated my last contract. I hoped that Heilbrun would offer up some pieces that fit into the Marshall puzzle, even if he didn't mean to. That's what I was hoping for—that and for Christy to look both ways before crossing the street from now on in.

On the other hand, I didn't want Heilbrun to see me helping her out either. If she raised a ruckus about Pamela Kay shorting Mama on the station buyout, it might look like I was taking sides against those best in a position to make sure I never worked in the Bay Area again. Not even waiting on tables.

My job today was to bust the bogus Mrs. Rubenstein, a.k.a. Rhonda Ridgeway. *Cherche la shill.* By my digs downtown it was almost cool enough to wear a Bogie-style trench coat and I was almost cool enough to do it, but it would be warmer in the Mission district so I stuck with a sweater I could pull off when I got there.

The Mission gets the lion's share of the warm weather in town. Maybe that's why the Latino community has grown up there, sunny Mexico and all that. The weather, the low rents and some pretty *laissez faire* enforcement about how many people can share an apartment. Still, the community has been moving up the economic ladder—young couples of all backgrounds, looking for affordable homes, are moving in. The Mission could be a roadmap to the American dream; a few more years and nobody will be able to afford to live there.

Right now though, English is pretty much a second language and the bodegas and taquerias are holding their own against KFC and Burger King. I found a parking spot just off Mission Street and could see the theater half a block down. The Mission Paradise was a neon dinosaur of a fifties' movie palace that had gone the way of every other single screen theater. Or dinosaur for that matter. Yet for now, the Nuevo Hispanic thespians had given it a second life, but unless they had a Latino Olivier or Gielgud in the wings, the wrecking ball wouldn't be far away.

The plaster in the lobby was cracked and the deco paint job had peeled a little. I doubted the Nuevo Hispanic crew drew much of a Nuevo Hispanic crowd, even with a Latinized version of Tennessee Williams. It probably hadn't been SRO since first run films starred John Wayne.

"ESTA-YAA! Esta-yaa!"

Ah, got it. Stella, south of the border. It must be Estanley Kowalski mooning for his wife. The door by the ticket booth was propped open so anyone from the street could walk in, although I seemed to be the only one interested enough to do it. Estanley's voice was coming through another set of doors to the theater proper. They too were propped open. Saves on the AC I guess. If they had AC.

I followed the voices into the theater. The stage was bare and the actors were sitting in a semi-circle reading from scripts. A few people were watching from the seats down front. I stopped about half way down the aisle so as not to interrupt the show. I stood there looking over the actors to see if Ms. Ridgeway just might be Estella or maybe even Blanca DuBois.

A guy who didn't look like Brando, or very Polish for that matter, stopped play acting and spoke to somebody in the cheap seats, "Carlos, I really have no view of the character's internal dialog...sure, it's about the Napoleonic code and all, but shouldn't this be the Zapatista Code or something? Did Zapata have a code? Did anybody south of Guadalajara have one?"

"Please, Bobbo, please," said a balding man in the fourth row. "Let the character just say the words as they are written. Leave the thinking to me."

The actor who didn't look like Brando rolled his eyes and said, "To hell with the code, Carlos; you've got the Napoleonic complex."

A few other players were having quiet side conversations, oblivious to the concerns of the lead. One or two people in the orchestra seats seemed to be dozing. Nobody noticed me standing in the aisle or if they did, they figured I belonged there. With the doors wide open, I guessed they got their share of the homeless or the underemployed slipping into the back row for a snooze. Probably not too different from the paying audience.

I was taking my time with each of the faces, straining my eyesight trying to pick out Mrs. Rubenstein. Rhonda Ridgeway might have a new look by now or be wearing no makeup or different make-up or almost anything. She had looked considerably older as Mrs. Rubenstein than in her pictures on-line. Now the harsh rehearsal lights on stage washed out the actors' features and masked their ages. Anyway, maybe she had a nose job or collagen injections. If I was lucky, she might have gone for the boob job.

So I hung back, eyeing the actresses, wishing I had binoculars. But Rhonda Ridgeway wasn't Stella or Blanche or the neighbor or any of the other characters. She wasn't even there. I began to ponder my next move. Maybe just see if anybody here knew her. But then again, they might not be too forthcoming, figuring me for a stalker or a bill collector or some such.

But then…. Maybe this *was* my lucky day.

The guy sitting two actors down from the left began to look very familiar. Maybe Mrs. Rubenstein sends her regrets, but if that wasn't Mr. Rubenstein, his golden youth melting into middle-aged spread, I'd eat a KPMT baseball cap. He was flipping through a script marking his lines with a hi-liter. From the number of times he marked things, his role didn't call for much talking.

The discussion on codes—Napoleonic, Zapatista or area codes—had pretty much petered out by now and everybody seemed to be concentrating on their pages while they waited for Bobbo to pick up his lines again. During the pause, I walked down the aisle to the folks watching the rehearsal.

Bobbo had just started up again when I walked into his sight line throwing him off. He stopped and asked Carlos who I was.

"Don't mind me," I said showing the charming smile. "I was enjoying your performance. You must be Estan— er, the lead."

Bobbo puffed up a little and gave me a nice return smile, "Yes, of course, you must visit my website, William Ortega dot-com. You may have heard of me. Are you from the media?" By now I was the center of attention, and when Ortega mentioned "the media," everyone's interest seemed to perk up.

"I am from the media as a matter of fact. Who's in charge here?" I asked. "Is there a producer or director in the house? A PR flack maybe?"

The balding guy stood up and held out his hand. "*Buenos días*, sir, I'm Carlos Sierra, the producer and the director," he said as we shook. "Formerly with the American Conservatory Theater, A-C-T," he spelled. "You the fellow that called from the Chron?"

"You mean the Chronicle, the newspaper? Even better than that, my friend. You've heard of talk radio, haven't you? You want to break out of the ghetto of Spanish language stations, don't you? I'm Jerry Jeremy and I'm your dream come true publicity-wise. I have the number one evening drive talk show on KPMT. I bring a listening audience of...well, I don't have the figures right now, but it's pretty big."

"Oh, I was expecting to have somebody from the Chronicle stop by."

"Sure, but this is radio. You have heard of radio? You know, like television only without the pictures. KPMT, Big Talk Radio, that's us, and I'm the biggest mouth there."

A couple of people seemed to recognize me. I'm sure they did. Probably even in a good way. Sure they did.

Even so, Mr. Rubenstein, who I knew to be a player in more ways than one, was packing it in. With hardly a look in my direction, he started jamming his water bottle and script and hi-liters into a backpack.

"Hold on," I said, moving closer to the stage, singling him out, "don't run away. I'm a big fan of yours. I saw a great performance you gave a while back. Marvelous performance, you and, let's see—ah yes, Rhonda Ridgeway."

His fellow thespians were looking at him now, maybe amazed that he was singled out. A woman with thick glasses, sitting a few rows down from me, spoke up, "Cruize, you can't leave. We haven't run your lines yet. You won't get rehearsal pay."

"Yes, hold on," Carlos Sierra joined in. "Apparently Mr. Jeremy is a fan of yours; he may want to talk to you. We need all the publicity we can get. Besides the guy from the *Chron* looks like a no-show."

The woman with the glasses said, "I'll give him a call, Carlos."

"Thanks, Mr. Sierra," I said and then addressing the group at large, "I'll need to talk to several of you to get a feel for your contributions to the production. Is there some kind of playbill with everybody's names on it?"

"I have a cast list someplace," Sierra riffled through his clipboard, papers slipping to the floor as he leafed through them. "Here, here it is."

"Great, that'll be a big help, but now I need to match the faces to the names. I already know Mr. Ortega," I said, "but if I can I get everyone else to just tell me their names, so I get some idea of who's who?" I signaled an actress in the far left chair to start. She was Asian, but her name, at least on stage, was Rosalie Jones.

"What about our roles? You'll definitely want to know who we are playing," Rosalie said. "That will tell you a lot about who we are. At least for the run of the show."

"Oh, yeah, sure. That's great too." I began to feel a little guilty as I searched for a pen, but maybe a plug or two for the show would make it all right. And the guy from the *Chronicle* might still show.

"A script, you'll need a script," a chubby actor said. "Otherwise you won't understand the significance of the parts as portrayed in our new version. We're bringing Williams out of the twentieth century and up to date, politically correct and all. You'll want to follow along when I do my lines later."

"Thanks, Wally, he can use my copy. I'll look over Carlos' shoulder," said a man sitting beside the producer-director as he handed his script over to me.

"Great, thanks for that suggestion. I can't wait to look it over," I said. "But for now, can we just have everybody stand up and identify themselves? And tell me the part you'll be playing, too. I know that's important."

So one by one, each of the players delivered their name and their character's name like they were auditioning for a place in a graveyard. I pretended to be making notes, but I was only interested in matching one name to one face. When we got to my boy, he didn't seem to want to look my way, mostly looking up towards the where the box seats would be if they had any. Carlos prompted him in case he forgot his name, calling him "Cruize" for short.

"Yes-s, I'm Alain de la Cruz, but everybody calls me 'Cruize,'" he gave Carlos a nod. "I am playing the part of the Doctor."

"Interesting...," I said being somewhat at a loss for words. Cruize found his chair and sat back down, but this time looked directly at me. Either he knew I knew or he thought I might have thought he wasn't the guy. But I knew.

"I don't want to break up your rehearsal," I said, turning towards Carlos and the rest of the orchestra seats. "How about I start off with a quick chat with Mister Cruize, er, de la Cruizer, while the rest of you carry on. You know, with the rehearsal."

"Wonderful idea, we won't need the Doctor for a while yet, and if necessary I can cue the others with his lines," Sierra said. "When you're ready to move on, just let me know. Don't you have a tape recorder or something?"

"Something."

Sierra squinted towards the entrance and said, "I wonder what happened to the guy from the *Chronicle*."

"I heard there's a big new production down at the Adam and Eve Club," I said. "Maybe he's interviewing the dancers."

"Nudity is so nineties," a shopworn ingénue said. "I haven't done any in years."

Maybe I'd interview her next. Meanwhile, I wanted to get de la Cruz to myself in case the man from the *Chronicle* did show up.

"Well, that would be one kind of exposure," Sierra was saying. "Okay, Cruize, go with Mr. Jeremy. You can use the lobby for the interviews. You can talk there okay without being disturbed, except for the occasional wino wandering in."

"Okay," de la Cruz said as he walked across the stage and down the proscenium steps. "Okay, a little buzz won't hurt my career. Let's do that interview, Mr. Jeremy."

We walked out to the lobby and I asked if there was any place nearby we could get coffee. He steered me next door, a place called the "Mexican Jumping Beans." We ordered and he let me pay without a fight. Cruize was more of a Brando type than the fellow playing the lead, but was getting a little past it, hair thinning, six-packs turning into a beer barrel. Not quite *The Godfather* yet, but definitely no longer *The Wild One*.

"Listen, Mr. Jeremy," Cruize started once we were seated,

the table wobbling on an uneven sidewalk, "I was wondering if you'd remember me. We've met before, sort of."

"Sure. Who could forget your wonderful performance as Willy Rubenstein in *Death of a Talk Show Host?*"

"Hey, com'on. It would have been a pretty big coincidence if you just ran into me here. But stranger things have happened; look at the role of coincidence in Shakespeare."

"Yes, but that's not really real. But then I guess neither were Mr. and Mrs. Rubenstein."

"I'm not sure what it is you want from me. I was hired to play the part and I thought it had something to do with a Halloween gag. An actress I was working with at the time offered me the part, but she never really explained what it was all about. I thought she had the hots for me. Maybe she did."

"Well I hope she treated you right, Cruize, because it was all about pulling a felony class rip-off." I let that sink in for a moment. If it scared him enough to take flight, I figured I could out run a pudgy, middle-aged guy. I wasn't too sure what I could do if I caught him though. Some of these actors know karate.

"She treated me right all right. She looks a lot better when she's not made up as Helena Rubenstein."

"Heather. Heather Rubenstein."

"Sure, Heather. So you're not here to promote our refried *Streetcar*. I guess I should have known. It's shit. The only work you can get in this town anymore is shit. A couple of years ago I was a regular walk-on on *Nash Bridges*. Uniformed cop, waiter, even a doctor once. Sometimes I got a line. Some commercials too. Now, it's all shit. But," Cruize eyed a young Latina mom walking by, "hope springs eternal." *Mamacita* was wearing designer sportswear and pushed an expensive-looking stroller built for two.

I said, "Lighten up, man. We'll talk about your problems in a minute. Right now, I want to talk about that performance you gave at the station." We paused to sip our lattes and Cruize asked if he could light up an herbal cigarette. It smelled pretty much like burnt pumpkin pie, so I figured the second hand smoke couldn't be any worse for me than a few thousand Thanksgiving dinners. Still de la Cruz got a few dirty looks from the passers-by. For all I know it's probably illegal to smoke on the street in San Francisco. I decided he'd had enough of a break and I picked up the threads of my pitch again.

"I believe you," I said, "you know, when you say you didn't

know what was going down last Halloween." I tried staring him down in case he was lying, but the smoke was making my eyes tear. "Anyway the past is the past, but to tell the truth, it hasn't been forgotten. As a matter of fact, I'm planning a little class reunion and I'm planning on having you there."

"You're going to do it again? Boost the ratings?"

"I plan to do it a little bit differently this time. Like, for instance, this time I'll know what's going on."

"You know that could make it less spontaneous."

"Sure, thanks for the tip. If I cast you in the part, you'll get a credit this time. Maybe get some buzz going."

"I could use that."

"Maybe pull you out of the shit. And if you decide to shine me on, you'll really be *in* the shit."

"Listen, Mr. Jeremy, you don't need to threaten me. If I did the wrong thing last time, I'm ready to make up for it. Would I get paid for this role? I got two hundred last time for about an hour of my time counting makeup and a run through."

"The pay? I'll have to call your agent, or maybe your parole officer, about that. But first, I need to know a little more about the casting of that last show. I want you to tell me how you got roped into the part in the first place and so forth. How did you get role of Mr. Rubenstein?"

"Well, at the time I had a small but pivotal role in a new adaptation of *Uncle Vanya*. In this version, Uncle Vanya is really Auntie Vanya, a transvestite." Cruize straightened up and puffed out his chest a little and said, "I was the understudy for the Auntie Vanya part too. God, how I hoped the lead would come down with some kind of shit, but for a cokehead he was healthier than a horse. But I actually moved better in heels than he did."

"So you're a man of many talents, including being a woman of many talents. Let's get back to the scam."

"Well, that was just a part. Any number of my leading ladies—before I gained weight—will tell you I'm all man."

"I can't wait for your memoirs. So remind me again, how did you get involved in this swindle?"

"It happened like this, one of the actresses, Rita Ridgeway—"

"Rhonda."

That's right—Rhonda—you know her?"

"Not really, but I've done some homework. But you're in the limelight now, this is your big scene. What about

Rhonda?"

"...well, like I say she was in this production with me, we really didn't know each other very well, but for some reason she and I started sitting together at the run-throughs. Then one thing and another, we started sleeping together. I liked that because she would make dinner instead of my having to eat out, what with the prices they charge in restaurants unless all you eat is McDonalds."

"So you got the part on the old casting couch."

"I like to think it was because I was right for the role. Rita, I mean Rhonda, said I should be cast as one of the leads in a little improv piece, sort of like a performance art thing, if you know what that is. One night only, improvising our lines. I just needed to act real angry and follow her lead, she said."

"Do a lot of this performance art stuff, do you?"

"Well, this was actually my first like this. I had done a good bit of street theater, acting at the Renaissance Faire doing different characters in jolly ole Elizabethan times, you know. Throw a little Will Shakespeare at the paying customers while you're selling them a turkey drumstick the size of a softball bat."

"I can guess who the turkey was. Let's forget the resume and get back to the Ridgeway gal and you doing the mister and missus bit."

"You mean the sex?"

"No, I'm like a monk—other people's sex lives don't interest me. Get back to the story."

"What? Well, anyway this was a paying job and I saw I could play it as a sort of angry Willy Loman. I figured since it was at a radio station, I might also get some kind of plug for 'Auntie Vanya'. Of course, that didn't happen."

"We try to limit the plugs to the real guests. A funny rule we have down at KPMT."

"I meant I thought we were legit. I wanted to get your audience to come to the play rather than sit around watching stuff on TV all the time."

"My listeners aren't watching TV. They're listening to the radio. That's why they're called listeners."

"So that's about it. She offered me a quick deuce and a chance to do some improv. I never actually heard anything about it once it was over, though Rhonda did drop out of *Auntie Vanya* soon after. I thought she was miscast anyway."

"So you lost touch with her and she could even have left the Bay Area?"

"I said she dropped out of the play, not off the face of the earth. After all, we both got the same agent."

Chapter 13.

AFTER dancing around a little more, I signed Alain de la Cruz, aka Cruizer, for an encore performance as Mr. Rubenstein. Only this time I would be writing the script. Well, Ronnie and I would anyway. In return, I got the name of his agent, Helen O'Hara, and her private number, the one she always answers. Before we parted, I told him to make my apologies to Carlos and to have him send me half a dozen front row tickets for opening night. For my part I'd plug the play, and with any luck, the audience would outnumber the cast.

The taco places in the Mission were inviting and the spicy aromas made my mouth water, but I decided to give Brad the Brat a break what with the close quarters in Studio B. So I collected the Beamer and did the stop-and-go behind a Muni bus most of the way back downtown. Most San Francisco buses are powered by overhead electrical cables, so no belching noxious fumes. Great for driving a convertible; I was only being gassed by the fumes from the delivery trucks and other cars stuck behind the slow moving Muni.

As I poked along I decided to give Christy some moral support. But she must not have needed any right then because she wasn't answering. I left a sweet message reminding her to listen to my show and suggesting we hook up after it was over.

I figured I'd better check in with Jeanne too, just to make my excuses in case she thought we had planned something for this evening. No luck there either, so I left a little more charm on her machine.

The Great Rondini was strike three—no answer there either. You'd think a mind reader would know I was going to call. I had wanted to let him know the progress I'd made and

100 Donald J. McGill

to plan our next step. I could always connect up later at the Blue Sphinx for a planning session, but I'd already done some planning for the evening. Now, if I could only connect up with Christy.

By the time I had made all my calls and checked all my messages in case somebody was actually trying to reach me, I'd made it back downtown where I dropped the car off at my apartment building. On the walk over to KPMT, I called Helen O'Hara on that special number that she always answers. I got the machine.

I left her a message mentioning Cruize, Ridgeway and possible work. If that didn't get her, nothing would. If I was George Lucas, I'd get a callback. As it was, even my own agent doesn't call me. Anyway, in thirty minutes I'd made eight calls, none of which got answered by a real person.

I had almost reached KPMT when the phone rang. Caller ID told me it wasn't anybody I was waiting to hear from though. It told me it was Pamela Kay. I stood there, right in the middle of Lombard Street, looking at the phone. I was trying to think of what to say when after ringing eight or ten times it rolled over to voice mail. Oh well, I guess I'm just like anybody else when it comes to that.

I wound up getting to the station with time to spare and darned if Michael the receptionist didn't recognize me on the first try. "Hey, Jerry! Mr. Tunney wants to see you! He said to tell you that when you got in. Maybe you stepped on somebody's toes."

"I have if I've done my job right."

I swung by Ned's office, but the door was closed and the voices from within didn't sound happy. I hung around for a while trying to hear what was going on, hoping it wasn't about me. I could identify Ned's voice, but then it was his office so that wasn't much of a leap. The other voice sounded familiar, but I couldn't hear well enough to place it. Then, the door suddenly opened, me stepping back just in time, and Tony bolted out. He barreled down the hall headed to his own office and I decided to follow.

"So Tony," I trailed him into his room, "were you and Ned going over our plans for a séance?"

"What? A séance?" It wasn't a hard question, but it seemed to have broken his train of thought. He relaxed a little, "No, uh no, Jerry. I'm sorry. I thought you were going to handle that end. Ilonya and I did do a little brainstorming on promotion though. But I have to run now, I'll call you over the weekend or we can discuss it on Monday."

He was stuffing whatever came to hand into his briefcase, looking for all the world like somebody who wanted to be someplace else. Maybe anyplace else.

"I thought I heard you talking with Ned, but not that, eh?"

"No, not that," Tony was jammed some old talk radio magazines in the bag. "Just some old business that won't stayed dead and buried."

An unfortunate choice of words. And the look on his face gave me a chill.

"Well, if that was about old news,' I said, "I'd hate to hear you guys when you actually get worked up about something. Anyway I've gotta run. Got a show to do. You know...."

"Thanks for looking in, Jerry. I'll call you tomorrow about the big show. It should work out great."

By the time I got back to Ned's office the door was closed again, but there were no voices. Back in Studio B I found a note Ned had left for me. It said he'd be back later and we should go for a drink after the show. Ned was buying.

"*Hey, folks, just the other day I had the boob tube on—something not recommended for intelligent radiophiles like yourselves—but I found myself surfing through about five hundred cable channels to see what to watch. It's amazing isn't it, all those channels and when you eliminate the talk shows—who needs those?—reality TV and infomercials, then take away the reruns of* CSI *and* The Golden Girls, *well, there's just not very much left.*

"And what about all those commercials—not to say there's anything wrong with sponsored messages on the radio —but on TV you see fifteen or twenty at every break. Could be some kind of Commie brainwashing thrown in with the shampoo ads. Anyway I thought I'd hit a time warp when Fred Astaire came on dancing with a vacuum cleaner. A time warp or I was seeing a ghost.

"The closest he came in real life—if you think movies are real life—was dancing with a mop and pail. But now he's tapping out a message from the grave and it says to buy this product, one that probably wasn't even around when...well, when he was still around. Astaire may be gone, but his spirit lingers on.

"Who knows who else may come back from the grave. TV technology has become Doctor Frankenstein, making Fred

Astaire into a video zombie. Not just the walking dead, but the singing, dancing, selling dead.

"Jenny Craig could bring back the Fat Elvis. Bela Lugosi could pitch for the Red Cross blood drive and Marilyn Monroe could—well, she could do anything and I'd buy it. Speaking of politics, just imagine Ronald Reagan rocking the vote for Sarah Palin. Maybe they'd both get elected..."

As it turned out Christy had to get her nails done or something, so she wound up missing my show again. I should have called her during a commercial break to make sure her radio was on and working, but I didn't talk to her until I was off the air.

"I'm so sorry, Jerry," Christy purred. Hearing her voice sent a thrill up my spine. Not to mention the thrill it gave to unmentionable parts. After all, I run a family show. She said, "I just returned from the lawyer's a few minutes ago with tons and tons of paper that Mr. Heilbrun had copied for me to go through."

"He didn't buy you dinner, did he?"

"No, he didn't do that. He's a little old for me as far as that goes."

"Well, I'm glad you're not one of those gals that go for the old guys. They usually want the early bird special anyway, two martinis and the meatloaf platter. You know, stuff they can gum. Say, you're not one of those gals that go for younger guys, are you?"

"Only when I was younger, but I just meant Mr. Heilbrun's too old to ask me out."

"Not even to rummage through your files?"

"Why, Jerry, whatever do you take me for. I keep those safely tucked away in my drawers."

"Thanks for the warning. But anyway, you must be ready for a break; you can't eat all those papers he gave you. Not even if you are from Tucson."

"I'm starving actually. You'd think Mr. Heilbrun would have had some tea and cookies to nibble on, being such a high-priced corporate attorney here in the big city."

"Didn't your mother warn you to stay away from lawyers? They're so cheap that in this town the homeless give *them* food. Anyway I like to think I'm better company than any old attorney. I have to a grab a quick drink with my station manager, but I can give him the slip. Then I'll take you out for a great dinner."

"That's sweet, Jerry, but I don't think you should blow off the station manager. That's Ned something, right? The old surfer dude? You better stay and work on your career. Besides, I can't wait; I could eat a wild mustang right now, or at least a big, green salad. Besides, I'm way too tired to be very much fun. I'll just order up room service and start in on these papers. I'll probably be asleep before you have your second drink."

"Hey, my career's doing okay. I can give Ned a bit of the old 'glad we could get together' and be out of there nineish. I can pick up a pizza on my way over."

Christy was saying, "You're irresistible as a water fountain in the desert, but I think we better wait until morning. Call me when you get up, if you're not too hung over."

"I don't think it'll go that far. I don't know that Ned will be in that much of a party mood. When I went by his office before the show, he was having some kind of an argument with Tony Paulson."

"Really? How interesting. Did you hear what they were saying?"

"I tried my best, but his door was closed. I thought about trying to put a glass against it like they do in the movies, but was afraid it might draw a crowd. I couldn't make out any words, but the tone of the voices seemed to say they weren't talking business."

"Don't do anything to get in trouble at the station, Jerry. I don't want to be the cause of you getting fired."

"Gee, Christy, if I'm going to get fired, I'd rather it was for helping you than for helping Tony. The Great Rondini's crystal ball says this will all come together and I'm gonna be a big name in Bay Area radio."

"You're very sweet, Jerry. I really do like having your help. Until I met you, I was feeling very much alone."

Chapter 14.

NED Tunney has been the station manager at KPMT, doing the old day-to-day ever since they painted the call letters on the door. In theory I worked for him, not Pamela Kay, although as the owner, she was his boss and therefore was my boss too somehow. If Mrs. Paulson was an aging beach bunny, Ned was the middle-aged surfer dude. Nowadays his sun-bleached hair was thinning and his swimmer's physique sported a bit of an inner tube, but twenty-five years ago Ned and Pammykins must have looked like the Frankie and Annette of Ocean Beach. The perfect teenage couple, except for her being a gold-digger and him being gay. I guess that would be the San Francisco version. I wondered where Tom Marshall fit in. Maybe he didn't, not in the movie version anyway.

Every morning Ned was up with the chickens, coming into the station early in case Freddy and Betty needed somebody to make fun of on the air. This way it also worked out that Ned could get away early enough to catch a wave someplace along the coast. About the time my show went on the air, he'd be hanging ten.

Although I had the impression that Ned liked me okay in my time slot, I realized that surfing didn't leave him much time to actually listen to my show. So I was hoping that he wanted to give me a few extra strokes after the last Arbitron book showed me moving up in the ratings. He was actually giving up the surf board tonight for drinks with me, so if Christy didn't want company, Ned and I could spend some time bonding. And drinking. Who knows—maybe he was getting tired of the morning nerds and I was the natural replacement.

At least that way he'd get to hear my show.

"HEY there, Ned, surf not up tonight?" I strolled into his office after the show. On his desk was a tangle of wires and scary looking electronics. He had some kind of magnifying goggles with lights built into the sides on his head.

"Jerry—good show," Ned looked up. "I hadn't realized how entertaining your show had gotten."

"Gee, Ned, my listeners say that all the time. I keep telling them that if they made better calls, I could get that big raise." With goggles and side lights, all Ned needed was a pair of green tights to look like your typical extra-terrestrial.

"I'm trying to get this old amplifier working," Ned said. "Believe it or not, we have been using it for one of our tower feeds since the day we went on the air. Not that we can't buy new equipment. We've got that too. The new ones are about a tenth this size, but you can't work on 'em. The new stuff you just toss out and replace, but maybe that's okay too when you consider the time it's taking me to fix this one."

"I imagine it cuts into your time on the old surfboard."

"Well, I try to keep things in perspective. A guy's gotta have time to surf. But if we can keep some of this old hardware flying, we might just save enough on the budget to pick up your option next year." Ned gave me a smile to show he was just kidding. Anyway he gave me a smile. "Everybody says your show is great. I wish I got a chance to listen in more often, but with my schedule...well, you understand."

I smiled back.

Ned found a good stopping place and took off the space mask. He grabbed me and an Oakland A's team jacket and bee-lined us for the door. Outside, he aimed us at the Bridgeview Grotto, a local bar tucked in next to Pier Twenty-nine and a half. The Grotto's about a block from the KPMT offices and not much further away for the liberal media elite that we malign so much during working hours. Radio and TV in particular hang out most nights, as well as folks from some of the newer ad agencies springing up in the area. Even some of the old-line agencies are represented at times, the Financial District a few blocks away imitating a ghost-town after six o'clock. Business deals, job interviews and romances have all started—and sometimes ended—at the Grotto.

Stepping through the door on a Friday night, the sound of the crowd trying to talk above the amped up music hits you like the Oakland Raiders' front four. Everybody's laughing at jokes they can't hear and trying pick-up lines that would be embarrassing to anybody who wasn't either drunk or crazy.

"Table at six o'clock," Ned yelled in my ear, pointing through the mob. He dove in like he was shooting the pipeline, landing an empty table by the restrooms. I was a little behind, doing more of a dog-paddle through the crowd. I got pinched twice, and it being San Francisco, I didn't know whether to blame the girls or the boys.

Our table had a good view of the KSF-TV women's softball team staked out at one end of the bar. In spite of its name, the girls were the only view the Bridgeview Grotto offered. You can't see any bridge even though the place is squeezed in between a couple of waterfront warehouses. From anyplace else around there either the Golden Gate or the Bay Bridge can be seen, but the Grotto offers only a view of the dredging scow moored out back. On a clear night you can see Alcatraz through its rigging. There's nothing like a romantic setting and at the Grotto there truly is nothing like a romantic setting.

"This place is jumping tonight. I didn't know it was so popular," Ned was saying.

"You need to get out more," I told him. "You know what I mean—drinking yourself silly, becoming a spectacle, maybe getting busted, film at eleven."

"I wonder if anybody will see us back here. Is there actually some one to wait on us?"

"Don't get nervous. Believe it or not, they keep this place open just to sell booze. I think that's our waiter over—er, maybe our waitress—over there." She was an older, taller woman with greenish hair and tattooed sleeves running down her arms. I waved to her hoping she really was the waitress—if she wasn't, I was headed into a very scary pickup.

"Keep your shorts on, honey," she softly bellowed, steaming past with a tray of empties. She exchanged the empties for a tray of fresh drinks and plowed back through the crowd, spilling booze with every step. I turned back to Ned, but before I could get a word out, she was hovering over our table trying to talk while she caught her breath. "I'm Maggie, your server tonight. Goddamn' sorry to have kept you two nice gentlemen waiting for close to forty seconds."

"That's all right," Ned started—

"Well Jesus Christ! I'm glad to have your approval on that. I was really worried you might complain to my boss. You know, butthead to butthead." She turned my way and asked,

"What's yours? Your buddy here apparently isn't drinking."

"I'm sure he wants to—"

"Are you talking for him now? All I want is a simple drink order from you and," she flicked her Bic in Ned's direction, "he's just gonna have to wait his turn."

I ordered a silver bullet, up, with three olives.

"Shall I make that two?" she smiled in Ned's direction. Her teeth were as green as her hair.

"Sure," Ned said, "as long as you're up."

While Maggie finished her rounds, pushing through the drinkers crowding the bar, Ned and I dished the office dirt, maligned the competition and spun some other girl talk. More than once Ned mentioned how much Freddy and Betty had opened up the advertising window for KPMT. Pretty boring stuff in my opinion. Maybe Ned had already had a few.

For my part, I tried working the conversation around to the things I liked—my show, my ratings, my time slot, my...well, you get the idea.

Our drinks came, amazingly full, in spite of Maggie elbowing through a gang of deckhands, balancing the tray over her head. Ned was telling me how he wished he could catch my show more often, "but you know man doesn't live by politics alone, Jerry. I just don't feel right if I don't get a few rides in every day, you know, like joggers or...well, you know."

"I know," I said, "but nowadays they have these waterproof radios you can hook to your wet suit. You could be catching a wave and my show at the same time."

"Well, I don't know, Jer, wouldn't something like that take quite a beating in the ocean? You know breaking waves pulling you way down, getting smacked by the board and stuff."

"Sounds like fun. Don't worry, I'll buy it, and if it breaks, I'll replace it. It's good for the ratings—every listener counts. Maybe you can get the other surfer doggies to tune in too."

"You'll have me calling in with the surf reports next."

"Hey, I wonder if that'll play with my demographic. 'Even the biggest wipeout won't knock your dentures loose when you glue 'em in with Super-grip denture adhesive.'"

"Sure, Jerry, it's great," Ned said slurping his drink to hide the smirk. "It's great to catch up with you like this, you know, away from the shop. I wanted to talk about something though that's probably better discussed away from work anyhow."

Ned looked like he was getting serious. I ran through the various possibilities in my mind. Well only one really—the possibility that my days at KMPT were numbered. And just when things had been going so good too, drinks with the boss and all. My martini high was suddenly going flat and I gave Ned my complete attention. He was explaining, "...Mrs. Paulson seems to be losing her grip on things. And since it's your show and all..." What was he saying? I seemed to have missed something.

I said, "I saw Mrs. P just the other day and she seemed to have a grip, a grip of iron even. She looked to be in good shape all over. Nice legs even. I'm sorry about the mistletoe, if that's what this is all about."

"Mistletoe?" Ned looked a little surprised. "You saw her just the other day?" He took a big swallow, emptying his glass, and grimaced as it went down, like maybe he swallowed the toothpick too. "Pay attention, Jerry. I'm talking about this idea of bringing back that medium, the one that cost us almost sixty thousand dollars—it's crazy, isn't it?"

Who told him? I was supposed to get him in the mood first. And how did Mrs. P know about it? Was Tony reporting on me reporting on him?

"Well, nothing's cast in stone so far," I said. "Never cast the first stone, they say. As a matter of fact, I was thinking of pitching the idea to you tonight, if we got around to talking business. Maybe after a few more drinks."

Now Ned signaled Maggie. She saw it and gave him a finger, meaning she'd be with us in a minute. The middle minute I guess.

Anyway, I decided to go into my pitch since the cat was already out of the bag. "Look, we've got a chance to turn that whole scam around. I don't know if they've spent all the money, but maybe we can even get some of that back."

I laid out the deal that Ronnie had put together. When Ned doubted that we'd ever be able to get the players back together, I said, "Never? I'll go double or nothing on my next contract that they'll be here. Except I don't want to take your money, because the cast is all lined up already. Think the old redhead can't pull it together, get the big names? Well, at least get these names?"

It might have been the gin, but I was getting pretty worked up about the séance. I was selling myself on it, so maybe I was selling Ned too. Rhonda was as good as signed, so I didn't mention I was still waiting for her agent to return my call. I also figured Ned didn't need to know that Tony and Madame Zoroaster were banged up together since that seemed to be a personal situation, not station business. For that matter I didn't mention Christy or her dad's murder either.

Somehow Maggie showed up with another round of drinks and Ned kept mumbling into his glass about how he wasn't sure the séance was such a good idea, but if Pamela Kay had signed off....

"Jerry! Hey, babe! Is that you hiding in the corner there? Is that Ned too?" Her voice cut through the din that was drowning out Ned right next to me. It was loud and sounded tipsy. And too familiar. It was a voice I had heard loud and tipsy on more occasions than one. And those times I thought it pretty much a good thing.

"Jeanne! Imagine running into you here. I didn't see you when we came in. You just get here?"

"Only about two hours ago. Where the fuck have *you* been? I left dozens of messages and e-mails and God-knows-what for you all over the fucking place."

"Jeanne, where the hell did you come from," Ned said, circling in on comatose. He tried to get both eyes aimed at her saying, "We'll buy you a drink."

He waved at Maggie who managed to smile back and ignore him at the same time.

"Hey, I've been trying to get in touch with you," I said to Jeanne. "Your voicemail box says it's full."

"Oh. Maybe that's why I didn't hear from you. Anyway I've been pretty busy." Jeanne pulled a chair up and sat close to me. "Is Ned okay? He looks like he's half-shot."

Ned said, "I'm okay, never better. Where's that big-assed waitress gone to?"

"She's on her way," Jeanne said not looking and only slurring a little. She sounded like Garbo in one of those early talkies, only louder. "You can get me drunk tonight, Ned. It's not a school night."

"We'll need to do something about that," I agreed. And Jeanne did look very agreeable, particularly after a few drinks. Her drinks, not mine. I didn't think the time was exactly right to bring up Christy though, and I wasn't sure there was anything to bring up yet.

Rather than have a difficult conversation with Jeanne, I was willing to just enjoy our time together. After all, she was still my official girlfriend and who says that that was going to change if I didn't solve Marshall's murder.

I still had to ask Ned about Tom Marshall though. He must have known him pretty well since they'd both worked at KPMT from the start. Up until Tom was killed, that is.

"More drinks, kids?" Maggie asked, looming over our table. "Some of you look like you can still stand up."

I didn't think she meant Ned. But Jeanne said she'd have the usual which seemed fine with Maggie, and over my protests Ned said to make it a round. I wanted to start working on an exit strategy and Jeanne seemed to be reading at least a piece of my mind, groping me under the table.

"I'LL be there," Ned said out of the blue.

"You will? That's wonderful. Where?"

"Your séance, where else?"

Jeanne said, "You're having a séance? You did that one time before, didn't you?"

"We're doing it again, kind of an encore, a repeat performance. Don't steal the idea for the morning monsters." I turned to Ned and said, "That's swell. We'll be glad to have you there, but maybe I'd better check out the surf report. I think it may be up that day. Maybe you can catch my show another time. Or maybe get that waterproof radio."

"No, I'll definitely be there. Where is it?"

"Where—what?"

"Where is the séance? Where's it being held, for Christ's sake?"

"At the station. On the air. On my show, Ned, we're doing it on my show."

"Aw shit. Not that again."

Chapter 15.

ANOTHER round delivered and another one ordered—this time I passed—and finally Jeanne and I were able to pour Ned into a cab. We walked along the Embarcadero back to my place, holding hands like a couple of kids. On the way I told Jeanne about Ronnie's plan to demystify Madame Zoroaster and expose the diamond bracelet swindle on the air. For the time being I decided to hold back about Tom Marshall's could-be murder and how I might be helping his daughter. No point in ruining the evening quite yet.

We passed Justin Herman Plaza which fronts on Christy's hotel. I picked up the pace a little there although it would have been tough to spot us at that distance in spite of the spotlights.

"Why are we running?" Jeanne asked.

"Skateboarders. They practice around here at night. Don't want to get run down by a pack of 'em." The free-boarders were still out, taking advantage of the empty plaza and its walls, rails and steps to practice banging their knees and elbows.

In this town, you're lucky not to get trampled, mutilated or spindled by the joggers, speed-walkers, bikers or skateboarders at almost any time of day or night. City sports. Half the people in the City spend their free time on sports and the other half on partying. A lot seem to do both. Ned Tunney seemed to fall into that category though I hoped he was better at surfing than drinking.

"Say, I've got a bit of a bone to pick with you," I said, trying to steer the conversation away from my behavior. "Whenever I call you lately, you never seem to be around. It seems like ages since we talked."

I figured Jeanne would counter-attack, but she surprised me. What she said was, "I know, I haven't been too available the past week or so what with my hours and all." She slowed to a stop at the foot of Market Street. "Last time I was over, you know, I set your DVR to record the KCTY morning show, *Bay Area Breakfast*. If you bothered to check, you'd see that it's been recording every day this week. And if you took the time to watch, you'd see that I've been doing the weather from Pebble Beach. I'm part of the PGA tour coverage."

"I've always wanted to know what the weather is in Pebble Beach. Around here I usually just look out the window. So how has the weather been in Pebble Beach? Your nose looks a little sunburned."

"It was great. The burn is because I spent all day following Tiger Woods around."

"You've turned into a golf groupie? I thought he was playing hard to get now."

"I wouldn't know. I took a leave from Freddy and Betty to try out on *Bay Area Breakfast*. They're trying me on weather, but I want to break into sports, so I talked the sports director into letting me do the weather and some background segments from the tournament. I've been on live TV every morning this week."

"Sports, uh? On the TV? Strange Ned didn't say anything."

"I kind of worked out the leave thing with Freddy and Betty. They covered for me and Ned always goes along with whatever they say."

"Freddy and Betty? That's even scarier than sports. What exactly do you know about, say pro football? Aside from your natural interest in the Forty-niner locker room?"

"Well, there is that."

"I don't suppose you had to share a room down at the Lodge with the sports director?"

"Well, there's that too."

"If you tell me you ever shared a room with Freddy and Betty, I'm leaving you right here."

"Whoa, there are things even I won't do, though they have been bricks about this."

"Thank God you know where to draw the line, dearie."

We cut through the courtyard separating my high-rise from its office tower twin, and punched in the access code at the door. The elevator was waiting and whisked us up to the eighteenth floor. I managed the locks to my apartment and steered Jeanne to the kitchenette, hoping solid food would absorb the alcohol sloshing around our tummies.

Cold pizza, sushi aging from God knows when, and rum raisin ice cream were about as solid as we could hope for. We moved to the living room where we sat looking at the lights shimmering on the bay. The living-slash-dining room is about as pristine as the day the decorator threw in the last throw pillow. It's seldom used because I do most of my serious entertaining in the bedroom. This night a full moon provided all the light we needed through the big windows. I was in the kind of mood that made me think I should spend more time looking at that view. After all, it probably kicked up the price of the apartment by an extra hundred large.

Jeanne finally broke the silence. "Were you keeping busy while I was down in Pebble Beach?"

"Oh well, you know," I said, "just the regular stuff."

"Let's see, Jerry. You spend three hours a day slaving over a hot microphone down at the station, maybe a couple of hours hanging out at Starbucks drinking lattes, and...what else is it that you do, sweetie?"

The moonlight illuminating her curves gave me an idea of how to fill the next few of those hours she was asking about. But for now I just said, "I'm working on a mystery."

"You're writing a mystery?"

"No, not that kind of mystery. A real mystery. Madame Zoroaster and her phony séances, a missing diamond bracelet, and maybe a murder."

"What murder? What have you gotten yourself into? Are you in any danger?"

"Hah. Danger is my middle name."

"You don't have a middle name. You don't even have two names. You're just plain old Jeremy Jeremy. Named after your filthy-rich uncle."

"Turned out he was just filthy."

Jeanne seemed to be getting worked up by my new persona. She bounced up on her knees next to me and in the moonglow everything bouncing above her knees looked great. Apparently the excitement wasn't sexual though. She pressed, "Who got murdered? What do you know about it? I could use this on the show, Jerry. My first scoop."

"Wait a second. What about Tiger Woods? Won't he be jealous?"

"The sports thing is still on, but this could be my break. Jerry, you have to let me in on this." Maybe the moonlight had been too revealing.

Anyway I busied myself clearing up the take-out containers and left-over leftovers to avoid a direct answer. While I stuck a few cups in the dishwasher, Jeanne drifted into the bedroom and by the time I got there she had curled up in the middle of the king-sized and was dead asleep.

Since she'd already hogged all the covers, I opened the pull-out back in the living room and having made my bed, I laid in it. Probably better that way.

Though Jeanne was normally a morning person, or at least a morning show person, minus an alarm clock she kept right on sleeping. For once I was up before her, giving me a chance to think about last night.

Bringing the murder up at all might have been a mistake if I had any hope of getting Christy to think of me as more than just a voice on the radio. I'm not ashamed to say I wanted Christy to really know me, to have some respect and admiration for me, and especially, to let me do with her what I had done with Jeanne in days past.

You bet I did.

I also wondered if Jeanne would try to scoop me on my own story. She was nothing if not a dedicated career girl. While she slept in, I went down to Starbuck's to pick up breakfast. A couple of *vendi* lattés, some croissants—chocolate for her, almond for me—and the morning papers. Jeanne was still sweetly snoring, so I took it all out to the patio.

Not even noon yet and the sky was blue and the sun had started warming things up. From my balcony I could see a dozen sailboats scattered around the Bay, gliding past Treasure Island and around Alcatraz, a few headed through the Gate into the Pacific. I glanced down at the street eighteen floors below and my stomach did a flip-flop. I stepped quickly back and stared at the hills across the bay until my world stopped spinning.

In spite of having a condo on a high floor, I'm not good with heights. Jimmy Stewart in *Vertigo* had nothing on me. Maybe mom was scared by the parachute ride at Palisades Park while she was carrying me.

I pushed a patio chair up against the living room door and sat down with the papers. I flipped though to the sports section, checking if the PGA tour had really stopped over down in Monterey. Not that I didn't trust Jeanne, but I like to verify my sources.

According to the paper, they were there in force. So Jeanne was working on her big break. I wondered what would happen to us if she made it big. Then I wondered what would happen to us if I made it with Christy. I didn't want to think about having to choose between Jeanne and Christy. I liked the time I had spent with Christy over the past couple of days, but Jeanne had been great to date when we could work out our schedules. For all I knew, maybe all Christy liked in the bedroom were ruffled curtains and patchwork quilts. But I did hope to find out for sure.

By now I had developed a headache, so I decided to stop thinking and enjoy the moment. I drank my latte and drank in the sunshine and tried to get Ronnie on the pipe. I needed to hook up so we could plan out the séance and maybe to see what he thought about Tom Marshall's death. I guess he was still sleeping though as his voice mail picked me up. I left him a message to call me back.

From the patio I could see that the bedroom door was still closed and there were no signs of intelligent life yet. I felt like calling Christy but didn't want Jeanne to come stumbling in on me.

I would need to get rid of Jeanne first. The problem being that Jeanne usually liked to spend most of the weekend with me. She hadn't started redecorating the apartment yet or giving me a list of honey-do's, but she usually planned on our rambling around the City together, squeezing tomatoes at the farmers' market or stopping for a late lunch at the oyster bar or maybe runnng up to the Metreon to catch a matinee and hit the video arcade. Sometimes I could get an hour or two off for good behavior while I went jogging in Golden Gate Park with Ronnie Green. I was thinking about using Ronnie as an excuse when my quiet time was interrupted.

"Good God, Jerry, how long you been up?" Jeanne padded onto the patio, flopping on a lounge chair. She was wearing one of my old tee shirts so her legs would get some sun.

"I got you a latté," I said, handling the cup to her, "it's already cooled down from scalding to merely tongue-blistering."

"How's your head; I feel like shit today," she said, not looking at all like shit. "You must have gotten me drunk so you could take advantage of me. After all, I'm a good Catholic girl; you want to see my rosary?"

"I'll bet the nuns loved having you," I said. "In school, that is. I would have come in to wake you up in my special way, but the sunshine seduced me before you got the chance."

"That's okay, I'm not sure I'd have been up to it with this hangover. I'm hoping the fresh air will have a beneficial effect."

"Really? Do the guys over at KCTY know you're such a light weight?"

"Do they know? Who do you think I was drinking under the table before you showed up last night?"

"Ah good, if your audition reel doesn't win them over, beating them senseless with Wild Turkey should do it. So what's on the agenda for today?"

"Well, honeybunch, I've got a carload of dirty laundry and nothing to wear on Monday. I know that your washing machine has never been used, so I figure I'd better just hit he laundromat. After that I'm going to need to get it together for KCTY. With any luck I'll have a new job by Monday."

"With nothing to wear, you should really turn heads. I have a lot of work to get through this weekend too."

"You? Work? Weekend?" Jeanne seemed a little taken aback. "Two plus two equals...how much again?"

"Jealousy is one of the seven deadly sins, babe. At least I think it is. Maybe I'm thinking of celibacy. Anyway, there's a little problem that Mrs. Paulson dropped in my lap. It's connected to our old friend, Madame Zoroaster, the psychic disaster. Ned and I were hashing it over last night."

"Let me understand this—Pamela Kay dropped Madame Zoroaster in your lap? That must have been some party— where was I?"

"The party hasn't happened yet. But it's on the way. We're holding a séance, only this time the seer is getting blindsided. The last time Madame Zoroaster swindled the station out of some serious cash. Now she's back and has her hand in Tony Paulson's pocket. And I don't think it's to give him a thrill. Anyway, Mrs. P wants me to find out what's going down."

"Holy batshit, Cowman! It sounds like you've stepped right in it."

"Yeah, and that's good luck only if you're a farmer. I was going to pump Ned last night to see if he knew anything about Tony that might help, but I think he was trying to see what I knew, so maybe he doesn't know all that much. Anyway, he got shitfaced before I got the chance to get anything out of him."

"Pamela Kay must have dropped a hint and Ned wants to make sure you're not checking up on him. He spends an awful lot of company time at the beach."

"Just my luck. If Pamela Kay doesn't fire me for the wrong reason, Ned will."

"Unless you can find out what the fortune teller has on Tony and use it as job insurance. If there's something to hide, you could be Tony's new best friend. You know, I always had the impression that Freddy and Betty knew where some bodies were buried."

"That's great—if I can't beat 'em, join 'em," I said. "Not only don't I get rid of the blackmailers, I turn into one. That's thinking out of the box; you'll go far in this business, babe."

"Just trying to think through your options, hon. Like they say, 'there's no business like in-the-know business.'"

"I suppose, but somehow I have the feeling I'll be the one who ends up getting the business. I need to have Ronnie think through my options. We have to sync up about this séance thing anyway."

"Good idea. He always does your best thinking for you. And like I say, I've got to get my shit together for this TV thing," Jeanne said tilting her head back for the last drops in her coffee cup. As she arched her back, I was reminded of a couple of the reasons I liked her so much. And for her mind too, of course.

"Like mother said," Jeanne said, "make sure to wear clean undies if you're gonna be on TV—it's only on the radio that you don't need 'em."

"Next thing you know, you'll be wearing a chastity belt."

"Well, *Bay Area Breakfast* does want born-again virgins," she said. "After doing the laundry and getting my nails done, I have to meet with my agent for drinks."

"Well, make sure you wear your underwear—and keep it on. Remember, you're a virgin again so—hey, since when do you have an agent?"

"You've got one."

"Yeah, but mine's an agent in name only. I claim him as a dependent on my tax return."

"Well, TV's newest sports babe is going need someone to look out for her interests. Nobody's blowing smoke up my ass if I can help it. Not unless they're paying for it."

"Gee, do I get a discount? Anyway, tell those TV guys to stay away from your ass. If anyone's going to go there, it's me."

"I'm afraid you'll need to discuss that with my agent. He handles all my affairs now." Jeanne stood by the balcony railing and pulled the tee shirt over her head and tossed it at me. My heart skipped a beat or two. She said, "I'm going to jump—in the shower that is. I need to get to the laundromat before the big driers are all gone."

"Why don't you just use a towel? Anyway, I'll scrub your back. I need the exercise." Agent or no, she let me close the deal. Before I knew it we were dressed and waiting for the elevator.

"You know, Jer, there's something in the back of my mind that I can't quite recall," Jeanne said as the elevator doors opened.

"It's probably just a hangover."

"No, Jerry, I seem to remember some kind of rumor about the KPMT's books being cooked. About a year or so ago. It was hushed up pretty quickly and no one ever mentioned it again, but I overheard Freddy and Betty talking about it."

I held the elevator open and asked, "Are you saying there might be a Tony-gate thing?"

"I'm not sure, but I remember hearing—or maybe overhearing—something."

"Come on, baby, give."

The elevator door was putting up a fight by now.

"It seemed like a big deal because the books were going to be audited. I think one of the partners was thinking of selling off part of the station. Like I say, it all got hushed up pretty quickly."

"I'll bet."

"Yes, I'm sure Freddy and Betty were dishing it, but with them it could just be bull." By now the elevator was bleeping in no uncertain terms.

"It's still might be a good lead," I said, thinking about Christy saying her dad had had the KPMT books audited.

"You *will* share if you dig up any other leads on this. Remember I'm willing to trade my body for hard news, sports-related or not."

"I'll keep that in mind, and seriously, I hope you don't have too many of your other sources on that plan." The door was closing for real now. "Anyway, how did you come to overhear Freddy and Betty talking about this?"

"Oh, it was easy. I had Brad the Brat bug their office."

Chapter 16.

BY noon I was sitting on Ronnie's stoop watching him lace up his trainers, his stoop being near Golden Gate Park. Where he lives is generally put-down as "out in the Avenues," reflecting its out of the way location. About half the City lives "out in the Avenues." So called because the streets are avenues rising numerically as you move toward the ocean. Unlike most places though, as you approach the briny in the Sunset District, the cost of living—that is, renting—actually drops.

In the Sunset, on most days the fog from the Pacific blankets the sky, shutting out sunlight and whatever else might be up there. Streetlights turn on at noon. Winter coats are worn in July. People throw parties if they can actually see the sun set in the Sunset. They tell me it was nothing but sand dunes until some real estate developer named it the Sunset District. Just in time for the influx of post-war prosperity. Welcome to sunny California.

This Saturday was an exception however, warm and sunny even there. So Ronnie and I warmed up some more by jogging over to the park and heading to the Polo Field along J.F.K. Drive. We tried to keep up a brisk pace. Even then, everybody passed us but one old lady in a walker. I got the feeling she wasn't really trying though.

"On your left," Ronnie huffed.

"Whassup?" I puffed.

The Great One head-pointed at a pair of leggy blondes pulling past us. He signaled me to pick up the pace to stay with them, but the gap continued to widen without much effort on their part. But since half the female population was taking advantage of the good weather, we had plenty of other viewing options.

With all the hot numbers in shorts bobbing around us, I figured it might be a good time to tell Ronnie I had a new dream girl. He slowed to a walk, holding his side like he'd cramped up. He looked a little bewildered and said, "I thought Jeanne was your main squeeze. What happened?"

"Oh, she's still around, but I think her new TV career is coming between us. She used to be okay when she was an associate producer, even if it was for the morning morons. But now I get the feeling she's ready to go into competition with me. I barely mentioned murder and she was all over me. And not in a good way."

"Murder?" Ronnie was definitely cramping up. He asked, "Where did murder come from?"

"Well, it's a long story. This girl Christy I like—"

"I should have seen that one coming. A person doesn't need to read minds to know if Jerry Jeremy's doing a good deed, there's a pretty woman in there somewhere."

"You don't know that. Without Satyra to feed you clues, you couldn't even read a newspaper. Anyhow, Christy's dad was one of the original partners in KPMT—"

"So her dad's your boss, too? I'm proud of you, Jerry, going after the boss's daughter."

"No, she's not the boss's daughter any more. While we were waltzing around with Madame Zoroaster last Halloween, his car went off a cliff into the cold, blue Pacific. And he went down with the ship, so to speak. Christy thinks he was run off the road on purpose, but she hasn't been able to get anyone to help her prove it."

"Until you came along imitating a bull in a china shop."

"Well, yeah, though I like to think of it as a damsel in distress kind of thing. Anyway, it all came together over at Tony Paulson's house a couple of days ago." So I gave Ronnie the play-by-play on how I saved Christy from being run down and about finding Madame Zoroaster chilling out at Tony's.

We flopped down in a shady patch that gave us a clear view should any more blondes come galloping by and I described for Ronnie how I tracked down the Rubensteins, aka "Cruize" De la Cruz and Rhonda Ridgeway.

Ronnie thought it over a while before saying, "So, Junior, you think that Tony Paulson is letting them sponge off him because he has something to hide and Madame Zoroaster knows what it is?"

"Sure, and Christy tells me there was something fishy

going on with the partnership agreement and the Paulson's stood to gain by it."

"And that might be the thing Madame Zoroaster is using on Tony Paulson? Maybe she tuned her crystal ball in to the Paulson channel?"

"And copied it to disc maybe. I don't know how she found out, but she did. Now she's putting the screws on Tony. Maybe he deserves to have the screws turned, but his Aunt has made me his guardian angel. I don't quite have all of it figured out yet, but I think I'm getting close."

"Close to doing the good deed you're doing for Pamela Kay? The operation was a success, but the patient's recuperating in the prison ward."

"Well, yeah, it starts to get all mixed up at some point."

"And why aren't they blackmailing Pamela Kay Paulson directly?"

"Hey, for blackmailing Tony they get me on their trail; with Pamela Kay, they'd be dodging a hitman. They don't need to read their tea leaves to know that."

While we tried to get our minds around the puzzle, we walked over to a sandwich joint across Lincoln Avenue. It was one of those shops with only two or three chairs and a counter recycled from Goodwill. But the bread was fresh-baked and the cold cuts were...well, at least cold. An Italian hero there cost me just a little less than a new pair of trainers. It must be tough being the only sandwich place within walking—or jogging—distance.

"So if we add it all up," Ronnie said, "we get a crooked spiritualist blackmailing the nephew of the station owner, probably because he cooked the books and maybe killed the former partner whose widow got shafted out of her share of the station by the killer's aunt as a result."

That's my boy. I said, "Come on, Ronnie, I may not have all the answers, but something's not adding up. Right now I don't know if two and two makes three or if it's adding up to five."

"Listen, Jerry, of course something's not adding up. You're not even talking about adding two plus two; you're doing the multiplication tables. At the end of the day the well-known radio talk show host, Jeremy Jeremy winds up with two girlfriends—Christy *and* Jeanne. You'll have one for each name, and what about your closest pal, Ronnie Green? He's left on his lonesome, someplace out in the cold."

"Maybe one of them will have a friend."

We had been strolling towards Ronnie's place while we ate. Ronnie swallowed with a gulp I could almost feel and said, "You just happened by in time to save the fair lady and take on her crusade, no doubt for your own dastardly reasons, namely because she's a looker and you want to play the knight in a shiny convertible."

"Well, I admit I'd like to play nights with her," I said. "But she really does need some help in catching her dad's killer. If I can do that, she'd be ever so grateful. Of course, if you help, she'd still be grateful to me and you'd just be a close acquaintance."

"So you think the fortune teller's got something on the Paulson boy because she has the power to see beyond this mortal plane. Maybe this Marshall guy came back from the great beyond and said to her," Ronnie's voice grew high and wavering, "he said 'The nephew done it. He done me in.' and he points his bony finger in the kid's direction."

"Hey, I don't want Marshall's ghost to give Madame Z the story. After all, it's my scoop; I'm the one pitching in to help his daughter. He could drop by in one of my dreams or something, let me know what gives. Or in this case, gave."

"You better hope he doesn't see what's going on in your dreams. After all, he is the girl's father."

"Hey, I might not want him dropping by when I'm dreaming about Christy, but I'm always a perfect gentleman even if I'm not awake."

"Sure, Red, let's just hope he wears a raincoat."

"Anyway, I'm gonna help the girl, and by 'I,' I mean 'us.' After all, it was your idea to bring back the Z-lady, and now, we—meaning you—need to go just a little bit deeper into the swamp. It's just a little further than you had planned on to begin with. And that leaves just one more thing...."

Ronnie gave me that look again, but at least he didn't clutch his side again. He asked me what more could be thrown on the fire—meaning his burning gray cells.

"How are we gonna get Jeanne off my back? She's trying to jump on this story with both her new Tory Burch's."

"Jeanne's on TV, eh? Well now, think about it, junior. Maybe she can do us some good. Maybe she can get us some TV exposure for the séance. Maybe even come by with a camera or two to catch us in action. And when I say 'us,' you know I really mean you."

I figured I'd be lucky to wind up in a crowd scene by the time Ronnie got through planning things. By now we'd finished off the subs, trashed the wrappers and were sitting on Ronnie's stoop again when my cell started ringing. I didn't recognize the caller's number, so I let it roll to voice mail. After a while, I checked for a message; it had to be a fan who'd somehow got my number or somebody who'd fat-fingered their way to my phone. I listened to the message, pressed the button to save it and hung up.

"I thought you were a mind reader," I said to Ronnie. "I guess AT&T is still a safe investment since ESP doesn't look to replace it anytime soon."

"Like the dream thing, I'm not sure I want to see what's on your mind. Who was that on the phone?"

"Another woman I've been chasing—Rhonda Ridgeway." I pulled Ronnie up by the arm. "We better take my car. She says somebody's trying to kill her."

Chapter 17.

I HAD phoned Christy before I'd hooked up with Ronnie for our run. Christy was already up and about when I called, having already left me a couple of messages. I guess I'd neglected to check thinking maybe they were from Jeanne. Even though I actually wasn't returning her calls, she was still glad to hear from me.

She was saying, "...so naturally Mr. Heilbrun's explanation got me to wondering, like I said in the message."

"Oh, uh, sure. I'll make sure I play it back a couple of times so I understand."

"Well, no need for that, Jerry dear. I'm explaining it to you now," she said using that voice like a guy might use to a telemarketer or some other kind of dummy. And I'm pretty sure she knew I wasn't a telemarketer. "Mr. Heilbrun gave me copies of a ton of legal papers. I have been looking through them, but since I only took one semester of business law, it's pretty slow going."

"I'd like to help, but I don't even understand my own contract. I just signed where they told me to. That is, after I heard what they were paying me. I'd have signed anything then."

"I don't think you're as naïve as you pretend to be. After all, you knew I had real problems right away."

"I knew that you were real, that was the main thing. And that truck was no mirage either. Just make sure you call me before you cross any more streets. After all, I used to be a Boy Scout."

"Don't worry, Jerry. You're my scout. I won't take a step without you."

My boyish charm seemed to be working. Too bad I wasn't hanging with her; I could have given her my best reassuring smile, dimples and all.

"Listen," I said, "how about taking a break today and letting this Boy Scout show you around the town. We've got all the best tourist attractions."

"Hey, Jerry, I used to live here, remember? Dad would drag me along when he took the out-of-towners around. I've seen everything from Fisherman's Wharf to the Crookedest Street in the World. But gee, I'll bet seeing 'em with you would be more fun than with my parents though Dad made it a lot of fun. In that way you're a lot like him."

"You're not turning me down, are you?"

"The reason I came back to San Francisco is to get to the bottom of Dad's murder. After that, I'll have plenty of time for fun, I promise. For now, I'm going to spend the day with a few reams of legal docs."

"Okay, okay, I get it. I need to handle a few things myself. You'll be hungry by dinnertime. Can we get together and compare notes then?"

"I'd like that. I'm sure I'll be ready for a break after plowing through this stuff all day."

So I wound up running Ronnie Green around Golden Gate Park. In spite of Tony Paulson somehow being at the center of all the dots, The Great One didn't seem convinced they were connected. Until Rhonda Ridgeway called to say somebody was trying to kill her.

Maybe she was going to help us put the kibosh on Madame Zoroaster's scam, but that wouldn't be enough to get her capped. Even Pamela Kay's not that vindictive. Madame Z might throw an evil spell her way, but that's about all.

Rhonda said she was holed up in the ladies' room at Nordstrom's in case the bad guys were still laying in wait. The store was due to close in another six or seven hours, but the line for the ladies' was getting unruly.

"Okay, Ronnie, it's time to save our leading lady's ass."

"That's my territory all right. But who's trying to kill her, did she say? We may need weapons."

"I thought you had the power to cloud men's minds. Or does that only work with women?"

"It always works on-stage, but these guys may not be drunk."

"We'll pick up a six pack on the way," I said. "Let's get a move on—she says somebody's trying to kill her and I want to be there when it happens."

TRAFFIC was light going downtown, so we made good time and were lucky enough to find parking in a bus stop on Fifth Street. The City Center is a high-rise shopping mall designed around circular escalators that carry shoppers up floor after floor. Nordstrom, of course, is at the very top. Just our luck.

We passed on the escalators and pushed our way on the express elevator instead. Ten seconds later we were in the store. I dialed Rhonda's cell and convinced her to meet us in Nordstrom's Café.

Last Halloween I had seen the frumpy Mrs. Rubenstein for a minute or two when she'd stormed into KPMT's lobby with de la Cruz. But now, I wouldn't have recognized her if I hadn't seen her on-line. She had morphed from frump to hottie. Rhonda didn't have any problem recognizing us though. Well, we hadn't changed all that much aside from our wearing baggy running shorts, having come from a run in the park.

We expected a big welcome, being the knights on white horses and all, but she really took us back with this one—"Where the hell have you guys been? I've been going crazy here, stuck in the john. Every time somebody flushed I jumped out of my skin."

"Jerry should have known better," Ronnie said, taking her hand. "I can't imagine his recommending such a busy crapper."

"Maybe it's not all his fault," she said. "I thought Bloomie's might not have been safe."

"You're safe now," Ronnie purred as he guided her onto a banquette and slide next to her. I got stuck with the chair opposite them. No matter, it gave me a chance to study Rondini moves with a babe who wasn't drunk.

While he made cooing noises, I made an effort to get things back on track. "Listen, Miss Ridgeway,—how about we call you Rhonda? Listen, Rhonda, what's all this about somebody threatening you? Your last show couldn't have been that bad...."

"You're safe now," Ronnie repeated, patting her knee.

"Thanks, I feel safer just having you here." She gave Ronnie a look like she'd been tied to the railroad tracks and he just showed up with a jackknife. Rhonda said, "My agent had just called me about being on Mr. Jeremy's show. Of course she didn't know anything about the radio job last Halloween, but I was a little worried that it was coming back to haunt me—no pun intended—when she told me that Mr. Jeremy had called her."

"Listen, call me Jerry—"

"And I'm Ronnie, Ronnie Green," I was waiting for him to drool on her shoulder. "But you probably remember me from that show. You know, The Great Rondini."

"He's great, if he's any judge," I said, "but what we need to do is get this all straightened out. Ronnie here is a mind reader—but me, I have to be told things before I can hear them."

Rhonda glanced at me and then said to Ronnie, "I need to make sure nobody's mad at me for that Halloween thing."

"We're not mad," I said, "at least not at you."

"We have a little gag of our own that we want you for, that's all," Ronnie added.

"Well, Helen—that's my agent—called this morning and said to call Jerry about being on his show. She called my cell right in the middle of my yoga class and totally broke my flow. But hey, how often does an agent call you?"

"If it's my agent, only when he needs a loan."

"After yoga, I had gone over to the weight room."

"The waiting room?"

"No, you know, the *weight* room, weight training, weight lifting. Like the Governator. I was doing bench presses when I see a couple of thighs on either side of me. They looked like tree trunks. Then the guys they belonged to pressed down on the barbell so I couldn't even move. I don't mind telling you, Ronnie, I was scared shitless. And that was before they even started to make threats. This, right in public. Well, it's really a private club, but there were people around."

"Why didn't you scream for help?"

"Honestly, I was too scared. I didn't know what they might do. Anyway, they said all kinds of really nasty things, but the upshot was that I'd be found floating in the bay if I did Jerry's show."

"Big thighs, eh? Could they be members of the club? Ever see them there before?" This was Ronnie playing at Sherlock Holmes. Not bad though.

I asked, "Would you recognize those thighs, I mean those guys, again?"

"Well, I was lying down on the bench looking up at them, but they were very short guys, so their faces were pretty close. It was at a peculiar angle, but if I was lying down again maybe I could recognize them."

I couldn't wait to see this line-up.

"I was really too scared to look at them, all I really know is they had big legs and were wearing those bicycle shorts, the stretchy, latex kind." She did puppy eyes at Rondini and said, "I noticed they weren't too stretched out in the bulge department though, if you get my meaning."

"You mean they weren't carrying any concealed weapons?" I asked.

"Don't pay any attention to him," Ronnie crooned. "He doesn't understand about how vulnerable you feel spread out on the weight bench like that. Just a little leotard to cover you. I hate to say this, but Jerry just isn't a weight room kind of guy."

"I don't eat my spinach either."

"You know," Rhonda said, "maybe I shouldn't say this, because I'm not at all prejudiced, but I noticed they were kind of,er, brown skinned, if you follow me. Not like African-American, more like, maybe Mexican, or like some Hawaiians. Definitely not a spray booth tan."

"What did they do?" I asked. "After they pinned you down with the barbell, I mean?"

"They didn't rough me up or nothing, just threatened me. Said if I didn't back off from your show I'd wind up floating in the bay. That's their very own words. Of course, it sounds a lot worse when they say it. Maybe it was they way they said it, the accent and all."

"Accent?"

"Yes, I didn't recognize what kind. As an actress, of course, I try to study accents, but this was one I didn't know offhand."

"Ever see any old vampire movie? You know like Bela Lugosi?" Ronnie asked.

"Sure, but it didn't sound like that. I know Count Dracula when I hear it." That let Vigo Czak and his relatives out. Rhonda continued, "Maybe some kind of Latino, but not Mexicano. I know a lot of Mexican actors and Mexican waiters. But that's pretty much the same thing, huh? I do a lot of hostessing between jobs so I know what they sound like."

"And after they threatened you?" I prompted.

"Yes. I was pretty shaken after that. I went to the locker room and stood under the shower until I stopped crying. I didn't want anyone at the club to see me crying. It's very exclusive there. And I'm not really a member. Some guy I know from my hostess job gave me some guest passes."

"So would these hoods have to be members to actually get in to threaten you in the club?" I asked. "I mean, you having to use guest passes and all?"

"I guess so. I don't remember seeing many scary looking members there before. It's mostly single women and gays. I guess the gays are mostly single too. Only members and their guests are allowed in though."

"Maybe they had passes too," The Great Sherlock deduced. "But somebody else, a member, would need to vouch for them, right?"

"Well of course. A member has to get the passes and be there to sign in the guests. Of course they know me, so I don't need to have my friend there, but I don't think they would know those thugs. Not at that club."

"So if they were guests, their names would be in the guest book or whatever?" I asked.

"Maybe not," Ronnie said. "If I were them, I'd just sign in with phony names. No paper trail that way."

"Does it matter?" Rhonda asked. "We don't even know their names, real or not, so if they were in the guest book, you wouldn't even know the difference."

We spent the next half hour making sure Rhonda Ridgeway knew that Ronnie and I would protect her from the musclemen who had visited her at the gym as well as anybody else that came along with ill intent.

I'm not sure how that would be done if the baddies actually caught up with us. We don't have much experience with physical combat, but maybe Rondini really did have the power to cloud men's minds. I wouldn't want to bet my life on it though. On the other hand, how hard could it be to outrun guys with short, muscle-bound legs?

While we still had Rhonda's gratitude, we gave her a quick rundown on the séance and her part in it. It took a little bit of gentle prodding to sign her after the visit from the thugs, but Ronnie seemed to be worming his way into her confidence. His imitation of a worm and the promise of big time radio exposure got the deal done though. Mrs. Rubinstein would make a return appearance.

To keep our leading lady in one piece, Rondini thought a little misdirection might be called for. Since the hoods probably didn't know Ronnie by sight—their not sounding like regulars at the Sphinx—he would take the Muni bus to Rhonda's apartment in the Marina and pick up a few necessities for her. Meanwhile, I'd drive Rhonda out to

Ronnie's flat, taking care that we weren't followed. She could hide out there and stick to Ronnie for protection. The protection mainly being that the hoods wouldn't know where she was.

While Ronnie slipped out to catch the 30 Stockton, I got Rhonda into the Beamer and took the return trip out to the Avenues. On the way I gave Cruize a call and warned his voice mail to be on the lookout for the two guys with big thighs. When he called back later, he said they didn't scare him—he knew Kung-Fu from working on a Jackie Chan film.

Chapter 18.

THE roses reached out and grabbed my wallet. The lady manning the flower stand wrapped up a dozen yellow for me. For Christy, that is. I was in Hyatt Regency lobby and while the florist wrapped and ribboned the flowers, I watched glass elevators float up and down above the atrium lobby. On each level rooms wrapped around the open lobby reaching all the way up to the Equinox Restaurant where tourists rotated three hundred and sixty degrees while they ate their dinners. It was great unless you didn't like heights.

Even the glass-walled elevators freaked me out. I felt like I was falling even when I was going up. To take the elevators, you need to have a guest key or be announced from the front desk. But having the desk call up kind of ruins the surprise, so I did what most people do and piggy-backed in behind a nice-looking couple in plaid shorts. If my luck was running, I'd catch Christy just coming out of the shower.

When I reached her door, I put on my dress smile and gave it the old shave-and-a-haircut. A man's voice answered, telling me to go away; he was sleeping. The voice had an accent and it wasn't Bela Lugosi's.

"Sorry, sir," I said. "Valet service. I have your wife's cleaning," I pitched my voice high, trying to sound bellhop-ish, or at least not like my radio sound. After all he could be a listener. "I'm sorry, the valet cleaners won't take it back if it's already clean."

The door opened a crack and I kicked it into the face peeping out. The peeper went sprawling and I came through the door swinging. I really hoped I had the right room.

Christy screamed from someplace inside and I heard

something breaking somewhere. I lashed out at everything that moved with sixty bucks worth of flowers. Beautiful roses, long stems, a lot of thorns—it was the peeper's turn to scream now. A couple of swipes though and I had to give up on the roses. I was looking for a loose baseball bat when suddenly the roof caved in on me.

I came to lying on the floor. Christy was cradling my head, stroking my hair and pressing my cheek close to her breast. For just a moment life was beautiful, the perfume, the touch of her hand and—well, let's just say I'll never wash my cheek again. Then that little man with the jackhammer started in, breaking things up inside my head. I felt it corkscrew down my spine all the way to the soles of my shoes where it bounced around a while before deciding to head back up.

When my eyes started spinning, at least Christy knew I was still alive. She lifted my head off her chest and told me a cold towel would help. "Will you be all right while I get one?"

"Ooh, no. No, don't let go," I snuggled up against her again. "If I'm dying, I want to go out with a smile on my face."

"You're not dying. I'm no doctor, but I'm sure of that. One time I saw a cowboy in the rodeo kicked in the head by a horse and he was acting just like you are now."

"Lucky guy, being held close to you as this."

"It was the rodeo clown held him until the ambulance arrived to cart him away."

Ambulance? I new wave of pain hit me, topped off by a bit of nausea. "Maybe you'd better get that cold towel. And maybe thirty or forty aspirins. Say, did that cowboy recover? Learn to walk again, that kind of thing?"

"Yes, he was a fine. Just a little goofy from getting kicked, but I'm sure you'll be okay; it was only a lamp."

"The horse was a lamp?"

"No, you were hit with a lamp. Don't you remember?" She stuck a pillow under my head and got up. "I'm going to run some cold water on a towel, and then I think I need to get you to a hospital."

"Have I lost much blood?"

"No, you're not actually bleeding at all, but you took a pretty good shot," she said from the bathroom over the sound of running water. "While the asshole at the door was punching you, the other guy let go of me and let you have it with the bedside lamp. Jerry, this is the second time you saved my life. I don't know how I can ever repay you."

"Don't worry about repaying me. I'm sure I'll think of a

way once the brass band in my head takes a break."

Christy sat beside me and pressed the cold towel against my head which by now was spinning and pounding at the same time.

"You're very special to me, Jerry. If it wasn't for you I'd be a total mess right now, not to mention the fact that those bastards would have dropped me right into the lobby fountain ten floors down. Good thing they smashed your head though."

"'Good thing' isn't exactly the way I would have put it, but if that's what it takes to get you to hold me close, I'm glad too."

"I didn't mean I'm glad they hurt you. Having your head to patch up keeps me from worrying about those bastards returning to finish the job. It keeps me from freaking out."

"Good. That makes one of us who's not freaking out."

By the time Christy had used all the towels and I had dosed out on aspirins, the pounding in my head was down to a slow drum-roll. Christy stayed close, holding on and hugging, as much for her, I suspected, as for me. We decided calling the cops wouldn't do much good and that I would probably live without a trip to the emergency room.

"Listen," I said, "I don't want to give you the wrong impression, but you're not sleeping alone tonight."

"Oh, Jerry, I don't think I'll be able to sleep here again," she replied. "Those guys might want to come back and finish things."

"Just what I was thinking. Pack your toothbrush; you're staying at my place. For your own safety, that is." I wondered how safe she'd be from me. I was almost sure she had nothing to fear—after all, I used to be a Boy Scout.

"Well, hon," she said, reading my mind, "I'd rather be fighting you off, than those jerks. Right now, I'm just a girl who can't say no."

Things were definitely looking up.

"Don't worry," I said. "You won't have to fight me off tonight. But I'm hoping you'll stay for a few days."

While Christy tossed a few things into an overnight bag, I got the lowdown on how the hoods had taken her by surprise. Just minutes before I arrived, somebody had knocked at her door. They claimed to be from housekeeping, bringing fresh towels or something, so Christy didn't bother with the peephole before unlocking the door. Two thugs pushed their way in and threatened to kill her if she screamed. Then they tore the room apart grabbing everything on paper short of the Gideon Bible.

The papers Christy had gotten from Heilbrun were spread out on the bed, every scrap in plain sight. Still, the punks emptied all the drawers and her suitcases, throwing everything on the floor. They shoved all the papers in one of the now-empty suitcases and were beginning to eye Christy when I showed up. When I knocked, they fell for the same gag that had got them in. Like they say, one good turn deserves another.

After I got lamped on the head, the hoods grabbed the suitcase with the papers, pushed Christy over an ottoman where she landed on her—well, I imagine it was a soft landing in any case—and they ran out. I wasn't in any shape to chase them, but they probably weren't just standing there waiting for an elevator either. No doubt they had taken the fire stairs to another floor where they could wait for the elevator.

If my head had been a little harder, we might have made it to the hall in time to spot them in the glass elevators and call hotel security. Then again, I wouldn't want the security guys to get hurt. They might put the doctor's bill on Christy's room tab. God knows the mini-bar is pricy enough.

As it was, Christy and I were fresh out of chase. So after she'd packed some of whatever it was she needed, we snuck over to the elevator bank. We'd left a sign on the door telling intruders not to disturb the occupants in seven languages. And just in case the baddies were still around, we pressed ourselves against the wall so we couldn't be spotted from the lobby, and we snuck a look around each corner before going on.

Before leaving I had helped myself to a bottle of beer from that mini-bar. It would make a dandy weapon if a weapon was needed. I could even things out for the dent they'd made in my noggin. I thought about two bottles—one for each hand—but at those prices, one would have to do.

As it turned out, the bad guys were nowhere in sight as we slipped out on the mezzanine level. We figured that was less exposed than crossing the lobby to the main entrance. So it shouldn't be a total loss, I popped the cap on the beer and we shared it to quiet our nerves while we headed down the block to my place.

One of the few public payphones still around is in the courtyard of my building, so I used it to dial nine-one-one. I told the emergency dispatcher that two suspicious characters were lurking around the Hyatt Regency and that they were...well, suspicious. I gave a thumbnail description of the perps and hung up without saying who I was. Maybe a visit from San Francisco's finest would put the hotel on the lookout for these guys in case they paid a return visit. I found thirty cents the telephone coin return and left it and the empty for someone who might need it more. Christy and I entered my building through the service door and rode the service lift up to eighteen.

In my apartment, I got Christy settled down on the terrace with a stiff drink. She finished it in two swallows and held the glass up for a refill.

"Gee, must be something wrong with this bottle," I said. "The label says it's supposed to be Tennessee *sippin'* liquor."

"That might be what it says, but a girl needs more than a sip after that close call," she said. "More like a gulp, I'd say. Those guys might have killed me. Or maybe raped me first. Or you, for that matter."

"Hey, nobody's raping me unless it's you." I filled her glass. "*Mazel tov.*"

"You should have one, too." This time she sipped first. Then gulped. "Aren't you having any? Or are you just trying to get me drunk?"

"Yes to both. While you have a re-fill, I've got to phone The Great Rondini. I want to warn him to be on the lookout for our pals." I left her the bottle while I went inside to call.

Ronnie answered about three rings in and sounded pretty chipper. I guessed having a pretty girl staying over did a lot for his morale. I know it did for mine. Still, I hoped my news would bring him down a little bit—I didn't want to be the only one scared to death.

I asked if Rhonda was still okay.

"She couldn't be in better hands, Junior. I'm keeping my eye on her at all times." I heard giggling in the background. "As a matter of fact, JJ, she's safe and sound here, protected from the cruel, cruel world."

"Got her tied to the bed, eh?"

"Now, now, old bean, no use being jealous. Dear Rhonda and I were just running through her part in the upcoming spiritual shenanigans."

Ronnie and I traded a few more jibes, and I filled him in on my adventures with Christy and the Huns. Ronnie didn't want to believe he was guarding Rhonda for no reason, the hoods having dropped her to try dropping Christy off the tenth floor of the Regency.

"Maybe somebody tipped them off about your record with the babes," I said. "With you watching over her, they figure she'll leave town without their help."

"*Au contraire*, old boy. I'm thinking this could be the one." More background giggling. "She's in show business, I'm in show business, she liked my place without my straightening things up, and though she didn't say it in so many words, I can tell she thinks I'm cute. You can be best man when the time comes."

"I thought I already was. Where is she now anyway?"

"Right here with me in the bubble bath."

"I thought you were a shower man."

"Somebody's got to scrub her back."

"Speaking of washing her back—I mean watching her back—where are you going to stash her when you do your show tonight? You're not going to leave her home alone?"

"No way. She'll be stashed at one of the Sphinx's best ringside tables. She'll never leave my sight and vice versa. After all, she's my biggest fan right now. I'm even waiving the cover charge."

"Hiding her in plain sight, eh?"

"Sure, it's all in the art of misdirection. Besides if those guys turn up at the show, Satyra can help out. She's a black belt in something or other. I heard somebody pinched her on BART and three passengers had to be hospitalized."

"Well, take care tonight," I said. "Those two cretins could be fans of yours."

Ronnie and I decided to meet at the Cliff House for brunch the next day. Once upon a time, Ronnie had dated the hostess there so he thought we could snag a nice table for four overlooking the ocean. Not an easy task with busloads of tourists showing up on typical Sundays. But it would impress our respective new girlfriends, and Lord knows, Ronnie needs all the help he can get. I'd charm the ladies over waffles while Ronnie worked out my game plan for the show.

Chapter 19.

As the evening fog chilled its way over the bay, I slipped out to join Christy on the balcony. Already the air was getting cooler. Inside of thirty minutes the lights of the City would be reflected softly from our fluffy sky as night came on. Sam Spade, Chinatown, fog horns, a pretty girl—romance and mystery.

"Don't get too near the edge."

Christy jumped at the sound of my voice. "Oh, Jerry, you startled me. I'm not going to fall, but my nerves are on still on edge." She leaned over the railing to watch the street eighteen stories down. "All I need to mellow out now is a handful of Valium."

"Sorry, I can check the medicine cabinet, but I'm pretty sure the strongest thing I've got is Tylenol. However, I am sure the booze cabinet is full; I *can* get you drunk. That fine Kentucky bourbon you've been downing is almost gone, but there's a quart of tequila. It was bottled just last week and I've been waiting for the right moment to break it out. Look—the worm is still doing the backstroke."

"Let's just finish the bourbon. That and having you close will make it all better." Sure, and the hangover won't be a problem until morning.

"Getting close present a problem." I eyed the balcony railing. "Why don't you take a few steps in my direction? I don't like to get too close to the edge. A sudden gust might blow me over, and with my vertigo, the trip down would be pure hell."

"I'll meet you half way," she said. "I'll think about going all the way later."

I took a few steps closer and she came a few my way and all of a sudden she was in my arms. We stayed like that a long time. I could have stayed longer, but finally she let go and pulled away. Not far away though. "This is nice, Jerry. Being here with you makes me feel much better. Either we need to slow down or you had better break open the tequila. "

"Why don't we go inside and build a fire? We can send out for a bearskin rug. While we're at it, let's get some food delivered too. Nowadays you can order any kind that strikes your fancy—Chinese, Italian, Ethiopian, Paleolithic, whatever—San Francisco's got it all. Besides it'll save wear and tear on my pots and pans. To be honest, the only thing I make in the kitchen is ice."

We moved indoors and I used the remote to turn on the fireplace. The perfect thing on a chilly summer night. Subdued lighting and a quiet jazz tune completed the scene. I speed-dialed a place that claimed to have steaks hot off the Pampas and ordered a pair. We curled up on the sofa and listened to the fire crackling under Miles Davis. It was shaping up as a pretty nice evening.

"It must be in the papers."

"In the papers?" I repeated. "You mean the *Chronicle*? The newspapers?"

"No, no, sweetie," Christy said. "The papers I got from Leland Heilbrun—the legal papers." I nodded, pretending I knew what she was talking about. "That's what those two bastards were after. They rounded up and took away every single piece of paper, paper clip and staple that Mr. Heilbrun gave me."

"They didn't want to leave a paper trail, I'd say. But I get it, maybe they weren't really after you. Bumping you off was just for fun. What they wanted was to erase the paper trail that might lead back to somebody connected with your dad's death."

"Sure. I hate to think the only reason they dropped by without calling was to toss me off the tenth floor," Christy said turning her baby blues on me. Jeepers, creepers, where'd she get them peepers?

She was saying, "I'd much rather think that it was just blind luck that they caught me in. Besides, they went after those papers like they were made of gold. That tells us the papers are important, doesn't it?"

"Maybe Freddy and Betty's contract was in there, no doubt signed in blood. I'd love to know what they have on the

Paulsons. Maybe I could get the same deal."

I snuggled closer this beautiful doll. Feeling her special softness took my mind off my aching head. Still something was starting to rattle around in there even as the perfume of her hair made me want to think of other things....

"Listen, Christy. How about this? Maybe they weren't trying to kill you because you're looking into your dad's death, but because they thought you might have seen something else that was in those papers. Something that might not even have anything to do with you or your Dad."

"Jerry, look, honey, I'm willing to believe it might not have anything to do with Dad's murder, but somebody's going to have to prove it to me first. It would be a hell of a long shot if it wasn't tied in. And even if there isn't anything in those papers, somebody thinks there is. And that somebody has got to be Dad's killer. I've got to get another copy of those papers from Mr. Heilbrun."

"Sure, I understand that.... But hold on—something's not adding up here."

"What do you mean? What's not adding up?"

"Why would the gruesome twosome go to the trouble of breaking into your room and stealing those papers if you could just call up Heilbrun and get another copy?"

"Maybe that's why I'm supposed to be dead now, remember?"

"But Heilbrun would know you had the papers. Wouldn't he wonder what happened to them? For that matter, so would I. And I told Ronnie Green what you were doing and he'd wonder too." Although Rondini wouldn't miss holding you like I would or miss the smell of your hair like I would.... "Any number of people might know about these papers. And want to see what's in them."

"True, but right now I'm the one who wants to see them," Christy said. "I need to get in touch with that lawyer."

"I don't know if we can reach him on the weekend. Mrs. Paulson might have his cell number in case she gets picked up for tax evasion or something. There might be something at the station too, but nobody's there on the weekend. Everything's run by computer. We could break in to Ned's office and hack into his computer or something to see if he's got a home number in his contact list."

"Jerry, do you know how to do those things?"

"Not really. I was hoping you did."

"Well, at UA once I watched a guy jimmy the door to the

Dean's office with a credit card."

"My, you did get a well-rounded education. Who was the guy, G. Gordon Liddy?"

"Just a guy I knew. I haven't seen him in ages, but we had some good times."

I couldn't believe Christy was thinking about another man at a time like this, but at least it wasn't Liddy. Probably one of those guys that's good at sports and wood shop. You know the type, those jocks that go around giving wedgies and jimmying into the Dean's office.

Christy added, "I was drunk when we did it, so it doesn't count, but I think I remember how he did it. Break in, that is."

"Well, as long as you were drunk, I can't hold him against you. That makes me feel a lot better. Anyway, I've got Discover, Visa, MasterCard and Amex. If one of those doesn't get us into Ned's office, we'll use a sledge hammer."

"I'm thinking a sledge hammer may not work on his computer, sweetie. In my experience, they usually need a password."

"True, but that may not be necessary. If I were a betting man—and I am—I'd bet Heilbrun's number is in the big Rolodex on Ned's desk. I'm not completely sure that Ned trusts computers or the information highway and all that stuff. The keyboard on his desk looked like it needed dusting."

"That takes care of one problem though we still need to get into his office. But I'm sure I can jimmy the lock."

"You don't need to get drunk again to remember how, do you?"

She claimed not. Too bad, we might have reenacted the action I was imagining on the dean's couch. She hadn't mentioned anything like that, but what's the point of breaking into the dean's office otherwise?

I got another brain wave: "Come to think of it, Ned's office is half full of file cabinets. He may have copies of some of those legal papers. Do you think you could recognize the papers if you saw them again?"

She thought so, having skimmed through them a couple of times. By now the delivery boy had dropped by with dinner, and while we ate, we finalized our plan to raid KPMT. We drank half the tequila to get our courage up and convinced ourselves that this was the right move for late on a Saturday night when lawyers were hard to reach anyway.

No one would be at the station until Monday's morning drive time when Ned came in for the Freddy and Betty snooze.

If we messed up his office he wouldn't know it until then so what did we have to worry about? Without the workday commuters, it didn't pay for KPMT to do local programming. Instead computerized black magic took syndicated feeds from back east, inserted local advertising and announcements, and broadcast them out over our signal.

Since the station would be just as deserted in the morning, it might have made more sense to get a good night's sleep before ransacking the place, but we didn't want to let time slip through our fingers. The sooner we had the papers, the sooner we would know who or what we were looking for. If for some reason the papers really weren't at the station, we'd at least get Heilbrun's home number and call him in the morning.

We gathered up a flashlight, some small tools Christy found under the sink, and I rummaged through my closet for dark sweaters and jeans so we'd look the part. Since Christy had left all her breaking and entering clothes back at the hotel, she had to make do with my stuff. They were kind of baggy on her, but I got to see her undies while we were changing. Nothing baggy there.

By midnight we were ready. Although Big Talk Radio is only a few blocks from my building, we decided to drive over since it was late and the streets didn't feel all that safe anymore. Besides, if things worked out right, we'd have a box full of papers to carry home.

I had never actually been in the station when it was dark before. From Monday to Friday programming is live from six A.M. until midnight so lights are on in the expected places. Also, the lobby doors are locked at five when Michael leaves the reception desk. If any visitor shows up late, they push a button that tells the board op to go let them in. Employees have a code they punch in to unlock the doors which lock again when they swung shut.

Back when I hired on, I had written the code on a yellow sticky and stuck it to my driver's license. Now standing in the dark by the entrance, I was trying not to drop the flashlight while I fumbled through the stuff in my wallet—credit cards, various business cards, an old locker combination, and a vast accumulation of other detritus built up over the years. Good thing I stopped carrying condoms in there when I left Passaic High. I didn't want Christy to get the wrong idea. I was saving that idea for later.

Behind a ragged snapshot from a distant branch of the Jeremy family tree I found a napkin with a phone number written on it in lip liner. The missing yellow sticky was stuck to the other side of the napkin although I never did find my driver's license.

Meanwhile, Christy had vanished.

I swung the flashlight around until I caught a baggy pant leg in its beam. I raised it to a baggy sleeve and a hand holding the door for me. "Come on," Christy whispered. "They haven't changed the code since Dad used to take me here on weekends."

"Some memory. I'll have to have Rondini tell me what else you've got in there." Inside the East Coast feed was playing through overhead speakers. Otherwise it was as quiet—and dark—as a tomb.

Christy carefully shut the door behind us and said, "You might not want to know what's in my mind. Besides you're chapter is only just beginning." She gave the door handle a tug to make sure it was locked behind us. And, I suppose, to allow that last remark sink in.

"I forgot you knew your way around here," I said.

"It's been a while, but it's coming back. Shine the light over there, towards the offices."

"Wait a second," I made a detour to the reception desk and gave it the once over with the flash in case Michael had left the office keys lying around. I emptied out a 'Big Talk' coffee mug that held a handful of pencils and some paperclips, but no keys. His desk drawers were all locked too. I couldn't help thinking that Michael didn't seem to trust his fellow man.

I turned back to find Christy and banged my knee on the corner of the desk. "Ouch," I whispered, "Christy, where are you?"

"Over here." A pale light came from the office area giving her a ghostly glow. She was navigating by the light from her cell phone. "Come on, Jerry. Is Ned's office still over here?"

The ghostly face disappeared but I headed toward the glow from her phone. Before I got there, she said, "Jerry, come on. Look at this, I think his door is already open. Come on, this is going to be easier than we thought."

I was pretty sure I had seen Ned lock up before we left for the Grotto Friday evening, but I guess was wrong. When I reached Christy, the door was wide open. I was thinking Ned must have come in earlier to pay some bills or take apart another amplifier, and had forgotten to lock up again. So much for our big break-in. And I was so looking forward to learning how to jimmy a lock.

This caper was beginning to feel way too easy. Next thing you know the secret papers would be pinned to Ned's bulletin board. I lit up the bulletin board with my flash just in case. No luck, just FCC notices and a calendar with a picture of a muscular guy on a wave.

"Jerry, look at this," Christy had her cell phone lit up again and was skimming through some legal-sized folders on Ned's desk. "The labels on these match the documents I had, I'm positive."

"They're the ones we're looking for?" This was even better than the bulletin board gag.

"No. They're empty. *Jesus-fucking-Christ!* Somebody beat us to them. How could they know they were here?"

"They might know if they were connected to the station. And we figured that was probably the case. Maybe they even got a little help from somebody watching us through her crystal ball. Our minds being a couple of open books to Madame Zoroaster." Paperbacks probably. If Madame Z wasn't a fraud...well, let's just hope she was.

I circled around the desk and added my flashlight beam to her phone's dying glow. The folders were empty all right. I swung the light around to the cabinets behind Ned's chair. They looked to be unlocked with a few of their drawers left ajar. No need to jimmy them open. No need to even look inside. Somebody had already taken care of that. Whatever secrets were here were now gone.

I was thinking we needed to find Leland Heilbrun's home number and give him a jingle before his office got cleaned out too. Assuming that wasn't where the crooks went first and—

"Oh! Sorry, Jerry," Christy said. "It's so dark in here."

"Sorry for what, babe?"

"Stepping on your foot, Jerry. I didn't realize it was there."

"My foot? I didn't feel a thing."

I beamed the flashlight down Christy's leg to see why and then I wished I hadn't. I even wished I hadn't come here looking for those important papers.

"Holy shit!" Christy plastered back against Ned's cabinets. As for me, I was paralyzed except for that churning in my gut.

The flashlight lit up a hand where Christy had put her foot. It was a man's hand, white and swollen, like something you'd find in rotten meat. Except for the diamond signet on his pinky finger. The hand was connected to a pudgy wrist sticking out from the sleeve of a nicely pressed blazer, said blazer on the pudgy man on the floor. He had his pudgy tongue sticking out too. Gray, sightless eyes stared up at me from a purple face.

From someplace I heard a caller on the overnight feed saying as how the country was going to hell in a hand basket and for all the same, old, tired reasons. It was an overdone, tiresome bit and the listeners were probably tuning out in droves. And I was thinking as how we wouldn't need that number for Leland Heilbrun now. We wouldn't be calling him about those papers after all. Nobody would ever call Leland Heilbrun again. There he was, at the end of my flashlight beam, with a length of recording tape cutting deeply into the folds of his pudgy neck.

Chapter 20.

"ALL right, sir, let me get your story straight," the woman said, with a look that could break a prime suspect or a cheating boyfriend. She had dark, almond-shaped eyes and was slim but in good shape, like maybe she worked out a bit. She had on a sweatshirt and faded jeans, but around her neck she wore a gold star. Written on it were the words "Inspector, S.F. Police."

"You're saying you just happened to stumble over the victim here? You work here, but you decided you needed to get some papers in the middle of the night? You had the lights off and were carrying burglar tools? You *stumbled* over the body? I'm just not getting it, sir—am I dumb or something? Do *you* think I'm dumb, sir?"

"No, no, absolutely not, Inspector. And it was my girlfriend that actually stumbled—er, stepped on the hand...but that's not the important thing—"

"And you have no ID, sir, unless I believe this spa membership card. A spa that I can't afford, by the way. And it shows the same name two times. Jeremy and then Jeremy again. No last name."

"That's right. I mean it's correct—my name's Jeremy Jeremy, first and last name's the same. I'm known as Jerry Jeremy on the radio. You must have heard my show."

"No sir, I never heard of you. And you don't have a California driver's license, sir? Or any state driver's license, sir?"

Homicide Inspector Janice Thé, the SFPD's dragon lady, had dragged me to one end of KPMT's business office and her partner, a detective named Estrada, had Christy at the other. I could see Christy and Estrada over Thé's shoulder. I couldn't hear what was being said, but they were smiling at each other like it was happy hour at the pick-me-up lounge.

Estrada looked kind of smarmy in his two hundred dollar jeans and a muscle shirt, and it looked like he'd turned Christy's third degree down to a simmer. So, at least we knew who got the good cop. That left me pretty much high and dry with the female Kojak no matter how much I gave her the smile or turned on the charm.

After we had recovered from the shock of finding Leland Heilbrun's body, Christy had dialed up nine-one-one from her mobile and the uniforms were banging on the lobby door in less than five. Must have been a Starbuck's still open near the studio. In the meanwhile, I had dialed up Ned to tell him there was a scoop brewing and he ought to get down here.

Christy and I had had only a few minute to agree on what we'd tell the cops. We decided to use Christy's dad being run off the road and the stolen documents Heilbrun had given Christy. We'd bring up getting attacked at the Hyatt Regency too. Maybe there'd be a little sympathy for my aching head, not to mention the damages to repair the damages to Christy's room. As actually happened, we would say that we came over to the station to see if there were any copies of the missing papers here.

It would only confuse the nice policemen (and woman) if we brought up the séance and Tony Paulson and the diamond bracelet scam. They might get sidetracked thinking there was a lot more than a double murder to investigate.

"ARE you listening, Mr. Jeremy?" Inspector Thé followed my gaze across the room to her partner and Christy. Then she swiveled back to me, eyeball to eyeball, saying, "Your friend's a pretty girl. So you don't think I'm a complete idiot, I imagine you wanted to get in good with her and played along with her theory about her father's death. But maybe this Heilbrun was taken with her too and thought she might return his feelings if he helped her out, just like you did. So he worked her with a few reams of paper from the recycling bin."

"Then how come the hoods stole the papers out of her room?"

"Maybe Heilbrun had them stolen himself, so she wouldn't realize he was putting her on. It could be the papers are pure bullshit. Then again, maybe you arranged the hotel fight so you could play the hero. Either way, I don't think you'd like the idea of Miss Marshall getting close to him or for that matter anyone else." She glanced at Estrada which caused me to look there again. Estrada and Christy seemed to be getting along. Thé said, "With the attorney out of the picture, you have an almost clear path."

Inspectors Thé and Estrada had shown up a half hour or so after the first uniforms responded and had immediately taken charge of the investigation. From where I sat at Rita Silvano's desk, I had a view of the lobby door so I was able to watch the comings and goings, but nobody had made the "goings" column yet. More cops drifted in, most with paper cups full of coffee, some with doughnut boxes from Krispy Kreme, others with cameras and crime scene tape and evidence kits. They all looked like they'd been awakened from a sound sleep. Which was probably true, it being two in the morning by now.

Ned had shown pretty quickly too with Brad and Kinta on his heels. Then the news director and Marsha Chung, a KPMT news reader, bustled in together like maybe they shared a ride over, like maybe they had been sharing more than that before deciding to car pool.

The SFPD let everybody set up camp in the studio side of the station. Ned made a few stabs at talking to the cops, but didn't get much, which was all right with me since the way I saw it, this was my scoop. After all, I found the body. I might even be a prime suspect. This could make my career. Freddy and Betty would be back to spinning golden oldies someplace out in Middle America.

Some of the boys and girls in blue gave me dirty looks as they put on paper pajamas and booties before crowding into Ned's office to give Leland Heilbrun's corpse a few dirty looks too. Like it was my fault—or his—their Saturday night got interrupted. Every now and then somebody complained about the broadcast audio coming through the office speakers. I couldn't say as I blamed them, the overnights being directed mostly to those people who sleep all day. Somebody must have searched out Brad the Brat with the complaint because suddenly the audio went as dead as the body in Ned's office.

Inspector Thé was saying, "You think you can recognize the guys who you allegedly ran into at the hotel if you saw them again?"

I told her sure, any place, any time.

"You, yourself, never laid eyes on these so-called papers?"

I said, no, not anywhere, not any time.

Since the only attorney I knew was lying dead in the next office, I decided—not to put too fine a point on it—to spill my guts. Occasionally another cop would walk up, listen to Inspector Thé browbeat me for a while, and then walk away again, confident I was going to get mine for having rousted them out of bed.

"Exactly when is your show on?" Thé asked.

"Every day from four to seven, except weekends. And the station may start doing 'best of' on the weekends. Come on, you must have heard my show. It's big—I even get coffee comped at Starbucks sometimes. That's pretty much the norm for cops I guess, but most people have to pay."

"I only listen to Asian top forty—songs to get me up when I'm called out in the middle of the night to see some jerk who went and fucking killed his lawyer."

"Sure, rock on. You know, I get a lot of crossover from classic rock, the seventies and eighties and the like. I'm big in that demographic, not that I remember it myself. But you might still like my show, we're big on law and order."

Sergeant Thé didn't say anything but something in the way she looked told me she might not be tuning in any time soon. Over in the lobby I saw a video cameraman and an audio engineer I knew hauling in their gear. Not one to look a sure thing in the mouth, Ned must have lined them up to get coverage for the website, and maybe cable news too.

About this time, Thé told me to stay put and headed over to confer with Inspector Estrada. I was glad to see her pull him away from Christy before they set up housekeeping. While Thé and Estrada whispered back and forth, I ambled past the lobby into the production end of the station.

Through the big window in Studio A I saw that Marsha Chung was already in full broadcast mode. The overhead speakers having been shut down, probably none of the cops realized we were carrying the story now as it was unfolding. I wondered how much of the office area Brad had wired for eavesdropping over the years. Normally Ned wouldn't be very happy about that, but now the news was being gathered the moment anybody said it.

What I wasn't very happy about was that this was my story and so far I was being cut out of it. I was hoping that Thé no longer desired my company and I could start giving my evidence to the listening audience. TV and the papers would be picking up on it soon and I wanted to be way out in front, what with the murder having happened right in Ned's office and all. The best scenario for us would be to have other media outlets pick up our on-the-air and replay it, giving us the spotlight. And when that happened I wanted to be the voice in that spotlight.

"WHERE did you run off to?" Inspector Thé's dulcet tones made the hair on my neck stand up. The last woman to get that kind of a reaction out of me was Mrs. Uberkrantz in the third grade. I said, "I'm not just a pretty face, Inspector. I'm a pretty voice too."

"And I thought you were mine until Monday at four," she replied. So, I gave her the pitch about how this was the story that would make me a household name. Maybe even in the Thé household. I also told her I'd make sure she came out of this with some good press, supposing I could avoid arrest for a while. Maybe she'd be a household name too.

"Inspector Thé, this is the hottest story in town tonight. That means you are too, you'll be all over radio and TV tomorrow."

"Not TV! I just got out of bed for Christ sake. I didn't even get to put my rollers in and I'm wearing a sweatshirt that says 'Forty-*fucking*-Niners' on it, for Christ sake."

"Don't sweat it, my crew can make a corpse look good— you'll look better than if you were alive. San Francisco, here I—er, here you come."

After that, we were practically on a first name basis. She called me Jeremy and I called her Inspector. Anyway, she told me not to plan on any long trips for a while and she promised to pry Christy away from her partner. She had started back to the lobby, but did a Lieutenant Columbo turn to ask one more thing, "About your friend, Miss Marshall—she was the one who knew the code to the station door, wasn't she?"

"Well, I had it written down some place, but—"

"I don't doubt you didn't know it, but she did, didn't she?"

"Sure, her dad used to bring her here as a kid and she still remembered it."

"And she believes the present owners gave her mother a raw deal on the buyout after her father's death?"

"Sure, her dad was going to sell it for a lot more before he died."

"And Leland Heilbrun did the legal work for the buyout and had all the paperwork? And Miss Marshall thinks that there is something in the paperwork that proves her point, doesn't she? And just maybe Miss Marshall and her mother stand to make a lot of money if the deal is thrown out and the present owners need to pay the going rate?"

I didn't have a ready answer for that, so I decided to do what I do on the show—answer the question I did know. "She couldn't have done this. Christy was with me all evening."

"Unless you were in on it too. But I doubt that's the case; after all, you're going to make me look good on TV. We don't, however, have a time of death yet, so she could have done it earlier in the day. She looks strong enough to stretch the tape around his neck. A pretty girl could make him lower his guard.... "

"Wha...hey, Inspector," I said, going along with the joke, "you almost had me on that one. Just like you made it sound like you thought it was me a few minutes ago."

"Maybe I still do. But you make me look good on TV today, and maybe you and your friend will be off the hook. You had better get to work while I get my lipstick; this'll be a big chance for both of us. And I'll send Miss Marshall over before Estrada and her start picking out baby names."

"I'M surprised to see you know Tom Marshall's daughter so well," Ned said. A statement that's really a question. All the subtlety of a brick meeting a plate glass window. He stated/asked it while I was finishing up the rundown with Dennis Hong, our news director, and suspected BFF of Marsha Chung, news reader. Radio being radio and Hong having some hopes of a career, he'd quickly abandoned any attempt to feature his girlfriend and jumped onto my bandwagon. As for me, I held back on Tony Paulson and on Tom Marshall's possible murder. There was something starting to stir in a far corner of my mind, but I couldn't quite make it out. Maybe Ronnie would be able to wake it up.

That's why I was only half listening when Ned said what he said, question or not. Then he said, "I thought she was at school someplace out of state. I wouldn't have guessed you would have known her, let alone been friends."

"Right now, I'm probably her only friend," was my reply. "Well...in San Francisco anyway."

"GOOD morning, this is Marsha Chung on KPMT, Big Talk Radio, with a KPMT, Big Talk Newsflash.

"Leland Heilbrun, KPMT's very own Big Talk Attorney,

was murdered right here at the KPMT studios tonight. At this time, police say it is too soon to have developed any firm leads or suspects. But KPMT's own Jeremy Jeremy was at the studio around the time of the crime. With Jerry at the time was a mystery woman who was said to be connected to the murdered man. Police have questioned both individuals but have yet to make an arrest...."

Even if she was boffing the news director, I decided right then and there that Marsha Chung would definitely not be my news reader when I took over the morning drive show.

"...now here next to the chalk outline in the Big Talk Radio studios is KPMT's very own murder suspect, Jerry Jeremy—"

I smiled into the microphone and deepened my voice slightly, knowing life would never be the same:

"Thank you, Marsha. This is Jerry Jeremy reporting from the KPMT studios where tonight yours truly and Christy Marshall, daughter of one of KPMT's founders, discovered the body of KPMT's legal counsel, Leland Heilbrun, minutes after his murder. Ms. Marshall and I will describe the scene and tie this to multiple murder attempts on Ms. Marshall herself..."

We were off and running.

The feed was live and the local media was picking it up by now, as well as stringers for cable news and the wire services. Video would be fed to the website as well as the TV and cable networks. KPMT's PR gal was working the phones, juggling calls from the world at large. The switchboard was inundated and I wondered if Ned had roused Michael from his coffin. Tony Paulson had already gotten the sales team in for a Sunday morning onslaught to squeeze any commercial opportunities dry. I worked in a few teasers for my weekday show and even gave Rondini a plug or two.

So far the only loser in this trudunit seemed to be Leland Heilbrun, but we'd get Mrs. P to say something really nice about him. Of course, Christy lost out on getting the papers that might hold a clue to her dad's death, but I wasn't thinking too much about that at the moment and I hoped she wasn't either.

The cops had turned Christy loose and I collared her in Studio B. On air we worked our way through finding Leland's corpse, not to mention yours truly saving Christy from almost certain death at the Hyatt Regency. I gave the hotel a clean bill of health though, hoping they might comp the room in exchange for a plug. This all led into Christy's suspicions about her dad's death at the hands of person or persons unknown. I skirted around any possible motives leading back to Big Talk Radio though. After all, I still had to pay the rent.

Kinta collared Inspectors Thé and Estrada, and we had a little roundtable to show our listeners how little the cops really knew. But done in a nice way since we were all pals now.

What with commercials and news alerts by Marsha recapping what we had just said, it was getting on towards sunrise sermon time before we knew it. We were dead tired, no pun intended. They'd hauled Leland out around three a.m. and most of the SFPD followed shortly thereafter. Ned's office was sealed off until further notice, it being a crime scene. I hoped the cops hadn't found the stash of Maui-Waui Ned kept in the office safe.

"...stay tuned as KPMT brings you the latest on its very own murder mystery. And don't forget to catch yours truly, Jerry Jeremy, Monday at four...." I was easing into a tease for my séance show when that tickle way back in my mind started up. I couldn't quite tease it into words though, but it knew it was a tickle that needed the okay from Ned or Mrs. Paulson, and maybe even KPMT's attorney assuming they could field a replacement. But there wasn't time for that, I had a career to build—*"...next Friday on the Jerry Jeremy show one of the leading psychics in this world or the next will recreate the murder of Leland Heilbrun, revealing the identity of the Big Talk Radio killer!"*

Chapter 21.

"WHADDAYA NUTS?" Ned's forearm pressed into my throat as he pinned me against the wall. "Did I hear you promo that damn' psychic finding Heilbrun's killer?"

His eyes were bulging out way too far, his arm slowly cutting off my air supply. Through clinched teeth he rasped, "I don't need a crystal fucking ball to know you won't have a fucking show by next Friday—"

Kinta tried wrapping his arms around Ned's head to pull him away but it came off looking like a group hug. Meanwhile, I was counting the spots forming before my eyes. Just as they were becoming one big spot, Inspector Thé hopped on, dislodging Kinta but not making much of a dent on Ned. Seems like there's never a cop with a nightstick around when you need one.

Suddenly the pressure on my windpipe was gone and as the spots faded I could see Estrada pulling Ned from behind. The tide was turning on our surfer boy. I could probably take Ned eventually but having Kinta and the SFPD in the brawl speeded things up. Luckily Estrada had decided to stick around and chat up my girlfriend.

"What'd you do?" Estrada wanted to know. "Screw his girlfriend?"

"You mean 'boyfriend,'" I said. "But no, I don't bat for that team if you know what I mean. Let's just say we have creative differences."

I took Christy's arm for support and so Estrada would know whose side she was on. I held on tight while running through the scales to make sure Ned hadn't bent the old tonsils out of shape. By now, he was slumped in a chair out in the lobby and Thé was whispering questions at him. It didn't look like she'd need the rubber hose or bright lights; Ned didn't have much fight left in him.

Estrada zeroed back in to ask what I meant by "creative differences." I guess the boys in blue talk through their differences instead of grabbing each other by the throat. Anyway, I told Estrada it was all in a day's work. "You heard me tell the listeners that I'd go with a clairvoyant to help break the case. I know it's kind of stepping on your toes, but you're not going to slam me into any more walls are you?"

"Hey, you're the one going out on a limb, not me. And your boss didn't like that, eh?"

"He said he'd fire me, if that means he didn't like it."

"Yeah, that's pretty strong stuff. Not to mention he tried to strangle you."

While Christy rubbed my neck and Estrada rubbed me wrong, Ned's cell phone interrupted his third degree. He did a lot of nodding and stammering into the phone, and after he rang off, I could see he was asking Inspector Thé if he could come back over where I was. I wasn't too crazy about that idea, but she must have had him to sign a non-aggression pact, because he was headed my way.

Turns out that it was Mrs. Paulson on the horn and she wanted to pow-wow around cocktail time, presumably giving Christy and me time to catch a few winks. Or maybe she just likes that time of day. According to Ned, she wanted heavy coverage on the murder and I was to be the star reporter. Ned—my new best friend forever—said she even wanted to know how the séance gag would work. She said to bring Christy along too.

I took it all to mean Pamela Kay wanted to be sure of how Tony and the gypsy twins fit into the picture before making any rash decisions. Meanwhile Estrada tried out a few more of his lines on Christy and Janice Thé, having nothing better to do, came by to watch. At some point we all agreed it had been a long night, so they kicked me and Christy loose with the promise we'd come by the Hall of Justice later. Sunday in the park seemed to be out.

Chapter 22.

CHRISTY and I were too tired to worry about the sleeping arrangements. I got the fold-out sofa-bed. I figured Christy deserved the queen-sized in the bedroom, having held up pretty well for somebody who had almost been rundown, nearly thrown off a ten story balcony and had stepped on a dead man. On top of all that, she'd put up with Estrada's passes and then turned on the charm for the folks out there in radio and TV-land. If I hadn't given her the bed, she'd have probably kicked my ass. Who says chivalry is dead?

The police had sent a couple of their finest to guard the offices of Cardwell, Heilbrun and Wilshire. They were going to make sure that nobody would be leaving any new fingerprints on the lawyers' files before they had a chance to dig out the missing docs. Apparently the legal beagles were not cooperating though, trotting out that old attorney-client privilege thing. Who knows what one might find rummaging through their drawers, so it might be a while before the cops got their hands on any new evidence.

This was just the kind of constitutional obstacle my callers love to complain about and I was thinking about using it on the show. I could tie it right into the murders, not to mention a big fat plug for the séance. All the pieces were falling into place.

Just as I was closing the drapes, shutting out the dawn's early light, Christy slipped into the living room to wish me flights of angels and all that. "Some negligee," I said, giving her the Groucho leer. She had on an Arizona football jersey, size triple-X large. "Wildcats, eh?"

"Oh, yeah. I think I got this off a linebacker at the victory party when we trashed USC."

"You knock him down and take the shirt off his back?'

"He didn't seem to mind. I think he was after a post-game ball...but he didn't get one."

"You seem pretty chipper for six in the morning. I've watched the sun come up before crawling into bed before, but I usually have a better time. We'll have to try it my way sometime."

Christy straightened the sheets I had tossed over the sofa and fluffed up my pillow. As she tucked and stretched, I developed a new appreciation for football attire. And she wasn't even wearing the shoulder pads.

I tried lightening the mood. "Hey, weren't you the chambermaid who turned down my bed at the Tucson Hilton?"

"Oh, sir, I don't think I've ever turned anyone down at the Tucson Hilton and I spent a lot of time there."

"So you're just a girl who can't say no?" I said to keep up my end of the banter. Three more lines and we'd have a TV pilot. "You really doing okay or just putting up a brave front?"

"You must be learning mind-reading from your friend. It's all just a front. Honey, if I wasn't so tired, I'd be sick to my stomach."

I took the pillow away before she fluffed it to shreds and I took her in my arms next. We held each other, nuzzling and hugging, in a clinch that told me I'd be missing out on something if I let go. But after a while sleep beat sex. I put her to bed in one room and went back to the other. I could still smell her perfume and feel her in my arms. I figured I'd toss and turn for hours.

I closed my eyes and when Christy woke me, it was past one in the afternoon. She had bounced out of bed at the crack of noon and I could smell the coffee brewing. Bacon and eggs sizzled in the frying pan. I was surprised I had a frying pan. I knew I didn't have any bacon and eggs.

"I made a quickie-trip to the quickie-mart downstairs. Pretty convenient if you happen to be out of absolutely everything."

"I don't stock up much since they started putting expiration dates on everything."

I noticed she had made a stop at the Hyatt also. She was wearing a new outfit, sort of an upscale down-home look.

She caught me looking and said, "When I went down to the market, I decided to walk over to the hotel and check out. I went up to get the rest of my stuff, and between the crooks and the police taking turns searching the room, it looked like a rock band had stayed there."

"I hope they didn't put it on your bill."

"The fingerprint powder and chalk marks were all over the place. The last time that many people went through my drawers was the *Alpha Bama* panty raid. I had to call that nice Inspector Estrada, to get them to let me take my things out. He sounded like I woke him up, but not grumpy or anything." Christy handed me a cup of the old fresh brewed. One sip and I hoped the bacon and eggs were her strong suit. The java not only put hair on my chest, I could feel it curling.

Still the moment was perfect. A taste of domesticity right here in my bachelor pad. Maybe I could get used to being waited on hand and foot. I could drop the maid service too.

"I hope Tommy didn't get the wrong idea," Christy said setting out the breakfast plates, "about me not staying in my room last night."

I was surprised I had plates.

"What idea would that be, babe? And who's Tommy anyway? Not another linebacker?"

"You know—Tommy Estrada, the detective. He said I should call him Tommy. And well, you know, people sometimes jump to the wrong conclusions when somebody sleeps over, Jerry. How come you're not eating?"

So it was Tommy now? I had a conclusion or two of my own to jump to. I tried the coffee again having lost my appetite. Big mistake.

"You know how much I appreciate all you're doing for me and Mom, Jerry." Christy buttered up both me and the toast. "But I won't have any time for personal things until Dad's murder is solved."

I tried to swallow, but the toast stuck in my throat. Even the coffee stuck in my throat. I said, "What about once we've solved your dad's...you know?"

"Jerry my love, you should already know I find you very attractive. Once all this is past, I hope you'll still like me too. Maybe all you see now is the damsel in distress side of me."

"You're great from all sides. And just wait 'til you see me without my shining armor. I mean...well, I'd put on something else, my street clothes or something. I mean I'm not really such a tough guy, you know."

"Oh, really? I thought that might be the case. But I do have to warn you that Daddy spoiled me. So you'll have a lot to put up with."

I was thinking I could put up with just about anything from her. Anyway—with or without the warning label—I was going to help Christy see that justice was done. I only hoped it wouldn't involve any more dead bodies, particularly not ours.

"I need to call Mom to let her know I'm okay. If she's already seen us on the news she'll probably be in a tizzy."

While Christy called home, I thought I'd better hook up with Ronnie. He'd have heard about the Heilbrun murder by now if Miss Ridgeway hadn't broke him of the TV habit already. He'd figure I'd be a no-show for the Cliff House, although he and Rhonda might have decided to risk the tourists anyway. I told his voice mail that we'd try to hook up at the Blue Sphinx later.

After our rendezvous the other night, I planned to send Jeanne some flowers and a cordial note. But she beat me to the punch. She had left urgent messages by voicemail, e-mail, instant message and probably would have thrown a rock through my window if she could have gotten the KCTY chopper to fly past the eighteenth floor.

Jeanne said she had an immediate need to talk with me. I hoped she wasn't pregnant. It had to be either that or she'd heard about the murder and wanted to give her career a boost with an inside scoop.

Christy was still on the horn to Mom, sunning herself out on the patio. Even so, I decided to wait until she wasn't around to return Jeanne's calls. I did hop on-line for a minute to send her eighty bucks worth of flowers though. I decided on the Hawaiian arrangement, not so romantic as roses, but leaving room to maneuver. I added a card saying that I got her messages to call and would do so soon. I hoped it sounded warm and intimate, but not too warm, not too intimate.

I DROVE to the Hall of Justice with Christy sitting next to me. Ah, that domestic feeling again; I might have to trade in the Beamer for a mini-van. The Hall of Justice is on Bryant Street squeezed in between the up-and-coming south of Market neighborhood known as SOMA and the Tenderloin district which is home to the homeless. SOMA aside, Bryant Street was still waiting gentrification. And it looked to be a long wait. Since there were plenty of cops around to watch the car, I parked in the bus stop out front.

The Hall houses police headquarters, a block of holding cells and the criminal courts. Homicide Detail is on the fifth floor. That's where we found Inspectors Thé and Estrada in a sea of paper cups and sandwich wrappers.

They looked pretty done in but seemed happy enough to see us. I guess they finally realized we were on their side. Either that or they planned to read us our rights and close the case early. But this time they didn't separate us for questioning or take out the rubber hoses. They'd have figured out that if we were cooking up an alibi we'd have done it by now.

Estrada seemed to be at a particularly low ebb, not even bothering to drool over Christy who definitely looked hot enough to get some spit going. Tommy-boy must have had a really long night or maybe just a reality check.

Meanwhile, Janice Thé plopped a tape recorder on the table, asking if we minded. I told her we didn't and I clicked on my pocket recorder which was...well, deep inside my pocket. I was sure they wouldn't mind since they were taping anyway and I could use a few sound bites for the station. You know the stuff, them questioning us, me questioning them about them questioning us, everybody questioning everybody, but nobody having any good answers. Brad and Kinta would have to edit something out of it later even if they had to make it up.

Estrada punched the record button while Inspector Thé gathered up the lunch debris and tossed it in a wastebasket. Christy and I took seats on one side of the table while Tommy and Janice sat across from us. I had pretty much thought Janice Thé headed the team, but Estrada took the lead in the interrogation. He probably wanted to show Christy that he was as good as Thé even if he wasn't quite as tough.

Estrada spent some time going through our personal histories like it was a job interview. The only difference being that I couldn't lie as much here. By the time he was done though I knew a lot more about Christy than before, the downside being that she knew a lot more about me. It was okay I guess, but finding out on our own would have been a lot more fun.

While Estrada covered the back story, Thé kept getting up and leaving the interview room only to return a few minutes later. Occasionally she said something to Estrada in police jargon or dropped some nugget of police gossip. She didn't seem too interested in what Christy and I had to say.

"Just for the record," Estrada said waving a leftover cookie for emphasis, "do each of you know the station owner, Pamela

Kay Paulson?"

We each confessed that we did.

Estrada followed this with more questions about Pamela Kay's partnership with Christy's father. If we only had the missing papers, this line of questioning wouldn't have been necessary. But we didn't, so it was. And while I was sure Estrada wanted to get everything straight, I didn't want to be late for cocktails at Pamela Kay's either. After all, doing the top forty at East Podunk wasn't in my career plan.

"So as I understand it, your father did want to sell his share in the company, but wasn't planning to sell it to Mrs. Paulson?" He was getting warmer. My watch said it was already twenty minutes to three. I wanted to get Inspector Thé on tape when she circled by again since Estrada was sounding like a poor man's Joe Friday.

"Any idea if they had bad feelings toward one another?" The good news was that he was working the Tom Marshall angle. I had planned on breaking the Marshall case myself and being Christy's hero, but having the cops on standby wouldn't hurt either. On the other hand, I didn't want Estrada to get overly involved at this point. Christy might wind up sleeping over at his place.

I asked, "Did they find anything in Ned's office that points to any one? Maybe our friends from the Hyatt Regency?"

"The crime scene investigators are concentrating on the empty file folders. But the office looked like it hadn't been cleaned in years, so there were too many prints and other traces to be of much use. But they're concentrating on things that the perps were more likely to have touched, the file folders, the desk...and of course, the murder weapon, that tape around the victim's throat."

"Yes, the tape," I had an unsettling memory of the tape cutting into Leland Heilbrun's neck. "I didn't notice at the time, but what was on the tape, anything special?"

"We haven't got that far yet. Why? You know something about the tape?"

"Not really. Most of our recorded stuff is on computer nowadays. Maybe it was one of Ned's eight-tracks, the Beach Boys maybe."

Estrada had a few more questions, revisiting things we had gone through last night and Janice Thé continued to swing by every now and then. She'd ask a question that Estrada had already covered and we'd answer it again. Little by little Christy and I managed to shift the balance of the interrogation until we were asking them most of the questions. I got a few sound bites though not much of anything new. At one point, Thé mentioned that they had been in touch with the Marin cops and the Park Service to see what they had on Tom Marshall's accident.

Finally Christy and I ran out of questions. I was down to whether Estrada followed the Giants or the A's, but instead he asked if we had heard the latest on the Cardwell, Heilbrun and Wilshire files. We said we hadn't.

"Turns out, they're gone," Estrada hooked a paper cup at the wastepaper basket. It hit the rim and bounced out.

"Gone?" Christy echoed. "The files in Heilbrun's law office? Not the originals? *The originals?* Don't tell me they've vanished too. Jesus Christ!"

"Sad to say, that seems to be the case." Thé had crept up on us again. The detectives watched our reactions while trying to conceal their own.

I said, "Don't tell me they broke in there too."

"I just did tell you," said Estrada. "But it's not quite like that. The story we get from Cardwell, Heilbrun and Wilshire is that Heilbrun signed out the originals and took them away. They might be the ones he had when he was killed."

I could see the tears swelling up in Christy's eyes. She said, "I can't believe that every scrap of paper that might have helped prove Dad was murdered has disappeared."

"It seems like an awfully big coincidence that somebody not only got the copies Christy had, but also the originals," I said. "And awfully fast work finding out on your part. I thought it was going to take some time to get the okay to even go through the law firm's confidential files."

"Normally. But we didn't want to wait until we had the subpoena," Thé said, brushing away the crumbs before resting her hip on the edge of the table, "Cardwell, Heilbrun didn't want to slow down the investigation into a name partner's murder either, so they agreed to get the papers together before we actually served them with a subpoena. It was one of their own that was killed. So they woke up Heilbrun's paralegal this morning to have her dig out anything to do with KPMT or the Paulsons, or for that matter your father, Miss Marshall."

"But when they got her on the phone," Estrada delivered the punch line, "she said she had already done it."

"When?"

"Yesterday afternoon."

"Heilbrun and the paralegal were in the office yesterday

working on another matter, even though it was Saturday—"

"Like rust," I said.

"Rust? What's rust got to do with it?"

"Oh. Sorry. Just like rust, shysters never sleep."

"Well, at least they work weekends," said Estrada. "Just like cops. Now to get back to *our* investigation.... Heilbrun got a call on his cell and then had the paralegal pull all the KPMT files. She says most of them were still on her desk from when she made copies for you, Christy."

"He took the originals?" Christy was twisting the life out of an empty soda can. For once I was glad we weren't holding hands. Thé and Estrada watched, probably thinking she had pretty good hand strength. But hey, she couldn't be the KPMT strangler—she was with me all the time. Without her, I wouldn't even have an alibi. She asked Estrada, "Why didn't she just copy them like she did for me?"

"It was late on a Saturday and they both wanted to get out of the office. Maybe Heilbrun planned to return with the papers or copy whatever was needed when he got to the radio station."

"Famous last words...oh, and I guess they were," Christy said.

"We figure Heilbrun was lured to the station by someone he trusted enough to bring these files to," said Thé. "But unless somebody else has copies and comes forward, we'll never know what was in them. And unless forensics comes up with a physical identification, like fingerprints or a DNA hit, we may never know who it was that disappeared the papers."

"Hey, how about this," I said. "I can't believe Pamela Kay Paulson and her taxman don't have copies of everything. Maybe a lot more than she'd trust Cardwell, Heilbrun and Wilshire with."

"No stone goes unheard. We called her this morning," said Inspector Thé. "She told us she would need to look around for the papers and would let us know if she found anything. As for letting us help her look, Mrs. Paulson said her lawyers advised her against it, unless we had a warrant."

"Cardwell, Heilbrun and Wilshire did?" I asked. "Or at least Cardwell and Wilshire? What about that losing one of their own stuff?"

"Maybe it's really about losing one of their own *clients*."

"How long will it take to get a warrant?" Christy asked.

"It's a little tricky," said Estrada. "We have to make a judge think that she may have evidence that would bear on

Heilbrun's murder. It helps if we can show that she's reluctant to cooperate or might have cause to destroy the evidence. She said she'd look around, so the judge might want to give her time to do just that."

Christy said, "I think the papers will show at the very least that she took unfair advantage of my mother after Dad's death. She might not want that to come out and that would cause her to destroy the evidence even if she's not connected with the murders."

"She could be building a bonfire right now," I said.

Janice Thé stood and stretched, her shirt riding up. A glimpse of mid-riff exposed a tiny pair of handcuffs tattooed in the vicinity of her navel. She shrugged and said, "There's no use crying over burnt milk. I'm pretty sure the crime scene techs will come up with something that will give us a break. If not...well, the perps have made two tries on Miss Marshall already so it stands to reason they may not be done trying."

"Wait a minute," I said, "I'm not going to stand here and let you use Christy for bait."

"Jan, I gotta agree," Estrada chimed in, "that doesn't seem like such a good strategy."

"Wait a second," Christy caught our attention, "I should have something to say about this. I'm willing to do whatever it takes if it'll help catch my father's killers."

Inspector Thé waved us all down, "Hold on, everybody. First of all, I'm not suggesting that we put Miss Marshall in any more danger than she is in right now. But we need to have someone watching over her in case an attempt is made again."

"Sure," I said, "that's what we need, police protection. Where do we sign up?"

"Well, there is one small problem," Thé said.

"Problem? What problem?"

"I don't have anyone available to provide protection for you right now. The captain needs to authorize the additional resources."

"Resources? What resources?"

"The peoplepower to keep Miss Marshall under surveillance. What detail they'll come out of, the overtime and so on. It's not cheap."

"So that's why there's never a cop around when you need one?"

"Don't sweat it. I'll have my initial report with a recommendation for protective surveillance on the captain's desk by eight hundred hours tomorrow."

"That's all right," Christy said. "Jerry's been doing okay so far. I feel safe with him."

She did? Her confidence gave me a lump in my throat. In spite of the lump on my head. Anyway, we were both still breathing. That's gotta count for something.

"Sure, I'll protect her," I said. "Just get somebody to protect me."

"First thing, Monday morning," Thé repeated.

"Sure, eight hundred hours. That's only about sixteen hundred hours from now. It sounds like ages."

Inspector Thé said, "The best thing for Miss Marshall might be to return home to Tucson. She should be safe there."

"The Tucson PD has been notified about the attempt on your life," Estrada said. "They're going to keep an eye on your mother's place, just in case."

"But we do think Tucson would be safer than San Francisco right now," Thé added.

"No, I'm not going home," Christy said. "I'm not going to let them run me off."

"You're sure about that?" Thé asked. "We can contact you there when we have any new developments."

"I'm not leaving until I find out who killed my father. I'll be okay. Jerry will watch out for me."

For some reason everyone looked my way.

I wasn't about to jump on any bandwagon that might take Christy out of town, especially since she was staying at my place now. I didn't think I'd be on the sofa-bed forever, particularly if I could unravel the mystery of her dad's death. And I thought I knew how.

After a beat or two, Thé said, "Okay, it's your decision. Until we can arrange for police protection, Jerry, I want you to stick close to Miss Marshall."

"Like a second skin," I said.

"Good," Tommy Estrada said, looking a little dubious. "You may not be much help in a gunfight, but it's possible they won't want to put a cap in you if they're not invoicing for it."

"That's good, I hate dealing with amateurs."

Around then, Janice Thé decided to change the subject. Just as well, I didn't like thinking about anybody "putting a cap" in Christy, or for that matter, me.

Thé was saying, "Here is what I see us doing: we set up a police decoy, a good looking undercover cop who can pass for Miss Marshall, a blonde or someone in a blonde wig. She'll check back into the Hyatt Regency as Christy Marshall. A few phone calls to get the word out maybe. Maybe Jerry has Christy on the radio program, then Christy slips out the back, dark glasses, dark wig, and the decoy goes back to the Hyatt. Something like that, I think. If the perps believe she's back at the hotel, they may pay her another visit."

"And then we'll nail 'em," Estrada added. Like maybe it wasn't clear?

"So the missing papers are yesterday's news, so to speak?" I asked, thinking about Pamela Kay and our upcoming appointment. It was time to pitch.

I went into the windup, "I'm no professional, but I guess it doesn't take a Sherlock Holmes to figure out that a person or persons unknown don't want something in the papers made public, and that person or persons is or are the perp or perps behind the Heilbrun killing and—the odds being what they are—also the death of Christy's dad."

"Better than even money I'd say you're right," Thé said. "However, Problem 'A' is making sure that nothing happens to Miss Marshall and you. We've been over that and the decoy may lead to a break. So that makes the papers Problem 'B'. Not that we aren't going to serve a search warrant on Mrs. Paulson—if we can get a judge to sign off. Problem 'C' is the fact that the papers may have been destroyed by now, and if not destroyed, we may not get our hands on them anytime soon if they can get the warrant quashed. We need to face that fact."

I had my own ideas about that though. Unless Madame Zoroaster really could channel Leland Heilbrun, I needed the papers to bust things open on my séance show. Even if she did channel Heilbrun, being a lawyer he'd probably plead the fifth anyway.

Chapter 23.

I WASN'T sure what we would be in for at Pamela Kay's, but I had the feeling that some of the people there might be less than enthused with the biggest media play Big Talk Radio ever got a piece of, let alone our having our very own dead body. After Christy and I left the Hall of Justice, we checked our messages, agreed to leave the Beamer's top up, and decided to wait to eat until we got to Mrs. P.'s. I figured Ricardo would have laid out some kind of spread, it being a near-wake.

There was a message from Kinta White and several from Jeanne. Hers ran the gamut from desperate to pissed to threatening. The good thing was she seemed to be focused on business, not romance. Come to think of it, she didn't even mention the flowers. I decided to call Kinta back first.

"Dude, we've just about worn through the acetate on last night's tapes," Kinta said, coming on the line.

"I thought we were digital now, that you put it in the computer somehow."

"We do. It's just a saying, Jerry. But listen, Brad and the rest of the crew have chopped those tapes into hamburger. We need some new stuff, the public wants fresh blood—and it might be yours."

"I think I've got it covered," I said. "I'll drop by the station on my way to Mrs. Paulson's place. I should be there in ten. Is Marsha still trying to take over the coverage?"

"No, man, we caught a break. She's out the way for now, up in Marin with Ned, but they could be getting the okay from the old lady to kick your sorry ass off the story."

"Don't sweat it, Kinta, no way that can happen. I've got this story all but wrapped up."

"You telling me you know who the killer is?"

"Well, no. I don't know that, not yet anyway."

"The police close to cracking it?"

"Well, not that either. But look, I'm on my way to there now with Christy Marshall and—keep this under your hat—I'm going to get something there that'll break this thing wide open. Film at eleven."

"But what can I air now? We don't want to lose our momentum to another station—after all, the guy was killed right here."

"Listen, kiddo, here's the deal—we just spent most of this afternoon with the cops and I had my pocket recorder running all the time."

I cut across Market into North Beach and double-parked by the station by the time I finished talking to Kinta. I dropped off the tape and got a refill from Brad. I also dropped off instructions not to air the part about the undercover decoy. I didn't think Thé and Estrada wouldn't mind their interview being turned into cop suey for air play, but I told Kinta he ought to make them look good. After all, I was counting on them to protect me and Christy from a gang of cut-throats.

I had left Christy in the Beamer so time was tight but I managed to record a couple of promos at light speed, telling listeners that I was the inside dope with the inside dope. "Try to run these as often as they'll let you," I told Kinta.

He said not to sweat it, by air time Monday people would be sick of hearing me. "Those eighteen minutes out of thirty we use for talk will be down to maybe ten by the time I'm done."

Kinta was doing a happy dance; it could be I wasn't the only one counting on this making his career. Jeez—careers! I'd almost forgotten Jeanne. While Christy waited in the car I made a quick call.

Jeanne picked up before I finished dialing. "It's about time you fucking called. I've been trying to get you since last night."

"Oh, hey Jeanne, how about those flowers, eh?"

"What flowers?"

"The ones I sent—"

"Never mind that now, you low-life," she said, very intent on something. "I promised the producers of *Bay Area Breakfast* that I'd have you on tomorrow morning's show for an interview."

"Well, you know there's a lot of demand—"

"Don't you dare screw me on this, you redheaded motherfuck—"

"It's not me. I need to clear—"

"You never cleared shit before, and don't say it's too early in the morning...and we're not sending a car!"

"Whaddayamean, no car?"

"We're on at seven-oh-five. Be early if you want make-up. They'll do the news report on the murder, then cut to us doing the interview—"

"You're doing the interview, not Tim Blanchard?"

"Sorry, it's a no-host affair. And speaking of affairs, if I'm good enough for you to shag, I'm good enough to do the fucking interview. And I didn't have to suck anybody's cock to get the interview, if that's what you're thinking. Nobody but yours that is, so you had better be here by seven."

I'm no Doctor Phil, but I didn't think breaking up was going to be all that hard after all.

GUEST parking was pretty tight by the time we got to Pamela Kay's. There weren't this many cars at the office Christmas party. As it was, I found a spot on the lawn not too far from the main house. For what Mrs. P paid the landscapers, I was sure a trim and a blowout in the morning would put the grass right again.

We strolled up to entrance and before I could finger the bell, Ricardo swung open the door. He was in perfect form, remembering Christy from years ago and was particularly solicitous to her—*"Miss Marshall, this! Miss Marshall, that!"* And he only stumbled a few times getting my name right. I'm sure Pammykins pays Ricardo to do that so the talent will know where they stand in the scheme of things. Finally he figured out who I was and told us everyone had been waiting for me. Murder brings out the best in some people.

Ricardo led us through a few miles of hallway into what he called the great room. It was definitely great, about the size of a basketball court. The sound system sounded like a million bucks, but why not? My voice was coming out.

"...killer has struck down one of KPMT's own. Now it's Big Talk Radio's turn to strike back! This is Jerry Jeremy and I personally will be presenting the facts behind the facts, the truth behind the truth and the lies behind the truth and the facts behind the lies and...well, you get the idea—"

"Please, no applause...." I said, getting the room's attention. Everybody watched us walk over to them. Our hostess and her earlier arrivals were grouped in front of a sixty-inch TV screen located just past the baby grand. Another sixty-incher was playing in a giant alcove by the fireplace. Both TVs were tuned to cable news but with the sound muted. The KPMT signal filled the room; the cable anchor-people's lips were moving, but my voice was coming out. It was like an electronic ventriloquist trick, only this time I wasn't the dummy. At least I hoped not.

Pamela Kay shared a white leather sofa with her nephew while Ned and Marsha Chung faced them across a massive chunk of glass that passed for a coffee table. My favorite sponsor, Charlie Wooten, and Dennis Hong, the news director, were in squishy suede chairs pulled up on either side. Charlie was probably worrying about his advertising rates going up as an unintended consequence of the rating spike. Dennis on the other hand was probably thinking Heilbrun's murder was news and therefore was his baby, him being the news director and all. And finally behind door number three, we had Jason Giles. He looked slightly uncomfortable, perched on a side chair that was more ornament than ottoman. Jason was the producer on Freddy and Betty's morning show. Around Studio B he was known as Jason the Rat-boy.

My guess was Pammykins didn't bring all these folks here just to make me the new morning drive guy. They were as guilty a looking bunch as I had ever seen. The question was what were they guilty of?

If they were talking about Christy or me, maybe it was only good manners to stop before we actually sat down with them. It took Pamela Kay a beat or two to remember that she called this meeting and to find her welcome mat. Then it was all hugs and air-kisses and telling Christy that she looked all grown up now. My, how time flies.

Anyway I put on my best smile as Mrs. P leaned close to me. I was braced for another round of air-kissing, but instead her breathy whisper said we needed to talk about "you know what." I didn't know what exactly, but figured I would soon enough.

Meanwhile, Christy was being welcomed by the Big Talk crowd and introducing herself around. Charlie jumped up and brought her over to take his seat at the table. Somehow I wound up in a chair that seemed to be made out of deer antlers. Fortunately it was a few points shy of making me a soprano.

"Glad to see you could make it," Ned gave me the kind of smile an insurance salesman gives a newlywed and I returned it in kind. He said, "We were just listening to the sound you got at the cop shop today. I can't believe how open they were on the record. It was on the record, wasn't it?"

"Uh, well, they never said anything about it being off the record, if that's what you mean. I know it's hard to believe," I showed off my pearly whites again, "but in radio hearing *is* believing, isn't it?"

"They probably didn't even realize what they were telling us," said Christy, giving me a look. "But I'm sure they'll have more to say to Jerry later."

"Really great stuff," Dennis Hong said just like I was one of the team. He gave me a smile too. "At this rate you'll have Marsha looking over her shoulder."

"Thanks, but I've already got a show." I looked Ned's way and asked, "I do still have a show, haven't I?"

"You're the man of the hour," Ned said, avoiding a direct answer. "We just were talking about how to take advantage of your inside position on this whole thing." Ned turned to Christy and added, "Of course, we also want to be sensitive to your position also."

"My position is that I'll do anything to find the people who killed my dad. So far, Jerry is the only one who has taken this seriously." She scanned the group trying to pick out a friendly face. "I'll do whatever Jerry thinks will help solve these murders."

"If it's really true," Tony Paulson chirped up.

"Of course it's true, dear," Pamela Kay stepped in, "Tom Marshall was more than my business partner—he was my very close friend. As Christy knows." Pamela Kay paused for affect, eyes down, then back up at Christy. Her voice cracked as she said, "I didn't take your belief that he was murdered seriously, but obviously that was a mistake that cost another close friend his life also." Pammykins used her cocktail napkin to dab at her eyes.

Between Dennis Hong's crocodile smile and Pamela Kay's crocodile tears, we might as well have been in a Louisiana bayou. The only difference being that the bayou was safer.

"Very well said, Pamela Kay." Jason Giles, the morning drive's head rat, put down his chardonnay and continued, "I'd like to get those police tapes on tomorrow morning's show. We could even cut in some of Jerry's original airchecks from the murder scene. Come to think of it, Freddy and Betty could even interview you, Pamela Kay. You know, the bereaved friend of the victim. And, well...of course," Rat-boy looked to Hong for support, "Marsha can use a few sound bites as breaking news."

Hearing her name, Marsha Chung decided to fan the flames, "You'll need to break Kinta White's arm to get the new tapes from him. He seems to think he's running the station now."

I said, "Remember, Marsha, possession is nine-tenths of the law and the victim was a lawyer."

"What's the law got to do with this? I'm talking about murder."

"Maybe you'll get to experience it first hand sometime soon."

"Whoa, everybody hold your horses." Ned, being the closest thing we had to a referee, held up his hands and signaled for a clean break. "Let's not have a wipeout here when we can all be riding the crest."

My pal Charlie, one of KPMT's biggest advertisers, threw in with me, saying, "Jerry's been doing a great job on this; it's really his story." Ah, money talks—at last.

And then he reversed field, "But no getting around the fact that the audience for the morning drive is a lot larger. We need to make the most of this God-given opportunity. Pardon the phraseology, God-given from a business perspective...."

Rat number two, this one jumping ship. My ship.

"From that perspective, I've got to say you're right, Charlie," Tony said, having never even been on my ship.

"Okay, okay, I'm a team player," I said, "I'll tell Brad and Kinta to hand over the tapes." I didn't really care if the morning drive's gruesome twosome brought in a few advertising shekels using my stuff. I still had Madame Zoroaster, the psychic disaster, in my back pocket. No, make that Madame Zoroaster, the psychic detective now. The psychic detective versus the KPMT strangler—what a match-up! "I'm such a great guy I'll even let Freddy and Betty interview me."

"I can do the interview on the news segment," said Marsha, deciding to be my new best friend.

"Sorry, Marsh, but it really needs to be a host to host broadcast," I hated to break that cold, bitter heart of hers. "Also, we'll need to schedule around my interview at seven tomorrow. KCTY TV, *Bay Area Breakfast*. I'll even put in a plug for Freddy, but Betty's been very distant lately."

Jason Giles, F & B's producer, finally started thinking like a producer. He said, "We'll do it maybe in the six o'clock hour and replay it on the later segments."

"That's a little early for me, but maybe someday soon...anyway I'll need my beauty rest tomorrow for the TV. Maybe I can call in," I said, "but I need something in return. I need to have complete control of my show this week. With Kinta and Brad, of course."

"Tell us what you want, Jerry," Ned said.

"It's really simple. I plan to cover the murders of Tom Marshall and Leland Heilbrun on my show. I will show them from a personal perspective using Christy's experiences and mine."

"Well, I thought that was the point," Charlie said.

"I can work the news to fit in with that," Dennis Hong said. "It really should almost be a magazine format, maybe Marsha—or even me—anchoring. News will support you fully, Jerry."

"But I really think we should leave anchoring to the air talent," Marsha said, kicking her boyfriend to the broadcast curb.

"But exactly, Dennis, Marsha, Jerry," Pamela Kay took command. "It's a given that this is a news story." She looked my way and her eyes tightened their grip on my throat. "Now tell us please, Jerry, what is it you are really planning to do."

"It's simple really. I'm planning to expose the killer or killers on my Friday night show."

"My God, that's great," said Charlie.

"What the hell—" Tony said, cheering me on.

"No fucking way!" Marsha Chung, star reporter, gasped.

"Jerry, you mean you know who it is?" Christy turned to me.

"No, not yet, sweetheart, but I will by the end of the week."

"Is that a police deadline?" Mrs. P asked while Ricardo tried to blot up the vodka she'd splashed over her cleavage. I said, "Let's just say the cops will be there. Somebody needs to bring the handcuffs."

"So the cops are just along for the ride?" Tony asked. "You're going to crack this case all on your own? In time for the Friday show?"

"You sound like you don't think I can do it." Not that he wouldn't want me to. "And I thought you'd be delighted to tie in all that advertising and promotion. This could make Big Talk one of the Big Boys."

Marsha said, "Not to mention making yourself one of the big boys too."

I was searching for a comeback when Ned, ever the

peacemaker, not to mention still our boss, waved us down again. "Let's get back to the basics. Jerry, please tell us how in the hell you are going to find the bad guys by four o'clock Friday afternoon."

"Ah, that's the beauty part, Ned—I don't have to. I'm just going to put everything in motion. You remember how in all those old detective movies William Powell gets everybody with a speaking part together for the unmasking, even if he doesn't actually know who actually done it? Well, that's kind of what I had in mind."

Marsha asked "Who's William Powell?" but I let that slide because Charlie was asking, "You think somebody will just up and confess if we roundup all the usual suspects?"

"Or will they just turn out the lights and pull a gun like in 'The Thin Man'?" Tony said.

"Neither one because I'll have a witness."

"A witness? What witness?"

"The best witness. The murdered man."

"WHAT the holy hell are you getting into now, Jerry?" Mrs. P gave me a look hot enough to singe the red off my head. Fortunately her private office was air conditioned to the point I could almost see my breath. "Stop jittering around, Jerry. Sit down and tell me what's going on."

She had pulled me free of the feeding frenzy my announcement had caused before I had really had the chance to bring the sharks on board. My guess was she didn't want Tony's clairvoyant ties to become office gossip.

"I want to talk with you about that thing I told you I wanted to talk to you about," was what she'd said before about-facing and dragging me down the hallway. We hadn't gotten too far, before she turned back having suddenly remembered her manners.

"We'll be back in a minute. Does everyone have a drink?" If anyone didn't, they weren't volunteering the information. They wouldn't dare. "Ricardo," she commanded, "make sure everyone's okay."

I had the feeling everyone would be okay but me.

I trailed behind Pamela Kay as she steamed out of the great room and down a merely marvelous hall. Her office was great too, but was only about the size of my apartment. Soft colors, plush chairs, and tucked in a clearing, a thick slab of glass that was used as a desk. Opposite a room-sized view of the Pacific, she had a wall of teak-faced file cabinets. I was thinking that an awful lot of papers could be kept here.

Meanwhile Pamela Kay was saying, "You swore to me that you were going to get rid of that crooked gypsy, but now it seems you've got the station's reputation staked on her and her shenanigans. You and I better still be on the same page here, because if you fuck KPMT, KPMT will definitely fuck you, mister."

"Same page, Pamela Kay? We're working on a whole book here," I said, trotting out a rakish smile. "My numbers are gonna go through the roof this week. It wouldn't surprise me if I was number one in my timeslot. By this time next week, we'll be the most famous talk radio station in the country. Already the cable news shows are all over us."

"They're all over us because Leland Heilbrun had the good sense to get himself killed at our place. The only reason you're even in the picture is that you were lucky enough to trip over the body."

"Sometimes you need to make your own luck."

"I hope you're not planning on somebody else getting bumped off. It's not like it's something you can count ever on happening a second time should your career takes a nosedive. And in my book, you're on the high board already. Stumbling over dead people—murders anyway—is not that common."

"I don't want to stumble anymore, Pamela Kay, not over dead bodies—"

"You and I had an understanding, a meeting of the minds—"

"Sure, Pamela Kay—"

"—unless I was totally mistaken, you were going to do something for me."

"Sure, Pamela Kay, I'd do anything for you." I was hoping it didn't involve mistletoe.

"You were going to find out what the hell that fucking fortune teller had on Tony. Then we—you and I—were going to run her and her boyfriend off. Didn't you say you had a gun?"

"Uh...no, no. I always try to back the NRA, but I don't actually have a gun myself. But about the show," I hoped to get back on track and maybe not get fired for it, "if I can play this out, Madame Zoroaster will get busted. She'll be out of Tony's hair, and if things go right, we'll shake something about the murder loose by setting up a phony séance bringing Heilbrun back for an encore performance. We'll say he's gonna name his killer. With the right promotion, the audience will go wild and our share will be huge."

"Listen, Jerry, these bastards are blackmailing my nephew. I don't want to tune in to hear one bit of Tony's dirty laundry being aired. Just remember you're right at the edge of that high board and about to take a triple gainer off it. And the fucking pool may just be empty this time."

"*No problema*, besides I forgot to bring my swimsuit anyway. Don't worry, Tony's laundry will be so white you'll think I took him to the cleaners." I didn't want to mention that his real dirty laundry might just be that he has a thing for women who were old and weird. After all, I couldn't recall ever seeing him chase any of the distaff staff around the office. But maybe he just didn't want to break any of those new laws my listeners always are complaining about.

I told Pamela Kay, "Here's how I see it playing out—it was Heilbrun that arranged to hand over fifty-eight big ones to Madame Z as a settlement. Even if it was your money, Heilbrun probably wouldn't like everybody knowing he got ripped off. Imagine how he'd have to feel having to face up to you—nothing personal—after getting burned for almost sixty grand."

"So he screwed up," she said. "Why would they kill Leland *after* he paid them off?"

"Don't you get it, PK?" In spite the AC working overtime, enough sweat was running down my back to float my kidneys. Or am I mixing metaphors? Anyway, I was saying, "That's the connection. When we nail them on the diamond bracelet scam, and the cops pop out to put the cuffs on them, they'll fold like a cheap suit."

"So they killed Leland? Over the scam they pulled? Did he even know it was a scam? He never told me as much." She shook her head. "What's that got to do with the Marshall girl and her father's death? And the partnership papers? How do they fit in?"

"I think Heilbrun must have figured it out and he thought he could scare Madame Z and her pal off himself. Instead, they, or more likely, some hired thugs wound up killing him. I think the legal papers might be a 'red herring.' That's when—"

"I know what a goddamn' red herring is."

"So probably Leland thought he could get Madame Z out of Tony's hair somehow," I said. "Maybe because he tumbled to the diamond bracelet con and threatened to call in the D.A."

"Okay," Pamela Kay leaned across her desk, "let's say you're right. Leland overplayed his hand and they killed him."

She smirked in triumph and said, "Why?"

"Why?"

"Yes, why?"

"Why what?"

"What do you mean why what?"

"Why did you say why?" Next thing you know we'd be doing "who's on first".

"I want to know why they would kill Leland over this. Why not just cut their losses and move on?"

"Because he had something else on them. I think he was trying to find out what they were doing with Tony and he found out something that scared them enough to have him murdered."

"And what happens if this something else does involve my nephew. I raised him like he was my own child. I would kill anyone who really hurt Tony—and that, my darling Jerry, can be worse than getting fired."

"For some people maybe. Listen, Pamela Kay, I'll find out what Madame Zoroaster's got on Tony before the séance. Honest, you can count on me. I'll make sure he's in the clear when this comes down. Trust me."

She looked at me and gave a laugh that sounded more like a snort and then said, "All right, I'll trust you because we need to make something of this murder and because I'm confident you're smart enough not to get on my bad side."

While the boss-lady was wrapping up the beatdown, I thought I heard distance chimes, possibly from a nearby cathedral. Pamela Kay had barely finished threatening me when Ricardo popped in to say Inspectors Thé and Estrada were cooling their heels in the library.

I gave Mrs. P a goodbye smile and started for the door. Before I made it though she called me back.

"One thing I don't understand, Jerry. The way you explain it, there's something I don't understand. What in hell do Tom Marshall and his daughter have to do with all this?"

I said, "Absolutely nothing."

Chapter 24.

It would be great to have all that swell private eye stuff you see on TV, like telephone taps and hidden cameras. Brad the Brat could probably do that kind of thing, but he'd had a long night wrapping up the murder broadcast. And sneaking him into the Paulson mansion might not be easy; Ricardo ran a pretty tight ship.

Still it would been great to hear the cops question Pamela Kay. Listening through an empty glass against the library door might work, but there weren't many empties around this place. Besides, I knew what the cops would be trying to pry out of her. Anything they could to track down those elusive papers. I also knew if the papers were still here where they would be.

Nguyen and Estrada hadn't shown up earlier because they'd had to wait for a judge to finish the back nine before signing off on the search warrant. If I was going to get a look at the papers, I needed to do it now.

Nonetheless I headed back to the great room and the KPMT hatchet squad. I wanted to set up my alibi in case Pamela Kay returned and I wasn't in there defending my turf. For the second time in less than an hour, the conversation stopped when I entered the room. This time even Christy stopped. The only difference being that Christy looked happy to see me; the rest stared at me like I was a pitbull at a cat show.

"Don't let me stop you. Just pretend I'm not here," I said. I noticed that Marsha was absent and wondered if she knew that water glass trick. "My ears are burning, but that's okay as long as my contract isn't."

Even Ned looked a little off-balance. Not ideal for a surfer. "It's nothing like that, Jerry," he said. "Christy here can tell you, the only plot being hatched is for tomorrow's Freddy and Betty show."

"You should be happy," Dennis Hong chirped up, "because you're going to be all over it."

"Don't forget I'm on TV in the morning."

"That's okay, man," Jason Giles said, "we plan on editing those tapes from last night like you were there being interviewed by Freddy and Betty. We'll script questions for them to match sound-bites from the tapes."

"Sure, cut me to ribbons. I'll be a virtual Jerry."

I leaned over to whisper a few words in Christy's shell-like and then told the gang to carry on while I went in search of a bathroom. Everybody jumped to say that Marsha had dibs on the one just off the great room—the crab hors d'oeuvres, I think it was—so I'd have to find my own. Just as well, since I didn't need a bathroom.

A trail of bread crumbs back to Pamela Kay's office would have been a big help. Next time I'd remember to grab a cracker or two off the spread back in the great room. I didn't know who else might be wandering the halls either. Ricardo might be dusting the rugs or something. If I ran into him, I'd use the line about looking for a bathroom. The problem being that he might just know where to find one.

If Ricardo happened to find me going Pammykin's drawers, he might not fall for the bathroom gag though. Ignoring that possibility, I found my way to the office. The door was open and the room was empty; Pamela Kay must still be trying to get Estrada under the mistletoe.

Just in case I did a quick look around to make sure some new corpse hadn't found its way here. As I checked out the filing cabinets, none of them seemed to be locked. Like they say an open drawer is an invitation. Or is that door? Anyway, I started rummaging through Mrs. P's private files.

About five minutes into my search I heard voices coming from the hallway. What's more they were headed in my direction. While Pamela Kay and the detectives entered from the hall, I was going out the door on the opposite wall. As it turned out, that door led to that bathroom I had been looking for.

I stood there in the dark, holding my breath. I had left the door slightly ajar, all the better to hear them by. And I did want to hear them. I thought about pulling out my little tape recorder, but passed on the idea. Getting caught taping Mrs. P, I might get fired; caught taping the cops, I might get fired on. Also, I was pretty sure nobody at KPMT would air Mrs. Paulson getting the third degree either. Not unless they wanted to join me in the unemployment line.

Through the crack I could hear them discussing KPMT's partnership arrangements. Pamela Kay apparently had known about Marshall's plan to sell off his share. She even said she knew which buyers he had lined up. Even so, Estrada sounded bored and Thé tired while they tried to think up new questions. In the end, they dragged all the facts of the buy-out from Pamela Kay.

Pamela Kay also let the detectives know that while their search warrant looked very impressive and all, she wasn't sure if it would stand up in court since she wasn't able to have her lawyer read it over. Obviously.

This seemed to make Janice Thé a little irritable, what with having been up for about thirty-six hours straight. She patiently explained they'd be glad to get Pamela Kay a court-appointed lawyer after they read her her rights and arrested her for obstructing justice. Coffee nerves, I guess.

In that case, Mrs. P said, they could damn well help themselves, the files were not locked. And while they were examining her privates, she'd go take a tinkle and hopefully that would still be private.

Uh-oh. Maybe not so private.

Pammykins stormed in like the dam was gonna bust. Either she was really pissed or really had to. Heels clicked across the tile and water started running in the marble basin. Thank god for the running water, I didn't want to hear anything else.

A quiet whoosh, some splashing in the sink and a burst of silence while she dried her hands, refreshed her makeup, and for all I knew, curled her hair, before I heard her heels clicking their way on out. I could hear Pamela Kay talking to Thé and Estrada, so the door to the office must have been left open.

That being the case, I was stuck in my hidey hole until they left in the office. And if they didn't get a move on soon, I'd be paying for my chiropractor's next vacation. As it was, I could pick up just about every other word from the office:

"...didn't find any...we expected...."

"...I told you Leland...kept them at his office....'

"...these files look...gone through already...."

"...nobody but me...."

Yeah, yeah, yeah. Blah, blah, blah.

Just when I thought they'd never stop, their voices began to fade away. They must have headed into the hallway and after a minute or two all I heard was silence. Carefully and quietly, I unwrapped myself from the plumbing and crawled out from under the double vanity. I had developed a new respect for plumbers and their cracks—er, backs.

The office lights were turned off but the wall-to-wall glass let in enough natural light that I could see fine. It didn't look like Thé and Estrada had done much of a search. No overturned tables or upended file drawers, no documents scattered all over the floor. The file cabinets were all tightly closed and each chair neatly lined up. The big glass desk gleamed in the late afternoon sun.

If I had my junior detective kit with me I could have dusted for prints, but the room was spotless. I could have taken out my magnifying glass to look for clues or tossed the place one more time for the missing files. But why bother? There were no secrets here anymore.

Chapter 25.

SUNDAY night at the Blue Sphinx is just right. Not crowded like on Saturday date nights or full of wild and desperate singles hoping to score on Fridays. The Sphinx is closed on Mondays and there's not a show on Tuesdays or Wednesdays. But on Thursdays everybody including The Great Rondini starts warming up for the weekend and on Friday and Saturday nights Ronnie Green earns his keep.

Sunday for most people means family or friends, hotdogs and beer, movies with the kids, or just doing whatever one does to get ready for the Monday to Friday grind again. So Sundays at the Blue Sphinx Rondini hands out the slight of hand to magic buffs and fellow conjurers who happen to be in town. And on this Sunday at least one person was there because she feared for her life.

The seven o'clock show was about half over when Christy and I got there. Ronnie had his head wrapped up like he was auditioning for *The Return of the Mummy*, his eyes covered over by several layers of cloth, while his assistant tiptoed through the audience.

Satyra took various personal items from people in the audience and held them up for all to see. Except The Great One of course, who had his head wrapped like a he'd sprained a memory bank. Even blindfolded though, The Great One could not only identify each item, but could also link them to some factoid only their owner could know. He was working hard to get a few laughs out of the set-ups and the crowd showed their appreciation. Applause greeted every correct answer, as well as a good deal hooting and whistling. Actually I think Satyra's tiny costume got most of the hooting and whistling.

I spotted Rhonda Ridgeway sitting at a small table close to the stage so Ronnie could keep an eye on her, blindfolded or not. Christy and I maneuvered through the audience and managed to squeeze in beside Rhonda. Since we'd created a big enough distraction settling in, we didn't spend a lot of time on greetings or introductions; we just traded encouraging smiles like guests at a funeral. And we used a lot of whispering and hand signals to order drinks which made more commotion than just talking out loud. I couldn't wait to see what we'd wind up getting.

All good things must come to an end and at last Rondini reached his finale, the one where the chain saw rips Satyra to pieces and the pieces are set on fire with a blowtorch. Once she's nicely *flambéed*, The Great Rondini pulls a fire extinguisher out of his sleeve and envelops the stage in a blue fog. When the fog dissipates, so has Satyra. I'd try it on my show but I didn't want to be the one ripped to pieces. Besides it might not play as good on radio.

After a few too many bows and an encore or two, Ronnie and Satyra joined us at our little ringside table. The best trick of the evening was trying to fit everybody in. Rhonda Ridgeway curled herself boa constrictor style around Ronnie. Satyra, a dressing gown covering her costume, wedged in next to me, cheek to cheek so to speak.

I introduced Christy around though the Ridgeway babe seemed to be monopolizing Ronnie's attention. We were still waiting on one of our players, so we small talked our way through a round of drinks. Nothing too heavy, just stuff like who thought the mayor's rug was too obvious and why the weather was so predictable.

"TV and radio weather reports—who the hell even needs 'em?" Satyra was saying. "It's always 'morning fog burning off by noon.'" Satyra circled her hand signaling for more drinks.

"Hey now," I said, "you're messing with my fallback position in case this séance gag doesn't work. Next thing you'll be saying 'Big Talk' should go to a music format."

Ronnie said, "Don't sweat it, Jerry. Even the music stations do the weather. You know, 'everybody talks about the weather, but nobody does anything to stop the conversation.'" Rhonda Ridgeway giggled up a storm at this.

While Rhonda regained her composure our round of drinks showed up and so did Alain de la Cruz. If we could fit him in, we'd have a quorum. The séance was less than a week away and everyone needed to know what was expected of them. Time was short so I couldn't wait to hear Rondini lay out the plan that would nail the bad guys, make me the hero and get me the girl.

"THAT'S it?" I gasped. "That's your friggin' plan?"

"Sure, what did you expect—a disappearing elephant?"

I suspected The Great One had been having too great a time with Rhonda Ridgeway to do his homework. Next, he'd say the disappearing elephant ate it.

The long and short of Ronnie's plan was that we'd get all the suspects in one room and flush out the killer like in some old *Thin Man* movie. I never thought what I had told the gang at Pamela Kay's would actually be the plan.

Anyway, we had to get our ducks in a row and Ronnie being the head quack started out by questioning how Rhonda was drafted to play Mrs. Rubenstein in the original production. Apparently a show she was in had just closed. "It was a Hawaiian take on *The Trojan Women*. There was an all-girl Greek chorus. We wore bikinis." Cruize was in it too. No bikini, his was a grass skirt.

"Yeah, that's the one," Rhonda was saying. "I understudied the second lead. So after it closed, this girl in my acting class tipped me to a job as a 'never met' in this hypnotist's act...."

"What's a 'never met'?" Christy asked.

"Someone you never met. Like the person from the audience who the hypnotist—or it could be a magician—" she gave Rondini a smile, "but anyway the hypnotist or magician always asks if you've ever met them before and you say you've 'never met'."

"Even if they've been married twenty years."

"That's show biz," I said.

"Well," Ronnie said, "the magic biz anyway."

"Not at all," Rhonda said, "I like to think of it as acting."

The kid was bound to go far. If somebody didn't club her to death first.

"Did it work?" Satyra asked. The question stopped us cold. Then she said, "The hypnosis. Did it actually work on you or were you just acting?"

"Let's just say I could do the act in my sleep."

"Why don't we get back to your séance story," I said checking my watch. "We only have five days until show time."

"Sure, dearie. Ronnie can put me in a trance later. To get back to my story, I began to get a lot of these jobs. At some point word must have gotten around and I got a call from this guy Vigo, Madame Zoroaster's manager or something, I'm not sure what. You ever notice how much he sounds like Peter Lorre? I thought it was a put-on at first."

"Did he happen to mention what the gig was all about?" Ronnie gazed into her lipid pools of blue. Pretty shallow pools at that, no chance of drowning.

"Well, he didn't say at first. The Peter Lorre guy said he was just lining up the players and asked if I knew anyone to be the husband."

So Rhonda brought de la Cruz into the picture, having just worked with him. Urged on by her new heartthrob, she gave us the rundown on the whole set up as far as she knew it. Ronnie nagged all the details out of her and she took the nagging in stride. Anyway, Ronnie finally got her to circle in on Madame Z's role in the scam. That's when Rhonda started throwing monkey wrenches—

She said, "Truth be told, I really never did meet with Madame Zoroaster. Everything was done through Vigo, you know, the Peter Lorre guy. We met with him twice."

The Great Inquisitor needed a big slug of margarita about this time.

"You say you never actually met Madame Zoroaster before the séance?" Christy took up the chase.

"Not before, during or after; I wouldn't recognize her if she walked in and sat down on his face." Thank God she nodded in Cruize's direction.

"You never met her," I echoed.

"Like I say, Peter Lorre set everything up," Rhonda signaled for a refill. "He told us what the premise was and gave us an outline of what we should say."

"It was improv, so Rhonda and I just ad libbed the dialog," Cruize said. "We ran through it once or twice with the little guy, and then—show time!"

"But did Vigo—Peter Lorre—tell you what Madame Z was going to say?" I asked.

"Not really," Cruize answered. "Just in general terms what her routine would be and that we should just play along. I really didn't even have a line until I worked some business out with Rhonda."

"So the clairvoyant on the radio—Madame Zoroaster— might not even have known this was a put up job?" Christy said.

"Well, I can't say about her," said Rhonda. "Peter Lorre said he worked with her, but maybe not."

"Oh, he's with her all right," I said. "She had to have known it was a set-up."

"Of course she did," Ronnie added. "It's what they all do. Plausible deniability—probably picked it up from Dick Cheney. She wanted to keep you from being able to point the finger at her at some later time."

"Like now."

"Go ahead, you guys, give her the finger," Satyra said.

"Point the finger," Ronnie corrected, but she was too busy stacking her empties on the next table to pay attention.

"Well, at least you can tie Vigo Lorre, I mean Peter Vigo, that is—Czak, to the scam," I fumbled. "You can say he set things up and we can show he's Madame Z's main squeeze." I shuttered at that thought as soon as the words left my mouth.

"Maybe the other guy could help," Rhonda said.

"Other guy? What other guy?" Ronnie did a triple-take. We all did, except for Cruize who was there and already knew. "You never mentioned another guy."

"I don't know his name but he seemed to be the boss. Peter Lorre kept checking with him that we were doing it right, doing what the other guy wanted. Like a director whose afraid of the producer. I'd say the other guy was the producer."

"Do you know who he was?" I asked.

Rhonda looked at me and said, "No, not really. We were never formally introduced. On purpose I think."

"Cruize, do you know?"

"Not really, but you probably do."

"Me?"

"Yeah," Cruize said, "after all, he works at KPMT."

Chapter 26.

"WHAT? Vigo and somebody at KPMT?" My head was spinning. "You mean back before the séance broadcast? Vigo Czak had somebody at the station—my station—connected with him?"

"Yeah, Czak said he was from KPMT," Cruize said. "At first I thought maybe he was you, since we were booked for your show."

"Sure, I might have thought that too," said Rhonda. "He was a good-looking, young guy, very metro, which probably means he's very gay. I remember Vigo calling him Tony."

What the fuck.

"*What the fuck!*" Christy jumped in. "Does this mean that Tony-fucking-Paulson was involved in this freak show from the fucking get-go?"

I'd have to make sure Brad the Brat was riding the dump button on Friday's show.

Meanwhile, Christy aimed a few more f-bombs at the Paulson family and KPMT and life in general before she calmed down, but I could sympathize. I was even glad real life didn't have a seven-second delay so nobody could bleep the emotion out of it.

"Well there you are. The fog lifts on another mystery," said Rondini as he flicked an imaginary speck of lint from his lapel.

"It's a surprise, but I don't know if we've solved the mystery yet," I said.

"Not *the* mystery, chum. A mystery. The part about two thugs warning Rhonda here not to replay the séance and also showing up at Christy's hotel so they could highjack a few reams of paper."

"Because they get around?"

"More than that, buster. Because the papers and the séance are connected. And I'll bet my last peso that Paulson is that connection."

Ronnie explained that once we exposed the diamond bracelet scam, we could pressure Madame Z into spilling the goods on Tony Paulson, which goods by Ronnie's calculation had to be the murder of Tom Marshall. And if he was responsible for Marshall, he would also be responsible for Leland Heilbrun.

"Do you really think it could be Tony Paulson?" Christy asked, her voice now hardly a whisper. She probably remembered how close she had been to being run down outside his house. I certainly was.

Ronnie said, "I'd bet on it. This has to be an inside job and the Paulsons had the most to gain. And to hide. We'll probably find out the thugs mow Tony Paulson's lawn when their not out threatening people."

"Okay, it all fits. Just remember though, if this doesn't go right I'll be sleeping in the Beamer."

"There's no way that can happen, Junior. After all, the first thing they repossess will be your car."

"Thanks, I wouldn't want to see anybody else out in the cold."

We kicked things around a little longer, adding Tony Paulson to the list of villains to expose on my show, and after a while everybody voted to hit the coffee place down the block before calling it a night. While we waited for Satyra to slip into street clothes, that tiny voice from deep inside of me began to nag. You know the voice. The same one I ignored skipping out on the cops a couple of years ago; you remember the commuter jam-up at Bay Bridge Toll Plaza back then.

The little voice reminded me that I was supposed to be doing a the old wash and fold on Tony Paulson's dirty linens not adding new stains. Maybe murder was what Ilonya Zoroaster had on Tony. If that was the case, exposing it would leave her with nothing to hold over him. Mission accomplished. The operation was a success, but the patient died.

The Hallowed Grounds was halfway down the block from the Blue Sphinx. It was run by a retired priest so I figured I'd better tell Christy to go easy on the f-word or she'd get ten Hail Mary's with her donut. Everybody sipped their decafs and half-cafs and such, not saying much, having talked themselves out by now. Even I had wound down and talk was what I do for a living. At about midnight we all told each other that we had early mornings and we all headed for home.

Just to be on the safe side Rhonda decided she better stay over with Rondini. And Christy ditto me, while Cruize and Satyra headed toward the Haight saying they'd share a taxi. Sure, and pigs can fly.

"JERRY, I've been thinking."

Uh-oh. That's almost as bad as when they say we need to talk.

"We need to talk."

"But I thought we were getting on so well."

"After tonight, I am more convinced than ever that those papers are the key to Dad's murder."

"The papers? Sure, I thought that's why we were after them."

"Jerry, listen to me." Christy was curled up on the sofa in my silk pajama top. The one I never even let Jeanne wear. The light cast by the fire danced over its silky stripes, not to mention Christy's lovely legs. I wished I was dancing with her too. Summer fog had sent chills through town, making it a perfect night for a fire.

Christy was saying, "Listen, sweetheart, Tony Paulson or Peter Lorre or Madame Zoroaster or even somebody else may be behind this all, but unless we get those legal documents, I don't think we'll have a leg to stand on."

I liked her legs just fine, but I knew that wasn't where she was going with this.

"Christy, I hate to say it, but I'd bet that convertible downstairs that those papers are already going up in smoke in somebody else's fireplace."

"Not every copy."

"We've looked pretty much everywhere. What's left?"

"The Tucson National Bank. I talked to Mom while you were at the station earlier. She told me that she'd put all of Dad's papers in a safe deposit box in the bank."

"Oh, baby, don't keep stuff like that to yourself. I almost had sex with a bottle of Liquid Plumber looking for those papers."

Christy and I kicked around various bank vault ideas for a while and absent Bonnie and Clyde knocking over the Tucson National, we agreed Christy should fly home in the morning.

First off she'd go to the bank with Mom. We talked about keeping an eye out in case she was followed, and Christy told me about some friends who would pick her up at the airport and provide local security. Christy seemed to know more than her share of cowboys and football players who were more than willing to watch out for her. I began to worry that she didn't have enough women friends.

The plan was for Christy to take the papers out accompanied by her posse and head for the nearest Kinko's to copy them. Then she'd return the originals to the bank vault for safe keeping and take the copies home to read through. She was sure she could find the connection. A good plan except for her being away for a few days. I wondered if the guy who showed Christy how to jimmy doors with a credit card was still around. Then they could just break into the bank whenever they felt like it. She needed to have the goods in time for Friday's show and I made her promise to be back by then whether she hit paydirt or not.

We wound up snuggling together in the big bed, too worn out to get nasty, too jumpy to fall asleep. Christy was curled in my arms and I stayed awake so I wouldn't miss a second of it.

THE elevator was stopping at every floor. The doors would open and Pamela Kay Paulson would get on, a new Pamela Kay at every floor, each new Pamela Kay wearing a different color nightie. As each one got on my anxiety level increased; I had an extreme fear of mistletoe.

The elevator filled with all the Pamela Kays, one more at each floor. Twelve Pamela Kays, then fifteen, then twenty, all in different color nighties, their bottoms and breasts pushed up against me. Who knew there could be so many colors? Their perfume made me dizzy, their bare skin burned against mine, my head spun, my knees buckled. I was dropping faster than the elevator. A soft, warm kaleidoscope wrapped itself around me....

I dreamed I was screaming and bolted up in bed. Panic shot through me like a bad burrito. Where was I? Where did all the Pamela Kays go? The alarm clock was shrieking. Nobody could sleep through that! I couldn't focus but I thought I recognized the sheets—I was in my bed in my own bedroom. No elevators in sight.

The shrieking stopped. Christy had punched the clock into submission. Silence. At last. No wonder I don't set the damned clock. For a moment I wondered if working the morning drive would be like this. Maybe it would be easier to stay up all night.

I looked at Christy and knew I would be all right if she was here to swat the alarm clock every morning. She looked great, a sleep-tousled, pin-up girl. I couldn't help smiling at her. I asked, "What are we doing up so early? Shouldn't we be cuddling or snuggling or something?" I was hoping she'd choose the *or something*.

"Now, Jerry, my dear, my plane doesn't leave until late morning you know," the pin-up said, "but I set the alarm clock so you could make your guest shot on *Bay Area Breakfast*. It's six a.m. and you've got to get moving. And I'm going to tag along just to make sure you don't fall back to sleep."

"Oh sure, *Bay Area Breakfast*."

Oh sure. A very, very early date with Jeanne. Somehow I had completely forgotten about it.

"C'mon, lover, I know this will be great for you and your show. And something might even come of it, maybe some witness will come forward or something."

If Christy and Jeanne never met, it would still be too soon. But my options were limited, maybe even non-existent—I had to go.

The pin-up had first dibs on the shower. As she headed to the bathroom she looked back over her shoulder and said, "There's a morning flight to Tucson I can catch after your interview. I need to get to the Tucson National before it closes at four o'clock."

"They close at four? Those guys have banker's hours."

"One of the advantages of working for a bank," she said over the shower. She raised her voice a little, "You'll have to drop me off at San Francisco International after the TV show. Or I can always take a cab."

"If we took a cab together, we could snuggle on the way."

I couldn't hear her reply over the water, but figured I'd better bring my car keys.

Since Christy was in the shower, I decided that morning coffee was my duty. I put on a bathrobe and slippers and— dream or no dream—took the elevator down. With any luck it wouldn't stop for any Pamela Kay clones. In fact, it was empty until the sixth floor where a guy in a suede jacket got on and then a well dressed lady at three. She looked me in my dressing gown, then at the suede jacket, then back to me. I could have explained that we weren't together, but by then we were at the lobby. The suede jacket gave me a very friendly smile as we got off.

There was a small line of early morning commuters at The Daily Grind, but in less than ten minutes I had a *gigante* latte in each hand and the *Chronicle* tucked under my arm. A few minutes after that, I was reading at the kitchen counter, sipping creamy Italian grind, no muss, no fuss. And I didn't even need to know how to work the coffeemaker.

Christy made her entrance fully dressed and ready to go. She was the Lady in Pink again—a cotton-candy dream floating into my very own breakfast nook. I could see an endless string of beautiful mornings like this and I didn't need a clairvoyant to help me. I might even get used to that darned alarm going off.

"Look at this," I waived the newspaper at her. "The *Chron* gave us four inches above the fold. Too bad they put it on page thirty-two next to the movie schedule."

"A lot of people go to the movies, Jerry."

"That's true and some of them even know how to read. You look great though."

"Yes, the picture did come out nice," Christy said looking at the paper, then she frowned. "It looks like they cut you out of it. I'm sure you were right next to me when that was taken."

"Thanks for reminding me. But I wasn't talking about the paper—I mean you look great. I'm going to go take a cold shower now. Then you can tell Mister DeMille I'll be ready for my close-up."

B*AY AREA BREAKFAST* is televised in a studio about the size of your typical warehouse. Once upon a time it actually was a warehouse, but most of the crates have been moved out. A large chunk of the floor space has been given over to bleacher seats for the live audience. The audience is separated from the set used for the show by a DMZ filled with equipment and technicians, microphone booms and cameras, assistant producers with two-way radios, big lights and really big lights, Teleprompters and fat cables connecting everything and everybody to everything and everybody else. There's a production crew that takes care of everything from make-up to those big video cameras on wheels. All this is focused on a brightly lit set where an anchorman and an anchorwoman are seen from the waist up at TV-style desks. I know for a fact that behind the furniture they have on cut-offs and flip-flops.

Off to the side is a green screen that Jeanne was hired to stand in front of, pointing to a non-existent weather map that's mixed in down the line for the viewers. Opposite the weather report, a couch and overstuffed chair flank a low table. From a distance, the entire set looked like something out of a doll's house, miniaturized and without any depth. The pleasant looking couple smiling at the cameras looked like Ken and Barbie come to life.

"Jeanne will be interviewing you at eight minutes after; that's six minutes from now," a nasal young woman in ripped jeans and a headset was giving us the rundown. "I'm Alice, and during the commercial break I'll take you out to the interview set and get you all settled on the sofa. Jim will mic you over there." She had a voice only Gilbert Gottfried's mother could love. "More than likely Jeanne will already be there, so she can set up the Q&A with you before going live. Jeanne told me to take real good care of you. Have a muffin?"

All of a sudden the light bulb went off over Alice's head. Gawking in Christy's direction, she said, "Hold on, didn't I see you on CNN? On Larry, maybe? No—I've got it—you're in this murder thing too!" Alice elbowed me out of the way to get a closer look at Christy. Then, into her headset she said, "Cary, did I get it wrong? Who is Jeanne interviewing—the man or the woman? Sure, I can do that...okay, okay...*no problema.*" Alice's glassy stare swung from Christy to me and then back to Christy. "Okay, I guess I'm just not myself today. I must not have had my Cheerios this morning. You're both being interviewed."

Jeanne was, in fact, already in her place sitting in the big orange chair. I wondered if I had actually ever seen her in anything but jeans and tee-shirts before. Well sure, I had seen her in considerably less, but today she wore a tailored pin-stripe that must have cost a week's pay. She'd only been away a few days, but radio appeared to be well in the past for Jeanne. She also looked a little bit unsettled, no doubt wondering why she was getting two for the price of one.

Alice put Christy at the end of the couch nearest Jeanne and I got stuck on the other far end, practically out of the picture. Somebody, presumably Jim, hung mics on us, had us count to ten for the man in the booth, and we were all set. There was still a minute until airtime, but if Jeanne wanted to prep us for the Q&A, or even give us an encouraging hello, she didn't bother to do it. Nerves maybe. An assistant director started the count down as we came back from commercial,

"Five, four, three…" and with only his fingers signaled two, then pointed at Jeanne. We were live.

Jeanne handled the set up smoothly except for introducing me as a radio announcer instead of a talk show host. Probably those nerves, her getting her big break and all.

"…and so, Miss Marshall, how did you come to be in a deserted office at night with Mr. Jeremy? Anything special we should know about?"

"No, Jeanne—may I call you Jeanne?—the reason we were there is that Jerry has been helping me investigate the murder of my father."

I tried to jump in, maybe plug my show, "So anyway, Jeanne—"

"Your father's murder? So—do you mind if I call you Christy?—so you and Jerry investigate at night?"

"We had been—" I started.

"Just a second, Jerry. Don't worry, I'll get to you. Don't you worry about that."

"Jerry had saved me from an attack in my hotel room—"

"Saved you from being attacked in your room? Tell us, how did he do that? By attacking you in the elevator?"

Elevators again.

"He interrupted the attack when he came up to my room. If I ever get my hands on those—"

"So, Jerry, what were you doing going to this young lady's hotel room in the middle of the night? Did she give you a key of your own?"

"Listen, Jeanne, we were trying to figure out how certain people and events might be tied into her dad's death."

"Sure, Jerry, and what's that saying about liars figure and something about figures like hers? Did you figure out how to get into—"

"A man was murdered, two men—" Christy started, but Jeanne kept going:

"And was Jerry Jeremy diddling while Rome was burning? And just who would he be diddling in your hotel room? Not me I'm sure."

Jeanne seemed to be getting a little off track, maybe even off the beaten path, maybe it was more than coffee nerves.

"Oh, Jerry has really taken me under his wing," Christy said. "He's let me stay at his apartment since I couldn't go back to the hotel."

"You don't say. I understand Jerry does a lot of entertaining up there. Did he show you the view, turn on the gas log?"

"I admit we curled up in front of the fire—"

"Jerry you curled this girl up on that couch!" Jeanne gave me a look she hadn't learned in TV-land. But I didn't want to lose the moment, everything being at a dramatic pitch and all. Not to mention what Jeanne might do to me if a commercial break happened along. So I went with my strength—I plugged my show.

"That's right, Jeanne," I acted like I hadn't heard a word she'd said. "This all revolves around a clairvoyant, a radio station, some mysterious papers and a University of Arizona linebacker who can pick locks."

"What?"

"Don't worry. All questions will be answered on my radio show. And asked too. Tune in to KPMT, Big Talk Radio, from four to seven, for the inside scoop on who got cheated, who got murdered and who's gonna have to run for the border. We'll even try to explain this interview."

"Sure. Tune in to Jerry's show. Tune in and try to find out what else he's been up to. I may even call in myself." Jeanne looked like the next murder victim might be me if *I* didn't make a run for the border.

"Thanks for the plug," I said as I untangled us from our mics and pulled Christy over cables and around cameras in quick step. "Gotta get this girl to the airport," I trilled over my shoulder, "Plane to catch, running late, gotta go."

We got to the Beamer, got in the Beamer, and got the Beamer out of the lot lickety split. I tried to think of a way to tell Christy what Jeanne was going on about. I could say it was because of a lingering brain tumor or maybe some kind of eating disorder. About then Christy leaned over and punched me on the shoulder in what I took to be a good way. She was grinning from ear to ear, practically brimming over with excitement.

"Wow, that was great," she said. "What's a girl got to do to get a job like that?"

I had an idea of what Jeanne might have had to do, but I didn't want to shatter any illusions Christy might still have.

"I'd love to do that," she continued. "Maybe I could start as a weather girl or a reporter and work my way up. Didn't you tell me you helped get Jeanne her big break?"

"Well, let's just say I helped her perfect her technique."

THE airport, SFO, was going at full tilt—planes coming, planes going, far-away places, strange sounding people, you get the picture. I could never figure out why the airlines were lining up at the bankruptcy court when so many people were trying to get to Grand Rapids or Kankakee or wherever. I'd have to remember to do a show about it, but for now, suffice it to say that the black hole of Calcutta had nothing on the departures concourse.

We left the car in the curbside drop-off zone since I planned to be back before the tow-truck came by. Then we walked together as far as the security gate and we had a major goodbye kiss. I hated to think that the next pair of hands on Christy would be Homeland Security patting her down. Anyway, my toes were still curled when I got back to the car.

Timing being everything, a parking cop was just taking out her ticket book when I got there. I gave her a law-abiding smile and said, "Don't worry, officer. That car's mine, I was just dropping off Willie Brown and he said it would be okay to park here."

"Sorry, man, I already got my pen out— Wait a second! Aren't you Jerry Jeremy? Oh my God! I saw you on TV during my break today!"

"Now that you mention it...."

She yelled to the passing crowd, "Hey, Jerry Jeremy from the TV show here!" She had a voice that could not only stop traffic, she could drown it out.

"I have my show on—" but I didn't get the rest out. She yelled some more, this time for cop further down the curb to come meet me, and then stopped a passing traveler and had him take a picture of us with her cell phone. The other cop and a small crowd gathered around us and I started signing autographs, hugging babies and kissing strangers. That must be what it's like to be Barack Obama.

I got off with a warning not to leave the Beamer in the drop-off zone too often and I promised to drop in at the next meter maids' ball. I was beginning to think TV might be okay, too.

Chapter 27.

"*GO-O-OD MO-O-oRNING!*"

"*I'm Freddy....*"

"*...and I'm Betty....*"

"*...and we're up to our arses—I mean, armpits—in a murder mystery. Not forty feet from where Betty and I are sitting KPMT's legal counsel—*"

"*No lawyer jokes, Freddy, this is serious!*"

"*—was murdered just this past Saturday night! It's a pretty chilling thing, don't you think, Betty?*"

"*Well, somebody's chilling in the morgue. What I want to know is what are the cops doing about it? Everybody knows the first thirty-six hours are the most important in a murder investigation.*"

"*The SFPD are just chilling too. Are these guys homicide dicks or just plain dicks? But we're not going to let them sweep this under the rug. There's crime scene tape all over KPMT's offices.*"

"*And speaking of KPMT, what about Jerry Jeremy, the station's very own evening talk show host? I don't think he's out of the woods yet, not by a long shot.*"

"*Betty, you're absolutely right on. I thought I noticed some liberal pandering on his show recently. Could that lead to some kind of weird psycho-fascist behavior?*"

"*You mean like bringing strange women to your place of work and then maybe bumping off somebody who catches the two of you knocking over the pencil jar on the boss's desk?*"

"*If the pencil fits....*"

I really hate Freddy and Betty.

I guess I could do a show like that too if somebody offered

me a prime morning drive slot along with a raise to match. It might be easier than doing my own show—no thinking required. But I don't know, I'm thinking that I might want to try that TV thing after I crack the murders.

I switched the dial to Armstrong and Getty. Like some kind of weird déjà vu, the boys were kicking around my murder with an ex-SFPD cop. A lot of speculation about what Christy and I were doing in the darkened office in the middle of the night and more than a few remarks on her good looks.

Anyway, they tell me that the only bad publicity is your obituary and I was hoping it wasn't going to come to that. The traffic back to town was slow, so I had a little time to think things through while I worked my way up the 101 freeway. Actually, I tried calling Ronnie to see if he had thought things through first. No use both of us thinking. He didn't answer though. I figured he and Rhonda had probably been up late talking or winding a few skeins of yarn while basking in the glow from the electric heater. So it looked like it was up to me to do this morning's thinking.

All things being equal, I should have gone home for a mid-day nap before my show since I had gone to bed late and gotten up way too early. Instead I drove to the KPMT studio and parked in a spot next to the building marked "Reserved for P.K. Paulson". It was still early enough that I hoped to catch Ned before he disappeared for lunch. I was amazed at how much could be accomplished getting up at the crack of dawn.

Approaching KPMT's front lobby, I was mini-mobbed by a couple of guys with cameras and a petite, young woman with a video shooter of her own. Everybody was shouting, probably thinking I wouldn't notice them if they didn't, cameras got shoved in my face, the petite, young woman banged me on the jaw with a mic.

"Over here, Jerry!"

"One question, just one...."

"Jerry, look here—"

The young woman shouted, "Where's the mystery woman? Buddy, roll tape! Where's Christy?" This time I ducked when she swung her mic my way, but Buddy almost got me with the camera lens. "Did you kill the lawyer?"

"You sure this is the guy, Joyce?"

She was small, but Joyce blocked the doorway like she played right guard for the Raiders. "Yeah, this is him," she yelled back, hanging on my arm.

"Hold on, folks, I just called for the morning paparazzi," I said to the assembled, hoping to give them a sound bite. But quick wit wasn't what they were looking for.

"Where's the girl?" the assembled asked, Joyce having become their unofficial spokesperson.

"Calm down now," I said. "I'm all about photo ops and sound bites. Make sure you get my dimples in the picture."

"I just want to ask some questions," said Joyce, as she pressed so close I think I might owe her dinner and a movie. "Take a shot of Jerry and me together."

She grabbed my shirt and pulled me down to her level, I put on my TV smile, and she started her spiel for the camera, finally asking, "Do you have any idea who might be behind this tragedy?"

"C'mon, You guys are making me blush," I said. "Tell your viewers to catch my show, four to seven, Monday through Friday, on KPMT, Loud Mouth Radio, where my mouth sets the standard...." I managed to tear away from Brenda Starr's iron grip, unkink my neck, and elbow my way into the station.

As I stepped inside, Michael announced over the paging system that Elvis was entering the building. It took me a moment to realize that he was announcing me. People stopped what they were doing and came over to the lobby, some running in from the offices. This was a big welcome since blasé is considered a job skill at the station. It takes so much to shake up these guys that they'd stop for coffee in an earthquake. Well, during working hours anyway.

A little applause, or some bowing and scraping, would have been nice, but you can't have everything. As it was, I got my hand shaken, my back patted and my cheeks kissed. Call me crazy, but I'd swear Miss Silvano gave me a meaningful look. At this rate, I'd have to ask Ned whether Freddy and Betty might be better off living and working in one of the red states, like maybe Canada.

Slowly everybody drifted back to whatever they were doing and the overhead speakers went back to the crazy afternoon guy pitching a fit over the City not patching the potholes leading up to Coit Tower, Lillie Hitchcock's phallic tribute atop Telegraph Hill to the City's firemen and their hoses. I myself drifted over to Ned's office.

I thought it would have police tape all over it, marking it as a crime scene, and maybe Leland Heilbrun's chalk outline on the floor. I could get Brad to take a few pictures of me by the outline, like I was Philip Marlowe working on a case. I also wanted to talk privately with Ned about what Heilbrun might have been doing in his office and whether he'd told Ned anything about the papers. His office being the scene of a crime, I figured Ned must have set up shop in the conference room. And since I was a star now, I figured no appointment was necessary.

Amazingly, Ned's office looked like it had before the weekend. No police tape, no body outline, no body, even the dust looked undisturbed. Maybe I could get Kinta to draw an outline on the floor later for those pictures. Ned wouldn't mind. After all he wasn't even here.

The office was empty and the lights were out.

After the morning drive show ended, Ned seldom went over to the working end of KPMT, so I didn't figure he was keeping the mid-day guy company. But he might be schmoozing in one of the other offices, figuring out how to wring every last buck out of a lucky murder. He was probably working out new advertising rates with Tony. Let's take a look.

"HI, Jerry, great audio of the cops yesterday," Tony said as he looked up from his computer screen and smiled without showing teeth. "Any new recordings? Any break in the case?"

I shook my head, and looked around his office. No matter where I looked, I didn't see Ned.

Tony was saying, "I couldn't make heads nor tails out of Freddy and Betty this morning. Or Marsha's news report for that matter. But they got a following."

"I didn't get much chance to listen today," I said. "You know, my TV interview and all. Plugged the hell out of it for the station. They'll probably bill Ned for commercial time."

"I doubt he'd pay it. He stuffs the seats in his woody with bills he doesn't want to pay."

"Think that's where he is now?"

Tony said he might be for all he knew. Or he might be getting a decaf soy latte at the coffee shop over in Levi Plaza. Why didn't we check it out? He'd buy.

The reporters had disappeared so I didn't get to show Tony what a big deal I was. On the other hand I didn't have to fight off Joyce and her buddy, Buddy. Maybe I'd tip them off when Christy was coming back so they'd make a big deal of me in front of the mystery woman. Only if they'd make a big deal of me in front of the mystery woman.

Tony and I walked across Levi Plaza to the coffee shop and ordered drinks that Juan Valdez could never have imagined back on the plantation. We picked a sunny bench to sit on while we drank them. Nothing like hot coffee in the hot sun.

"So, Tony, it looks like we are locked and loaded for the séance to blast off on Friday's show."

"Good. I know that Ilonya and Vigo are really up for it. No missing jewelry this time; of that I am positive."

"So you're still in close contact with Madame—er, Ilonya? She's not actually staying at your, ah, place, is she?" I wanted to put it discreetly. "I mean, no reason she shouldn't be, of course."

"Well, Jerry, I think you've been having a house guest also, haven't you? A young, single woman, alone with you in your toney bachelor pad?"

"Oh, only because we couldn't use her hotel room—that is, she couldn't—she couldn't use her hotel room, you know, thugs breaking in and such." I sipped the steamed milk floating on the coffee and licked the foam off my lip.

"Sure, Jerry. And I saw Jeanne interviewing her on Bay Area Breakfast."

"Technically, that was me she was interviewing."

"You seemed a little tongue-tied. Come to think of it, aren't you and Jeanne an item? How does Christy fit in?"

"Well...."

"Maybe you are just a nice guy sharing your penthouse with the poor country girl."

"She may be from cow country, but she knows how to jimmy a lock."

"Come to think of it, that interview this morning was pretty impressive."

"The way I got my stuff across?"

"No, not you exactly...."

"Christy?"

"No, Jeanne. She handled herself pretty well. I think TV's going to be her thing. Maybe yours too, someday."

"I thought you were listening to Freddy and Betty."

"I can multi-task."

"Well, about Jeanne and Christy...." I took a desperate swig of coffee.

"Just kidding you a little, Jerry. I've got to get even for your making me an item with Ilonya."

"Well, Ilonya's not my type, but one man's poison as they say...."

"Well, she's really not my type, Jerry."

So Tony and I swapped a few lies about who were our

respective types and drank our drinks and after a while headed back to the office. I never got a straight answer about Ilonya and Vigo's attraction to Tony, just that he had gotten interested in the paranormal after my show with them. He really didn't sound like he enjoyed it though.

Chapter 28.

"*So here's what you've all been waiting for—over the past two days, you've been wondering why a man was murdered here in KPMT's studios. Some of you may not have picked up a paper or listened to the radio or watched anything but the Giants on TV, so I'm going to bring you up to date on not just one, but two murders today.*

"*Call in. Give me the third degree. Or just listen to what I have to tell you. I have one week to name the killers and by the end of my Friday show, you will know who they are. Maybe the cops will beat us to it, maybe not. I hope they do, but they don't have any suspects yet, except maybe me.*

"*But I know something they don't. I know that I didn't do it. Now you know it too.*"

My show was taking a different tack from usual; most of the time, I hope to get callers who are a little over the top, like:

"*Jerry, I have sources who say that Hillary is a victim of deep mind control by an evil mastermind.*"

"*You mean Bill?*"

Ah, talk radio politics. Five minutes of enlightened debate on the great issues of the day is as exciting as reading the fine print in the Grasslands Preservation Act. Kinta White describes a "good" caller as one who will start a screaming match or sends our collective blood pressures into outer space. We like callers who take our listeners' out of the gridlock and into the imaginary world of politics.

But today was different. The idea of solving a mystery on the air gave our audience something real, yet something that was more exciting than the old day-to-day. A kind of reality radio. For a change, we got great calls from people who actually weren't nuts.

Sure, there were still some wacky theories about the murders, like the lady who thought she recognized Heilbrun as somebody she knew back in the sixties. She said he was still on a secret government hit list started by Nixon. It's possible, but I think our killers got to him first. Maybe saved the government some coin, but we're not talking politics today.

As it turned out, I never did find Ned before airtime. The surf must have been up or something, but I had wanted to get a few sound bites for Tuesday's show. Have him tell me what a great guy Tom Marshall had been, how Tom and Leland had taken a meeting or two together. It would give the murder angle a little human interest and maybe suggest some kind of a link.

I thought Christy might like it too, although she'd have to go on-line to catch the show since our signal doesn't get past Fresno. Maybe I'd have Brad put it on CD so I could play it for her over the phone.

Anyway, all the TV and radio news and the papers were full of the Heilbrun murder. But the connection to Tom Marshall's nosedive off the Marin headlands—which most people including the police didn't even know was murder—was all mine. I was going to play this hand through to the end, but I hoped that Christy's hunch about her dad's safe deposit box would fill my inside straight. Otherwise, it would be one hell of a bluff.

"JESUS Christ Almighty, Jeremy!"

Nice to hear your name linked with the Big Guy, but I almost dropped the phone anyway. I wasn't sure why Pamela Kay Paulson was calling on my cell and that's always cause for concern.

Brad, Kinta and I were in a booth at Fog City Diner where I was springing for some after-show grub when my cell rang. I knew it was Mrs. P because Brad had programmed a special ringtone for her—the Godfather theme. Sure enough, up popped a picture looking like Pamela Kay's last mug shot. But appearances can be deceiving; the way she led off made this look to be a good call.

"I heard your show and you are finally hitting your goddamn' stride, my love."

"Really...my, er, stride..." I said. "I mean, Pamela Kay, I'm really putting my all into the show, what with the murders and all that stuff."

Upbeat call, but with Mrs. P you never knew for sure. I was nervous about the old bait and bitch, er, switch, good news, bad news, how's your wife and kids, bang—you're dead.

"Keep using that trumped up Marshall mystery to take attention away from Tony. You know what I mean, Jerry."

Did I?

I wondered if Ricardo had spiked her milkshake. Pamela Kay's mood might swing the other way if the spotlight landed back on Tony after all. Would she blame me or just think I was dishing out a little Dr. Phil-style help? If I was a hit, would she can me anyway? Would I care? Who died and left her in charge anyway?

Tom Marshall, I guess.

"You still there, Jeremy?"

"Oh, hello? Hello? PK? You there? I must of hit a dead spot. You hear me now?"

We batted the "can you hear me now?" thing back and forth for a while, establishing the fact that we were both on the line. She had the dulcet tones reserved for the more pissed-off kind of bull moose. The guys had gotten their food by now and were wolfing it down like they had been marooned someplace without a decent diner. Maybe Bakersfield. Mine came too and was slowly growing cold.

Pamela Kay was still saying nice things about me and I was agreeing, so it was hard to get her off the phone. Then she spent a few minutes reminding me that I needed to get rid of Madame Zoroaster, at least as far as Tony was concerned. I told her not to worry, I didn't think they'd be picking out rings anytime soon.

I had been wondering why Heilbrun had the only copies of all the station's legal papers, like partnerships, licensing and so forth, but I couldn't think of how to work it into the conversation in a subtle way.

So I just asked her.

"That's none of your business," she explained. "But if you must know, that's the way it was supposed to be."

"Really?"

"Leland didn't want copies of copies floating around and getting lost or in the wrong hands. Not that they contained any great secrets. Whenever any one wanted to look at them, Leland would check with me, and depending on who and what they wanted, I'd give him the go ahead or not, or maybe I'd check with the other owners first."

"What other owners? I thought you owned the station."

"I do. Most of it anyhow. I bought up Tom Marshall's share when he died, and that gave me controlling interest. But you know Charlie Wooten bought in, guaranteeing us a certain amount of advertising as part of the deal. And there are a couple of other shares, like Tony has a small piece, and of course, Ned Tunney."

"Ned's an owner too?"

"Sure, Jeremy, he's the 'T'."

"The tea? Like Earl Grey?" I almost knocked over my iced...uh, tea.

"Don't be silly, Jeremy. When we started the business, we used our initials for the call letters, 'PMT'—Paulson, Marshall and Tunney."

"Sounds like a rock group."

Pamela Kay spent a little more time trying to shake something out of me about the Tony-Ilonya hookup, but since I didn't really know anything, she came up empty. Still she managed to drag it out until my burger was cold and the tea was lukewarm. The waitress was clearing when Mrs. P called it quits. All I got for dinner was the check.

BACK at my place a little later I tried to watch TV, flipping back and forth between Letterman and an old Bob Hope movie. Seemed like Dave was aging pretty fast, but Bob looked young as ever. Somehow though I couldn't get interested. It was a too late to call Christy and I didn't want to take a chance on her mom answering. Mrs. Marshall might think I was just another one of Christy's thirty or forty college chums. I thought about calling Ronnie, but decided to wait until morning. Right now I pictured him doing something magical with Rhonda Ridgeway.

I plucked up my courage finally and checked my recorder. The interview was right there along with the cable news coverage of the murder. Despite Christy's enthusiasm, I wasn't too sure that Jeanne had taken things in quite the right spirit. But at least I could see the girls live and in person. Or at least live to DVR. I thought about muting the sound, but decided a little tough love might make me feel better about dropping Jeanne. The images flickered and the voices merged and the interview was a lot shorter on the replay than it seemed in person.

All told though, it wasn't too bad. The girls looked both

lovely, and to the knowing eye, in love. The funny thing is that Jeanne's interview didn't seem so much about the murders when you just watched it on the tube. Not at all what I thought we were doing. Still, I got a good plug in for the show. Ned would love that. I replayed it a few times and it still looked good.

I dozed off in front of the set and this time I dreamt about Christy and me. Only in this dream Christy looked more like Jeanne; I kept getting confused about who I was with. I was kissing the dream Christy who looked like she might have been Jeanne while another Christy that looked like Christy but might have really been Jeanne stuck a microphone in my face—I know, I know—and kept asking questions. We were surrounded by photographers snapping pictures and popping flashbulbs. The flash bulbs became sunlight pouring through my living room windows. Christy and Jeanne...I think I was dreaming....

Just then my cell went off. Jeanne. No dream.

"What are you, psychic?" I said. "I was just thinking of you. To tell the truth, I had been dreaming of you."

"Only me?"

She must be psychic.

"Of course, just you. Hey, thanks for the interview yesterday. I'd really like to thank you in person."

"Oh, yeah, I bet you would. What happened to the shitkicker?"

"What? You're not jealous, are you? Hey, I'm just trying to help the poor kid out. She's practically an orphan, all alone in the big city."

"Sure, she's little Red Riding Hood and you're wearing grandma's clothes again."

"I only play dress-up with you, dear."

"Not a good move with your legs."

"Hey, what's wrong with my legs?"

That got a laugh out of her. "Oh, Jerry, I'm really going to miss you."

"What do you mean? I told you I'm just helping Christy find out who killed her dad."

"I'm hoping you do find out and if there's anything I can do to help, let me know. 'Though I don't know how much help I'll be down in LA."

"The Santa Monica Open coming up, is it?"

I was closer than I knew, but far from right. Jeanne's interview with Christy and me was the tipping point. She told me that a spot was open on ESPN and whoever it is that does the hiring and firing liked the interview enough to make her an offer she couldn't refuse.

"I've always liked sports," my ex-girl said as she began to fade away before my very eyes. "And this will be right down my alley, lot's of locker room interviews. Talk about a dream job."

"Gee, well-toned tush and a load of dough."

"Well, actually not that much dough, hardly more than a weather girl gets, but there's a lot of exposure."

"Sure, and people will get to see you too. Speaking of which, maybe we can get together before you head down south."

"I'd love that, Jerry, but I'm catching the afternoon shuttle. Besides I heard there was a new girl in town."

I could've said that she wasn't actually in town at the moment, but decided to leave it like that. Radio to TV, weather maps to locker rooms, I hoped that somehow I'd helped.

WITH Christy in Tucson, I figured this would be a good day to get my ducks all lined up for the Friday night fright. I didn't know if Christy was going to turn anything up or not, but I had Rondini in my back pocket just in case. I was sure The Great One could stir things up enough to shake things loose.

Using Rhonda and Cruize to pin the diamond bracelet swindle on Madame Z and Mister C, Thé and Estrada would pull out the handcuffs and threaten to throw away the key unless they agree to rat out their pal Tony. If we had to, Ronnie could do some channeling of his own, conjuring up Marshall's ghost. All we needed to nail down the coffin, so to speak, were the secrets hidden deep inside the Tucson National Bank.

Blackmail, murder and motive. It looked like it was all coming together. If the radio gods were with us, I might get Tony to confess right on the air. Pamela Kay would know it was the right thing to do. Anyway, I'd be a pretty hot property after the show. I thought maybe Brad the Brat could hook up a hidden camera to catch the fat lady singing for CNN.

I tried Ronnie's cell, but it went to voicemail. I stopped calling after leaving five or six messages. He'd know how to get me when he came up for air. Anyway, I'd try him again later. No luck with Christy either, so she got a message too.

Since no one seemed to be around, I figured it wouldn't

hurt to show up at the station a little early so I could go over Friday's setup with Brad and Kinta. I liked the idea of playing candid camera. There really would be film at eleven.

To the best of my recollection I had never been at the station before noon, but today was special. The setup for the setup. I had never realized that Brad and Kinta didn't actually show up at KPMT until shortly before my show went on at four. Ned must pay them by the hour.

I bribed Michael to call them at home and say Ned wanted them to come in early. There was some talk about overtime, personal lives and working elsewhere, but Michael turned out to be amazingly persuasive coming up with concert tickets originally intended for a listener promotion. I was sure Ned wouldn't mind, this being for my show's big showdown. Besides he was out of the office, God knows where. At any rate, Brad and Kinta were finally on their respective ways in.

I was thinking maybe Michael could order up some sandwiches for us when my cell went off.

"So that'll be the Crab Louie," the waiter recited, "a rare New York strip steak and one chicken salad on toast." I was the chicken salad. I was also sitting across from Inspectors Janice Thé and Tommy Estrada at a sidewalk table outside the Ferry Building. A big yellow umbrella protected us from the sun, not to mention the sea gulls circling the restaurant.

The sidewalk there is wide enough that most of the Embarcadero's exhaust fumes never got to our table, although the noise made up for it. Thé had called wanting to go over Friday's show. She said they'd feel better with some idea of what was supposed to go down. Fair enough. I wanted the cops there for the bust, so the least I could do was to pick up a lunch on my KPMT expense account.

Not that I actually had a KPMT expense account, but without the threat of a perp walk, Madame Zoroaster and her pet toad might not cooperate.

The cops and I all said what a nice day it was, beautiful weather, light sprinkling of tourists and all. Tommy Estrada was saying, "I love working outdoors on days like this. Give me a drive-by shooting out in Hunter's Point on a sunny day—you know, they got the best weather in the City out there."

"It gets kind of windy late in the day," Janice Thé said. "And like most of the City, it's cold after dark, but who would dare go there after dark."

"Still on a sunny day, it's great. Sometimes when we're stuck in the fog out in the Avenues, I pray for a nice drive-by in the Point."

"Sure," I agreed, "just don't forget the sun tan lotion."

I felt a just little bit guilty having bailed on my production team, but felt good about bonding with the cops. We ate and had refills on our ice teas and lemonades, and the talk turned to the Heilbrun and Marshall killings.

"We know that Tony Paulson doesn't have an alibi for the time of Mr. Marshall's death," Janice said, "but at the time of the Heilbrun murder, he was at a house party with about a dozen very prominent witnesses."

"Sure," I said, "that figures. He would want an alibi if he thought we were getting close to him. Anyway, I can't see him actually strangling anybody himself, unless it was a sponsor."

Between bites, Janice said, "He was at a party up in Pacific Heights at the time. And he happened to bring along your lady friend, Ilonya Zoroaster, and her companion to entertain or educate the party-goers with all that medium unity bullshit."

"Seems she was a hit," Estrada said. "She lined up several personal consultations there."

"Like shooting fish in a barrel," Janice said. "Wealthy fish."

So I filled them in on the diamond bracelet scam and how we had the actors to back up our story, and what we thought would happen if we could get the Inspectors to put a little pressure on Madame Z and Vigo concerning that. Anyway it was better than any plan they had.

Estrada thought it might be a little tricky pressuring a couple of citizens during a live broadcast where everyone could hear, but I pointed out we wouldn't be using real rubber hoses. I promised they'd get their names on the air and I'd make it look like it was all about them. So they agreed to come along, for the ride if nothing else. And the plug of course, this being radio.

Dessert, coffee and the check arrived and were duly handled. We said our farewells until Friday or until they got a break in the case, whichever came first, and I headed for the cable car turnaround just up Market Street.

The California Street cable car goes right by Charlie Wooten's dealership out on Van Ness and I wanted to drop in to say hello. It's a fun ride on a nice day and even the locals mix in with the tourists. I stood in line until my turn came and hopped on as the car began the long pull up Nob Hill. I did the

San Francisco thing and stood on the running board holding onto a strap, all the better to lean out for the view and get the breeze from the oncoming traffic.

Even heading up the steep hill, the cable car managed to pick up speed. A delivery truck with "Royal Fish Company" painted on its flanks came speeding downhill, brushing me back, but not brushing me off, thank God. I was so busy ducking the fish truck, I didn't notice a chunky tourist in tank top and flip-flops on the run for the moving cable car.

Tank Top made it on and started pushing through the crowd. Half of us turned to look when a woman shouted that he stepped on her corns and he should watch out. I noticed that he didn't take much notice though. He just kept plowing through kids and shopping bags and people's feet. From the passengers' reactions, I guessed people didn't behave like that back in Peoria.

Tank top? Built like a tank? Built like a Filipino tank?

Holy Hyatt Regency, Batman! I wasn't on the tenth floor anymore, but I had the feeling I'd still be flying. Hopefully not in front of another fish truck. Tank Top had his eyes on me and the only reason he wasn't choking the life out of me right now was the tangle of people in flowered shirts blocking his way.

"Hey, watch where you're stepping," somebody shouted.

How come there's never a cop around when you need one? And I had just sprung for lunch too.

I started pushing my way further to the front, hoping to maintain a comfortable distance between me and my pursuer while the good people from the red states were all yelling for both of us to find a seat or get the hell off and leave everybody in peace. The gripman was ringing the cable car bell to restore order. Maybe it was some kind of gripman's S-O-S. Still Tank Top waded through the crowd like the 49ers front four wading through the salad bar at T.G.I. Friday's.

By now I was as far forward as I could go. Any further and I'd be sitting on the cow catcher. The car seemed to be going extra fast, practically rocking off it's tracks while a huge Muni bus rocketed by downhill.

If I jumped I'd probably only break my legs, get a concussion, and maybe get run over. It seemed like a better idea than waiting for Tank Top to get his hands on me. I pulled the cord to let the gripman know I wanted the next stop, but we must have been on an express.

With all the bell ringing and buses blasting by, I almost

didn't hear the angry buzz-saw sound until it was right beside me. From out of nowhere Tank Top's twin brother came buzzing up by the cable car on a Vespa. He pulled close, but on the motor scooter he only came up to about my knees. The right level to grab my leg though. I managed to kick free and then climbed on the bench. I wound up standing between newlyweds from Sheboygan. I had a sense of déjà vu catching a glimpse of Thé and Estrada running uphill after us. Maybe I had forgotten to leave a tip. But now wasn't the time to think about that.

The guy on the scooter was still trying to grab my ankle and his pal had gotten a lot closer. I dodged around a husky kid in shorts who wasn't helping at all. Tank Top reached around a solid, corn-fed hausfrau, but he couldn't quite get to me—his arms were muscular but short. He did get the attention of the hausfrau's husband though, a six-foot two testament to hard labor and clean living. Back in Des Moines, squat, dark-skinned body builders just didn't put their arms around your wife.

While Paul Bunyan proceeded to hammer Tank Top into the floorboards, Number Two was teasing my shoe laces. There was no where to turn. The fight behind me had cut off that escape route and the guy on the scooter was just waiting to get a good grip on me. The spectators had blocked any way out and a little old lady was pounding on my toes with her umbrella even though we hadn't seen rain since March.

Vespa-man pulled along side me, close enough to count the gold caps sparkling on his front teeth as he smiled. If he stretched another inch or if the scooter hit a bump, I was a goner.

Suddenly the Vespa spun away, bouncing off a parked car and wobbling to a stop. Thank God for potholes! I'll never badmouth the Mayor again, at least not for that. But Tank Top had gotten free of the tourists and was fighting his way past the old lady.

By now I heard ringing in my ears. Not heavenly chimes calling for me, I hoped. Not our gripman's bell either. It was our mirror-image coming the other way, a cable car running back downhill. It was headed toward us fast, not leaving much time to think things through. Tank Top straight-armed the white-haired lady out of the way. But she was tough, I'll give her that. Tank Top pulled free and coiled himself to spring. I pried my fingers off the pole I had been gripping, and closing my eyes, took a giant step into open space just as Tank Top lunged.

His brawny arms reached out for me but all he grabbed was air.

Chapter 29.

WHEN the Big One hits—that catastrophic quake that tumbles the City by the Bay into the bay—any true San Franciscan wants to be here for the ride. It's the gospel that makes San Francisco special. At least that's what everybody says. We're known for our "been there, done that" attitude. Naked ladies run in the Bay-to-Breakers marathon along side men wearing tuxedos. For that matter, men dressed as naked ladies run too. In the clubs, gals are trying out pick-up lines on guys too cool to care and the real hook-ups are made at the Marina Safeway. Nobody looks twice at anything. Everything is just taken in stride.

So all the conductor said was, "You gotta have a transfer, fella, or you gotta pay the fare. City's cracking down on free rides." I went through my pockets in case I did have a transfer, but no luck. If I hadn't been in shock, I guess I wouldn't have bothered looking. Tank Top and his pal had slipped my mind at the moment, let alone my plan to visit Charlie Wooten. All I knew was that somehow I was still all in one piece and that was all I had on my mind.

Maybe the conductor had seen it all before, but I was still amazed. You know that thing about still being in one piece, that was amazing. As Tank Top zeroed in on me I had stepped off the cable car going up the hill and onto the one passing us in the opposite direction. Rondini has a gag about his hands never leaving his body; in my case it was hands, arms and legs, and boy, was I glad I didn't lose any one of them. The tourists even gave me a little well-deserved applause. They must have thought I was some new kind of mime. If I'd had a hat to pass, I bet I could have gotten the cost of the fare.

Instead I coughed up five bucks and found a seat facing the street. I felt very relaxed. Sit back, boy, enjoy the ride, check out the view over to Alcatraz. The car lurched a little and I started to scream, but caught myself.

I thought about a big, icy martini at the end of the ride and that helped a lot. Or it could be a Manhattan. Or both, just throw it all in one glass. Just the thought of it relaxed me. I couldn't wait to see what the real thing would do.

I watched the traffic with detached interest, keeping an eye out for Vespas. We passed a squad car stopped in the middle of the uphill lanes, picking up a young couple, an Asian lady with a big dark haired guy. They looked like I should know them, but how could that be? They had to be tourists from Detroit or Memphis or someplace like that. Where else would tourists be from?

Anyway, now I knew where the cops were when you needed one—riding around with young honeymooners from out of town.

I took Manhattan. Beautiful amber liquid with a candy-red cherry in a frosted glass. The second one as beautiful as the first, it pretty much brought me back to life. I'm pretty sure it was the second one. I had a couple more after that just to nail it down. But, somewhere through the second or third one I remembered that the young couple getting into the cop car weren't honeymooners.

They were my cop pals—Thé and Estrada. Tired of running uphill and no cabs in sight, they called a cop. One of the perks of being on the force I guess. Somewhere in the recesses of my alcohol-soaked brain, I wondered if they knew how close they had been to catching Leland Heilbrun's killers.

I never drink before a show. I have a tough enough time doing it sober. But today, I planned on spending the afternoon in the cool, dark confines of the Bridgeview Grotto, chatting up a barmaid named Sheila, telling her about my close call on the cable car. And I planned to stay there all evening too.

I knew Sheila would protect me if the Filipino leg breakers showed up. I once saw her arm wrestle the audio guy from the evening news. Not only did she beat him twice in a row, she had more tattoos. Someday she'll make somebody a fine tag-team partner.

I could have called Christy and told her about my narrow escape, but decided not to. She might catch on that I was under the weather, three sheets worth, and not only because of today's misadventure. I was missing her already. Not like I missed Jeanne when she wasn't around to help with a tough crossword puzzle. I missed looking into Christy's eyes or smelling her hair. I missed holding her in my arms.

Two o'clock, two-thirty, three. Mickey's hands kept on turning and after three or four or maybe five wonderful Manhattans, I was beginning to feel better. Sheila and I made plans to run away to the South Seas and find a deserted island to set up barkeeping on. But first I needed to make sure Brad and Kinta could come with us so I could do a remote for my show.

My show.

Oh Mama! Reality rears its ugly head. I called off my engagement with Sheila and headed across the street to KPMT. Just as I was dodging traffic on the Embarcadero, my cell started ringing. Inspector Thé as it turned out. Strangely enough she and Estrada were waiting for me at the station. Not the police station, the radio one.

When I got there they were hanging with Kinta White, maybe getting the tour, or I suppose they could have been pumping him for my whereabouts on the night of...jeez, I hoped it hadn't gone that far. We greeted each other like the old friends we had become, shaking hands and hugging, checking to make sure we had our wallets and all our fingers after. I was a little woozy from the afternoon's refreshments, but what they had to say brought me back to the here and now.

"Tommy spotted them following you when you left the restaurant," Janice Thé said. "So we figured we'd better tag along since they matched the description of the hotel perps."

"If I follow you, you followed them following me?" I was trying to grab on to the story in spite of my haze. Kinta handed me a large mug of black coffee and shoved a couple of aspirins into my mouth. I gulped the coffee, choked, sprayed and coughed for about three minutes and started to feel better. As far as the KPMT coffee was concerned, Starbucks had nothing to worry about.

Janice dabbed her face with a hanky, saying, "The only problem was that we missed that damned cable car. I do five laps on the Marina Green every day, but running straight up Nob Hill is more than I'm used to."

"Not that Jan and I can't keep up with somebody on foot," Tommy said, "but running uphill against a cable car...."

"We were able to wave down a patrol car," Janice said.

"Funny, how when you need help, a cop always pops up."

"Sure, I'll have Kinta remind me to do a show about cops being around when you need 'em," I said, hardly worried about seeing two of everything. "Anyway I was probably going downhill by then. I think I may have seen you guys, but basically I was in a non-alcoholic stupor. But I fixed that; now I'm in a real alcoholic stupor."

"We were surprised when we caught up with the cable car," Tommy said. "We saw you get on and you didn't get off, but you were gone. A real disappearing act."

"Turns out we were able to grab the two punks that were after you. Jan ran down the one that was on the cable car and the other one was picked up later at San Francisco General. He came to the emergency room with a busted knee, said he hurt it in a motor scooter accident."

Janice Thé finished her Coke and crushed the can, one-handed. Meanwhile, Kinta gave me a refill on the coffee and a handful of Tums. The room had slowed to a low tumble now.

"The perps aren't talking yet," Thé said, "but my guess is that they're undocumented. If we can tie them to the hotel attack, and maybe something on the Heilbrun case, we may be able to make a deal with them."

"They turn in whoever hired them in exchange for some leniency or a reduced charge, maybe just send them back to the islands," continued Estrada, fleshing it out. "It's not like they're mobbed up and need the witness protection program if they talk."

So maybe the cops would get something out of the hoods. They seemed to think it looked likely. I hoped it would happen before show time on Friday, but Janice Thé declined to predict the future. She wasn't the crystal ball type anyway. Thé agreed that they would be there Friday in case somebody needed arresting. I told her to bring enough handcuffs to go around.

"*So, folks, politics plays second fibber, er, fiddle to murder on today's snow...that is, today's show...*" The Manhattans hadn't been entirely dissipated by four cups of black coffee but I sure was wide awake. "*Listen, you folks out there, today has been mother, uh, murder, not least because they tried to spill me—er, kill me—twice in the past couple of days. The last time seemed like only today...I want you all to know the dangers of riding public transit....*"

I could see the words floating around in my mind, but they

tended to be all jumbled by the time they got to my mouse, er, mouth. Anyway, I kept rambling on, it being my show. I tried to focus on the murder story and on plugging Friday's séance. Kinta pumped me with even more coffee and put through almost every caller to give me some breathing room. We repeated some commercials two or three times while I worked on my rehab.

By the time I signed off, my head had stopped spinning, my vision had cleared and that interesting little slur had disappeared. My mind was clear as a bell except for the bombs going off in the top of my head. I hate getting a hangover when it's not even the morning after. Not that I have too many since being incoherent on the show isn't really considered good form.

Surprisingly, Brad and Kinta thought it was a good show. To hear them talk I was better than ever. On the other hand, they could have been building up my confidence before Ned called in to hammer me down. But when even the news reader said it was a good show, I wondered if I should burn my twelve-step card and join the bottle of the mouth club.

I began to feel a lot better about things as the fog lifted. Mine, not the one covering the City. The Filipino thugs were in jail, I had had a good show, the aspirins were kicking in, and most amazing, I was still alive. I called Christy to let her know that the bad guys wouldn't be visiting Arizona any time soon. After some lovey-dovey stuff, I told her how I had practically collared them myself. I didn't want Christy to worry about me, so I pumped up my part for her benefit. Well, for my benefit really.

Christy told me about her day too. She had done the open sesame routine on Tucson National's vault and gotten her dad's papers. She had made copies and returned the originals to the bank. Now she was reading through them, but it was slow going, a lot of lawyer-speak. Luckily, an old college chum of hers was back in town from law school and would know all the theretofores and whereasis. Christy thought she might get him to help. Something about all they had shared together.

Anyway Christy promised to be back with the goods in time for the séance, even if she had to be with her old chum day and night. I didn't like the sound of that, but kept it to myself. I just told her I couldn't wait to see her and the papers. My career was riding on it.

Chapter 30.

"YOU betcher ass, absolutely." Charlie Wooten was being expansive having just had a three martini lunch. Charlie wasn't one for celery sticks and carrot juice. Not until his next heart attack anyway, and probably not even then. Still he never forgot a car or the driver it belonged to. "Yeah," he was saying, "Tony drove a real sweet 745Li back then. Dark blue. I remember he traded it in just before Christmas for the Lexus."

"The one he has now?"

"Sure. I figured he was buying himself an early Christmas present," Charlie said, his mood as sunny as the weather. Although I doubted he would even know if it was raining after all those drinks, but on the other hand, I didn't come to talk about the weather. "I remember we had just done a real good fix-up on the BMW. I think the side was all fucked up."

"You got some memory."

"I keep track of most things that go on here. Somebody's got to, if you want to keep the goddamn' people coming back. If I remember right, you're overdue for service too, Jerry."

I promised I'd bring the Beamer in and declined Charlie's offered of a big green cigar he'd pulled from his pocket. It looked a little sat-on, but Charlie didn't seem to notice. He bit off the end, spitting it in the general direction of the shop door, then pulled out a lighter with about a pound and a half of gold wrapped around it and flamed the Corona until it was burning just right. He might have been playing for time, trying to remember if I'd gotten my tires rotated recently. By the time he was done breathing life into the cigar, I was lightheaded from the smoke and the smell of gas and oil from service bay.

Charlie was maybe five feet inside the big roll-up door.

Some cop driving a Hyundai might be angry enough to write him up for smoking indoors, but then none of the cops on Charlie's beat would still be driving Hyundais. Charlie's a pal, but I was still tempted to rat him out for polluting the atmosphere. That stogie oughta come with a catalytic converter.

"Sure, you bet I remember that car," Charlie's mind finally clicked into gear, "it being Tony Paulson and all, I wanted to make sure he was taken care of. That, I do remember. After all, I had just got KPMT to put you on not long before. I didn't want another disaster."

"Right, good thinking, Charlie. So what was the deal on the 745Li? The side was damaged, you say?"

"Oh, you bet. Tony had some cock and bull story about it getting side-swiped parked outside his place. But at the same time, he didn't want to make an insurance claim. We see a lot of cars come in here and Matarasso, my bodywork guy, sees even more of this stuff."

"I'll bet. But exactly what stuff are you talking about?"

"Fuckin' automotive bodywork," Charlie said. "What the fuck are we talking about here, Red? Paulson sure didn't get that damage parked in front of his goddamn' house. I remember it was a bad scrape on the front quarter panel and the bumper was bent a little. In other words, Paulson had to have been the swiper, not the swipee, if you get my meaning. I got pictures if you don't believe me. Steve Matarasso took some photos in case we decided to use the insurance after all. Sometimes people want to keep it off their record, but change their minds when they hear the cost."

"Did Tony?"

"No way. The station was paying, so it was no skin off his nose. But I remember I called Ned Tunney just to make sure he didn't want to run it through the insurance anyway. His car was in for new tires come to think of it. He had me put the cheapest tires I could find on his own car, so I was surprised when he said to just fix Tony's ride and the station would pick up the tab."

"Really? You got some memory, Charlie."

"Like I say, in this business, it pays. I'm hoping you're not going to do anything with what I told you that will make me regret having such a good memory, are you?"

"Let's go look at those pictures."

AFTER my visit to Wooten Imports, I was feeling the day was shaping up as a decent one for playing detective. It had started out great with the intense blue sky that stands in when the fog takes a day off. I had gotten up around ten-thirty which is pretty early for me. I did some deep knee bends and a few crunches before breakfast, breathed a little of the clean city air eighteen stories up, careful not to get too close to the edge. It's a long way down, so I decided I'd better take the elevator. I got coffee and the weather being so nice, I picked a sunny sidewalk table for my first coffee of the day. Summer in San Francisco and no jacket needed. Imagine that.

Before planning out my visit to Charlie's auto palace, I decided to call Christy and almost spilled my cappuccino when she picked up on the first ring. This time I would buy a lottery ticket. After all, I might need a little nest egg if everything worked out with us.

"Hey, babe," she answered. Her voice sending the good kind of shiver up my spine. And she called me 'babe'.

"Hey, babe, yourself. How's the paper chase doing? I was hoping you were about to wrap things up and head back to the Barbary Coast," I said.

"You know, Jerry, there are some very interesting things in Dad's papers. But I'm not sure what it all means yet."

"Any hints would be appreciated, read me a few clauses and sub-clauses and sub-sub-clauses. Maybe we can get a sound bite to tease Friday's show. You know, party of the first part and all that kind of thing."

"Oh, well, I don't actually have the papers anymore."

"I didn't quite hear that—a truck just rumbled by. I thought it sounded like you said you didn't have the papers anymore."

"That's right, sweetie, that is what I said."

The missing documents gone missing again. My stomach was doing that thing it does when I'm looking over the edge of a bottomless well. I'm no clairvoyant, but I could see a certain séance taking the plunge. Along with my ratings, my show and my way of life.

"Uh, how can I put this gently," I said, "but I thought we thought those papers held the key to a couple of murders, your dad's included."

"Oh, Jerry, don't be a butthead. The papers aren't lost or stolen or anything. I gave them to a guy I know to analyze, a former classmate of mine."

"Not the lock-picking quarterback?"

"No, not Mark. He's a teacher now, he doesn't know anything. I gave the papers to Peter Rebutto. He's in second year law school and interning for a judge in town. He'll do anything for me."

"He will, eh? You two were like brother and sister, I guess?"

"Now don't be jealous. There's no reason to be, Petey and I are just good friends now."

"So has Petey found anything to help us in your dad's papers?"

"Well, I think so. It looks like maybe somebody was fucking around with the station's finances. Before Dad could sell his share of the station, he had the books audited to determine the asking price. It looks like the audit turned up some funny stuff in the accounts. The books were cooked according to Petey."

"So can Petey tell who the Emeril Lagasse of the income statement was?"

"Not exactly, but there may be some clues. Petey says 'follow the bread.'"

"What? He's a part-time baker too?"

"No, the bread, the dough, the *money*. It's the trail to the bastard who killed Dad. There's an accounting whiz I went to school with who knows all about computer systems helping Petey on it."

"Jeez, what did you major in? Interpersonal relations?"

"Don't be silly, Jerry, my friend's name is Sally and we were freshman roommates."

A Muni bus screeched by, drowning out the conversation for a moment. "What? I couldn't make you out, Jerry," Christy was saying. "What was that noise? Did you...that? I think...losing the signal anyway."

"Hey, I'm still here. Can you hear me now?"

"Jerry...before I lose...completely." A sound like crackling cellophane drowned out her voice. "Sally and Petey think...documents show...in time...."

I lost her signal but I was pretty sure she was gonna say how crazy she was about me and that she couldn't live without me. Maybe she'd even forget about those old college chums if I cracked her dad's murder. I checked my messages before heading back to my apartment to get ready for my trip to Charlie Wooten's showroom. The only message was from Dennis Hong checking whether Marsha could hang out during the séance; they must have put their egos away and patched things up.

By the time I was through pumping Charlie about the car business it was getting on towards air time so I headed directly to the KPMT studios. I was hoping I might get a minute or two to ask Ned what he knew about Tony's old car, but he was tied up in some kind of meeting with Freddy and Betty and their manager. Poor guy, all that surfing and the only sharks he sees are on land.

"YOU know it's a given that the President of the United States is literally the most powerful man on earth. And of course, some presidents are stronger than others, but when it comes to raw power in politics—or in government for that matter—I always say that once again California leads the way. Boxer, Feinstein, Pelosi—they're all sissies when it comes to real bulk. In my opinion, a really powerful politician should be able to bench press at least three hundred pounds. Most of the wimps on either side of the aisle spend way too little time pumping iron. They're always out campaigning or writing up new laws.

"But California was blessed with our very own Conan the Republican. Sure he's making movies now, but he's shown he has the power to do a clean-and-jerk with something as heavy as the state budget. And just look at the size of that cigar he hauls around—let's see Jerry Brown suck on that.

"Now maybe when Jesse Ventura was governor of Minnesota, Arnold would have had some competition. Not only a powerful governor, Jesse could execute the flying drop kick on his political opponents. On the other hand, our guy is pretty good with the two-handed broadsword...."

I promo'd the Friday show every chance I got with an occasional plug for Ronnie's gig at the Blue Sphinx thrown in for good measure. After all, what's a pal for. If Ronnie ever made it big, he could return the favor by sawing me in two or something. The show moved along smoothly, callers calling, commercials irritating, news and traffic ditto. And then I signed off and was free for another twenty-one hours. Plenty of time to sit at Miss Silvano's empty desk and use her phone to call Ilonya Zoroaster. Rita's perfume still lingered in the air, maybe from her drawers. Not that I'd check out her drawers without her wanting me to.

Vigo Czak answered. His Peter Lorre was almost perfect, if

only Lorre had had more of a lisp. Madame Z was busy marking the tarot cards or something, but I had a nice chat with the boy troll. Ilonya and Vigo had been able to set up housekeeping in a place of their own recently.

Lucky Tony.

Turns out the spiritualist business was thriving in spite of people living longer. Apparently the Madame had a pretty busy schedule what with the society friends that Tony had introduced her to, not to mention the friends of the friends, and the friends of the friend's friends and so on. But lucky for me, according to Czak, the Madame had foreseen a little get together and we should be there at noon tomorrow. I guess they sleep late too. Up 'til the witching hour no doubt.

Leaving KPMT, I ran into Brad the Brat. He was headed over to the Grotto and wanted to drag me along. The word was Jeanne would be wrapping up ESPN's game coverage from the Dodger locker room. I hoped Jeanne had somehow set my recorder to catch it. I'd love to see the girl I loved hanging out with a room full of naked men. But then Jeanne was always ready to put out a hundred per cent. But I had to pass on Brad's offer to let me buy him drinks, let alone see a naked baseball team. I had no time for that kind of foolishness right now.

I had a magic show to see.

Chapter 31.

For a Tuesday night the Sphinx was jumping. I guess my plugs were working. At this rate, Ronnie would be able to give up doing tricks on street corners. On a good day he probably gets ten, fifteen dollars in the hat. Not enough to get a real rabbit yet, but maybe in a couple of years.

I found a spot at the bar and ordered a club soda, no lime, no ice, no glass. I take it straight from the bottle. Rhonda Ridgeway was sitting at a small table near the stage, her eyes watching The Great Rondini's every move. Most other eyes in the place were glued on Satyra who was in the audience again picking out the rubes whose minds Ronnie would read. The deepest secrets were like an open book to Ronnie, large type edition too.

"And where are you from?" Satyra waved the mic in front of a pretty face.

"Chicago," the face said, reaching for the hand of the guy sitting next to her. "Actually we live right outside of Chicago—"

"I am beginning to see a house...no, I lie, it is more than a house, it is a home," The Great Rondini intoned, "...light yellow paint...with green shutters...a two car garage..."

"My God! That sounds just like our place," said the woman.

"Okay, shall we put The Great Rondini to the test?" Satyra said, throwing out a challenge. The audience burst into applause while the couple from right outside of Chicago smiled and nodded a little shyly. Maybe they were thinking Rondini might know a little too much about what went on in bedroom communities outside Chi-town.

"Before the show tonight, The Great Rondini wrote a

234 Donald J. McGill

message on the blackboard you see behind him. What he wrote will be revealed in a moment, but first—" Satyra paused let the suspense build, then asked, "Rondini, can you see the names of our visitors from Illinois?"

Like a beginner in phonetics, Ronnie sounded out the parts, "Ma-Mar-Mart—I am getting the name Martin. Maybe a first name or maybe a last. And I see G-Gi-Gi—no, it's a J. Ji-Jim and another J-Ju-Judy. Jim and Judy Martin." The out-of-towners were jumping and twitching in their seats now. They owned up to being Jim and Judy. Then Ronnie started in seeing numbers, one by one he put them together, "four-seven-three-one."

"Do these numbers mean anything to you?" Satyra asked Jim and Judy.

"Yes," Jim agreed that they did. Then Judy blurted out, "They're our house numbers, forty-seven thirty-one West Elm Street."

"God, I hope you cleaned," Jim said, "before he looked inside."

"Well, I'm sure he'll find your shorts on the floor right where you left 'em," Judy fired back.

AH yes, Rondini strikes again. Another happy marriage shot to pieces. From honeymoon to divorce court, all in one easy illusion.

"Ladies and gentlemen," Satyra's voice filled the room as she walked back on the stage, "will you please direct your attention to Rondini's blackboard—we will now reveal the message written before tonight's show!"

Moving to the right of the board while Ronnie took the left, with a flourish Satyra flipped it over, showing the audience the words written on it—

JAMES AND JUDITH MARTIN
4731 E. OAKRIDGE AVENUE
ITASCA, ILLINOIS 60143
USA

"He got everything but your bra size," Jim Martin said to Mrs. Jim Martin. She in turn gave hubby her back. But she did give The Great Rondini a big smile. If our boy played his cards right, he might just find out Judy Martin's bra size.

Ronnie and Satyra bowed and curtsied, twirled their capes and tassels, thanked the audience for showing up, did a quick encore and finally made good their escape. I finished my club soda and wandered backstage to chat up Satyra while Ronnie changed out of his waiter's tux in the restroom. Rhonda Ridgeway was apparently helping him although there seemed to be a lot of giggling going on.

I cornered Satyra in the backstage hallway. She was still in her showgirl outfit, so I didn't mind Ronnie taking his time. Rondini had picked up her costume second hand from an old Vegas revue, but it worked its kind of magic in San Francisco too.

"Good show tonight, love," I said, giving her an appreciative smile. "The bit with the honeymooners was a new wrinkle."

"Ronnie and I worked it out this afternoon," she said as she slipped off her six-inch heels. Minus the heels we could see eye to eye and I'm a six-footer. She gave me a smile and eye to eye, she told me, "Jim's a cousin of Ronnie's hair stylist. Ronnie gets free haircuts for breaking the kid into the business."

"Gee, I thought Ronnie cut it himself, you know, looking in the mirror."

"Don't take that smoke and mirror stuff too literally," she said. "Can you unzip me a little? This outfit's a little tight around the chest."

Absolutely I could do that.

I told Satyra that the cousin and his squeeze did okay, but that she was the one who really carried the act. "Ronnie's my pal," I said, "but we need to face facts, he's getting a little long in the tooth. What is he now? Thirty-four? Thirty-five? Practically middle-aged. He's on AARP's mailing list already."

"I thought you guys were the same age, went to school together and all."

"Same graduating class, but he was left back a few times. He was the only kid at Garfield Junior High old enough to date the teachers."

"AN ambush," Ronnie was saying, speaking just above a whisper. Everybody looked around the pizza place for gypsy eavesdroppers who might be in the employ of Madame Zoroaster. "Not my style really, but it's the only way to break this case open. Take JJ here, he's in the media so he does it all the time, he thinks nothing of it...." I was feeling a little ambushed myself at this point. Ronnie was probably trying to impress the Ridgeway babe.

He said, "We'll catch Madame Zoroaster and that spooky Czak off guard by springing your return appearance as the Rubensteins on them." Rhonda Ridgeway and Alain de la Cruz were hanging on his every word.

Cruize had joined us at a late baking pizza parlor not far from the Sphinx. The owner, a guy named Angelo, threw a good pie, not to mention he scored extra points by recognizing me from TV. Of course I acted suitably embarrassed when Mrs. Angelo insisted on taking my photo with hubby in front of the oven. They said the picture would go over the cash register along with Gavin Newsom and Don Johnson. I told Ronnie he might make the wall of fame if he wore the turban next time.

Back at the Sphinx, I had given the gang the rundown on yesterday's encounter with Tank Top and his pal and how we could breathe easier now they were behind bars. Thanks to my quick thinking, etc., etc. I did manage to work Thé and Estrada into the story, but what the hey it was my story, wasn't it. It was good news for Rhonda anyway no longer having to share a room with Ronnie.

The pizzas began to roll out of Angelo's kitchen, some of the classics like barbequed chicken with hosan sauce and then some not so typical. Cruize got a pie with avocado and jalapenos, while Satyra had ordered a combo that included mangos and coconuts. Since almost everyone had their own preference in the beer department too, we wound up with about a half dozen pitchers to finish.

We agreed to turn the screws on Dracula's daughter and her midget with the diamond bracelet swindle. To get out from under that, we were sure they would roll-over on Tony.

"The thing that still puzzles me," I said, mopping the suds off my lap, "is how come Tony almost knocked Christy and me off to keep us from seeing the papers, and he did have Heilbrun killed for them, but hasn't done anything about Ilonya and the hunchback? They're the ones bleeding him dry."

Ronnie emptied the pitcher of Belgium brown ale into a few of our glasses, saying, "It's the old safe deposit scam. They tell Tony that if anything happens to them, the evidence will be turned over to the cops by a mysterious third party."

"Oldest trick in the book," Cruize said. He must have been

an extra on *Nash Bridges*. Or maybe put on the tights for *The Merchant of Violence*.

"What Madame Zoroaster is holding over Tony must be in the Marshall documents," Ronnie said. "If every copy gets destroyed, maybe there won't be anything left they can use against Tony."

"Unless she really has a copy in the bank," Satyra said.

"Ain't that the truth," Cruize said, and with a burst of insight, he added "and there isn't any way for Tony to know, so burning all the other papers just helps Madame Z's position."

"Well, I don't think Madame Z will go down for the diamond bracelet scam without using Tony as a bargaining chip," I said. "However, she might not want to finger herself as a blackmailer. Even if murder trumps blackmail, she still may want to keep it to herself."

"Sure, we need to break her down," said Sherlock de la Cruz to Satyra's cleavage. Maybe he thought she had a microphone hidden in there. Anyway, she didn't seem to mind.

"Let's think this through," said Ronnie. "What else can we get on Tony? If we have enough evidence, Ilonya may throw in with us to make the bracelet fraud look like part of Tony's master plan."

"I don't know," Satyra said, planting an elbow in the Cruizer's ribs to get a little more...uh, elbow room. "It seems like a lot going on for one night, the bracelet caper and also a murder all the way up in Marin."

"Maybe that was the idea—the radio hoax creates a diversion so that nobody would think too hard about the murder," Cruize suggested. Okay, so maybe he wasn't so goofy. Satyra rewarded him with a smile. But he was still rubbing his ribcage.

"Point well taken." I smiled at Satyra like it was her idea. "But I'm going to need all the ammunition I can get if I'm going to try to nail Tony. Mrs. Paulson will skin me alive if it winds up looking like we sandbagged her nephew by mistake."

"We'll be sandbagging him on purpose," Ronnie said.

"Pamela Kay Paulson has to absolutely believe we did the right thing," I said. "That we have exposed the guy behind the murders of her business partner and her attorney. Not to put too fine a point on it, we need to give the cops enough reason to hold Tony and keep some slick lawyer from springing him."

"Except that lawyer's dead," said Rhonda. "Now they'll need to find a new one. That should keep him locked up a little longer."

"Sure, every cloud has its silver lining, but try telling that to Heilbrun."

"If we need to get a line on Paulson, why don't we set something up? Like having Rhonda accidentally on purpose run into him someplace," Cruize said. "A bar or something, and she turns on her charms, makes a play for him. If they get cozy, she might get him to say something that will help us."

"What the hell? What's with you, Alain?" Rhonda said. "You think I'm some kind of a hooker?"

"Come on, Rho, it happens all the time, you want to nail down a role or something. I can't believe you won't do this for the show."

"Listen, I'm as good a sport as the next guy," Ronnie spoke up, "but I don't think Rhonda's that kind of girl."

"Thanks, love," Rhonda said. "It's a stupid idea, Cruize, but anyway Tony knows who I am, it'd ruin the surprise for him if I showed up early. Now, has he ever met Satyra?"

"Hold on," Ronnie and Cruize said together.

"Hold it, everybody," I said. After all, somebody needed to get this train back on its track. "I don't think either of you are going to put the moves on Tony anytime soon. As it turns out he's gay."

I explained how he told me he didn't particularly try to hide it, but felt it was best to keep his personal life separate from the office. I could just imagine the damper this might put on him taking Charlie Wooten out to the local strip club.

"Sure, you guys are something else," Rhonda said. "As soon as Cruize has to suck his dick, it's off the table."

"Please, nobody wants to see his dick on the table at all."

Ronnie ran everybody through their paces again. We were all pinning our hopes on Christy. Her and a guy named Petey. I knew she'd find some hard evidence in her dad's papers, but we also tried out a few backup plans just in case. None of them were any good though if Ilonya and Vigo were willing to take the fall for the diamond bracelet gag. If Mrs. Paulson kicked in to the Transylvanian defense fund to protect her nephew, I'd be lucky to get a job doing overnights in the Prague.

We finished the evening with Angelo's special coffee. He had whatever you wanted as long as it was regular or decaf. Then Ronnie and Rhonda headed over to her place, since there was no longer any chance of the hoods hanging about. I wondered how she would unload the Ronster, since by now he'd be repeating his usual tricks. Anyway, she'd find it easier to break it off with the front door between them.

Meanwhile, Cruize was cruising after Satyra as she went looking for a cab. I was hoping he wouldn't catch up with her because we needed him in one piece until Friday.

Chapter 32.

THURSDAY was another beautiful day. An amazing string of good weather for the City. In San Francisco you can seldom count on nice weather for more than three days in a row before the fog takes its turn again. The great, grey lady, but for now she was nothing but brightness and light—we were all living on borrowed time.

I had told Ronnie to meet me at Madame Z's place in Pacific Heights. Ilonya and Vigo had moved from Tony's upper-middle 'hood to the heart of the gold plate district. Their flat was in a tidy-looking Victorian but it faced the wrong way for a really good view of the bay. That probably knocked down the monthly by at least a grand in this neighborhood.

The closest parking space was a few blocks away so by the time I got back to the house Rondini was already pacing the sidewalk. Either he used some hoodoo to materialize a parking spot or he had taken the bus here.

"Well, Junior, this is the final go-round before the big day. You all set?"

"I was born set, er, ready. Like I told you, I have photos of the car, we know Tony staged the diamond bracelet scam, Madame Zoroaster apparently has something on him, and Christy thinks her pals will have the legal docs nailed today." And it goes without mentioning, I was counting the minutes until Christy returned. About twenty-four hours worth.

We climbed a dozen steps to the elaborate entryway and found a doorbell with "Celestial Seeings" taped next to it. This had to be the place so we gave it a push. I thought they would buzz us in, but Vigo showed up in the flesh, if you can call it that, and signaled us to follow him up a flight of stairs. On the second floor he stopped in front of a oak paneled doorway and gave a couple of sharp raps. I wondered why he needed to knock at his own place but didn't get a chance to ask, because almost immediately Ilonya Zoroaster cracked the door slightly, paused to check us out, and then she swung it open.

Ronnie and I both got European-style air kisses and were ushered in with a sweep of her arm. The small sitting room was furnished with well worn, overstuffed furniture in a faux-Victorian style. I looked around for any clairvoyant trappings, like Ouija boards or astrological charts, but was disappointed. The flat could have belonged to a retired dot-com millionaire for all it showed.

"So, Ilonya, you moved out of Tony's," I stated the obvious. "Probably easier to entertain clients here, eh?"

"We did move out—reluctantly, Jerry. Tony is such a good host, very generous. But as you know, Jerry, it is not good to wear out your welcome, as they say."

"Your business must be off to a good start with a place like this," said Ronnie.

Vigo Czak, firing up a small cigar with a large flame, said, "Yes, as Ilonya says, Tony is very generous and he has many contacts. People who have great needs for Madame Zoroaster's gifts."

"I would have thought Tony would have been kind of sore about how things turned out before," I said. "You know with the diamond bracelet and the station and all. Personally, I got quite a talking to after that one."

"Oh, Jerry, I hope you are not holding us responsible for that thing," Madame Z protested. "That had nothing to do with us—we could not help it if someone stole the jewelry. When my spirit guide calls on me as his channel to this plane, I cannot control what comes out. I only know that it is the truth."

"Oh yeah, well about the truth—" Ronnie started to say when I headed him off. I didn't want Ilonya to get a sudden case of laryngitis.

"Of course not," I said. "Nobody would expect you to push around the ghost of Christmas past. We want the truth. We want you and your ghosts to help us get the truth."

"Sure, my thoughts exactly. Jerry took the words right out of my mind," Ronnie said. "We need this séance to be on the up and up, all the way up. We need a real-time connection to the other side to help solve a couple of murders—we want you to contact the victims themselves."

"An interesting approach, although I would not trust the American police to believe in my power to do this."

"Don't sweat it," I said. "I have a prediction of my own—the cops *will* believe you when you name the killer. I mean when the spirits do, and we are counting on you to make that happen."

"If everyone is willing to join their positive energies into a powerful force field, I can be successful in communicating to those having passed over. Perhaps even your victims."

She sounded like she was in a trance already.

"It's all about networking."

Everyone looked at Vigo Czak who had just spoken.

"Oh, sure," said Ronnie. "Networking?"

"Must be the very long distance network," I said taking a step back.

"Vigo knows how these things work," said Ilonya. "Spirits having passed over to the other side can be located by my spirit guide and channeled through me for their loved ones still in this world. You must think of it as a cosmic network of souls, both good and bad. To-Nohwa is the firewall protecting us from the malevolent spirits."

Czak gave us a smile, showing off his yellow teeth, and said, "Networking." I felt like smacking his stupid face.

"Speaking of networking the dead, I thought we'd just run down the program for tomorrow's show," I said, smiling my own self just to show what good dental hygiene could do. Ronnie laid out the agenda we wanted Madame Z to think we'd be following, one that gave her room for another scam if she felt like it. If Madame Z really could see into the future, she would have known to steer clear of an encore performance.

Instead Vigo practiced his English on us and Ilonya treated us like a couple of pals. It was hard to think of them as ruthless blackmailers willing to look the other way at murder—perhaps even suppress evidence—for mere money. Well, as reasons go it's not bad.

We finished the set-up, shook everybody's hands, gave Madame Z more air-kisses, and before we knew it, they had shut the door behind us.

At the entryway we paused while Rondini picked the lock on the Celestial Seeings mailbox. All we found were a couple of advertisements and a utility bill addressed to the former tenant. Her e-mail might have held a few more secrets. I'd have to ask Christy if any of her former schoolmates was a hacker. Maybe psychics just sent the good stuff telepathically.

You know, person-to-person.

Ronnie told me he had left Rhonda soaking in the tub and wanted to get back before she dried off. So while he went to find a Fillmore bus, I tried to remember where I parked. I wanted to drop by KPMT to tell Ned that my séance show was a go. I'd hold back on the surprise ending though. Ned might have some wacky desire to tip off Pamela Kay and that might put a crimp in the show, not to mention my career. PK had an obvious blind spot where Tony was concerned, but once we had the goods on him I was sure she'd see the light.

I also wanted to catch Ned because he might remember something about the bodywork on Tony's car. Ned had signed for it, so KPMT would foot the bill. As tight as Ned was, I was sure he would know what Tony's explanation was for the work. As it turned out, the joke was on me. Breaking my record for coming to work early, I found that Ned was breaking his record for leaving early.

Michael the receptionist—the kid who idolizes me for bringing murder and gore to the station—tipped me that Ned had snuck out for an afternoon riding the waves. Michael said that I'd find him out at Ocean Beach.

DESPITE unseasonably sunny skies elsewhere in the City, Ocean Beach looked like the North Atlantic during a hard winter. The only thing missing were icicles hanging off the tourists who somehow confuse these beaches with the ones you see in all those beach blanket bongo movies made in SoCal.

The waves were giving the shore a terrific pounding and the wind was beginning to blow spume and sand across the walkway at the top of the beach where I was standing. I didn't see Ned anywhere though. There were a couple of specks bobbing way out in the water, but they couldn't be surfers, not in weather like this and not if they valued their lives.

I approached a girl standing next to a van full of surf boards and asked where to surfers hang out. What could she say but, "Usually over their Speedos."

"How's that?"

"That's a joke. Hanging out over their Speedos, get it?"

"Oh yeah," I said, "pretty funny. It would be even funnier if you actually knew where they did hang, you being in the business and all." I pointed to the sign on her van. "Eva's Surfboard Rentals" was hand-lettered on scrap plywood. Concise and to the point. Eva herself looked concise and to the point, and ready to go in a lime colored wet suit unzipped and pulled down to her waist. It showed off a good tan, but mainly it showed lots of gooseflesh from the chill blowing off the water.

"How was I to know you didn't have a sense of humor? Sure I know where they hang," she slide a board out and leaned it against the van where the wind blew it over. "But right now nobody's just hanging out, they hanging ten." Eva pointed out to the specks in the water.

"I thought those were seabirds."

"Surfin' birds is more like it."

"You ever see an older guy out here. His name's Ned Tunney. Probably comes out once or twice a week."

"Ned? He's out here more than that. You're not his boss are you?"

"No, and I'm not the truant officer either."

"What's a truant officer?"

"Don't you watch Little Rascals? Well, never mind, it's not important."

"I can tell, you're the boss."

"No, Ned's the boss actually."

"Wow, he's got some gig."

"Anyway, I've got to talk to him. How long is it before these guys catch a wave and come back here?"

"All depends. Waves come in a chain, building up to the sweet ride, the really good wave, then slack off again. The doggies hope to catch the sweet one, but if they wait too long and the waves slack off, they wind up having to wait for the next chain to build up."

I should have brought a translator.

"I don't suppose these guys carry their cell phones out there?"

"Dude, this is one place where you go to get away from cell phones, X-boxes, iPods, whatever. It's all about man and wave. Or it could be woman and wave." Next thing you know she'd be lecturing me about man, woman and waves.

"I need to talk to Ned."

"Well, it looks pretty slow out there now. They probably won't be in for a while, but you know, if the mountain won't come to Muhammad...you know what I mean?"

"No, what?"

Five minutes later, I was inside a day-glow orange wet suit and Eva was pushing me into the surf on one of her rentals. The main instruction she gave me was to keep paddling and don't come back without the board. I wondered if Muhammad really started like this.

I tried paddling through the breakers, hoping the sweet ride wasn't about to smack me down. I was trying to keep one eye on the specks, one eye out for sharks and one eye on the receding shoreline. I managed to splash around a lot, gain a little ground, and then a wave would push me shoreward. I could see the specks weren't seabirds now though and the shoreline was beginning to look a long ways off. My teeth began to chatter and I was hoping it was from the cold. Up ahead I could see six distinct bodies bobbing upright in the water which seemed to be getting a bit rougher. One of the bodies—the second one over from the left—looked like it could be Ned.

I paddled some more and could now recognize Ned in spite of his goggles and nose clip. With his hair plastered down, he seemed a lot balder than he did at work, and the waistline of his wet suit bulged more than I would have thought, but it was definitely him. Out here the wind seemed less strong and Ned heard me when I yelled his name. I kept on paddling, slowly making my way over to him.

"Jerry! Can that be you? What the hell are you doing out here?"

"I'll go anywhere if it'll help the show." I spit out a mouthful of salt water and grabbed onto his board to keep from drifting past. Ned was able to pull me into a sitting position astride my board, but I seemed to be backwards, looking out to sea while the surfers faced the shore.

"What the hell are you babbling about? What about your show?"

"I'm zeroing in on the killer of Tom Marshall and Leland Heilbrun, Ned," I said, gasping a little as the swell bounced us up and down. My stomach didn't seem to be getting the hang of it. A little bigger wave did an encore and I gripped the board with hands and legs and anything else I could use. I said, "Tomorrow night my listeners will be the first to know who the killer is."

"What makes you think that you know who it is?"

"What? Well, look, Christy has found some incriminating papers of her dad's back in Tucson, and we have some very strong evidence about the car that ran Tom off the road."

"You have all that?"

"Sure, that's why I almost drowned myself to get out here to talk with you. Christy will be flying back here tomorrow with the goods and we'll bring the cops in on the air. They'll find out when everybody else does, and we'll have an arrest right there on my show. I'll be *numero uno* with a bullet after that."

Ned accidentally bumped into my board and I had to grab onto him to keep from sliding into the deep blue. His board then began to tip, upending him. Ned's feet broke the surface, sending plumes of water into the air. His head went under at about the same time with barely a splash.

"Jesus, Jerry!" the water spewing out of his mouth made the rest undecipherable.

"Jesus, Ned, grab on," I said. "I'll pull you up."

"No, just stand back," Ned did a neat kip up and mount onto his board. "If anybody's going to drown out here, Jerry, it's not going to be me."

"Don't worry, Ned," I was struggling to stay on myself as the board tipped and bucked. "I've got a survivor's instincts."

"So Marshall's little girl has solved the mystery," Ned had to yell as the wind picked up again. "And you know whodunit, eh?"

Ned's surfer pals had found a variety of perfect waves and were speeding atop them toward the shore by now, crouching for balance, feet dancing, arms outstretched. A board flew high in the air as one of the surfers wiped out.

"Christy's having some people go over her dad's papers," I yelled back, "and she'll be on tomorrow's afternoon flight from Tucson. She'll make it just in time for the show."

I was sprawled on the board now with my arms and legs wrapped around it. I think Eva gave me a child's board when what I needed out here was one of those really big boards. Sails and a motor won't hurt either.

I held on and shouted, "Until she gets here we won't have the last piece of the puzzle, but just you wait...."

Ned's voice was drowned out by the wind, but he pushed up on his knees and took a few strong strokes in the water, picking up the momentum of a large swell. As he stood, his board came alive, swerving close to me as he charged by. Its wake rolled me over so I was clinging to the underwater side of my board. I held on tight though and held my breath too for as long as I could. Then, I let go and struck out hoping I was headed towards the surface.

I don't like opening my eyes under water, so I just hoped I was swimming in the right direction. After what must have been ten or twenty minutes I still hadn't made it to the top so I was about to turn around when suddenly I was gulping fresh air having broken through the surface waves. Maybe it only seemed like ten or twenty minutes; still I didn't like thinking about what could have happened had I turned around.

I tried to tread water while coughing out plenty more of the stuff, trying to catch my breath between spasms. Slowly my panic from being on the wrong side of the surface was replaced by my panic at being all alone far from shore. I tried to give it my best flutter kick but something was pulling me back. My right leg was fine, but something had a grip on my left ankle. Something I couldn't kick loose.

Oh my God! I tried to stifle a scream as I realized something had a hold on my leg. From the corner of my eye I could see a big torpedo shape behind me following my every move. A great white! A man—and Jeremy—eating shark. Its pointy nose breaking through the waves, those red and yellow stripes on its back.

Kind of odd for a shark.

Sure, it's okay, I knew it all the time. What a gag. It's the surf board. I remember Eva tethering it to my ankle. No shark. No white death. Not yet anyway.

But I still had drowning to worry about.

I got to the board and held on to stay afloat, figuring I could kick with my legs until I got to shore. Except being low in the water, I couldn't exactly see which way the shore was. The only thing I could see in any direction was the blue Pacific. I figured if Ned had seen me wipe out, he would be back soon. Momentarily, I hoped and with help. Did they have a Ski Patrol out here?

If Ned had seen me....

I had watched Ned pull himself out of the water onto his board and it looked pretty easy, but after trying a dozen or so times with no luck, I figured there was more to this surfing stuff than it appeared. Anyhow the trick eluded me. One of those things you're supposed to learn back on shore I now supposed.

The sky looked darker, but it couldn't have been more than two o'clock. I make it a rule never to miss a show and I still had time to get to mine if the Coast Guard found me in the next hour or so. Presuming I was still above water by then.

"Dude! Hey, whatcha doing in the water? You're supposed to be on the waves not under 'em."

"Eva! You've come to save me," I shouted.

"No way, dude, I'm here for my board. I should pull that

wetsuit off your bony ass and leave you out here."

"You can have the wet suit, but I'm not giving up this board—I go where it goes. Help me up so I can ride in style." I was splashing around in circles as Eva tugged on my arm. The board refused to stay in one spot, but the good news was that Eva was a whole lot stronger than she looked. Somehow she muscled me onto the board. Then Eva snapped a tether to my board and told me to hang on. Like I needed convincing.

With her pulling and the ocean pushing, we moved in fast. As the waves broke near shore, I did a few underwater rolls and swallowed a lot more seawater than I was sure was good for me. However before long, lo and behold, I was kissing the sand of Ocean Beach. I abruptly stopped it when I thought about what might have gone on in that sand. I wouldn't want to walk barefoot on the beach, let alone put my lips on it.

Eva managed to pry me off her surfboard, got me dried off and in my clothes about sixty bucks lighter for the rental and the tow. Not bad, I thought. Maybe I could do a show on the politics of surfing. Eva said she'd come on the air if she could plug her business. I might get Ned on too, if he wasn't out actually surfing. Gnarly, dude.

Speaking of Ned, I wondered where he'd disappeared to. I had taken a quick look around when I reached shore hoping the regulars hadn't seen my triumphal return. Then or now, Ned was nowhere to be seen. Most of his surfing buddies were still there, some going back out for another ride, others just hanging out, comparing boards and shivering. In spite another brush with death, it looked to be just a routine day at the beach.

"*IT'S* another beautiful day in the Bay Area. We're having a great summer, folks, but autumn going to be a little early this year on KPMT, Big Shot Radio. Tomorrow we're going to have our special Halloween show. You'll want to pick up a couple of carpoolers for the ride, because you won't want to be alone. Tomorrow I will reveal the identity of a real ghoul, one who walks among us, a murderer who killed on Halloween and again just days ago.

"Full moon or not, tomorrow the ghosts of victims past will not only rattle their chains, they will rat out their killer, here on KPMT, the murder station...."

So I waxed poetic less than twenty-four hours before I would solve the double murder and win the girl. I certainly hoped Rondini knew what he was doing.

Chapter 33.

I DON'T know why but it always happens—everybody calls my cell while I'm on the air. I don't know if they ever try our call-in line, but my voicemail takes a beating whenever I'm working. Tonight, they were merciless. Mrs. Paulson had called twice, telling me I'd better get back to her before she made it three times. News travels fast, so maybe she heard about my surfing adventures and wanted to make sure I was okay. Or that my train hadn't totally jumped its tracks.

Inspector Thé and The Great Rondini had also called and left messages. But instead of calling Pamela Kay back, or even Janice or Ronnie, I pressed the speed-dial for Christy and left her a flirty message. I also tried her Mom's number just in case she had decided to give her old school pals a pass tonight. I suspected the boys might need a break by now. I got Mom's machine. This time I left a message that Hallmark would be proud to put on a card just in case Mom picked it up first.

I tried Ronnie, but he was probably working by now, so he got a message too. Not flirty, but not printable either.

I called Janice Thé back on her cell—she had said day or night—and she picked up on the first ring. She had a kind of a good news-bad news thing going. The bad news was that they didn't have enough on Tank Top and his pal to keep them from making bail, which they did. Or somebody did for them.

The good news was that there wasn't more bad news.

The thugs stood on their rights and insisted on a lawyer, the Philippine consul and an interpreter, and for all I knew, a tax accountant and a book deal. Janice's only words of encouragement were: "These guys will probably be on a freighter to Manila before your show goes on. By the way, what time does it go on?"

We spent the next ten minutes going over the séance gag and how it would get the goods on all concerned. Thé and Estrada had tried to sweat the truth out of Manila's most wanted, but hadn't gotten anywhere. However, if Tony broke down and confessed, they could extradite them from the Philippines, provided the local Guardia Nationale could flush them out of the jungle.

After I got off the phone with Janice, I tried to think of a good reason not to return Pamela Kay's call when my caller ID told me Christy was on the line. That was as good a reason as any. It was out of my hands, I had to answer.

"Christy honey, at last it's you. I was sitting by the phone waiting for your call. No food, no water—thank God, I've had enough today—and no other women—just waiting for you."

"Jesus, Jerry, I've been trying to get through for twenty minutes, don't you have call waiting?"

"Uh, I thought I did, but maybe I didn't set it up right. I was on the phone with the Homicide Detail."

"And I thought you could never call a cop when you needed one. Is everything all right? You didn't find another body, did you?"

"No, Thé and Estrada are backing us up on Friday's show. You know, chips, dip, handcuffs."

"That's a good thing, Jerry. My pals found some very incriminating evidence. I'll be bringing notarized copies of them with me. The originals are in the bank vault."

"So give, what did they find?"

"It's a little complicated, but somebody was cooking the books at KPMT."

"And when your dad's auditors were checking everything before he sold his share, they smelled something fishy and it wasn't clam chowder."

"I'm afraid they did find something and it cost Dad his life."

"A motive if I've ever heard one. I'm sorry about your dad, sweetheart. It was a lousy turn."

"I know but I feel better that we're going to put the bastard behind bars. I can't wait to get there. And not just for that, Jerry. I miss you a lot. My old college pals— well, they aren't funny at all compared to you."

"Gee, thanks...I think. I miss you too. When's your flight get in? I'll pick you up."

"That may be a problem. I couldn't get on a flight until the one forty-five. That gets me to SFO after your show has started. I should be able to grab a cab and make it before the séance segment starts though."

"I was planning a nice re-union before going to the station, isn't there something earlier? Try Oakland? San Jose? A Greyhound Bus?"

"'Fraid not, partner. But I'll have the goods there in time for the showdown."

We spent a few minutes saying lovey-dovey stuff, then Christy said she'd see me tomorrow and I said I couldn't wait and we rang off.

It was all coming together. I was a little concerned about the thugs making bail, but as long as they left the country, I'd be happy. I didn't think they'd add much to the show unless they burst in with guns blazing. But that might be a little too much.

I couldn't put off calling Pamela Kay any longer, not if I wanted to keep my job. From deep inside that little voice was telling me to steer clear of anything specific about tomorrow's program. After all, Pamela Kay had said to clear up the Madame Z problem, but I didn't think she meant for me to do it by wrapping the long arm of the law around Tony. My only excuse was that Tony could really use the kind of help they only give out at San Quentin. Maybe twenty years to life's worth.

I was sure that Mrs. P would see just how important it was to do the right thing. Murder was more than some childish hi-jinks. Even if the child was her only nephew.

Anyway Friday's show would put me in the big time. Ned and Pamela Kay couldn't argue with boffo numbers. I clicked her speed-dial.

"You can drop the research on that fortune teller, Jerry."

Pamela Kay's words knocked the wind out of me. What did she mean by "research" anyway? She had ordered me to do anything to get rid of Madame Z short of dropping her into the bay. And that hadn't been ruled out either. Now, two murders later it was just "research"?

"Jerry, I finally got to meet Ilonya this afternoon and she is fucking fabulous," Pamela Kay was bubbling along like George Clooney had just called for a date. "You know, it seems that Tony just got in a little over his head with the house and everything, so he was trying to raise some quick cash. As I suspected, he didn't come to me because he didn't want me to know. Goddamn' ridiculous what these kids will do, isn't it,

254 Donald J. McGill

Jerry?"

She made it sound like all she needed to do was give that young rapscallion a good talking to and it would fix everything. Maybe ground him for a week or two.

"Great, marvelous news," I said. "I guess he only rented out his spare room to get some pocket change."

"What the hell are you talking about, Jerry?"

But it wasn't really a question. Not when she added, "Everything is okay now, so drop it."

"Sure, no problem, PK. Madame Z's got a couple other bank accounts now to fall back on. She can even afford to have her own place now and plenty of treats for her pet monkey. Too bad those bank accounts belong to somebody else."

"Oh, Jerry, who gives a shit about those gypsies now? You and your buddy, you know—the phony mind reader—can have them on your show like you wanted. Show them up as a couple of fucking frauds for all I care. Just leave Tony out of it."

That didn't sound like a question either. It sounded like my job heading south. I echoed her words, "Leave Tony out of it...you betcha."

"I don't want any embarrassment for him or the station, or least of all, for me. I doubt if my friends listen to your show, but I don't think you should go out on any goddamn' limbs, if you get my meaning."

"Whaddaya mean your friends don't listen to my show?"

"I mean keep things straight between us and you'll be fine."

"Don't worry, really, I'm feeling fine already...."

Chapter 34.

*"T*OOOO-*NOOOHWAAAA!"*

Madame Zoroaster was in fine voice, not hers, but doing fine nevertheless. She was howling down the airwaves for a dead Indian. *"Hear me, To-Nohwa!"*

I wondered if Mr. Nohwa was screening his calls, maybe shining her on to that big answering machine in the sky. So far the séance was about as interesting as listening to moss grow on a tombstone.

"Feel our energy! We await your guidance! Toooo-Nooohwaaaa!" Behind her chair Vigo was whispering that maybe she should try it in Hungarian. The audience would really love that. *"You must hear our call, must you not?"*

This was almost as good as dead air. The doorbell's ringing, but nobody's home. The good news was that Ned wasn't here to hear it. Michael said he hadn't shown today and wasn't answering his cell. Probably because it was still on the shore with his beach towel. At least he wouldn't be listening when the show changed directions. Like I said, that was the good news.

The bad news was that we were into the six o'clock segment already and no one had seen hide nor beautiful blonde hair of Christy. Her flight had arrived on time according to Kinta who checked on-line. I had him look over the traffic wire for major accidents or tie ups, but it was just a typical shitty Friday commute. It's always heavy, but not two hours' worth.

"Toooo-Nooohwaaaa!"

I looked at Ronnie hoping he would jump in to save the day. He was sitting on my left and to his left was Ilonya

Zoroaster, facing me. Satyra filled the space between me and the not-too-clairvoyant clairvoyant. The four of us were holding hands around a card table Kinta had set up in the KPMT lobby. Vigo Czak was impersonating a nervous stage mother while Tony Paulson had pulled a chair up behind Satyra, close to the mic but not taking part—yet.

Rhonda and Cruize were stashed in Ned's office with Janice Thé and Tommy Estrada. They could listen to the show without being seen until they got their cues. Time was ticking down and Madame Z was dicking around too long trying to get a dead Indian on the psychic blower. Even if we figured on ditching the six-thirty news break and traffic report, we still had the diamond bracelet scam, a phony medium, two murders and fifty-eight commercials to get through before the top of the hour.

"I can feel your presence!"

That was more like it. Now if she could only reel the old bugger in.

"To-Nohwa, make yourself know to us."

The Z-lady began to tremble, finally shaking to the point that we had to hold the mics to keep them from bouncing off the table. Satyra looked ready to slap Madame Z back to reality and Brad the Brat was getting ready to jump in and save the equipment.

"Send us a sign! Show us you are here!"

Madame Z was looking like a bobble-head doll on a dune buggy dashboard. Vigo was fanning her with an old copy of Radio Today he found lying around. By now Ilonya's eyes were bugging out in two directions at once. As a matter of fact, all our eyes were bugging out.

Suddenly, Madame Zoroaster froze. I was guessing maybe a stroke. That would be just my luck. Killers on the loose, my girl missing with the goods, and now my psychic throws a spoke—

A deep voice came rattled across the room, *"Who calls for the dead? Who needs the wisdom of the infinite spheres? Let all who seek the truth know that To-Nohwa is in now on line."* Czak gave me the giant yellow smile. I was hoping this wasn't just a plug for her website

I leaned into the mic and said, *"Well folks, here we are, reaching out with about forty zillion kilowatts of power, beaming our signal to that big gridlock in the sky, that road trip we'll all be taking someday. Big Chief To-Nohwa is on the psychic radio line. Noh-man, it's Jerry Jeremy here on*

KPMT, Ghost Talk Radio..."

So we introduced everyone again, and had the usual round of plugs. *"That's right, Jerry, half off the cover to anybody who mentions your show...."* Next thing you know, Ronnie would be handing out free-drink coupons. He was getting famous off me, at least for giving away free stuff. He was doing so well he might wind up in the morning drive slot.

Madame Z and her invisible friend burned some air time ditzing around before finally getting down to business. In her To-Nohwa voice, she said, *"Someone seeks the truth from souls that have been taken violently from your plane. I can feel these spirits are uneasy. They too desire justice be done. I will summon them and they will come to you...."*

"Kind of like a heavenly paging system," I said. *"To-Nohwa, the first spirit that I need to interview, uh, that is, commune with, died last Halloween when he was run off the cliffs above the Pacific right into the Pacific. Tom Marshall murdered, maybe by someone at KPMT, maybe someone in this very room. Tom's spirit needs to tell us who."*

How's that for turning up the heat. I got some startled looks from Tony and Vigo, but Ilonya was a trooper, carrying on with the act. *"A life will hang in the balance tonight,"* she baritoned. *"The one with two of the same will need to rise to new heights to tip the balance one way or the other—"*

Ronnie covered his mic and whispered, "Let's get on with it, Junior. Ask who did the deed, who ran Marshall's car off the cliff."

"—tip it the wrong way and happiness will elude you; tip it the right way and who knows what the future will bring."

I hated to break up the soliloquy but I had a show to do. I said, *"Listen, Chief, I know the union says you've got to be cryptic, but I'm not sure I'm following you. Does this have anything to do with the Freddy and Betty show?"*

"This is ridiculous," Tony Paulson muttered from the peanut gallery.

"—you will face the one who seldom listens, but hears you now."

"'One who seldom listens' you say," Ronnie echoed. *"That covers a lot of ground on this show. Oh, Deep Throat, may I address you directly? We've got a murder to solve here."*

"Speak to me," the deep voice commanded. *"Ask what you must know, tell me who you seek."*

Tony Paulson looked like he was getting a bad case of agita. He could probably see what was coming without a crystal ball.

Ronnie said, *"I want Tom Marshall to name the person who killed him. Who ran his car off the road into the Pacific?"*

This wasn't exactly like we had laid it out. The plan had been to tie Madame Zoroaster to the diamond bracelet scam and then get her to spill what she knew about Tony. But we seemed to be edging in the right direction anyway. Maybe Madame Z really had seen the future and didn't want us to go there.

Even so, we were hanging on her and To-Nohwa's every word as though what came next would reveal the truth. She began to bob again and Vigo looked a bit concerned, like maybe he expected her to blow at any moment. Tony shook his head in disgust and Kinta frantically signaled it was time for a commercial break.

"He remembers what he saw on his journey home," To-Nohwa, er, Madame Zoroaster said. *"A passage through thunder and lightning—yes, even in the Bay Area, lightning. In the end, he was blinded by the light. This is all he knows."*

"He doesn't know who did it!" Satyra bounced out of her chair and practically out of her low-cut dress in the bargain. Rondini barked out a laugh like he'd expected the switch all along. Vigo and Tony just looked surprised, but not unhappy.

Madame Zoroaster, the psychic disaster, had stuck it to us again. Then, in her phony To-Nohwa voice, *"The spirits do not always deliver hope, but always bring the truth! You have your answer; your circle is weakening so I must leave you now...."*

"Wait, don't go!" Oops, I'd forgotten this was all a con job, the same one that got me in hot water over a diamond bracelet. At that point, Ilonya Zoroaster pitched forward onto the table and Vigo jumped into action. While Madame Z let out several loud sighs, Vigo carefully cranked her back into an upright position.

Her eyes blinked open and she looked around trying to get her bearings. She looked my way and asked, *"Did anything happen? Did we penetrate the veil?"* A nice touch, an improvement over her performance last Halloween.

"We reached somebody," Ronnie said, *"but I don't think it was from the other side, unless you mean somebody from the other side of an ocean."*

"What are you trying to say to us?" Vigo Czak gave Ronnie the evil eye.

"I said—as Jerry might say—I said what I said. And I'd

like to offer some proof. I'm a bit of a spiritualist myself."

"Amen, brother," Satyra offered up.

"The Great Rondini will now show how these things are done," I added, since it was my show and all.

"I will now conjure up the ghosts of Halloween past," Rondini said. *"The last time Madame Zoroaster appeared on this show, she divined the location of some family jewels, you should pardon the expression. In particular, an expensive diamond bracelet that Pearl Strathan allegedly had left to her daughter Heather. However, since the bracelet's location was broadcast over the air, Heather's evil twin, Cheryl, beat her to it and vanished."*

"That was not my fault," Madame Z piped up, *"although I could have predicted it. I believe I mentioned that there was some danger."*

"I have listened to the tapes of the show and you didn't," Rondini said. *"However, let's not argue over spilled diamonds. Satyra—"*

"The Great Rondini will now summon those wacky Halloween spirits," Satyra read her lines off a three by five card, *"right here in the KPMT studios, Heather Rubenstein and her Dick."*

"Her husband, Dick, that is," I added.

At this point Rhonda and Cruize stepped out from behind the office plants. The effect was pretty good on our studio guests, but some flash powder and a cloud of smoke would have been better. Either way it was lost on the radio audience, so no use worrying about that now.

"Who are these people?" Vigo Czak demanded.

"These are the folks who showed up here as Mr. and Mrs. Rubenstein just as our Halloween séance was going off the air," I said. *"They had quite a row with Kinta White, my producer, and although they wore make up and dressed a little differently, Kinta can verify they're the same couple. You must have seen them too."*

"Will the couple who originally appeared here as Mr. and Mrs. Rubenstein please reveal their true identities?" Ronnie said over protests from Tony and Vigo. Madame Z sat quietly looking like she was still in a trance. Kinta waved a mic under Rhonda's and Cruize's respective noses and they gave their names. The Cruizer put in a plug for the Nuevo Shakespearians. Rhonda, not having a show, plugged Ronnie's gig again.

"Now then," Rondini continued, *"did someone in this room*

hire you to portray the Rubensteins?"

"Absolutely, we didn't know anything was up. We were told it was just a radio stunt." The two poor, duped thespians described how they had been roped in and the way they improvised world class performances from a pig's ear or words to that effect. I pitched in with, "These actors did not realize what was to happen next—a scheme so underhanded you'd think it was put together by the Democrats.

"A week later," I continued giving it my best March of Time voice, "the station was contacted by someone who allegedly represented the alleged Rubensteins and threatened to sue KPMT for broadcasting the alleged location of the bracelet. That wasn't you playing the alleged caller was it, Mr. de la Cruz?"

"No, I was totally committed to rehearsals by then."

"Good boy," I patted his head. "To make a long story short, KPMT paid out a large sum of money to settle out of court and make things right with the fictional Rubenstein clan over the missing diamond bracelet.

"Now, I turn to Rondini the Great and his lovely assistant, the lovely Satyra, for the answer to the question that will answer the question my listeners are asking themselves— namely, who wound up with the diamond bracelet?"

"Well, Junior, nobody has the bracelet because there was no bracelet." Kinta was the only person in the room who looked surprised at this. "Remember the Rubensteins were just made up for the gag, so her mother didn't really exist and neither did the bracelet."

"That's right, no one ever saw it or her mother," I said. "We just took the word of Heather Rubenstein that it ever existed, and as we now know, even Heather never really existed."

"Although I thought I did bring the part to life," said Rhonda. "It fooled you guys for a while."

"Thank you, Rhonda, you're truly a woman of many talents," Ronnie said, having spent time auditioning her over the past few days. "The scam was to make it look like there was a bracelet, then blame the station when it couldn't be found."

"I saw the bracelet," Vigo volunteered. "I definitely saw the bracelet. I cannot be held accountable if these poseurs did something with it." He put a protective hand on the clairvoyant's shoulder.

"Aside from Madame Zoroaster's visions, there is no

evidence the diamond bracelet ever existed, which it didn't," said Ronnie. "Now, Rhonda and Cruize, please tell us who in this room put you up to this fraud."

"We didn't know it was fraud," they said in unison. Rhonda gave the magician a kind of hurt look too. What an actress! But the plan wasn't supposed to nail Ronnie's main squeeze.

"Holy (bleep)—" de la Cruise said, Brad neatly clipping out the s-word during the seven second delay. "We were hired, by this guy." Cruize pointed to the mastermind. "He said he represented the station. Had a business card and everything. Of course it could be made up at Kinko's."

"I've heard of that," Rhonda said. They were both staring at the guilty party who just smiled and shook his head. Tony looked like he couldn't believe they had accused him.

"For the listening audience," Satyra pitched in, "they are pointing at a KPMT executive, Tony Paulson."

"I knew he worked for the station," Cruize said, amazed. "Maybe it's not fraud after all...and Rhonda and I did a legit job then."

"What in (bleep) is all this in aid of?" Vigo Czak said to the wall, the mics barely picking him up, but Brad bleeped him just in case.

"Okay, everybody, settle down," I tried taking control before I lost control. "It's not a crime for the station to hire some actors for a dramatic reading, but probably KPMT wouldn't come off too well if it was done to fool the audience— that's definitely cheating. But in this case, everybody at KPMT except for Tony Paulson was fooled as well."

Kinta stuck a note in front of me saying that Pamela Kay Paulson was on line two and wanted to speak to me, pronto. I might have a call-in show, but this was one call I wasn't going to take. I needed to keep it going until we exposed the murders, otherwise both me and my career would be toast. I waved Kinta off and hoped he wouldn't pick up the line to tell her. If he did, she might order him to kill the transmitter feed thereby taking us off the air. (Bleep) I said to myself.

"Listen everyone," I said, deciding to go for it before I was stopped, "the real fraud started much earlier. We have documentary evidence on the way and it will be arriving before this show is over, but here's how I figure it went down.

"At some point, Tony Paulson needed money; we don't know why yet, maybe gambling debts, a coke habit or just home prices in the Bay Area. We all know what that's like.

Anyway, he cooked KPMT's books to cover money he funneled into his own accounts. It wasn't a huge amount, probably just enough to fix the roof and paint the house. An amount he could pay back quickly. But he wasn't aware that one of the owners of KPMT was planning to sell his share of the business. To do so, the books would need to be audited and that would uncover the embezzlement.

"*So Tony Paulson—*" I started my wrap-up, but Kinta was going crazy, signaling me to pick up the phone. I tried waving him off again. I was sure Mrs. P would lighten up once she found out the truth. At least I didn't think she'd shoot the phone screener, so Kinta's pitching a fit was putting me off stride. "*So as I was saying, Tony came up with a scheme to get a payoff from KPMT in order to put back the dough he'd embezzled from the station. Sort of robbing Peter to pay Paulson.*"

"*Is that when he decided to run the séance scam on your show?*" Satyra asked, somehow reading my mind. We were on a roll.

"*Last Halloween,*" Ronnie picked up the thread, "*Tony arranged for Rhonda Ridgeway and Alain de la Cruz to play the parts he had scripted for them—*"

"*That had nothing to do with Madame,*" Vigo Czak interjected.

"*Well, I do a lot of illusions that appear to be magic, but they only work if every element is controlled,*" Ronnie said. "*For example, if Heather Rubenstein and her dead mother were totally fabricated by Paulson, how could Madame Zoroaster know about a diamond bracelet? How could she describe the room and location to find it if there really wasn't any such house? How could she 'see' a bracelet that was made up just to fit into the scam? Of course, it went missing— it never existed!*"

"*I only relay what I see,*" Madame Z said softly. "*I am in a hallucinatory trance and simply repeat what my guides communicate to me. It cannot be influenced by mere mortals. These two here, pretending to be actors, are probably the crooks. Maybe they planned it as a joke and then when it turned out as it did, they decided to cash in. It's been done before.*"

She dabbed at her eyes with her scarf, being careful not to smear the heavy mascara. An imitation of an injured party. She declared, "*People have tried before to discredit Madame Zoroaster. And they have lived to regret it.*"

Vigo helped Madame Z to her feet, saying, *"(Bleep) it. Madame Zoroaster and I, we are out of here."* Pulling her by the arm, he started towards the exit.

"Hold it! Not so fast, you two," Inspector Thé barked. The command cut through the hubbub, silencing everyone in the room. The detectives stepped into our makeshift studio, showing their badges. *"Both of you, back in here and sit down. This show's not over."*

"Until the fat lady sings," we all said eyeing Madame Z.

From the studio window I could see Brad giving me the thumb's up that it had all gone over the air. I gave the radio audience a quick recap, introducing Thé and Estrada. Satyra gave another plug for the Blue Sphinx and Ronnie's website. Kinta was adding more chairs and waving the wireless mic around trying to get what everybody said on the air. We were ten guests now and Christy hadn't even shown up. With all that was going on, I had forgotten that she was almost three hours late from the airport. That's some traffic jam. I hoped the taxi driver was tuned to KPMT instead of Radio Pakistan.

"Now, while the handcuffs are passed around, we'll take a short break for a few messages from the folks who make all this possible."

The Brat queued up the dozen or so commercials we had missed and I tried calling Christy's cell. I left message number eight on her voice mail. The traffic guy said he hadn't heard about any problems coming up from SFO. Some traffic guy he was, what with Christy still mired in gridlock. Meanwhile Mrs. P was back on line three insisting on speaking with me during the break. She told Kinta that if she had to come down personally, it would be to run my contract through the shredder. What a kidder she is.

I told Kinta that a threat like that was a good thing. "That means I'm not fired yet. Go bolt the lobby door so she can't get in until the show is over."

"I don't know, Jerry," Kinta said. "I don't think you work here any more. Or at least you won't when Mrs. Paulson gets done with you."

"Just bolt that door. I don't want anybody getting in—or out. I've still got a job until seven o'clock tonight."

The bumper music was playing us back from commercial as I sat down again. We all crowded around the table. Madame Z and Vigo Czak were looking pretty desperate, Tony was looking pretty glum, Satyra and Rhonda were looking pretty. Off-mic de la Cruize was telling the detectives about

Don Johnson and his walk-ons in the old Nash Bridges TV show. Only Ronnie seemed to be paying attention.

"Welcome back to our listening audience," I led off. *"You've just heard how KPMT, Big Spender Radio, was swindled out of close to sixty thousand dollars for an imaginary bracelet."* Maybe Heilbrun deserved killing after falling for that one. *"However, now the fun stops. Somehow the scam escalated into murder. Tony needed cash to cover up his fiddling with KPMT's books. But someone discovered the accounting fraud."*

"What?" Tony screeched.

"That's right, maybe you realized that your fraud had already been discovered by Tom Marshall or maybe you thought it wouldn't be covered up in time to prevent its being uncovered, but—"

"You cannot be serious!" Tony said. I wouldn't want to take his blood pressure at that moment. A tick higher and we'd be at code blue. I'll give him this though, he put on a good front—like it was all news to him.

"I'm not standing for this! I'm a vice president here and you're fired, Jeremy! This show is off the air as of now! Brad—cut the feed."

"Nobody's doing any cutting!" Inspector Estrada said, his voice carrying over the clamor as he lightly tapped Tony back into his seat. *"This is an official police investigation and we're going to play it through. If the listeners get to hear it, okay, but I want to wrap this crazy thing up. WQhat I wouldn't give for a nice, quiet drive-by shooting right now."*

I looked at Brad, who just shrugged and looked at Kinta who looked at the flashing hold button imprisoning Pamela Kay Paulson. Kinta looked from me to Brad and shrugged too. We were good, so I picked up the ball.

"As I was saying, something happened to panic Tony Paulson, maybe it was Tom Marshall meeting with Tony's aunt who owns a major piece of the station. The meeting took place at Pamela Kay Paulson's cozy, twenty room estate in Marin County last Halloween at about the time Madame Zoroaster was conducting a phony séance on my show. Perhaps, the scam was too late, maybe Marshall had already found the accounting fraud and was already sharing it with Tony's aunt.

"At any rate, Tom Marshall's Mercedes was run off a cliff as he returned to the City. Tom was killed and the embezzlement was hushed up. The following day, Tony

Paulson brought his car into a garage to get the scrapes from the collision fixed."

Everyone but the listening audience was looking at Tony now. But he seemed to be amazingly relaxed for someone on the fast track to Folsom. He looked around the room, meeting each of our stares. He finally spoke, asking, *"That's what you have? That's all you've got?"*

"Not quite," Ronnie answered. *"We know that Madame Zoroaster and her pal have been blackmailing you over this."*

"Not again," Vigo Czak had a vein bulging out of his forehead. If it popped, somebody could get hurt. *"No more again! We are not crooks or blackmail people or what have you."*

Nothing bothering him that a handful of Prozac wouldn't fix.

Kinta signaled me that we were running over, but I waved him off. No commercials, no station breaks, no seven o'clock news—we were the news tonight.

Vigo was dancing up and down now. *"Madame simply asked Tony for help to get started when she came back to San Francisco. Madame spent the winter working the cruise ships out of San Diego, giving readings and holding private séances for the passengers. Mr. Paulson was the only person in San Francisco that knew Madame, so naturally I contacted him when we returned and he graciously let Madame—and me, of course—stay at his house for a while."*

"And that's all there is to it," Tony said. *"I'll admit I took a small loan out of the office accounts. I needed some quick cash to pay off a builder's lien on my home. I had some unexpected costs in the re-model. I didn't want to ask my aunt just then and I fully intended to put the money back. Which I did."*

"Wow, we actually got it in one," Satyra said. *"It's just like we thought."* I don't know why she sounded surprised. Okay, I was surprised too. Our plan was actually coming together.

"Well, Jerry, I think that wraps it up," Ronnie said. *"There's your motive for knocking off Thomas Marshall. Of course, the Marshall killer then had Leland Heilbrun murdered to keep from being exposed. Officers, do your duty."*

"What the (bleep). Are you (bleepin') crazy or something?" Tony exploded. *"For the hundredth time, the hundred thousandth time, I did not kill anybody.*

"I covered some expenses when I was temporarily short of

cash. My aunt knows about the books—I told her—and yes, I wound up making good the money from the bracelet con, but it was mostly my aunt's money anyway and she's down with it now. I don't think Marshall wanted a scandal, he was trying to sell his share of the business and finding the books were off wouldn't have helped get him the price he wanted."

Janice Thé leaned into Tony's face and asked, *"Then why were the Bobbsey Twins here blackmailing you?"*

Aha! Game, set and match.

"What the (bleep) are you talking about? They weren't blackmailing me. I've known them for a while and we've become friends. When I heard about their appearance on Jerry's show, I asked them to help me out with the séance thing, so when they came back to San Francisco and needed a place to stay, I helped them out."

Thé drilled in, *"You tried to get a loan against your KPMT stock. What was that for?"*

"How did you find out about that? The Heilbrun thing, I suppose. I had just re-modeled a house that was built over ninety years ago. You have no idea how expensive that is. I can show you the bills, believe me."

"Fair enough," Janice shot me a glance like I'd better be ready with some backup. *"Before I read you your rights, let me ask you one more question—where were you on the night Thomas Marshall died?"*

"I was at someone's house, a friend, listening to Jeremy's show—the Halloween show—to make sure the séance went okay."

"You had a lot riding on it," Satyra said. Tommy Estrada patted her shoulder, welcoming any support in a storm.

Thé gave me another look, the kind you get when you're caught pissing in the soup. Not that I ever have. Anyway, she turned back to Tony and said, *"So now you have an alibi?"*

"How come you never said anything before now?" I asked. *"And what about your car?"*

"Look, Jerry, look everybody, I was in a relationship with one individual, but I was dating someone else on the side," Tony said. *"I spent that evening with the one on the side and didn't want it to get back to the first person."*

Tony looked at me and said, *"I'm sorry, Jerry, I didn't think things would get out of hand like this. I didn't bring it up because, although I've tried to break it off, the guy I was in the relationship with still doesn't want to end it. I hoped it all would stay buried—no pun intended—and not stir up any* more bad feelings."

"*So where was your car all this time? How did it get banged up?*" Estrada asked.

"*My lover had it.*"

"*Your lover? I thought you just said he was with you all evening.*"

"*Not that one, the first one—the one I had the serious relationship with—*"

"You really need to take this call," Kinta hissed in my ear.

What the hell? Why was he interrupting at a time like this? I didn't think having Mrs. P fire me over the phone was all that important. After all, I had been fired once already.

"It's Christy," he hissed.

"Why didn't you say so? Have Brad patch her through."

Kinta gave Brad the thumbs up and my girl's beautiful voice came over the speakers, "*Jerry, are you there?*"

"Hi, er, hello, Christy, you're on the air. Where are you anyway? When will you be here?"

"*Well, Jerry honey, something's come up. I may not make it to the studio.*"

"What? What do you mean not make it?"

"*Well, Jerry, I've been kidnapped.*"

Chapter 35.

"*WHAT!*" Even my ears couldn't believe my ears. "*How can you be kidnapped?*"

I felt the room swaying and a purple fog began to cloud my vision. The last time I felt like this was under Pamela Kay's mistletoe. Ronnie and Satyra had to hold me up to keep me from collapsing. Satyra tried to bring me back with a slap on the cheek and then she slapped me again. I figured I'd better get it in gear before I got slapped silly.

"*Christy, who's got you? Where are you?*" I said, trying to get my head on straight.

Estrada pushed in at my mic, "*Christy, play along for now, don't do any thing to upset the kidnapper. Do you know where you are? We'll come and get you.*"

"*Who kidnapped you?*" I said. "*What happened?*"

"*Jerry, I've been kidnapped by Ned. You know, your station manager, Ned Tunney. He met me at the airport and said you sent him to pick me up. I'm in his car now.*"

"*What'd he do, put you in the trunk?*" Estrada asked.

"*No, of course not. I'm right here in the passenger seat next to him.*"

"*And he doesn't know you're calling us?*"

"*Sure he knows. He asked me to call. He said it was a call-in show and this might liven things up.*"

Finally the bastard takes an interest in my show.

"*Christy, this is Inspector Thé with the SFPD. I'd like you to ask Mr. Tunney to come on the line.*"

After a bit of background conversation, Ned's voice came over the speakers. "*Hellooo out there in (bleepin') radioland. This is the (bleep) mad killer of (bleepin') KPMT.*"

Ned wasn't sounding like his usual laidback self. It was a good thing Brad the Brat was riding the dump button on the seven second delay, bleeping out anything not suitable for family listening. Kidnapping and murder are one thing, but foul language? No way.

Ned gave us the radio confession we wanted, *"I (bleepin') admit it. And I'm (bleepin') smart enough to know that I won't get away."*

"He's the one—my ex-lover—who took my car last Halloween," Tony Paulson said. *"I never put it together; I thought Tom Marshall just had an accident."*

Rhonda and Satyra looked at each other and both said, *"An office romance!"*

"My God," said Janice Thé.

"Ned, if you know you can't escape, why not just pull over and let Christy go?" I pleaded. *"I'm in good with the cops, I'll see you get a fair shake."*

"Jerry, you couldn't give your (bleep) a fair shake after a good (bleep). However, since you ask, I'm going to get even with Tommy Marshall's little (bleepin') girl. She stirred this whole thing up after it was put to (bleepin') bed.

"And let's don't forget you, Jerry. Number seven in your (bleepin') timeslot. You deserve something too, but I regret that can't give it to you personally, you little (bleep). But I do know you're crazy about little Annie Fannie here, so your punishment will be to know that you and your meddling made me kill the (bleep)."

"Don't do anything to make your situation worse, Mr. Tunney," Inspector Thé said. *"Right now you're probably not facing a capital charge, but if you kill Ms. Marshall, it will be a felony-murder with special circumstances."*

Estrada was on his cell rallying the police or tracing the call or something. At least it kept him from shoving me off mic again.

"You won't live to stand trial if you hurt her, you rat—"

Tony pushed in to my mic, *"Ned, listen to me babe, like the cop said, you don't want to make it any worse."*

"Make it worse? You (bleepin') whore! I killed Marshall to (bleepin') protect you. He told me that he would go to the DA with the evidence if it messed up his (bleepin') sale. I did it to protect you, you ungrateful (bleep)."

"But, Ned...." Tony trailed off.

"Don't do this," I said. *"Christy didn't do this to you—"*

"Your spirit will find no rest until you make an act of

contrition," Ilonya Zoroaster joined in. *"Let the girl go or you will never rest!"*

"Mr. Tunney," Janice Thé used the voice they must teach you at the Police Academy, the one that could stop your hair from growing, *"I want you to pull over to the side of the road and let Miss Marshall go—now!"*

"(Bleep) you, (bleep)." A terrible banging came from the speaker, then silence.

From a distance we heard a phone ringing. Once, then twice. We were stupefied. The Brat got it on the third ring. We watched him talking to the caller, dead air going out to the world. Brad was punching buttons on the control board like crazy now.

"Jerry, it's me," Christy's voice came back over the speakers.

"What's going on? Are you okay?"

"Ned dropped the phone. Jerry, listen, my battery may be dying, so listen—I know where we're headed—there's nothing else up this way. We're headed right above the station. He's taking me to Coit Tower."

Perched atop Telegraph Hill, Coit Tower looms above the Embarcadero visible to most of the downtown area. A tribute to the firemen of San Francisco, the tower is modeled after a giant fire hose nozzle. Or as some say, a giant fireman's nozzle.

KPMT's offices were a sheer drop down the hill from the popular tourist attraction, but unless you were a mountain goat there was no way up our side. To get to the top, almost a hundred yards straight up from KPMT, you need to take twisty, narrow city streets winding through the North Beach neighborhood on the other side. The forty-niners apparently never thought about getting someplace in a hurry. Least of all, the top of Telegraph Hill.

Estrada and Thé were already out the door, orders to call 9-1-1 hanging in the air like dust trails in a Roadrunner cartoon.

"Wait for me," I shouted.

"Don't worry, Jerry, we'll handle your show," Satyra and Ronnie yelled after me.

I caught up to Thé and Estrada a couple of steps outside the studio. They had stopped in their tracks and I came up short too. We looked out over a hundred or so gleaming bikes and helmets, multi-colored latex and more stretch shorts than you'd ever want to see. Bike after bike after bike crowded the streets.

We don't block the traffic, we are the traffic.

Sure you are. The traffic jam you mean. The Critical-Motherfucking-Mass.

Chapter 36.

IT would have taken something on the order of an M1 battle tank to wade through the jam-up of bikes and riders. An unmarked police car didn't stand a chance. Estrada got the lights flashing and was punching the siren every few seconds, but could only move an inch at a time. At this rate by the time we got going we'd be too old to chase bad guys.

Nearby bikers just stared as Thé leaned out of the passenger window waiving her badge and trying to shout over the crowd. If they took any notice at all, they looked at her like she was some kind of crazy person, like the people you see on the street talking to imaginary friends. Not to be confused with the people on their mobile phones.

If anyone had actually wanted to let us through, they were blocked anyway by the bikes in front of them who were blocked by the bikes in front of them and—well, you get the idea. I was considering a run at the ancient wooden stairway running up the face of the hill by us. But they were probably condemned for a reason, not to mention how high they went. Even before they were closed off, just thinking of climbing them gave me a panic attack. Now my heart was pounding; I was caught between a rock and a tall place. I looked at the bikers and then up at the cliff and then at the car, not sure what to do. Then fate or luck or divine intervention stepped up to the plate— salvation appeared and was heading in my direction.

I could see it down the block, past the bikers, a half dozen heads and shoulders floating towards us. As they passed the Critical Mass mess, I could see their bodies gliding smoothly along the sidewalk. Once again, it was tourists to the rescue as they drifted silently along on what appeared to be giant lawnmowers. Each one, moms, pops, kids, balanced between a set of wheels, holding on to the lawnmower handles.

Janice Thé was on the hood of the car by this time deafening the close-in crowd with a bullhorn. From up there she saw them too slipping smoothly past the gridlock. By the time they reached the bus stop where her car was parked, she was blocking their path, waving them to a stop with her badge.

"Halt! S-F-P-D! We need your scooters for police business. A woman's life is at stake!"

"They're not scooters," said a skinny guy in a tie-dyed shirt. "They're Segway Human Transporters."

"Who the fuck cares? Get off the scooters," Thé commanded.

The tourists looked a little put out and nobody made a move to give up their ride. "Human transporters," said the tie-dye guy.

"You can walk back to the rental office and ask for a refund," Estrada said. "Maybe you'll get tickets to the Alcatraz tour."

"I don't know, Mister, we left a deposit for these," the head rube said. Then, he turned to Mr. Tie-dye and asked, "Jason, will we get our deposit back? And what about—"

"Give us the fucking wheels or I'll haul your skinny asses in!"

For emphasis, Thé pulled a service revolver from somewhere under her shirt. Estrada backed her up and I stood in back of him. The bikers near us finally showed some interest; maybe next month they'd do scooters.

"Look, I'd like to help," Jason said, "but I'm in charge of this tour and I'll get my ass fired if I let them out of my sight."

"These folks will be okay as long as they don't play in traffic," Estrada said nodding at the Critical Mass.

"Not the people, the scooters," Jason looked torn between his skanky job and being an accessory to murder. Estrada moved in with a nose to nose glare and Jason caved, saying, "Look, okay, but I'll have to come with you to keep an eye on the Segways."

You lean forward, you go; you stand up, you stop. Easy enough. Six of us—Jason and a two of his customers came along to keep the fleet together—were gliding along at a snappy eight miles an hour. Folks who thought it safe to be on the sidewalk, maybe window shopping or just lollygagging, found themselves jumping left and right to get out of our way. We were like a motorcycle gang, only in slo-mo. Estrada took the lead, a natural born-to-be-wild kind of guy. He also knew the neighborhood from his days as a beat cop. Narrow alleys, side streets and a few backyards turned into shortcuts.

I had gotten the earpiece of my cell on and speed-dialed the show while trying to keep up. Brad said Christy was still on the phone and patched me in. I heard Christy's voice and she sounded rattled, but still bearing up, *"We're getting out of the car now,"* she was giving a play-by-play of her own kidnapping. What a trooper—the ratings had to be through the roof.

"We're parked right next to Coit Tower.... We cut the line of tourists waiting.... Ned wants to know if I was ever here before.... Yes...yes, Ned, a long time ago, with some folks from out of town once...."

We were running down a back alley when my Segway hit a rut and jumped, twisting onto one wheel. I toppled off and the cell phone went flying. The Segway came to a gentle stop next to a large cardboard carton. I looked around for the phone, my only link to Christy, but couldn't spot it in the weeds and junk. A raggedy woman climbed out of the big carton for a closer look at the Segway. She looked ready to take it for a spin when Jason and the tourists bounced up to her through the weedy lot.

"Police business," Jason proclaimed, "step away from the Segway!"

"The wha'?" the homeless lady said. "You mean this scooter?"

"Here," I gave her a ten-spot and stepped onto the Segway again. They say if you get bucked off, the best thing is to get right back on. I never heard what to do if you get bucked off again. The cops were well ahead of us by now, but Jason, the tourists and I were leaning on the gas. Well, we were leaning way forward anyhow.

A few minutes later, North Beach, the homeless lady, Critical Mass and all that was left behind and we were climbing up Lombard Street toward a tower and a damsel in distress. I hoped she was still only in distress and not in something worse.

Chapter 37.

THE high fog was rolling through the Gate and throwing a soft, grey shadow across the City. Jason and the Segways were left at the edge of the parking lot and a handful of visitors— those who hadn't run off when Ned started waving his gun— peeked out from behind their rental cars. Thé, Estrada and I stood by the door to Coit Tower itself. We looked up at the tower like Ned and Christy might pop out from the observation deck and give us a wave. I felt dizzy just looking up, let alone looking down at the bay.

Estrada was on his cell to somebody back in HQ; apparently they no longer used those police radios you see on TV. Janice Thé paced back and forth, every now and then stopping and straining her neck to look up. I could hear sirens from a ways away and I guessed the SWAT team would be here soon if they could blast their way through the Critical Mass crowd. On the other hand, I tried not to think of the possibilities involved if it came to a shootout between a bunch of police yahoos and a mad station manager-slash-murderer with a hostage.

Ned's car was parked next to the stairs leading to the tower entrance, doors open, engine running, but no Ned and no Christy. Her purse was on the floor with its contents scattered around, but I didn't see her cell phone. At least not in the car, but some out-of-towner late for a dinner reservation might have picked it up on his way out. I walked back to Jason and the two guys in shorts who were shivering on the side lines. They could have been waiting to see if something was going to happen or maybe just wondering how to get all the Segways back down the hill. One tourist had his camcorder out just in case.

"If anybody has a cell phone, I'll give you a hundred bucks to borrow it for a while."

Three hands with phones shot out. I checked the battery and signal strength on each one. Jason's had three bars, so he got my personal IOU. I let him hold one of my credit cards for security; I gave him the one that was over the limit already. My earpiece and mic worked okay so I dialed the show's private number.

"Brad, I'm at Coit Tower with the cops. You have anything from Christy or Ned? I think she still has her cell."

But either her signal or her battery had died about the time Ned dragged her into the elevator. I was hoping the signal and battery were all that had, well, you know....

Meanwhile, The Great Rondini and Satyra had been filling the airwaves with a recap of the kidnapping and plugs for their act at the Sphinx. Brad thought he'd like to catch their show. He also mentioned that Pamela Kay was there and wanted to pull the plug, but Dennis Hong, KPMT's News Director, was rallying the news team and was trying to talk her into treating us as breaking news. So far they had wrestled each other to a standstill. I guess normally Ned would have been the tie-breaker. Maybe he still was.

Tony Paulson and the gypsies had moved away from the microphones and were talking to each other in whispers. Brad alternately tried to tune them out of the broadcast or pot them up so everyone could hear; neither worked, so they were just background noise. With the news team coming in and some cops to keep an eye on things, the station lobby would look like the Marx Brother's stateroom scene soon. All they would need were a few guys from room service and Kinta was working on that.

While I got the 411, I watched a remote news van from KSF-TV pull up behind Ned's car. The cops might not get through, but the TV guys made it lickety-split. The sirens were getting louder though; the cops must have heard there was media coverage. Other stations would be pounding in as the word spread.

So once again it was show time.

"Brad, can you still patch me into the broadcast?"

"So far. I still have the board."

"Put me on and then call Christy's cell again," I gave him her number and he brought up the show on my line, Ronnie and Satyra doing a Regis and Kelly impersonation. For my ears only, Brad counted down my cue. At "two," Ronnie's voice faded down and at "one," I was on the air. Brad only mouthed the "zero", but I knew what was happening even if couldn't see him. After all, this was my show.

"This is Jerry Jeremy joining you once again. I am at the base of Coit Tower where Ned Tunney, jilted lover, disgruntled station manager, and dirty, rotten murderer, is trapped on the observation deck of San Francisco's famous landmark—"

"It's Jerry!" I heard Satyra say in the background.

"—San Francisco's famous landmark—"

"Where is he?" Marsha Chung's nasal whine came over. What the hell was Brad doing? This was supposed to be my show. At least for a few more minutes.

"—as I was saying, famous landmark, Coit Tower. We cannot see anything from the ground level, but the police look like they are preparing to storm the stairs."

"Ready with Christy on line two, Jerry," Brad's voice floated into my ear like my very own spirit guide.

"Jerry, is that you?" now Christy's sweet voice reached out to me and the seventh largest audience in Bay Area radio. Probably number five or six tonight.

"I'm here. I'm just outside Coit Tower," I said to Christy and the listeners. *"Inspectors Thé and Estrada are on the scene and several police vehicles are now arriving."*

I gave a little color commentary describing the growing pandemonium as cops in flak jackets and helmets double-timed up to Thé and Estrada inside the tower lobby. They all bunched up at the door to the stairway that went to the observation deck. Locked, naturally. So the attendant was dispatched to find the key. Automatic rifles, tear gas guns, a truck full of barricades to keep out the curious, not counting the media. TV vans were arriving in force now, crews setting up their lights and cameras, stringing cables, satellite antennas rising from the vans, reporters primping against the breeze off the bay. News helicopters circled above us. A few days ago the cameras would have been all over me, but tonight was the cops' show. The cops and Ned and Christy. Tension blanketed the hill, something big was about to happen.

"Christy, tell us if you can, what Ned is up to now."

Jesus, I sounded like a CNN anchor handing off to a reporter on a remote assignment, not a guy whose girl was in danger.

"We're by one of the windows overlooking the bay. Ned

broke the lock off and has opened it." Her voice echoed in seven second delay from a dozen radios, turned low, that the news vans were monitoring the drama on.

"Is he threatening you?"

"I'm not really sure. He seems to be crying. Ned, don't cry, we can get out of all this okay."

One of the choppers had its spotlight on a window that must be the one Ned opened. A couple more were hovering above the observation deck looking down on them. I wished Jason's phone could stream the TV feed so I'd know what was going on up there.

"How's he doing, is he going to come down?"

"Ned, how are you doing? Do you know what you want to do? He says not. He's still got a gun. Want me to hold that for you, Ned? No, no, it's okay, I was just asking."

While Christy got the interview with Ned, I stepped into the lobby to make room for one of the TV reporters to get the tower in the background of his remote. The SWAT team filled most of the small lobby. Even Thé and Estrada had body armor on now. The cops were beginning to move slowly up the stairs so I tried to keep out of their way too. I stepped back to avoid getting trampled and banged my funny bone against the elevator door.

Open sesame.

We all figured the tiny elevator would be stopped at the top. Instead a dozen pairs of eyes looked cautiously out at me. To say they were packed in like sardines wouldn't be an understatement, it would be an insult. They were sightseers scared off the observation deck by gun-toting Ned. The elderly elevator operator was crushed into the corner holding the brass knob that apparently drove the thing. While the tourists unpacked themselves, I stuck a Hamilton in the operator's hand and told him I was borrowing the car tonight.

"Going up?" No takers all of a sudden. I pushed the metal grill shut and the outside doors closed. It seemed to have only two speeds—up and down. The old buggy wasn't the fastest thing in town, taking what seemed like two hours to get to the top, but was probably two minutes. Like an old pro, I only took about five tries back and forth to get it parked within a foot or so of the floor. When I stepped out, a bunch of out-of-towners swept me back in.

"Please, folks, getting off. I'll probably be going down on my own soon. Just close the grating and swing the handle. You can do it, I know you can."

I was in a circular stairwell just below the observation deck. As slow as the elevator was, I still beat the cops up which was just as well. Amazingly, Jason's cell phone was still connected to the station. I'd have to get one like this if I lived long enough. I gave the studio a little play by play as I crept up the stairs and when stuck my nose above floor level, both Christy and Ned were staring at me like I had materialized in one of Rondini's magic tricks.

"*No smoke, no mirrors, just me,*" I said, stepping onto the deck. Ned held a largish pistol in one hand and was clinging to Christy's arm with the other. The narrow window behind them was open. It looked like a long way down. Christy held her cell phone up by their faces.

"*I knew you were coming,*" Ned said, nodding at the cell. "*You're on the radio. Are you alone? You were talking cops earlier.*"

"*You know me, Ned. Never one to share the spotlight.*"

Brad's voice in my earpiece cued me that everything was going over the air. Ned was being picked up by Christy's phone. I hoped they wouldn't be hearing any gunshots in the next few minutes.

Ned said, "*You really should be on the morning drive, Jerry. You always wind up in the hot spot.*"

"*Well, we could go downstairs and discuss my contract,*" I said. Somehow I really didn't think he go for it.

"*You're great. I wish I had listened to your show more, somehow I didn't appreciate you until now.*"

"*Well, we have the future ahead of us. You can listen then. You can make up for the past.*" I was pretty sure he'd get the signal in San Quinton.

"*Well, I'll just have to make do without that pleasure, because you won't be around to do any more shows.*" I felt that chill running down my spine again, this time all the way to my socks.

Over the cell I could hear the threat echoed in seven second delay. In the background, there was a constant chatter from the crystal ball gang as they all talked over each other's words. For some reason, it crossed my mind that Marsha Chung would never make it as host if she couldn't keep the guests under control. Then Brad whispered over the feed for my ears only, "Tony says the psychic had a vision that Ned's gun ain't loaded, he says she says so. If it's true, maybe you and the girl can take him down."

If it's true? God Almighty, what an if! So okay, let's say

Madame Z is right. Ned was probably fifteen years older than me, but he swam and surfed everyday so he was in pretty good shape, while I never lift anything heavier than an extra large coffee. On the other hand, Christy must be in pretty good shape from fighting off all those old college chums.

What was I thinking? What made me think that Madame Zoroaster—the psychic disaster—could even predict the sun coming up in the morning? Ronnie had said it was all a scam. She was probably trying to get me shot in order to stop any further exposé. Besides, Ned was practically leaning out the window already.

"Ned, you have the gun," I said. "I can't hurt you. Let go of Christy. She just wanted to get closure on her Dad's death. Let her go, you can kill me instead."

I wasn't sure that came out the way I wanted. Filling dead air is one thing, but I didn't want it to be with a dead talk show host.

"Closure? Jerry, you're sounding like one of those (bleepin') pinko-stinko-shrinko's you always go on about. You weren't just kidding the audience were you?"

"Oh, no. Oh no, Ned, I'm still against all that, but maybe there are some good ones. Some that could help you, maybe some that don't believe in fluoridation or higher education, maybe set you up with a good defense—"

"Jerry!" Christy shouted, giving me a look. "Don't help him out!"

"Hang tight, Christy, I just—"

"Had your fingers crossed, did you, pinko," Ned said in a way that made me think I wouldn't be getting his vote for the morning drive slot.

He waved me over with the gun as he stepped to the side. I moved to the window, a glance down made me feel really bad. I was less afraid of falling than of looking down. Brad the Brat was talking in my ear again, but I was too scared to listen at first, praying that Madame Zoroaster was right about the bullets. "Jerry...Jerry...Tony Paulson says to give Ned a phone," he whispered. "He thinks he can convince Ned to give up if he can just talk to him."

"Now he tells us!"

"Well, boss, we might be doing great radio, but you're not really getting anywhere with Ned. You know how you always thought he really didn't like you...maybe you were right."

I had to give Brad his due—we were doing great radio. But I wasn't ready to get shot just for a shot at the morning show.

"Ned, take Christy's phone," I said, pointing at the cell. "Somebody wants to talk with you."

"Who? Not Pamela Kay? You didn't bring her in on this did you?" Ned took aim with the pistol.

"No! No! Not Pamela Kay! I heard she's having a big party up in Marin. Probably not even listening. Take the phone—after all, it's a call-in show."

Christy held up her last connection to the real world and Ned slowly let go of her arm and took the phone. He said hello and I could hear Tony's voice over the radio hookup. As Tony spoke to him, Ned lowered the pistol and Christy carefully slipped over next to me.

It seemed like several lifetimes since I got off the elevator. I had a feeling it wouldn't be coming back for me. But maybe we wouldn't need it. Ned's pistol was by his side now and he was talking intently on the phone. I could hear Tony making progress over my cell, the broadcast of this going out to the world. Ned had turned his back to us to get some privacy, but we heard the radio feed through the phone anyway.

While Ned was busy on the phone, Christy and I slowly edged backwards towards the stairs. Then—

Everything went topsy-turvy.

We were pulled from behind and bodies jammed the observation deck, pepper gas blinded and choked us, there was shouting and the pounding of feet, men in black, choppers closing in, their floodlights bathing the observation deck. Christy and I were dragged down the staircase and pushed down on the elevator floor. For the second time inside an hour, a cell phone had gone flying out of my hands. I could hear Ned shouting—frustrated or angry but not in pain. No shots were fired. I held tight to Christy and as the doors closed I heard somebody saying, "Son of a bitch, this thing isn't even loaded...."

Chapter 38.

"HI-YAA-YAA-YAA, hi-yaa-yaa-ooo..."

I swung the tomahawk over my head with one hand and flapped the other one over my mouth in proper Indian call style. At least that's how we did it as kids back in New Jersey.

"Listen up, folks, this is Big Chief Crazy Bull saying it's time to come on down for a cra-a-azy deal at Rootin' Tootin' Bronco Billy Wooten's used trucks and cars. We buy, we sell, we trade, we take you for a ride. We'll put you on four wheels—

"Watch the ice cream, son," I smiled, looking around before shoving the little monster into the traffic on North Sixth Avenue. "The suit's a rental and they charge extra to take out stains."

I was got up as a cigar store Indian from my feathered head-dress down to my beaded moccasins. I doubted the outfit would pass muster with Tony Hillerman though, it being more like something off the Warner Brothers back lot.

"Whether you're a college kid, a cowboy or chorus girl, Bronco Billy can put you behind...er, behind the wheel."

Who would have believed it? Charlie Wooten's uncle has a used car lot right here on Tucson's auto row. You can't make up this kind of stuff.

"Chief Crazy Bull is pounding his tom-tom and will be pounding it all day long, right here at Bronco Billy's big lot. And believe me, Bronco Billy's got a lot of lot.

"I'll also be spinning your favorite country tunes throughout the day here on Tucson's chip-kicking radio KICK. Bring down the whole family—" Just watch the ice cream. "Yessiree, the entire family will enjoy the big Labor Day sale out at Bronco Billy's Used Trucks and Cars. The B-man will personally take twenty percent off the Blue Book, twenty percent off the tax and twenty percent off the odometer.

"Pick out a pick-up and take the little woman for a test drive. While you're kicking the tires, the Big Chief will be glad to kick—I mean, entertain the kids."

It was already a hundred degrees in the shade and my headdress didn't provide much shade. I was sweating like a Presbyterian in a nudist colony. At this rate, I'd look like I'd had a rain dance with real rain.

But all in all, it was great to be back on radio.

I was the weekend deejay on KICK's remote from Bronco Billy's used car lot, his being one of their bigger sponsors. The rest of the week I spent selling the rattletraps Billy stocked the lot with. Charlie Wooten had given me a reference, so his uncle had me talking farm boys into splurging on cars they couldn't afford, saying their folks would bail them out if they couldn't handle the payments. I had to ride shotgun on test drives, wishing I had a shotgun on most test drives. Anyhow the radio show was tied into the deal, so I didn't much care. I was back on the air.

Of course, Pamela Kay fired me the second I got down from Coit Tower. Maybe if I had been able to nail the murder rap on Tony, she would have seen the light. But Ned being the villain ruined that.

It turns out he had borrowed Tony's car, that 745Li Charlie Wooten remembered so much about, to drive up to a meeting at Pamela Kay's place. But Pamela Kay didn't show. Turns out she had decided to ride out the rainstorm at an exclusive little spa she was visiting down in Carmel-By-The-Sea. So it was Ned that Tom Marshall told about the books.

Unfortunately for Tom, Ned and Tony's office romance was either kept too discrete or else the office gossip machine was on the blink. Tom didn't realize that they were hot and heavy when he told Ned about the embezzlement. Ned panicked, thinking Tony might wind up in the slammer soul-kissing some biker named Elvin. When Ned spotted Tom on Route 1, he figured, what with the rain and all, he might be able to solve all Tony's problem with no one being the wiser—including Tony.

The problem that he didn't solve was Tony's desire to branch out with a new man. And when Ned tried to hold him back, he got dropped like the proverbial rock. Tough break for a killer, but I guess karma evens everything out. Anyway Ned looks likely to get off with a plea bargain and a few years in the booby-hatch. One victim being a lawyer, that must count for something.

Tony Paulson got off with probation and a stern talking to by a liberal, Democratic appointee to the bench. Pamela Kay—blood being thicker than money—made Tony KPMT's General Manager in Ned's place. I wouldn't be too surprised to see Madame Z and Vigo replacing Freddy and Betty on the morning drive someday soon. But maybe that's just wishful thinking on my part.

I cued up an old Buck Owens favorite for my listeners to give my war whoop a rest. About a minute later, Christy rang my cell.

"How're ya' doing, Paleface?" she said.

"The outside temperature's down to about ninety, but when I talk to you I'm about twenty degrees hotter." We traded some baby talk and I let another cut play. As Buck yodeled his way through the tune, we set a time to meet for dinner. I back-timed our good-byes to the end of the song, just to show how good I was.

After Mrs. P gave me the brush, I had followed Christy back to Tucson. So here I was whooping it up at Bronco Billy's. There was a sticky patch when my Native American listeners threatened to picket Bronco Billy's lot, but once they saw me live, they decided I wasn't a threat. I think Billy offered to throw in a couple of used pick-ups at cost. Though he never said whose cost.

Christy and I have been talking about getting serious about talking about getting serious, but right now she has to spend a lot of time with her mom. She's also taking a couple of post-graduate courses at UA on the nights she's not mommy-sitting. Or washing her hair or getting her nails done. Busy girl.

But when I'm with her there's a magic that Ronnie Green could never conjure up. Of course, I still keep in touch with Rondini and like I always tell him, there's nothing like true love. He should try it once or twice.

The Great Rondini and Satyra are still headlining at the Blue Sphinx, but Rhonda Ridgeway isn't around anymore. Seems she wanted to be the magician's assistant, but this time Satyra read her mind and made up Ronnie's mind for him.

Ronnie keeps saying he wants to get a club date in Tucson sometime. I'd bet Bronco Billy would love to add a magic act to his Saturday car sale—an Indian chief, a mind reader, and Satyra. With a little Hank Williams Jr., we could start our own

Wild West show.

Still, I often think about that last show on KPMT; it really was great radio. If the cops had been a little slower breaking into the observation deck at Coit Tower, I think I might have been able to take Ned in myself. Not because of what I could do though. It was because of what Tony said to him on Christy's cell phone. Just between the two of them and several thousand listeners.

Talk radio gets in your blood and they really need something better out here in the desert. Whether the morning drive or the cattle drive, they could use some great radio.

Oh, yes—in case you were wondering what Tony said to Ned, he swore he was still in love with him, and of course, "...I'll be waiting for you when you get out."

Well, what can I say? It's a San Francisco love story. And all along, you probably thought it was a mystery.

And now a word from our sponsor—

We hope you liked ***Tune in to Danger*** and if you did, we'd appreciate any kind words you might care to write in a **Goodreads** or **Amazon** review or wherever you purchased this book.

If you would like to see other forthcoming mysteries, sign up for our mailing list at

www.Donald J. McGill.com.

Tune into Jerry's next adventure
with these excepts from

Talked to Death

Yessir, there's something special about chasing a little white ball around ye olde and ancient on a sunny Saturday morning. We were playing at the Canyon Country Club just north of Tucson and that "something special" I mentioned could just be a case of heatstroke.

Summertime in this line of country is so hot the local cowpokes are wearing tank tops and baggy shorts out on the back nine. If Mother Nature had her way, this place would be one large pile of sand with a few grass traps just to make it interesting. But here at Canyon you'd never think you were in the middle of a desert. As far as that goes, you're not actually in a canyon either.

You might say they've made the desert bloom. That is, the developers and the money-men behind the club have. Acres of manicured lawns, palm trees and tropical flowers carefully tended to distract the membership as they hook one off the tee. In the rough? You should have it so rough.

Overlooking not just one but two championship golf courses is a gorgeous tile roofed clubhouse. Medi-terranean in style, so they say, though it looks a lot like the local adobe. But hey, at these prices it's the south of France. And just so you don't forget where you really are, a couple of vultures ride the thermals high above the parking lot. Just in case some rich geezer kicks next to the Mercedes, I guess.

At any rate, they haven't air-conditioned the fairways yet, so in the good ol' summertime you need to tee off before the sun comes up. With luck you'll finish your game before the heat finishes you. With red hair and fair skin I go from freckle to burn in one easy lesson, so coming straight from work is my style. It's the one advantage of getting off at six a.m.

I work when most people are sleeping, which is a bit of a problem for a radio talk show host. You probably knew that already—at least you would if you lived in Tucson and had insomnia. My driver's license says I'm Jeremy Jeremy—try explaining that at the local DMV—and from midnight to six in the morning, I'm KICK's top talk show guy. I have the same name front and back because Mom and Dad couldn't afford two different ones when I was born. Talk about the lasting effects of an economic downturn. Meanwhile, with five bucks a hole on the line, I was slowly playing myself into the poorhouse.

"Christ Almighty, Jeremy. We oughta be in the lounge by now, downing a couple o' cold ones."

That's Bronco Billy Wooten talking, the king of Tucson's used car trade, and a major sponsor of mine. He was loud enough to make a fellow shank his tee shot on the next hole. Billy added, "Horsin' around waitin' for you, we didn't tee-off until goddamn' near six-fuckin'-thirty."

Guilty as charged.

"Don't I know it," I said hoping Bronco Billy would mellow a bit if I played along. Billy and the other guys had beaten the sun up to get that early tee time. But me—I was already up; I had spent the night working. "It's already so hot I need an oven mitt with these metal shafts. Next time I think I'll skip your last three spots and put on a hour or so of Boxcar Willie tunes so I can cut out early."

Billy groaned while Dale Andersen, KICK's program director, tripped over his five iron trying to smooth thing over. "Jerry's only joking. You know what kidders these on-air personalities are." What a kidder Dale is. He's born-again, doesn't smoke, drink or lie, but still pretty much runs things at the Talk of the West. And he's pretty much the talk of the Talk of the West, as we kidders like to say.

When I started at KICK, Dale pretty much as said to keep my slick, big city background as far in the background as possible, so on the night owl shift I try my best to be a down-home, right-wing, all-American buckaroo for all those night watchmen, long-haul truckers and other graveyard workers who make up my audience.

Did I mention Dale was born-again?

Since we were playing for five bucks a hole—gambling with sponsors apparently not being a sin in Dale's book—I had been taking my time lining up a tricky seven-footer on sixteen when Dale spoke. I could swear he said something about moving my show from night time to prime time. For a second I thought it was just the heat, but when Bronco Billy back-slapped me and shouted, "Holy shit, Jerry, ain't you the man now. Or more to the point, you're *my* man now. You're gonna be Tucson radio's goddamn' voice of the pre-owned vehicle. At least from seven to ten ever' evenin'."

Since Billy was pounding my back, I figured I must have heard Dale right the first time. And if Billy said I was the goddamn' voice of the pre-owned vehicle, that made it official. After all, he's the sponsor. I was now the evening man. A big step up; after all, real people might be tuned in at that hour.

"Gee, thanks, Bronco Billy," I said. "You too, Dale. For once I'm speechless."

"Bit of a drawback in a talk show host, ain't it, Jerry?" This from Henry Sequero, my golfing partner. Everybody's a critic nowadays. Where was he when Billy was moaning about the heat being my fault? On the other hand, as the Canyon golf pro, he was keeping our score within sight of the big guys'.

Let him talk. Dale—and more likely, Bronco Billy—had made my day. Until now, I'd been consigned to matching wits with nutballs at three a.m. Not just nutballs, but the kind of nutballs who make phone calls to radio stations in the middle of the night. It was either call me or the suicide hot line.

I had wound up in the all night penalty box after being blackballed out of San Francisco radio, but that's another story. You may have seen it on CNN, all about murder and romance. Besides it had a happy ending when I followed the girl of my dreams out here. And now I was on the comeback trail as the trailhands say.

"Nice try, Jerry," Henry said my putt rolled past the cup. He'd barely winced. "Maybe Dale's just trying to put you off your game."

"Sure," I said. "He's liable to do anything at these stakes. After all, he is a program director." I gave Dale a nice smile since he was still *my* program director and I didn't want to go back on nights before I had gotten off them.

"I ever tell you fellas, about how I heard Dale got to be the PD?" Billy asked. "It was on the championship course down to

Silver Hills. He was playing with Joe Galoosa and they were all tied up after eighteen so's they went into sudden death." Bronco Billy was piling it on at Dale's expense.

"That's right, Billy," Dale conceded. "If I hadn't won that round, I would have had to take the General Manager position and Joe would be having all the fun as PD." Everybody chuckled, Dale being the boss and all, and Joe G. being Dale's boss. Everybody chuckled but Billy, that is. Being the sponsor he didn't have to chuckle. Dale added, "It was a darned close call if I do say so myself."

"You don't say," Bronco Billy said. "But wait just a damn' minute, you *did* say, didn't you? Right in the middle of my fuckin' story." Dale tapped in a twelve-footer bringing a smile back to Billy's face.

Bronco Billy was Tucson's largest used car dealer and one of KICK's biggest clients. His nephew Charlie Wooten, my sponsor back in the City by the Bay, had told me to look him up when I came out here, and I did. I wouldn't have thought it possible for anybody to be as rough around the edges as Charlie, but as it turned out, Billy was, only more so. On the other hand, his partner in today's foursome was a squeaky-clean, Young Republican, all tanned and blonde, blue-eyed, and just about no fun at all. His idea of a big weekend was a morning spent mowing the lawn and taking the kids out to the waterpark later.

Henry Sequero, Canyon's golf pro extraordinaire, on whose sixteenth green I had four-putted, was one of the really good guys I had gotten to know during the short time I'd been living in Tucson. He even introduced me to a few of the regulars who hung out at Canyon. I wasn't a member, so having a few pals who were got me the occasional round of golf and more than a few rounds at the bar.

As it was, by the time we finished seventeen, Henry and I were down about forty bucks. Not too bad, but enough to let them know we knew who was boss. I'd figured having the club pro as my partner I'd be on the winning side, but now I was pretty sure my partner was holding back a little. He must have figured Bronco Billy would be good for a lot more in future tips than losing a few holes would cost. As for me, the only tip I ever got from Billy was not to buy a used car off his lot.

I was teeing up on eighteen, a par-four dogleg to the left, when Dale mentioned that the guy I was replacing on the evening show had taken a job pushing Bronco Billy's jalopies out at the lot on North Sixth Avenue. Dale was saying, "...he spent too darned much time talking about the old days. Not that we don't revere the memory of Barry Goldwater, but let's face it, that kind of thing really doesn't spark ratings any longer."

"Sure, of course not," I said. "Remember, I'm new in town, I hardly know a thing about the old days with Barry. The '64 landslide and all that. I thought he still ran the department store. I hardly know anything about back then."

"And you know even less about selling cars," Bronco Billy chimed in.

"Yes, but I liked the Indian costume."

Bronco Billy's was the elephants' graveyard for broadcast talent coming and going in Tucson. I had spent a little time out on the lot thanks to my pal Charlie Wooten, but it didn't take long for Billy to agree I'd probably sell more cars reading his commercials in the dead of the night.

"You won't be sorry, Dale," I promised. "Back in San Francisco I had one of the top shows on KPMT. I do have one question though—if I was losing ten bucks a hole to you instead of five would I have a shot at the morning drive time slot?"

[...a short time later Jerry finds himself hooked up with his long time chum, The Great Rondini, and getting ready for a working vacation at a nearby dude ranch...]

"...*THIS is Jerry Jeremy signing off on KICK, the Voice of the West. And just to prove we are really the Voice of the West, next week my show will be coming to you from the Circle-K Ranch and Spa near beautiful downtown Kirby, the liveliest ghost town in the big A-Z.*

"*We'll be staying compliments of the Circle-K management and we'll be getting there in one of Bronco Billy Wooten's fine pre-owned Jeep Cherokees. Stop by and let Bronco Billy put you in one of your own; they come in sizes for all shapes and in a variety of boudoir pastels—oops, that's the Lydia's Lingerie copy—but not to worry, Bronc Billy will be glad to put you in something sexy too.*

"*And if you happen to drive that brand new—to you, anyway—jalopy down Kirby-way, make sure you drop on by and watch us do the show live from—did I mention this before—the Circle-K Ranch and Spa. Even better, Jerry's old saddle-pal, The Great Rondini, will be pulling ten-gallon rabbits out of five-gallon hats down at the Silver Birdcage Saloon, the west's only certified haunted beer joint."*

IT had been a week since I got the magician's call and I was settling quite nicely into my new seven to ten timeslot. It fit like a custom-built golf cart. I'd pop out of the sheets around noon, maybe hit an air-conditioned driving range, check-in with Christy to see where to meet after the show, then detour past the line next door at Tacos-To-Go and be on the way to the station. At last it was all falling into place.

Except for one unforeseen cloud on the horizon. My new hours.

I know, I know—a guy who only works three hours a day shouldn't go around bellyaching, but who knew they started those post-grad classes so early in the day? Nine or maybe nine-thirty? When do the professors find time to flirt with the coeds? Don't they have a life of some kind? Not one that goes past ten at night apparently.

"Jerry dearest, I already told you I'll listen to you on the air every evening, just as soon as I'm done with my homework."

So much for my number one fan. I'd call during the seven-thirty news break to get a fire started for after the show. But higher education was getting in the way. Christy went to class during the day and between her homework and my evening show, there wasn't much time left before she headed to bed. To sleep. Alone.

We spent so much time calling each other, my cell phone needed a cell phone. I was telling her, "...baby, I need to be able to reach out and touch you, smell your perfume, nuzzle your neck...we're spending so much time apart, I may have to matriculate. I think that's the word."

"Better stop there, Jerry my dear, or I'll be up late finishing this paper. I know you wouldn't want me to drift off during the Sexual Ecology lecture, would you?"

"Hey, some of my best shut-eye was during class. I'd still be in school today if they hadn't asked me to wake up and leave."

"I don't believe that."

"That they woke me up? I couldn't believe it either. But really, babe, when you're not at the library or on a shopping run with Mom, you're rehearsing for the school play or getting your nails done. How many times a week do you need to do your nails anyway?"

"Now don't get sore, darling, blah, blah, blah...." I won't go into the mushy stuff, but I decided having Christy over the phone was better than not having Christy at all. Still I did wonder how fast the average woman's nails grew. I'll have to remember to Google it. As it was, I had to get back on the air. The show, as they say, must go on. Otherwise you don't get paid.

Later that evening I hit number one on my speed dial again, "Hey babe, I didn't get a chance to tell you before, but I'm on to something that I—er, I mean you—will really like. But you'll need to play hooky for a few days."

"Is this the one where I dress up like a school girl and you play the truant officer?"

"Sure, I'll even bring the handcuffs. But that'll have to wait until you're back here in school again."

"But if I'm in school, you won't be able to arrest me."

"Don't worry. I'll think of something—but hey, that's not why I called. If your mom let you stay up to catch my show you'd already know me and a guest of my choice are being comp'd for a week out at the Circle-K dude ranch. I'll be doing my show from there while The Great Rondini—you remember him—headlines in the local ghost town. Have mic, will travel."

I gave Christy the backstory the way Ronnie had explained it to me. The Great One's road show had been making the rounds and wound up being booked into the Silver Cage Saloon, a renovated dance hall that the Circle-K used as a tourist attraction-slash-nightclub for the visiting dudes. Ronnie said they'd renovated and fixed it up so even the ghosts had new sheets. The ranch even brought in clean dirt for Main Street.

What with Rondini and me being pals and all, and this bump in the trail being a part of KICK's broadcast area, Ronnie had somehow managed to soft-soap the head dude into letting me come over and give him a million bucks worth of free publicity. In return I got a week's free room and board. Ronnie also figured that in return for setting it up, his old pal might throw a little plugola his way too. Well, that wasn't exactly how he put it. For one thing, he didn't say little.

So I'd be plugging Rondini and plugging the dude ranch, plugging their spa and plugging the ghost town, and hoping the FCC didn't unplug me. With a little luck I might be able to squeeze in a paying sponsor like Bronco Billy. I didn't mind bending the rules a little to get a week alone with Christy. I was sure Mrs. Marshall would enjoy some alone time too. So what if there were a few strings and maybe a government investigation attached?

[...and after his evening radio show on location at the Circle-K, Jerry tries to get some time alone with Christy Marshall even if it means a nighttime journey by horseback...]

THE desert by moonlight. Even though I was getting chapped around the chaps, I had to admit that a nighttime ride in the great wide open was pretty high on the scale romance-wise. Christy had pulled me over to the corral after the show since it looked like Mom was staying in tonight.

The nags knew the way, following the path down the arroyo we had come through that morning. When we got to the cottonwood stand we had passed earlier in the day, Christy pulled up. A natural spring fed a pool of cool, dark water shadowed from too much moonlight by the trees.

"This is great," I said. "Let's have a picnic?"

"Sorry, Jerry, but I forgot to pack the food."

"I wasn't really talking about food?"

"Well, I'm talking about going for a swim," Christy said.

"But I forgot to pack my swim trunks."

"And I really wasn't talking about clothes."

"Now, that's more like it!"

Christy swung a leg over the saddle and slid off Buttermilk like she'd been riding all her life which I think she had. I couldn't quite match her style, having to get down more gingerly. The only ponies I had grown up around were out at the track on those days dad decided to skip taking me to little league practice. Looking back, I'm sure that knowing how to bet a trifecta has come in handier than learning to swing at a curve ball.

Christy and I stripped off our duds scattering them over and around the boulders, playing a little hide and seek by the light of the moon. Ducking behind a big chunk of red granite, Christy spotted a silver arrowhead glowing in the moonlight, probably left by some medicine man skinny-dipping here way back when. We played a grown up version of tag as we splashed into the water—cold as an Artic wind against our sunburned bodies. We frolicked in the shallows for a while, stopping every now and then to share a little body heat. It didn't take long even with the warm-ups to start to chill a bit though—gooseflesh and shivering and all that stuff.

"If we get deeper in, we'll be warmer," Christy said, wading in up to her chin.

"Seems like it should be the other way around," I said as she faded into the darkness of the water. The overhanging trees and a couple of transient clouds cast inky shadows over the deep end, but I could just make out Christy's white form floating ahead of me. She was just beyond my reach, waiting for me to catch up. I knew there would be some real body heat generated when I did.

"Jeez, babe, you really are cold," I said, moving in for the good stuff.

"Jerry, what are you talking about? I'm over here. Where are you?"

Uh-oh.

"Christy? If you're over there, who am I holding over here?"

Seems like a guy can never find a match when he needs one. Even treading water, I felt my pockets for one until I realized I didn't have any pockets either. I was hoping for a swarm of fireflies when old man moon found a hole in the clouds. And after the black of night, the moon now lit up the place like it was high noon. Light enough anyway to make me wish I hadn't wished for more light. A wide, pale torso floated in front of my eyes, kind of roundish with her hair spreading gently out in the water. She was face down, but I didn't need to see her face. Even by moonlight I could recognize that brassy red hair. Not to mention that less than an hour ago she was sitting just across the table from me.

"You'd better get your clothes on, babe," I said not able to look away from Mrs. Edelbaum. "Turns out we're not alone here. We may be a million miles from San Francisco Bay, but nonetheless, I think we've found a floater."

"Oh God, Jerry. You mean...."

"Yes, I'm afraid so. We got to stop meeting dead bodies like this."

Just for drill, I figured we should whip a little CPR on the old girl in case there was a spark of life left in her. I took one of her cold arms for balance and tried to pull her up by the hair.

"Jeez, I think she's been scalped!" I froze, holding a tangles mass of bloody hair in my hand.

"It's her wig, Jerry." Christy bobbed up next to me. And believe me watching Christy bobbing usually would take my mind off anything, let alone Bev Edelbaum, but it didn't seem to be working now. Christy said, "You must have known that red hair couldn't have been real."

"Sure, sure," I said. I could see now that Bev had short silvery hair, except for a dark spot about the size of my palm—not very brassy, but definitely blood red. I looked at Christy standing nipple-deep near me and said, "Let's try to float her over to shore, near the horses. I think we can skip the CPR though."

With Christy pulling on one of her arms and me on the other, we steered and swam and pulled Bev to the far side of the pool. Floating in the water she moved easily, but getting her up the rocky bank was a bitch.

"My god, Jerry...she must weight three hundred pounds."

"She's certainly dead weight."

"Jerry!"

"Oh, sorry...I wasn't thinking."

Resting her on the high bank, Christy and I walked a few steps away before flopping down to catch our breaths. Two naked people sitting on some pretty uncomfortable rocks and desert sand. I thought I felt a cactus down there too, but I was too blown out to move.

God, Christy was beautiful. Too bad Mrs. Edelbaum had gotten to the ol' swimming' hole before us. Too bad for Mrs. Edelbaum, too.

After resting a minute, we started gathering up our clothes. They were still there anyway, so with some reluctance we got dressed. Sometimes it's just one damn' thing after another.

Things being what they were—a murder and all—I figured I'd better use my cell to call the Paleface Suite. Out in the middle of nowhere and I still had three bars of good reception; the Native Americans must have all the iPhones. Anyway, I wanted to get Ronnie on the blower to see if he had any ideas on how we could make some hay before the sun did shine on this murder. As it turned out he might have, but all I got was his voicemail. And leaving a message wasn't the idea I wanted. It looked like I was all on my own this time. Well, actually me and Christy, but I wasn't sure she appreciated the media possibilities. After some mental wrangling, I came up with a plan of action.

While I was formulating the plan, Christy called her mom to check in and reassure her it was only a murder, not an elopement. Meanwhile I looked up Dale Andersen's home number.

"Hi, Mrs. Andersen? Betty? I hope I didn't wake you...I

need to speak with Dale right away.... Me? I'm Jerry Jeremy, the seven to ten show? Must be a bad connection, you not recognizing my voice and all...." Seems I had woken up Betty and the kids—must be they don't stay up for Leno—but finally she got Dale to pick up.

"Hey, Dale, get ready to print up new rate cards, the Voice of the West is about to have the Scoop of the West."

"What? Jerry, have you been drinking?"

"No, I'm just high on death. I've stumbled across a murder out here in the high desert. And it's all mine, I'm right here with the body."

"Jerry, steady yourself, man. Are you okay?" Dale seemed a little disturbed by the news. I hoped he was all right, but he asked me first.

"Sure, I'm fine. I admit I was a little nervous about the scalping, but there wasn't any reason to be as it turned out."

"Just stay calm, boy.... Is Dakota there with you? Is she all right?"

"Dakota? No need to worry about her. She's not going to let it out. As a matter of fact, I'm pretty sure she's all tied up right now."

"Listen, Jerry, the station will stand by you, but we don't want anybody else getting hurt. Where are you right now?"

"Down by the creek a mile or so from the hotel. The creek bed turns here making a deep pool. We pulled the body out of the pool though, so she's drying off now."

"She? But not Dakota? Jerry, listen...it's not that girl you brought up there?"

"Christy? Not on your life, I wouldn't be this calm if it was her. As a matter of fact, Christy's right here. She's in on this with me."

"Christy's in on it with you?"

"Don't worry, Dale. I'll make sure she doesn't let anything slip. After all, for a lot of people murder is a once in a lifetime thing."

"Sure, Jerry. Uh...there wasn't anything sexual about the murder was there."

"Well, not since I got to her, but I doubt it anyway. She didn't look the type."

"Good. But you don't really know the victim, do you? You just got there yesterday."

"Yeah, but I'm a fast worker. She was a guest on tonight's show—Mrs. Beverly Edelbaum, the art patron."

"A guest! My god, Jerry."

"Well, you did hear the show didn't you?"

"Uh, sorry, Jerry. My wife's mother's birthday. But I'll listen to the sound checks first thing. You just stay calm. Believe me, help is on the way. Betty called on the other phone. Just don't put up any kind of a fuss when they get there."

So after one or two more pleasantries I finally got Dale off the phone. For a radio exec he seemed kind of namby-pamby, letting a murder throw him like that. I doubted Mrs. Edelbaum was even a steady listener.

Christy and I sat with our backs to Mrs. Edelbaum and looked out at the moonlit desert. Someplace out there was the ranch, but all we could see was barren land spotted with the occasional tumbleweed. The desert stretched as far as we could see which in spite of old man moon wasn't very far. We huddled together for warmth and security while on some unseen ridge a coyote howled causing the horses to shuffle nervously. Christy and I huddled closer.

Christy was snoring lightly in my arms and only the chill of the desert at two a.m. kept me from drifting off. Even under the circumstances, the smell of Christy's hair and the warmth of her—

"Freeze, motherfucker!"

Blinding light exploded around us. Christy screamed, waking up to the nightmare.

"Don't move, asshole!"

"Hands above your head!"

Shouting came from all directions, khaki arms and legs pulled us apart. I was suddenly face down in the dirt, my hands cuffed behind my back.

"Don't move...cocksucker!" He probably meant me, but nonetheless I tried to see what was happening to Christy and got my face jammed back in the dirt for my trouble. "I said don't move!"

Who were these guys? Indians? Mexicans? Bev's killers?

"Speak English? ¿Habla ingles? You have the right to remain silent—" It dawned on me that it probably wasn't Indians. "You have right to have a lawyer present..."

"Okay, you guys, slow it on down now," a deep voice rumbled through the havoc. "The gal says they're together. Circle-K dude ranch. She says he's on the radio, some kind of deejay."

"Talk show...talk show host," I spit the dirt out of my mouth. "Jeremy Jeremy...law and order talk show...."

"Take his cuffs off and get him on his feet if you ain't broke any bones on him."

Pulled to my feet, I found myself staring into the steely gray eyes of the Marlboro man. Slightly older now, his long hair and walrus mustache turning white, but he looked like he could still step out of the west and onto a magazine cover. But maybe lose the mustache first.

"I'm Sheriff Darrell Lee Redhawk," the Marlboro man said. "You do any podcasting? Ya' know, streaming audio or something? I can't pick up the Tucson stations for shit out here."

"Podcast— Sure, I'm almost positive I do that. Computers and all that stuff. Sure, the Internet. I'm sure I do."

Christy stepped over and slipped her arm around me. That made me feel a lot better. That and an idea that was starting to float around in my head. The Marlboro man had a voice made for the airwaves. He made Sam Elliott sound like a teenager. If I could talk him into coming on the show, and with Rondini to supply some brain-power, this story could go national. Shades of KPMT San Francisco, only this time I wouldn't get canned—though I might be moving up and moving out after the networks got a load of me.

By now, Dale probably had the entire news crew in the KICK van heading my way with board ops, engineers, producers and God knows what all. Not that the Voice of the West really had more than four or five staff they could send here and still stay on the air. But after all, Bronco Billy was sure to get more than his money's worth with his name right up there next to the killer's.

For now though, Darrell Lee seemed to be doing the talking, "...so this head man from the radio station had his wife call down here telling everyone that you might just be a homicidal maniac." He gave me a squinty look that made me wonder if he didn't still believe it. He added, "If she's really your boss's ol' lady though, you probably want to start working on your resume."

"Hey, I'm not afraid of that. The message probably just got lost in translation. I've got the inside track on this murder. He can't fire me until I solve it...er, until it's solved, that is."

Redhawk aimed a stream of tobacco juice just south of my shoes.

"That's right," he said, "'until it's solved'. And the solving will be done by the Cochise County Sheriff's office, not some tenderfoot from Tucson."

"Don't worry, Chief. I'm not really from Tucson."

"The only-est thing I'm worried about is that body over there—" Mrs. Edelbaum was lit up like a movie set and surrounded by people in paper clothes "—that and the county elections coming up."

"Of course, Sheriff Redhawk," Christy said. "Jerry and I will give you our complete cooperation."

"I know you will, ma'am." Darrell Lee gave me another look, but this time his face crinkled into what passed for a smile. "Tell me a little more about that show of yours, Jeremy. You ever do anything on politics?"

If You Enjoyed This Preview...

Visit **www.DonaldJMcGill.com** to find the full

Talked to Death and other terrific Jerry Jeremy

adventures in Donald J. McGill's Talk Radio

Mystery series.

About the author

DONALD J. McGILL writes and publishes the Jerry Jeremy Talk Radio Mystery series. He lives with his wife just across the Golden Gate Bridge in Marin County, California. Like most native San Franciscans, he started out someplace else—in his case, a bump in the road called New York City.

WHEN not plotting new murders, Don works in the Bay Area's IT industry, including companies with radio, TV and news outlets. His love of talk radio came about during the time he commuted by car to the Silicon Valley. Those radio personalities made the time fly by—even if the traffic didn't. Jerry Jeremy is a light-hearted take on what one of those great talk show hosts might be like.

DON now travels to work across San Francisco Bay by ferry. But talk radio still keeps him company, only this time the words are his. The *Talk Radio Mystery* series are written on these daily crossings and there are more stories to come. So like the big guys on the radio say, *stay tuned!*

About the cover

THE cover for *Tune in to Danger* is homage to the poster used for the 1943 Ray Milland-Paulette Goddard motion picture comedy, *The Crystal Ball*.

For the latest scoop on Jerry and his pals, including free samples, visit **www.DonaldJMcGill.com** and please follow **@tuneintodanger** on Twitter.

Again, thanks for tuning in!